D. B. Thorne is a digital entrepreneur and founding member of a highly successful tech start-up in the UK. Thorne has long been fascinated by the intersection between the digital and real worlds, inspiring him to write the acclaimed thriller *Troll* and the brilliant follow-up, *Perfect Match*.

PERFECT MATCH

D. B. THORNE

CORVUS

Published in Great Britain in 2018 by Corvus, an imprint of
Atlantic Books Ltd. This edition published in 2019.

10 9 8 7 6 5 4 3 2 1

A CIP catalogue record for this book is available from the British Library.

Paperback ISBN: 978 1 78239 599 7
E-book ISBN: 978 1 78239 598 0

Printed in Great Britain by Clays Ltd, Elcograf S.p.A.

Corvus
An imprint of Atlantic Books Ltd
Ormond House
26–27 Boswell Street
London
WC1N 3JZ

www.corvus-books.co.uk

PERFECT MATCH

ROBBIE, THOUGHT TIFFANY, WALKING ALONG HACKNEY ROAD past shops that had once sold wholesale leather goods but now hawked artisan coffee at prices just the wrong side of crazy, could go screw himself. She was going on a date. If the date went well, anything might happen. She was ruling nothing out. And if Robbie parked outside her flat one more night, she'd call the police. No, scratch that, she'd go one better and call her brother, and there was only one way that was going to end.

The evening was warm and every other car seemed to have its roof down, each one pumping out different music, samba then rap then something African, diversity filling the rich city air around her. Somewhere up ahead was Shoreditch and her date, a guy who was unknown beyond a brief message exchange. And a photo, which she'd admit hadn't exactly blown her away, but he had the right amount of eyes and noses, and she liked blonds, so that was a start. Anyway, pretty much anything beat Robbie White.

As she walked, she knew people were looking at her, men mostly, but she didn't care. Hell, it was her job to have men look at her, so it wasn't like it was anything new. Fact was, she looked amazing, and the long walk in preposterous heels wouldn't do her calves any harm either. No, she felt good, as good as she'd felt for a long time, and if tonight wasn't a success, it wouldn't be for lack of trying.

'Hey, darling, you want a ride?' A car slowed next to her, a Golf with some kind of exhaust upgrade on it that made it sound, well, ridiculous, she thought. Exactly the kind of thing Robbie went for. She'd bet this guy had a decal on the rear bumper. What was it Robbie had had, until she'd made him take it off? *Louder than your girlfriend last night*. Sad didn't begin to cover it.

'No,' she said. 'Thanks.'

'Where you going?' the driver asked, his urban patois betrayed by his skinny white face.

'I've got a date,' she said, almost sang, and did a small pirouette on the pavement in celebration. The driver, barely more than a boy, tried to think of a comeback but instead just laughed, said, 'You have a good one, my darling,' and drove off with a throaty snarl of his ill-judged exhaust. Yes, thought Tiffany, tonight's going to be a good, good night.

She'd never been to Convent before, didn't really do trendy bars, or at least the Shoreditch hipster brand of trendy. She didn't like men with beards, which kind of ruled out eighty per cent of the available talent, she figured. She turned off Curtain Road down a side street, but before she got to the lit sign, red neon spelling out *Convent* in cursive, a voice called to her.

'Tiffany?'

She turned to see a man, blond hair, cross the street to catch her up. 'Yeah?'

'Tobes. Hi. Sorry. I didn't book and the bar's full. Since when was it all hen parties around here?'

'Oh.'

'I recognized you from your picture. You're ...' He paused. 'You're really pretty.'

Tiffany giggled and pretended to fan her face with a flat hand. 'Whatever. Where are we going?'

'I've called an Uber. You know the Rooftop?'

'No. Listen, I don't want to be driving ...'

'It's close.' He paused. He wasn't young, was older than she'd expected, but there was something immature about his face, and Tiffany felt sorry for him. Maybe he was out of his depth. Maybe he just needed a bit of mothering. 'Look, I know, I feel stupid because it was my idea ...'

'It's no problem,' said Tiffany. 'Though I'm gagging for a drink.'

'Hold on,' he said. He held out a hand. A car stopped, and the driver said through his open window, 'Sam?'

'We're in.' He opened the passenger door and held it for Tiffany, who slid in showing as little thigh as possible. He got in next to her and said to the driver, 'Got the address?'

The driver turned and nodded, said, 'Verona Street?'

'That's it.'

Tiffany relaxed into her seat and decided to let things go, to just enjoy the night, see where it took her. It looked like her date had it under control. She looked across at him and he wriggled out a hip flask, said, 'You were saying?'

'What?'

'About gagging for a drink?'

He unscrewed the top and handed the flask to her, and she took it and drank, then he took it and put it to his mouth and handed it back to her, and this happened again and again, and as the taxi drove them through the busy, alive streets of east

London, the night closed in around her like a warm blanket and she no longer cared where they were going, or why, or what was carrying her there, because she'd rarely felt so good in her life and things were going to be wonderful, just wonderful, of that she had no doubt, though actually, no, no, stop, why was it that the taxi driver had called her date Sam? Wasn't he called Tobes? Wasn't he?

two

HIS SISTER HAD BEEN VENTILATED BY A TUBE DOWN HER throat, and a cardiac monitor blipped her steady heart rate in green waves across a black screen above her head. Solomon kept an eye on her blood pressure, which looked reasonable, the systolic number on top holding fairly stable at around 101, the diastolic below maintaining a steady 63. Not bad, both a little on the low side, but what did he expect? She was in a coma, and both numbers were within the acceptable range, or at least the range that scientists had decided. Who knew?

He looked down at her sleeping face, her closed eyes and delicately arched nose, which also looked normal. Directly past her and in his line of sight was his brother, whose nose fell well outside any range that could be termed normal, bent and misshapen and broken he couldn't guess how many times. The ventilator hissed and sucked and the cardiac monitor blipped quietly and it could almost have been peaceful, here in this room, if it hadn't been for his brother. Solomon had never seen his brother calm, but right now he was a lean, shaven-headed vessel of barely controlled rage.

'So tell me this, since you know everything,' his brother said, as passive-aggressive an opening as Solomon could imagine. 'If it was an accident, how come she's missing teeth and her arm's broken? Tell me that.'

Solomon didn't answer, instead he turned and looked out of the window onto the hospital's car park. An old man was helping an unsteady woman – Solomon assumed it was his wife – into the passenger side of an old-model something-or-other, it was hard to tell from up here. Maybe a Nissan. Yes, it was a Nissan. Good.

'One hypothesis would be that it happened when she fell,' he said, without turning around. This was the first time he had left his apartment in twenty-two months. Twenty-two months, one week and three days, to be exact.

He watched the old man start the car and navigate his way out of the car park, as carefully as if he was piloting a tanker through a crowded harbour. In his mind, Solomon idly transformed the car park into a geometric framework, planes and axes and angles, placing every car in theoretical motion and modelling a possible future in which each and every one was simultaneously attempting to find the exit. He played out alternative pathways and trajectories and velocities, a complex yet elegant piece of mathematical choreography.

'That,' his brother said behind him, 'I'm not buying. What, she goes out for a drink, nearly drowns, ends up in a coma and it's an accident? Please, Solly. Do me a favour. You know who did this, don't you?'

Solomon was spared from answering this question by the sound of the hospital-room door opening. He still didn't turn around, instead let his brother deal with whoever had come in. The room was well lit and the day was bright outside, which meant, Solomon knew, that light was refracting efficiently through the window. Which meant there was very little reflection, something Solomon was perfectly happy with.

'I'm sorry,' a woman's voice said, 'but we're going to need you to leave.'

'How come?' Solomon's brother said.

'Hospital rules,' the voice said. 'And we need to change your sister's dressings.'

'Don't need to leave for that. We'll stay.'

'Luke,' said Solomon, still facing the window. 'You must allow the lady to do her job.' He raised his voice slightly and said, 'Don't worry. We're going.'

'I'll give you a couple of minutes,' said the voice, and Solomon waited until he heard the door close behind her before turning.

'Please, Luke, don't be difficult,' he said. 'They're only following the rules.'

'Not being difficult,' said Luke. 'Just saying.'

'We'll be coming back, remember that. Upsetting the hospital staff won't make it easier for us to see Tiffany.'

Luke thought for a second, then smiled. 'Point. Best to keep the wardens sweet, isn't it?'

Something like that, thought Solomon, although probably not the analogy he would have deployed. But then, he wasn't Luke, was he? Not even close. Taxonomically close but a metaphorical species apart. He put his hood on, took his Ray-Bans out of the pocket of his running top and put them on. 'Are you ready?'

Luke stood up and leant over their sister's sleeping face, giving her nose a quick kiss, careful of her broken arm in its plaster cast. 'Later, Tiff.' He paused, bent above her, and Solomon could sense his internal struggle, his unwillingness to leave her here, alone, in this room. But eventually he stood, picked his jacket up from the back of the chair and headed for the door. Whatever his brother's faults, Solomon thought, he loved his sister. But then, with Tiffany, what wasn't there to love?

It had been Solomon who'd got the call from the police, the landline of his apartment ringing for what might have been the first time ever. Not that he didn't get calls, people did call him, now and then. Occasionally. But on his mobile. He only had the landline because the phone networks ran an inelegant but efficient scam in which you needed a landline in order to get online. Probably a way of future-proofing their business, Solomon imagined, since landlines were as doomed as the Neanderthals, but it hardly mattered. Solomon lived his life in the virtual space. As far as he was concerned, the rise of the online community was the only thing that made his existence bearable, and he'd willingly hand over a kidney for an internet connection, never mind thirty pounds a month.

'Hello?' he'd said.

'Solomon Mullan?'

'Yes?'

'We have you down as the next of kin of … Tiffany Mullan.'

'My sister,' he said, an unexpected wobble in his voice he tried to control by swallowing.

'I'm afraid she's at Royal London Hospital,' the voice said, a man's. By the detachment in his voice, this wasn't the first time he'd made this kind of call. 'In intensive care.'

'Can you tell me what happened?'

'She nearly drowned,' the man said. 'She's in a coma, that's all I can tell you.'

'Drowned? How?'

'Sorry, I don't have that information.'

'Well, is she stable? Has she been ventilated?'

'I ...' The man on the other end didn't seem used to this level of informed questioning. 'I really couldn't say. She was found in a canal, that's all I can tell you. You'll need to come in.'

'I'll be there,' said Solomon. 'As soon as I can.' He hung up and stood for some time with his back against the wall of his hallway, trying to process what he'd just heard. His sister, Tiffany, in a coma. He'd need to go to her, need to go outside. How did that work? Shoes, he'd need shoes. Where were they? He hadn't worn shoes in well over a year, had had no need to. And a coat. Did he need one? What month was he in? He felt anxiety flood his chest, anxiety for his sister but also for himself. He'd have to go out of the front door and into the world, where people were, where they talked and laughed and looked, always looked. God. Money. Did he have any? People still used it, right, out there? Of course they did. He rubbed his face and tried to think calmly. It would be okay. People did it all the time. Went out there, got things done, functioned as social animals. He could do it too.

He walked through to his bedroom and found his mobile. He looked through his recent calls, found his brother's number. It was about the only one in there, the only person he spoke to, him and Tiffany. Before he thumbed the call button, he looked at the time: 3.15 a.m. He listened to the ringtone, wondering at the same time what exactly his brother would be up to at this time of the morning.

Outside the room the hospital corridors smelt clean, and that reassured Solomon slightly about his fear, which he acknowledged as irrational, of MRSA, the tabloid spectre of entering hospital for one ailment and rapidly dying of another.

'You want a lift home, Solly?' said Luke, walking slightly ahead of him. It made it easier not to make eye contact, Solomon suspected.

'You drove here?'

'Yeah. Why?'

Given the smell of booze on his brother's breath when he'd arrived at the hospital at just gone five, he shouldn't have been anywhere near a car. He probably shouldn't even have been standing. But with Luke, the normal rules had never applied.

'No,' said Solomon, though he did want a lift, he really did, in fact he would have endured however many hours of his brother's angry company if it meant avoiding public transport. Avoiding the public in general. But he had somewhere to go and he didn't want Luke to know anything about it, so he'd just have to suck it up and face the world.

'Sure?' said Luke.

'I'm sure.'

'Suit yourself,' said Luke. 'I'll call you, yeah? We need to get this sorted.'

Get what sorted? Solomon almost said, but stopped himself. He wasn't ready to hear about his brother's plans for revenge, whoever they were aimed at. Instead he gave a non-committal 'Yes,' and watched his brother walk away, or aggressively swagger to be more accurate, before he turned a corner and disappeared. His brother, a promising career criminal. His sister, a comatose stripper, sorry, burlesque dancer. And Solomon, whatever he was. The white sheep? As far as family dysfunction went, the Mullans were running away from the competition. He sighed, pulled his hood lower over his forehead and headed for the hospital exit, counting the black and white tiles beneath his feet as he walked.

three

'WHAT HAPPENED?' ASKED INSPECTOR FOX, KEEPING HER EYES on Solomon Mullan. She hoped that she came across as concerned, rather than intimidated by what she saw.

'What matters is what happened to my sister,' Solomon said quietly, his head bowed. 'That's what I'm here for. I'd appreciate it if we could talk about that.'

Fox would rather have talked about Solomon Mullan's brother, Luke. He was the family member of interest as far as she was concerned. As far as the department was concerned. Not the sister. But there you were, and here Solomon Mullan was. And she had a job to do.

'Fair enough,' she said, and looked down at the notes she'd made about the case. They didn't amount to a whole lot. 'So Tiffany Eloise Mullan is your sister,' she said.

'You know she is.'

Fox looked up sharply at Solomon, who still had his head bowed. She didn't need this attitude, was accustomed to dutiful respect from juniors and civilians. She was an inspector, after all. A young one, but as far as she was concerned that only meant she had more talent and ambition than the rest. She tried for her most condescending manner. 'Are you in a fit state to do this?' she asked.

'Yes,' said Solomon. 'Why do you ask?'

But she didn't bother answering, just went back to her notes. After a moment she said, not looking up, 'She was a stripper.'

'Was?'

'Is.'

'Yes, she is.'

'How is that?' Fox said. 'For her?'

'I believe it's a living.'

Fox looked up again. She had very blue eyes and had developed a direct gaze that she knew people found hard to meet. But Solomon Mullan seemed equally practised at looking anywhere but at her, his face always averted. 'Are you going to continue to be abrasive?' she said. 'I am here to help your sister.'

Solomon nodded down at the edge of the desk nearest to him and audibly swallowed. 'Understood. I apologize. Please continue.'

'Does she have any other sources of income?'

'Such as?' Still Solomon didn't look at her, kept talking down to the desk in front of him. Fox sighed.

'Such as, I don't know. Waitressing. Minicab driving.' She paused. 'Prostitution.'

Solomon shook his head and rocked slightly forward. Fox watched the hair on the top of his head – black, wavy, thick – and waited. 'Mr Mullan?'

'No,' he said eventually.

'No?'

'No, she isn't a waitress, no, she doesn't drive a cab, and no, she doesn't solicit men for sex.' There was an edge to his voice now, and Fox knew that the prostitute barb had stuck, and had hurt.

'As far as you know,' she said, giving it a twist.

'Let me ask you a question,' said Solomon. 'Are you conducting an investigation into my sister's attack, or her reputation?'

He looked up at this and Fox forced herself to maintain her gaze. She even smiled slightly, allowing him his objection. 'Point taken,' she said, and looked down, away from Solomon, back at her sparse notes. 'Though there is, so far, no evidence that she was attacked.'

'Or that she wasn't.'

Fox nodded quickly. 'That's what I need to find out.'

Her phone rang and she picked it up without speaking. She listened for a few seconds before saying, 'No, I can't do that.' She listened to the reply, closed her eyes and said, 'At once.' She replaced the handset, picked up the notes she'd been reading from and said, 'Excuse me,' before walking out of the office.

Inspector Fox's office was in a police station in east London made of rough grey concrete that looked as if it had been poured sixty years ago, in a hurry. The reception was lined with posters warning against car theft and burglary and mugging, and populated with exactly the demographic of people Solomon suspected carried out those very acts. He had been called by Fox just after he'd arrived at the hospital, and it was now gone two in the afternoon. It felt as if he'd been up for a long time, and he'd sat in the reception with his head hung between his knees, a forlorn posture that hadn't looked out of place.

'Mr Mullan? Solomon Mullan?' A uniformed officer had opened a door next to the reception desk and waited for Solomon to pass him before showing him down a corridor and up a flight of stairs, eventually to an office with frosted glass on it and a name card: Inspector Fox. He'd knocked on the door and waited for a female voice to say, 'Come in,' before opening the door and stepping inside.

Now, with Fox gone, Solomon looked around her office. There wasn't a lot to take in: a monitor and keyboard on her desk, a pile of papers, a desk tidy with four identical black pens in it, a telephone. She was young, couldn't have been that much older than Luke. Thirty? Young for an inspector. She was probably on some fast-track programme, held a first in PPE from Oxford and the force couldn't believe they'd managed to get hold of her. But they had done, and to prove it, there was a certificate on the wall behind the desk telling Solomon that Helen Fox was, beyond doubt, an officer of the Metropolitan Police. Just as his sister was indubitably a stripper and, as far as he was aware, nothing else. Not a waitress or a cab driver or a prostitute. Extra work wasn't in her character. Tiffany had never been what people would term a grafter.

The door opened and Fox came back in, sat behind her desk and without a pause looked over at Solomon and said, 'And your brother is Luke Michael Mullan.'

'Yes.'

'We know about him.'

'I imagine you would,' said Solomon. 'He has a record.'

'Quite a record,' said Fox, a laugh in her voice that might have been an attempt at levity, at building rapport. Or it might have been simple malice. 'What's he doing nowadays?'

'He collects,' said Solomon.

'Collects?'

'For wayward women and afflicted children,' said Solomon, knowing as he said it that he shouldn't, but finding it enjoyable nonetheless. Why did he want to goad this cold, uninterested woman? 'Rickets, that kind of thing,' he added.

'I see.' Fox was silent for some time and Solomon wished he had the confidence to meet the gaze he was sure she was levelling at him. 'I think,' she said at last, 'that we should talk about your family.'

If he had to choose one word to describe the Mullan family, Solomon thought, that word would probably be 'motley'. His father had been an amateur boxer in his youth, but he'd had more desire than skill, or in his words, 'I liked fighting, but fighting didn't like me.' During Solomon's upbringing his father had worked on offshore rigs, coming home at unexpected moments with large presents and a lot of noise. Solomon had adored him, but he'd been dead over ten years now, his mother soon after, apparently deciding that life wasn't much worth living without Sean Mullan in it. Solomon was twenty-three, an orphan since the age of thirteen. But at least he'd always had his brother and sister.

For a time they'd been taken in by distant family, travellers who had treated the three of them like their own, which essentially meant, Solomon now realized, as indentured labour. After several months, an exasperated social worker had had them removed and they'd been placed in care, left feeling like aliens recently landed on a faraway planet. But almost immediately their father's sister Dorothy had, in her words, 'sprung them', and taken them with her to live on her farm in the Essex countryside. In the car on the way there she had explained to them that she was happy to give them somewhere to stay, but she didn't have any money, and any she did have she wasn't keen on sharing. So they'd have to pay their own way, something the eldest sibling, Luke, immediately saw to, mostly via burglary.

'How is my family relevant?' said Solomon.

'It's unconventional,' said Fox.

'Hardly unusual nowadays.'

'And you,' said Fox, frowning. 'You're not what I'd expect.'

'You mean ...'

'No, no, I mean ...' She paused, tried to find the right words. 'You seem educated.'

Solomon frowned. 'I shouldn't be?'

'I wouldn't have expected it, no.'

'Would you mind explaining why?'

Fox looked at the monitor on her desk. 'Parents deceased, chaotic upbringing, limited education. The three of you.'

'Books are freely available,' Solomon said. 'There's no tax on reading.'

'You don't have a record.'

'I'd need to commit a crime in order to have one.'

'I'm just surprised—'

'Inspector Fox,' said Solomon. 'Please. My sister is lying in a coma. Most of my family is dead. I'm tired, both physically and of this line of questioning.' He took a breath. 'I would like to know what happened.'

Fox raised her eyebrows and sat back in her chair. 'I told you as much as I know on the phone,' she said. 'Someone saw her and raised the alarm. A passing couple dragged her out, attempted resuscitation. The ambulance crew took her to the Royal London, where she remains. Her blood alcohol level was high, which suggests she had been out beforehand.'

'Do you know who raised the alarm?'

'No.'

'Well, was it a man? A woman?'

'We don't know.'

'Have you spoken to Robert White?'

'Not yet.'

'You're aware that there's a restraining order out on him?'

'Yes,' said Fox, in a way that suggested no.

Solomon shook his head at the floor. 'You don't think that would be a good place to start? Looking for the man with a record of violence towards her?' He took a deep breath and tried to will himself calm.

Fox was silent for a moment and he heard the sound of pen on paper, the inspector making a note. Then she said, 'We do know she had been on a date.'

'Oh?'

'She had an app. On her phone.'

'Do you have a picture? Of this date?'

Fox opened a drawer in a pedestal beneath her desk and pulled out a plastic ziplock bag. She opened it and took the phone out. 'You do much online dating?' she said.

'Do I look as though I do?'

She turned the phone around so that Solomon could see it. 'Know him?'

A picture of a man, young, blond hair. Not bad-looking. Nice eyes. Something about the mouth, pouty, sullen. Solomon had never seen him before. He would remember. 'No. Has he got a name?'

'Tobes.'

'Tobes?' said Solomon. 'I'm assuming that's short for Toby?'

'We don't know.'

'You don't have a surname?'

'We're looking into it.'

'Well, that's reassuring,' said Solomon.

'They'd arranged to meet. Had some communication.'

'Could I see?'

Fox picked the mobile up, swiped at it, put it back down. 'This was the exchange.'

Drink?

When?

Can u do Saturday?

Day off! Where shall we go?

To a convent.

???

Convent. A bar. Dwkd. I mean awkward. Have you been?

To Convent? No.

You should!

OK ...

What hour now?

??? Hour?

Time. What time.

Oh. 9?

C u then.

Solomon looked up. 'That's it?'

'That's all we've got right now.'

'Did anybody see them there?'

'At the bar?' Fox shook her head. 'No. Not on CCTV either. Looks like they either changed plans or he stood her up.'

'I can't imagine anybody standing Tiffany up.'

'Is that right?' said Fox.

'And you can't match the photo? You've tried social media, I imagine?'

'We know what we're doing,' said Fox. 'We've run the algorithms. Nothing's turned up yet, but we're still working on it.'

Solomon nodded. 'Is that all?'

'You've definitely never seen that face before?'

'No.'

'Then there is just one more thing. Where were you between, say, eleven p.m. and three a.m. last night?'

'At home.'

'Can anybody vouch for that?'

'You could check my building's CCTV,' said Solomon, 'if you have the time. Apart from today, I haven't been outside for years.' He stood up. 'But I'd appreciate it if you used that time to find out what happened to my sister.'

Fox opened a drawer and retrieved a card, holding it out to Solomon without looking up. Dismissed. He took it, then pulled his hood over his head and found his Ray-Bans. But before he put them on, he looked down at Inspector Fox and waited for her to acknowledge him. When she did, he met her gaze properly for the first time. To her credit, she didn't flinch.

'My sister is one of the finest people I have ever known,' he said. 'Whatever you think of my family, please do the right thing by her.' He didn't wait for a reply. Putting the inspector's card into his back pocket, he turned and opened the office door and found his own way out.

four

ONCE, IN BETTER DAYS, YEARS AGO, SOLOMON AND HIS OLDER brother Luke had been close, bonded by common misfortune and the need to grow up fast. He supposed they had been a team, one the brains, the other the muscle. And I wasn't the muscle, Solomon thought as he let himself into his flat, feeling a surge of relief at its safe familiarity, its order and predictability. He hadn't realized how on edge he had been, every second that he had been outside. How anxious, how scared, how terrified of other people's reactions.

On 1 January just over two and a half years ago, Solomon had woken up in Luke's spare bedroom after a New Year's Eve party that still hadn't finished when he'd gone to bed at four. As he walked downstairs that morning, his brother's house had had the look of a post-apocalyptic disaster, sleeping bodies arranged randomly on chairs, sofas, under tables, propped against walls. He hadn't been drinking, didn't drink, never had. He got to the kitchen and put on coffee, checked the fridge for milk. None. Obviously. He'd walked to the front door, not imagining that there would be any waiting on the doorstep, but living in bleary post-party hope.

He opened the door, but before he could look down he sensed movement in his peripheral vision and then felt something splash in his face, a cold feeling to begin with, freezing, but that sensation soon turned to burning and his heart began to beat so quickly that he thought he would pass out. He turned and felt his way back to the kitchen and found the sink, splashed water into his face as fast as he could, kept on and on and on until he felt hands on his shoulders and realized that he was screaming, a sound he didn't recognize as his own, that couldn't be coming from him. He turned and could make out his brother, Luke, and he saw the look on Luke's face and he managed to stop screaming and said to him, an animal moan, 'How bad is it?'

Of course Solomon knew that *bad* was a relative term and that he hadn't died, hadn't really come close, certainly after the medic had shot him full of adrenaline. But he had lost the sight in his right eye, which now looked like a small white half-boiled egg. The skin on that side of his face was shiny and had the texture of a plastic bag that had been screwed up and rudimentarily straightened out. Half of his ear was gone, and one side of his mouth was almost lipless and pulled down into a permanent expression of sardonic disapproval. How bad was it? It was bad, very bad, and a year of operations had only made it worse, the closer each procedure brought him to normality, the more obviously the project was doomed to failure. He would never look human again, and nobody would ever be able to look at him without surprise, dismay, disgust or, in most cases, fear.

What made it worse was that he knew, and Luke knew, that he had never been the intended victim. Luke had been the target, for any of a number of reasons, and Solomon had done nothing, nothing at all to deserve it. But neither had said anything and it was only because they were brothers, and needed each other, that they hadn't drifted apart, each repelled by the force of that denial.

He'd had a place at Cambridge lined up, reading philosophy. He'd given it up. He'd had a girlfriend, or at least kind of, but that hadn't lasted beyond the first viewing of what was left of his face. He'd had a future, friends, had escaped the fetters of his upbringing, but that was all lost. All he had left was a flat, which was crucial, because as soon as he could, he made sure he never had to leave it again.

Solomon was late back, and so he headed straight for his living room, which to any outside observer would have looked more like a laboratory with easy chairs. One wall was taken up by a large desk, several laptops, four flat-screen monitors, speakers, routers and a Gordian tangle of wiring. He opened a laptop and waited for an animated spinning wheel to catch up. He tapped softly at keys, and on the central monitor an image of a table appeared, four people at it, drinking. They all met together twice a week in the same pub. Well, all of them except Solomon.

'He lives,' said a man, enormously bearded, in his fifties. He raised a pint of beer to the screen.

'I'm sorry,' said Solomon, sitting down. 'There was a family emergency.'

'Oh my good Lord,' said a grey-haired woman. 'What in heaven's name happened?'

'My sister,' said Solomon. 'She's in hospital.'

'Nothing serious, I do hope,' she said.

'The words "emergency" and "hospital" would rather preclude that, don't you think?' the bearded man said. Which effectively summed this group up, Solomon thought, pedantry trumping sentiment every time.

'For God's sake,' said a younger woman, pretty, with long hair in ringlets. 'Phil, don't be a pest. Ignore him, Fran.'

Phil, the man with the beard, raised his eyebrows at this unwarranted accusation, but kept quiet.

'Welcome, welcome, in any case,' said a middle-aged man, raising a glass. 'We extend to your sister all the best.' Masoud, as cultured a person as Solomon could hope to meet.

'Thank you,' said Solomon. 'I've interrupted.'

'Oh, not really,' said Fran. 'In fact you've arrived at just the very moment. We were debating ...'

'Gently discussing,' said Phil.

'... the merits of this question,' Fran continued, ignoring Phil. 'Ready?'

'Yes.'

'Kandinsky was a member of which Munich-based art movement?'

'Kandinsky?'

'Yes.'

'I should know this,' said Solomon. He paused. 'I should. This is irritating.'

'That's what I said,' the younger woman agreed. 'Kind of.'

'What is it for?' said Solomon.

'A new show,' said Masoud, then added importantly, 'Channel 4.'

'Arts based?'

'No, but it's got specialized sections, and art's one of them,' the younger woman said. 'Think Trivial Pursuit, with some kind of overcooked elimination mechanic.'

'With you,' said Solomon, closing his eyes. 'Kandinsky.'

'Yes,' said Fran patiently.

If Solomon had ever known the answer, he'd still know it now. But he didn't, which he found surprising.

'Die Brücke,' he said. A guess, not like him.

'No,' said Phil, delight in his voice, no attempt to hide it, Phil being Phil.

'Unlucky,' said Masoud. 'That was Berlin. Ludwig Kirchner.'

'Who shot himself in the face,' said Phil.

'Thank you, Philip,' said Masoud. 'So the answer is Der Blaue Reiter. But please, do not feel bad. Nobody else got it either.'

'Which means it's too difficult,' the younger woman said, in a way that suggested she'd been advocating the same view for some time.

'Kay is right,' said Masoud. 'It is too obscure.'

'Or people are too stupid,' said Phil.

'Considering that you also got it wrong, I imagine you would need to place yourself within that bracket,' said Fran. Phil began to reply but thought better of it and went back to his drink.

This was the Brain Pool, or alternatively what Solomon could accurately describe as All the Friends I Have in the World. He joined them two nights a week, although the relationship was one-sided in the sense that they'd never met him, not face to face, had had to make do with an avatar of a spinning question mark for the past eighteen months. He dialled in remotely, but given the varying levels of social ineptitude within the group, Phil occupying the furthest reaches, it wasn't an issue. They'd asked why to begin with, but ultimately they were more interested in the questions they set together for TV programmes and radio shows and newspapers and any other quizzing forum they could find.

Solomon did know that Phil was an anarchist, though that didn't qualify as a profession. Fran had told them that she had a private income, which meant she was rich and didn't have to do anything. Masoud was an Iranian refugee who had been a nuclear physicist in Tehran but wasn't allowed anywhere near a British nuclear facility so drove an Uber instead. And nobody really understood what Kay did, something at the intersection of neurology and computer code, biological algorithms or organic computation or bio-organic algorithmic computation. It was complex, even for Solomon.

Solomon had never questioned why he knew so much, or how he retained such vast amounts of knowledge. He just did, storing complex information in ways he considered normal even if nobody else did. Chronological sequences lived in his mind as abstract many-coloured landscapes, whole swathes of history reduced to patchwork configurations he could recall at will. Entire knowledge systems, geometry or thermodynamics or organic chemistry, lay coiled up in elegant multi-threaded helixes, springing into words and facts whenever he called upon them. Names, events, physical laws, anything he ever learnt was absorbed, converted into abstract forms and patterns, complex polyhedrons and kaleidoscopic panoramas. He didn't know why. It just was. He never forgot anything, and he had learnt a lot. A whole lot. Which was why the Brain Pool felt so right when so much in his broader life now felt so wrong.

Fran had the contact that had got them this new Channel 4 gig, and she spent the rest of the time explaining the format, the kind of contestants they could expect, the level of questioning. Just below PhD level, she rather thought: think enthusiastic amateur, probably professional, likely postgraduate with some kind of failed-doctorate axe to grind. Their kind of contestant. Meant they didn't have to demean themselves with questions on characters from Dickens or the periodic table. Yawn.

Last orders came and the meeting ended and Solomon hung up, the picture on his monitor switching back to his desktop image of Diego Maradona facing down five Brazilian players. He sat staring at it for some time, knowing that he should eat, drink, do something, but too drained to move.

A notification slid onto the screen, just to the right of Maradona's head. From Kay. It read: *Hey.* Nothing more. Solomon looked at it without moving, without expression. After a long time, minutes, he leant forward and typed:

Hello.

Sorry about your sister.

Thank you.

Any news?

No.

The last news Solomon had had was that afternoon, the ward sister telling him that no, there had been no change, yes, Tiffany was still stable, and yes, visiting hours were the same the next day, ten until four. Would she call if the situation changed? Of course, she had him down as next of kin. Who else was she going to call?

Well. Good luck.

Thank you.

Kay had never messaged him before, not directly, and Solomon typed his replies as if each key of his keyboard might be wired to an IED. A new message appeared:

Hey, I wanted to ask you a question. Questions.

Okay.

Do you mind?

No.

Okay. So ... Are you married?

No.

In prison?

No.

Hmm.

Hmm?

I have another question. But I have no right to ask it.

You can ask.

Sure?

Sure. Go ahead.

Are you differently abled?

Sorry?

You know. Do you have ... Are you in a wheelchair or something?

Oh. No.

Okay ...

Solomon didn't reply, just watched the ellipsis that Kay had left, its implication that she hadn't finished, that there was more to say.

Then why? Why can't I see you?

I. Solomon looked at the word, the single letter. Not *we*, not the group, the Brain Pool. *I.* Why can't *I* see you? He had no idea how to answer, what to write in reply. It was as far out of his grasp as thermodynamic engineering. No, it was a lot further than that.

It's complicated.

Sorry. I shouldn't have asked.

That's okay.

It's none of my business. I'm sorry.

No, really. It's fine.

You might be horribly disfigured!

Seriously, forget it.

Solomon stared at Kay's last line, read it again and again. Did this mean he had a moral duty of disclosure? She might have meant it as a joke, but there it was. The question was implicit. *You might be.* Meaning, if you are, you should say. Wouldn't ignoring it constitute a lie? He was so tired that he didn't know, had no way of telling. He told himself to stop thinking. He did too much of it, and how often did it help? He blinked, then typed:

Horribly is a relative term.

He sat back in his chair, immediately wishing that he could unwrite the words yet at the same time infused with an almost indecent release, as if he had just shared something exciting, taboo. He could not take his eyes from the screen, but when the reply came, it was agonizingly prosaic.

Oh God. I'm sorry.

There was nothing left to say, and Solomon simply waited until Kay's status went inactive. He was left with an anticlimactic feeling, like that of an unsatisfactory first sexual encounter, a leap into a tantalizing unknown that had proved shabby, embarrassing and unfulfilling. He lost track of how long he sat, staring at those last words, but eventually he stood up and went to bed. He needed to be up to see his sister. She was what mattered.

five

LUKE WAS SITTING IN THE HOSPITAL CHAIR, BADLY REGRETTING most of the events of the night before, when his brother walked in, head to the ground and hood up, dragging himself along, Luke thought, like a walking apology for existence. Luke winced at the stabbing pain in his head and managed a rough 'Here he is.'

Solomon turned his head minutely towards him and said, 'It sounds as if you had quite a night.'

'Needed to let off some steam,' said Luke. 'You know.'

'I'm not sure that I do,' said Solomon, and Luke watched him carefully, trying to work out whether there was any judgement implied in that answer. Solomon walked to the window and said, his back to Luke, 'How is she?'

'Same. Listen, you're here now. I'm going to get myself some coffee. Something stronger. You be all right?'

'Of course.'

Solomon waited for his brother to leave before turning around. Two years without going outside, he thought, and now he had done it twice in two days. His sister looked the same apart from a bruise on her cheek that had been purple the day before but was now changing colour, Solomon imagining the haemoglobin breaking down, producing biliverdin, turning the bruise green like a flower going putrid. The blip of the cardiac monitor and the suck and hiss of the monitor transmitted its illusion of calm, a calm that could be broken at any moment by a frantic bleeping as any one of a million internal human processes failed. Solomon hated, no, despised uncertainty. Hated processes beyond his control.

'Mr Mullan?'

He looked up, surprised by the voice, and saw a doctor in a white coat, carrying a clipboard. 'Yes?'

His face caused the doctor only a moment's pause, and the first thing he said was 'Acid?'

'Sulphuric.'

'Looks like it hurt.' The doctor was young, and Solomon could not help but smile at his clinical humour.

'A little.'

The doctor smiled back briefly, then looked down at his notes. His name tag read *Dr Mistry*. 'Well, we're not here for you, are we? I have some questions about your sister.'

'I'll help if I can.'

'Does she use drugs?'

'Recreationally? I imagine so,' Solomon said.

'You imagine so?'

'She's young, she's pretty, her job is ... unconventional. So yes, I imagine so, now and then.' He paused, remembered he wasn't talking to the police. 'Why do you ask?'

'The amount of pentobarbital in her bloodstream was high,' Dr Mistry said. 'Be good to know if she had any kind of dependency.'

'No,' said Solomon. 'I'm sure of that. How long do you expect her to be unconscious?'

'At the moment we're keeping her under,' the doctor said. 'Induced coma. She'd been in the water for a while, and until we know more … What she's been through, we don't want any seizures. No sense risking it.'

'Which doesn't answer my question. How long?'

The doctor raised his shoulders, not quite a shrug but as good as. 'Comas are strange things,' he said. 'Meaning there's a fairly hefty chasm in our knowledge of them.'

'Right,' said Solomon, grateful for his honesty. 'I was aware of that.'

'Best we can do right now is keep monitoring her and hope for signs of change. Change for the good,' Dr Mistry added.

'You said pentobarbital,' said Solomon. 'Which is a barbiturate.'

'Right. You're a medical man?'

'No, just, I must have read it somewhere,' said Solomon. He paused, then said awkwardly, 'Thank you.'

'No problem.' The doctor looked at his face, a professional scrutiny. 'How do you cope with that?'

'Cope?'

'It must be difficult, out here.' He nodded towards the window. 'In the world.'

'I do my best to avoid it,' said Solomon. 'Unless I absolutely can't.'

The doctor nodded, then put his head to one side, still looking at Solomon. Eventually he said, 'Well, don't give up on it. The world, I mean.'

'And if I already have?'

'That's not the impression you give,' the doctor replied. He tapped a pen against his clipboard, then said, 'Good to have met you.' Solomon was still wondering how to respond when he turned and left.

Luke arrived back half an hour later and immediately slumped into the hospital-room's chair, closed his eyes and groaned, long and loud.

'Are you all right?'

'Solly, Solly, I'm not,' his brother said. 'I'm a long way from. Any news?' he asked, opening one eye, the one nearest their sister.

'I saw the doctor. He told me that she'd tested positive for barbiturates.'

Luke didn't answer, slid forward in the chair so that his head rested on the back, his legs straight, feet crossed. 'Oh?' he said eventually.

'Does that sound like Tiff to you?'

'Course it doesn't,' Luke said. 'But she didn't take them herself, did she?' He settled his chin onto his chest, eyes still closed. Solomon watched him for a while, wondering if he was asleep, but then Luke said, 'Fucking Robbie, wasn't it?'

'Maybe,' said Solomon.

'Maybe? Ain't no *maybe*, Solly.'

Solomon didn't answer, knew there was little point arguing with his brother. And Luke was probably right anyway. Robbie White was as nasty an individual as he could imagine, and he wouldn't put a lot past him. But still. It didn't feel right, even though he couldn't exactly say why.

Luke shook his head, chin rubbing the front of his Adidas top.

'Boy's going to wish he could crawl back inside his mother, start all over again.'

It was strange how, in this hospital room, his brother got the chair, his sister got the bed and Solomon got to do the standing up. Got to do the right thing, the expected thing, which was to be subordinate to the needs of his siblings. Hadn't it always been the same?

'I don't know.'

'We'll know it soon's I ask him,' said Luke, as if to himself, sprawled on the chair. 'It's the way you ask, that's what I've always said.' He said nothing for a long time and Solomon thought that he really had gone to sleep, right up to the point when he said, with a lack of humanity that made Solomon close his own eyes in dismay, 'Fucking Robbie. I'll be seeing you.'

Robbie White had been Tiffany's on-and-off boyfriend for years. Almost four. Three years, nine months and a number of days, depending on the official start date of their relationship, which wasn't confirmed, as far as Solomon knew. Which was nearly four years too many, if you asked Luke. If you asked anyone, Solomon supposed, or at least anyone who cared about Tiffany. Because Robbie White was one of the most unpleasant, unpredictable and manipulative people Solomon had ever met, and during his chaotic upbringing he'd encountered more than his share.

He wasn't big, or imposing. He wasn't aggressive in his demeanour. He had a job, a normal job installing satellite dishes. He had no police record, at least nothing serious, and had never been near prison. Yet there was something wrong with him, something Solomon had difficulty articulating. Adjectivally, he was narcissistic, malignant, sadistic. And he simply would not, apparently could not, listen to reason.

Take Tiffany's twenty-first birthday. Luke had gone the extra mile for her, hired a venue, a hall outside an Essex village. She'd pulled up in a stretch limousine pumping music, and Solomon had watched her tumble out with a happy shriek. Robbie was with her, glued to her as usual. Sometime during the evening he'd taken exception to Tiffany speaking to another guest, Solomon forgot who, which meant he'd never known. Robbie's reaction had been to backhand her across the face in the middle of the dance floor, then drag her out to the still-waiting limousine, which had then taken them both home, from her own twenty-first-birthday celebrations.

It wasn't this, though, that was so disturbing. It was the next day, when the pair of them had turned up at the venue as Luke was paying off the PA hire company and Solomon was helping load gold-sprayed chairs into a Luton van. Robbie had pulled up in his tuned and lowered hot hatch and stepped out. So had Tiffany, but he'd gestured at her to stay where she was. It was sunny, and the area in front of the venue was gravelled, and Robbie had crunched across to where Luke was handing over a thick wad of notes.

'Luke.'

'Fuck do you want?'

'Lost my sunglasses. Last night.'

'So?'

'So I'm looking for them, aren't I?' He wore a sly smile on his face, closer to a smirk.

'Tell you what,' said Luke, taking a step closer to him. Robbie didn't flinch or make any move backwards, in itself incomprehensible. 'You leave right now and I'll try to pretend last night didn't happen.'

Robbie looked down at the ground and pulled at his nose with a finger and thumb. He laughed softly and looked back up. 'But I still wouldn't have my sunglasses, would I? And they weren't cheap.'

Solomon had watched Luke in fascination, wondering just how long it would take before he lost it. He knew that Luke respected their sister's life choices, as far as possible. But there had to be a limit.

'You hit my sister.'

'That's between us. Me and her.'

'You really think?'

'She's a big girl. If she doesn't like it, she can leave.'

'You don't hit her. Never.'

'Yeah, well,' said Robbie. 'These things happen, don't they?'

Luke looked away and nodded up into the blue sky, as if thinking, though Solomon knew he was only trying to control his rage. And controlling his rage wasn't something Luke had a glowing record on. Or any record at all. Eventually he looked back at Robbie's half-amused smile. 'Why doesn't Tiff come over? Tell me about it herself?'

'Nah,' said Robbie. 'We've got somewhere to go. I already told her, she hasn't got time.'

This, Solomon knew, was a provocation too far. But before Luke could do something regrettable, the guy from the PA hire came back and said, 'You've given me too much.'

Luke told him to piss off and count himself lucky, but by the time he'd turned around, Robbie White was walking back to his car, their sister watching him over the roof. Luke went to go after him but changed his mind, decided to leave it, wait for the right time. And as they left, Solomon wondered just why Robbie had come in the first place. Had it really been for his sunglasses? Or some other reason? Solomon didn't understand people very well, didn't have a natural feeling for their instincts or motivations, but it seemed to him that he might have come back just to rub their faces in the fact that he, Robbie White, exercised more influence over their sister than they did.

'Shit,' said Luke, rubbing his eyes with the tips of his fingers. 'Need to go.'

'Now?' You've only just got back, Solomon thought but didn't say.

'Something's come up. Nothing good, either.'

'Oh?' said Solomon. 'Is it anything you want to share?'

Luke shook his head, hard, like he was trying to rearrange everything inside the way it was supposed to be. 'Doesn't matter. Not now.'

'Are you sure?' Solomon looked at him curiously. It wasn't like Luke to mention anything about his dealings. Activities. Whatever you could call them.

'Sure. Don't worry.'

But Solomon did, because it wasn't often he saw Luke worried. Luke could handle himself. Luke handling himself wasn't an issue and never had been. That was the understanding.

'Are you sure that you're sure?'

'Fucking said so, didn't I?' It was said without anger, without heat, but still, it wasn't like Luke to speak to Solomon like that. Solomon nodded, didn't reply, noting mentally that it appeared that his brother was into something more than usually dangerous right now. Though what that was he didn't know and wasn't anxious to find out.

'Well,' he said. 'If you need me ...'

'I'll call. Don't worry.' Luke stood up, and said, 'Forget about it.'

Visiting time was over soon after Luke left, and Solomon kissed his sister goodbye before heading home. On the way out of the hospital he called Fox, with a feeling of trepidation. Solomon had a weird capacity for visualizing data, for organizing and retaining facts, but he had no such affinity with people. He tried to understand them but often found himself reverting to clumsy and broad metaphors, lacking in nuance. He imagined Fox as a tall, precipitous mountain, cold and covered in ice, impossible to scale or get a grip on. This was about as far as he could get with her, where his understanding ended.

Fox picked up after a couple of rings.

'Inspector, it's Solomon Mullan. We met yesterday.'

'We did,' she said, without warmth. She left an uncomfortable pause, then said, 'And how can I help you?'

'I've just been at the hospital. Were you aware that my sister had tested positive for barbiturates?'

There was a pause on the other end, then Fox said, 'I heard. Yes.'

'Then I assume you are taking the case more seriously now.'

'Oh?' Solomon pictured Fox, her frank gaze, short hair, her sharp, unfriendly features. 'Why is that?'

For a moment Solomon didn't have an answer. 'Because why would my sister give herself a potentially lethal dose of barbiturates?'

'Mr Mullan,' said Fox, 'your sister leads, as you yourself told me, an unconventional lifestyle. Probably unhappy, given her profession. You tell me why she might voluntarily ingest a substantial quantity of sedatives.'

'She didn't try to kill herself, if that is what you're insinuating,' said Solomon.

'Didn't she?'

'No. I know my sister.'

'Unfortunately I never had the luxury. So instead, I'm going on the most likely explanation, given the information I have. And I'm treating your sister's situation as either an accident, or attempted suicide.'

'Which it isn't.'

'Which it may or may not be, but for the purposes of the investigation right now, that is the working hypothesis.'

'And her date? Her non-existent date, what was he called?' Solomon pretended to have difficulty recalling his name. 'Tobes?'

'No record of them having ever met, and she never made it to the bar. Instead she was found four miles away, near her home, in a canal. So it's not a priority.'

'Not a priority,' repeated Solomon, his voice suggesting that Fox had just attempted to pass the earth off as flat. 'And Robert White?'

'We'll get to him,' said Fox. 'But again, no suggestion that he had anything to do with it.'

'I imagine that asking him would be a start.'

'I've got your number now,' said Fox, as if he hadn't spoken. 'I'll call you if anything changes.'

'I would encourage you to look at her date again,' Solomon said. 'There's something about that message. Their exchange. There's something there.'

'I'll keep you posted,' Fox said. 'I need to go.'

Solomon walked out into Whitechapel, its street stalls and tide of people, his dead phone still pressed to his ear, and was so outraged by what Fox had just told him that he hardly registered the shocked faces of the people pushing their way past him, or more accurately, away from him.

six

SOLOMON DIDN'T LIKE TO THINK OF HIS APARTMENT AS A prison. He reasoned to himself that its luxury and privacy, its connection to the outside world, and its front door, which he was free to use at any time even though he didn't, were all inconsistent with a penal institute. On the other hand, he knew every square centimetre of it, in far more detail than the longest-serving lag was likely to know his cell. He could mentally reconstruct each room, map out its dimensions, calculate its surface area, its volume, perform any number of three-dimensional mathematical tricks. He could convert the total space into polygons of various shapes and build them into elaborate structures, all the while remaining true to the sum of its original measurements. All this he could do without even needing to open his eyes.

Rather than a prisoner, he preferred to liken himself to an Arctic scientist, stranded at some remote outpost, entirely free to venture outside but unfortunately penned in by hostile and indifferent forces. This felt a more positive and precise analogy, although in the case of the scientist, those forces were polar bears and shifting ice floes and sub-zero blizzards. In Solomon's case, they were people, basic interactions, the challenge of buying milk without unwanted looks and judgement. And so like survival at a distant outpost, Solomon relied on the reliable delivery of supplies, his connection to the outside world dependent on robust communication networks. He had no need to leave the safety of his apartment, provided he planned well and nothing went wrong.

But opening his apartment door and seeing the note on the floor, he was reminded of the conditional fragility of his existence. *Sorry we missed you.* His weekly grocery delivery, gone back to wherever it'd come from. Which meant the only food he had for the next week was frozen. Unless he wanted to visit a shop, which he didn't. He didn't know how close to starving he'd have to be before he faced a busy supermarket, but he wasn't there yet, wasn't even close. He sighed, bent down and picked up the note, crushing it in his hand. Screw it. He would live. He could always ask Luke.

But then, hadn't he just received a long-awaited message, a faraway transmission of hope and opportunity? He checked his notifications, but there was nothing more from Kay. That beacon had blinked out.

What hour now?

That was what Tobes-no-surname had written to his sister. *What hour now?* The phrasing was strange, archaic. Solomon sat at his desk, searched *Convent, bar, London*, the place where his sister and her date had arranged to meet. It existed, that was certain, a converted warehouse building in Shoreditch that had never actually been a convent, but he guessed the idea of getting smashed in a defunct house of God must appeal to trendy twenty-somethings' sensibilities.

Solomon couldn't help thinking that there was something wrong with the whole exchange. Something odd, stilted, artificial. But then, what did he know? It had been years since he'd dated, and he never would again. Emojis, abbreviations, acronyms, all of this was a grammar that he wasn't hard-wired to understand.

He sat back and thought. The untraceable name, the unmatchable profile shot, the strange phrasing, *What hour now?* Even Tiff hadn't understood that one, had answered with a string of question marks. He didn't care what Inspector Fox said, something about this was not right. Not right at all.

The other characteristic that Solomon shared with an Arctic scientist was that, in the solitary time he had, which was the entirety of it, he researched. He read and watched and listened and learnt. Learnt and learnt and learnt. And since he had nothing better to do and nowhere he felt comfortable in going, he figured that he might as well start doing the research that Inspector Fox didn't seem to want to.

A search of crimes linked to dating apps returned thousands of results, telling him that violence against women had risen seven-fold in the last year. Soared. Skyrocketed. Headlines gave more detail:

WOMAN CLAIMS SEXUAL ASSAULT FOLLOWING DATE

COLLEGE STUDENT KIDNAPPED AND BEATEN

WOMAN DIES FLEEING HER DATE

ONLINE DATE MURDERED AND DISMEMBERED

That last result related to a crime in Mexico, and so he refined his search to the UK. It gave him a slight reduction in results, but not much. It had been three years since he'd last dated, and he felt out of touch, disconnected from this online ocean of available singletons. He pictured a vast network, millions of connections firing like synapses, every nanosecond, all across the world. He felt diminished by it, disorientated by this new neural dating system, his sister suddenly reduced to collateral damage of twenty-first-century romance. Was that all this was? The inevitable fallout from too many random hook-ups?

More from a lack of ideas than anything else, Solomon typed in the search terms that best matched his sister's attack. *Online date. Drowning. Canal. Barbiturates. East London.* But before he could look at the results, a notification appeared at the top of his screen. From Kay. A question:

Can we talk?

Solomon paused for a second, then replied:

Of course.
I'm sorry about yesterday.
It's fine. Don't worry.
I do worry. I enjoy speaking to you.

He looked at the two sentences like they might be a trap, dangerous, a beautifully wrapped parcel that made a ticking sound. He typed:

You can still do that.
You're sure?
Of course.

Another notification appeared: *Incoming call.* He chose *Answer without video*, almost a reflex reaction, and Kay appeared on his screen looking like she was still at work judging by the background, white desks, monitors and swivel chairs. She was wearing a lab coat and glasses, her blonde hair pinned up. Solomon had never seen her in glasses or with her hair pinned up before and it gave him an irrational jolt of surprise, as if he'd always known her for one role, and here she was, cast in an exciting yet incomprehensible new one.

'Hey,' she said.

'Hello, Kay. You didn't have to call.'

'I wanted to. Am I interrupting?'

'No.' There isn't a great deal to interrupt, thought Solomon.

'I didn't sleep. I kept thinking what an idiot I was. Well, what an idiot I am. I say stupid things, so it's not just with you, I do it all the time. People say I talk too much, that I should just learn when to shut up, but ...' She ran out of words. 'See? I'm doing it now.'

Solomon smiled, though he knew it wouldn't reach her. 'It's fine,' he said.

'And I haven't even asked about your sister, so now it looks like I'm just thinking of myself, which makes it worse, right?'

'She's the same.'

'Oh good. I mean, not good. But you know what I mean.' She paused. 'Don't you?'

'Yes.'

'Good. That's good.'

'Yes.' Solomon had never spoken to her outside of the Brain Pool, where getting a word in past Phil and Fran counted as an achievement. This was a side of Kay that he'd never seen. Or heard.

'So,' she said, then stopped. Solomon tried to think of something to say to help her out. 'Anyway, I just wanted to—'

'What do you know about online dating?' said Solomon.

'Sorry?' Kay looked surprised, flustered, and Solomon thought with a sudden panic that she'd misinterpreted his question as some kind of come-on.

'I mean, my sister, she'd been on one. A date. Before she was found, in the coma. An online date.' You idiot, Solomon thought. A more mangled sentence you'd be hard pushed to invent if you had a week.

'Oh. Well, yes, I've been on some. One or two, I mean, not lots. Not my thing really, swipe if you think I'm pretty, like some kind of beauty contest.' She stopped, winced, eyes squeezed tight in mortification, then remembered she was on camera. 'Oh God,' she said.

At this Solomon could not help but laugh, a genuine laugh at Kay's heartfelt discomfort. It wasn't often he laughed. 'It's okay.'

'You think this date, it has something to do with what happened to her?'

'Maybe. I don't know. The police are trying to treat it as an accident, avoid an investigation. They found high levels of pentobarbital.'

'Is that like her?'

He thought of his sister, her laugh, the toss of her hair, her reckless, defiant spirit. When she was out of reach of Robbie White's gravitational pull, at least. 'No,' he said. 'Not at all. Plus, they can't match her date's photo, or find his name.'

'Plenty of impostors out there,' said Kay.

'He asked her what time to meet. He said, "What hour now?"'

'Strange phrasing.'

'I know. I can't get past it. It just sounds ...'

On the screen a man came into view, handed something to Kay, a folder, papers. She looked up, then back to Solomon. 'Listen, sorry. Got to go. I'll message you.'

She hung up and Solomon watched the *Call ended* screen for a couple of moments before closing it. Beneath were the results of his search, *online date drowning canal barbiturates east london*. He scanned down the results, and stopped at the fifth:

WOMAN FOUND DEAD HOURS AFTER ONLINE DATE

He followed the link to a story in a local north London paper:

A woman, named as Rebecca Harrington, was discovered dead in the Grand Union Canal in the early hours of the morning of 15 July. Traces of barbiturates were found in her blood, but police are keeping the investigation open. 'We are aware that she had arranged to meet a man online,' a police source told us. 'We are hoping to speak to him.'

Solomon knew enough about norms of distribution, standard deviations from the mean, outliers and various other statistical models to have little time for coincidence. And what he'd just read had too many similarities to his sister's case to seem merely chance. The online date, the canal, the barbiturates. And the timeline, only three weeks apart. At the very least, it should force Fox to do some proper investigating. He took out the card the inspector had given him and started to dial her number, then stopped. He thought of her indifference, her hostility, and ended the call. Instead he looked up the address details for all the Harringtons he could find in Islington, and started making calls himself.

seven

KAY MOST LIKED THE IDEA OF KNOCKING DOWN DOORS AND
taking down names because it gave her something different from the lab, which involved, generally: watch thing grow,
enmesh thing, introduce electrical current to thing, watch thing
die, start growing thing again. Okay, it was more complex than
that, but since there were, as far as she knew, only three (possibly four) people in the world she could have a conversation about
it with, it wasn't something she often talked about. But this, this
was different. This was the real world, not theoretical, and real
results could happen here within days and minutes, rather than
months and years. Basically, it was exciting, and there wasn't a
lot of excitement in her life unless you counted her bi-weekly
Brain Pool meetings, which she frankly didn't.

Rebecca Harrington's parents lived in a third-floor council
flat on a red-brick estate in Archway, just off the Holloway Road.
Kay called the flat number on the intercom at ground level and
waited to be buzzed up, climbing three outside flights of stairs
and walking along a balcony that fronted the building until she
got to their door. It opened before she had time to ring.

'You're Kay?'

The man who stood in the doorway was large and balding

and holding a can of cider even though it was only just gone eleven in the morning.

'Yes.'

'You can come in, but I warn you we haven't cleaned.'

'That's okay.'

The man stood to one side. 'Walk past the kitchen and head to the end,' he said. 'Jean's there.'

'Thank you.'

The day was bright outside, and inside the flat it was dark and gloomy. Kay felt as much as walked her way down the corridor and got to a room at the end, the door open, the curtains inside closed. To begin with she couldn't make a lot out and wondered if she'd found a storeroom instead of the living room, it seemed so chaotic. But soon the chaos reconciled itself into a stack of boxes, and past them two armchairs and a sofa, an indistinct woman sitting on one of the chairs.

'Just be careful of those,' said the woman, Jean, not getting up. 'It's Rebecca's things. We were having a sort-through, but ...' She stopped and Kay could hear her breathing. 'Well. We haven't finished.'

Kay edged past the boxes and found herself standing over Jean sitting in the armchair, the space was so cramped.

'Please,' Jean said. 'Go on. Sit down.'

Kay sat down, and only now, her eyes accustomed to the light, could she see that Jean was crying, gently weeping, a handkerchief crushed in her left hand. For the first time since she'd set off from home that morning, she wondered just what she thought she was doing.

*

It had been Solomon who'd called Kay back the day before. She'd been surprised but not in a bad way. She seemed to have this way of always saying the wrong thing to Solomon, making herself sound thoughtless and clumsy. Hell, she had that way with everyone, what was she thinking? Maybe it was just because she liked him, even though she hardly knew him. He was quiet and considered where she was loud and, well, not. Not usually, even though she tried. She did.

'Solomon.'

'Hello, Kay. Am I interrupting?'

'No.' He wasn't. She was reading a peer-reviewed paper on artificial neural networks, which was almost exactly as interesting as it sounded.

'I wondered ...' Solomon paused. 'I wondered if I could ask you something. To do something for me.'

'Course,' said Kay. She'd be glad to, happy to do something that might score a point, make a contribution to the credit side of their account. 'What do you need?'

Solomon had been uncertain on his theory, the similarities between his sister's case and that of Rebecca Harrington. But Kay liked a theory, had no problem with them, however outlandish. Weren't unlikely theories what she traded on pretty much every week in the laboratory? Maybe this will work. Nope. Maybe this. Nope. This? Uh-uh. Etc.

'And they won't talk about it over the phone?'

'No. And if I go ...' He paused again. 'It's usually better if somebody else does the face-to-face.'

'Are you ... I mean ...' This time Kay paused. 'How bad is it?'

Always the same question, thought Solomon. And how to answer? 'It's pretty bad.'

'What happened? Sorry. If you don't mind me asking. If you don't want to talk about it, that's fine, I just, you know. Maybe it might help. Isn't that a thing, talking about it, isn't it supposed to help?'

'I'd rather not,' said Solomon.

'No,' said Kay. 'Sorry. I, yeah. Forget it.'

'It's okay.'

'I'm intruding.'

'I'm asking you to knock on a stranger's door and get details about their daughter's death.'

'True,' said Kay. 'Very true. So okay, what's the address?'

'Jim can't deal with it,' said Jean. She was maybe fifty and her short hair was dyed blonde, and with her legs tucked underneath her on the chair she looked as small and fragile as a fairy. 'He started boxing up her things and next thing I know he's given up and he's drinking again. Which ain't like him. It ain't.'

'Can you tell me anything about the investigation?' said Kay. 'Do you have any details?'

'Investigation,' Jean said, a derisory laugh in her voice. 'Do me a favour. Three weeks and they've done nothing.'

'Solomon told me they never found the man she was supposed to be on a date with.'

'No, they never found him. But then they didn't exactly look very hard. Left a lot of stones unturned, that lot.'

'Why was that?'

'Why? Because my Becky weren't rich and she weren't perfect. And when it all looked like too much hard work, they thought sod it, she's tried it in the past so she must've tried it again.'

'Sorry, tried what?' said Kay.

'Topping herself,' said Jean, sudden hostility in her voice. 'Overdose. What d'you think I mean?'

Kay didn't know what to say, felt out of her depth, missing vital information. 'Sorry,' she said, 'I didn't ... I mean, I wasn't aware that ... that Becky, I just ...' Stop talking, she thought. Just, stop.

'Anyway, Jim kept on at them but they didn't want to know. And now ...' Jean closed her eyes and willed herself not to start crying again. 'It's done.'

Kay kept silent, and the only sound in the room was the ticking of a clock over the unlit gas fire.

'Do you have anything you can share?' she said eventually, as gently as she could. Think about each sentence, she told herself. Work it out in advance, test it in your head. 'About this date she had? It's just, Solomon, he thinks there are similarities. With his sister.' She paused, planned the next sentence. 'And if there is, perhaps it'll help everyone.'

'Sounds ridiculous to me,' said Jean. 'But he had a nice voice, your Solomon.'

'We're not ...' Kay began, then stopped. 'So, was there anything?'

'Only what was on her phone,' said Jean. 'The police made posters. Of the picture. Of him.'

'You have one?'

Jean reached over the arm of her chair and found a sheet of paper. 'Here.' A copy of a photo, a man's face. Dark hair, long. Slight smile. Nothing remarkable. But Kay might just have swiped on it, who knew?

'Do you know his name?'

'Caesar. Least, that's what he called himself. C-A-E-S-A-R.'

'Were there any messages?'

'That's how they do it now, isn't it?' said Jean, for the first time showing some animation, sitting up straighter in the chair, which seemed too big for her. 'They look at a photo, send a couple of words, and that's it.'

'It's easy nowadays.'

'Too easy, you ask me. Anyway, yeah, there was. They were read out at the inquest.'

'Do you have them?'

'No. They're on her phone, on Becky's phone. The police have still got it. Odd.'

'What is?'

'The messages. They were odd. Sounded odd, I dunno. Can't explain.'

'Can you remember anything about them?'

'They were meeting at a bar. Called the Gypsy Queen. He was taking her out for cocktails. That's all I remember. That, and thinking that there was something odd about it.'

'Odd, like what he said? Rebecca's date?'

'More the way he said it. Or wrote it. It just didn't sound right.'

Kay nodded and was about to thank Jean when there was the sound of smashing from another room, again and again, and a man's voice bellowing, like an animal gone berserk, with the note rising higher and higher until it more resembled a cry of pain. Jean stood up, said, 'Jim. You'll need to go.'

'I ...'

'Now. I don't want him seeing you. Not like he is.'

Kay took the copy of the photo and stood up too, surprised by how much taller she was than Jean. 'Thank you.'

Jean nodded, distracted, and pushed at Kay to get her moving. 'Just head for the door. Don't stop. He doesn't need talking to, not now.'

Kay headed for the front door, keeping her eyes focused ahead of her, though as she passed the door to the kitchen the keening sound from Jean's husband seemed louder than was possible. She fumbled with the opening but got the front door open and let light in – she'd forgotten how bright it was outside – and for a moment, stepping out into the sunshine, it felt like she'd escaped something, though she did not know what.

eight

IF THE DISPOSAL OF BODIES WAS SOMETHING YOU COULD actually rely on, if they'd stay drowned and never rise to the surface, if they'd stay buried and never get dug up, if sniffer dogs and forensic scientists and grasses never led you to them, then Luke would've got rid of Robbie White a long while back. And cheerfully, too. He'd probably have whistled while he shovelled, lost himself in the joy of the job, dug an extra-deep grave to wrestle the fucker's body into.

But the problem right now was that he couldn't even get hold of Robbie White's all-too-alive one. He'd disappeared, gone off grid, which was suspicious enough, he figured. Tiff ends up in hospital and Robbie White vanishes off the face of the earth. As if he needed any more convincing that Robbie was behind it anyway. Solomon could say what he liked, all he wanted was an easy life, to rot away quietly in his apartment. Luke wasn't like that.

'Well if you see him, don't tell him I'm looking for him,' Luke said, talking to his dashboard, hands-free Bluetooth fuck-knows-what putting his mobile over the speakers. 'And call me. Yeah?'

'Count on it,' said the voice on the other end of the line, a supposed friend of Robbie's, except that Robbie wasn't the kind of person who exactly had what you might call friends. Because he was an arsehole, basically.

'Do that,' said Luke, and hung up. He was on his way to his lock-up, or what he still called his lock-up, though things had changed from the time he was starting out and could only stretch to a single garage in a line of other garages behind a housing estate in Dagenham. This was bigger, a lot bigger, two corrugated-iron-sided barns and an office, behind a gate you could only open if you knew the code. Which he did, and could count on the fingers of one thumb the other people who did. Which was how he liked it.

He indicated and took an exit off the A127. He was driving an Audi but had had the RS badges taken off so that it looked like an ordinary exec-mobile, rather than a four-litre monster that could outrun any police car. Would give their helicopter a run for its money too, come to that.

He tapped his phone's screen and called up Solomon's number, hit call, waited, but his screen told him that the user was busy. Luke wondered who his brother could be speaking to. As far as he was aware, he didn't know anyone. Apart from him and Tiff. He tried him again, got the busy message again. He'd try later. Right now, he had Robbie White to find.

Inspector Fox hadn't particularly wanted to call Solomon Mullan back, not just because she didn't have any news for him, but also because the case of Tiffany Eloise Mullan wasn't at the top of her list of priorities. Or to put it another way, she had better things to do. But eventually she'd found a ten-minute window and had called his number.

'Hello?'

'Mr Mullan? It's Inspector Fox. You called.'

'Yes. Thank you for calling back.'

'How can I help you?' said Fox, not somebody who had time for civilities. 'I've got five minutes.'

There was a brief pause on the other end, then Solomon said, 'Have you heard of a woman named Rebecca Harrington?'

'No. Who is she?'

'Who was she. She went on a date with a man she met online. She was found dead, in a canal, with barbiturates in her blood-stream.'

Oh here we go, thought Fox. Here we go. A member of the public with too much time on their hands. Spare me. Jesus, Allah, Buddha, one of you, any of you, please. Spare me. 'Oh?' she said.

'And the police never managed to trace him. The man she met. They never found him.'

'And you think ...' She left the sentence hanging. She wasn't going to give him any help, wasn't going to supply the oxygen.

'I don't think anything. The similarities are self-evident. Wouldn't you say?'

Don't encourage him, she thought. 'On the face of it? Maybe.'

'I think you need to hear this.'

I'm sure I don't, Fox thought, but said, closing her eyes in anticipation, 'Okay. What have you got?'

Kay had taken shots of Rebecca Harrington's date. She'd called him up and messaged them over as JPEGs.

'That's his name?' said Solomon.

'It's what he calls himself,' said Kay. 'I guess it might not be his real one.'

'Caesar. That could be, I don't know, Italian?'

'It could be. It could be anything.'

Solomon looked at the man's face. Dark. Not blond, not like Tobes. 'What do you think?' he said.

'I don't know,' Kay said. 'I never saw the other one.'

'There's something about the mouth,' Solomon said, mostly to himself. 'Maybe.' He thought back to the face he'd seen on his sister's mobile, in Fox's office. Wondered if he remembered it right, if it hadn't been distorted by his own wishful thinking, reshaped by his conflicted interests. But Solomon had never misremembered anything, as far as he knew. Certainly he'd never forgotten anything. It just didn't happen. Everything he'd ever read or seen was there, ready, waiting to be whistled up from the vast vault of his memory in a moment.

'And you don't have the messages?' he said.

'They're on her phone, and the police have still got it. But Jean did say that they sounded odd.'

'Odd in what way?'

'She couldn't say. All she remembered was that they were meeting at the Gypsy Queen. For cocktails.'

'And that definitely exists?' said Solomon.

'Passed it on the way home,' said Kay. 'Looks okay, actually.' Stop talking, she thought. Don't invite him. She watched her screen, his question-mark avatar, as close to Solomon's face as she'd ever got.

'Mmm,' said Solomon. 'It's possible that I'm mad.'

'We all are,' said Kay. 'It's a question of how far we embrace it, rather than how far gone we are.'

Solomon nodded at Kay, aware that she couldn't see him but doing it anyway, feeling unexpectedly in tune with her, with her offbeat worldview. But not to the point that he'd let her know, because then some kind of rapport would be established, which might lead to affection, which in turn might lead to her, eventually, wanting to see him. And she mustn't. She couldn't.

'Maybe,' he said, his tone dismissive.

He saw her face close and wished that he hadn't said it, but knew that he'd had to. He'd see her at the Brain Pool meetings, and that was enough. This, all this, was a mistake. He could see it now.

'Well,' said Kay. 'I've got, you know ...'

'Yes.'

'So, if there's anything else ... You know where I am. Here, I guess. You know, if you want ...'

'Thank you,' said Solomon. 'I appreciate it. What you've done.'

'Then ...' She paused, then quickly said, 'Okay, well I'll see you,' and closed their link, leaving Solomon with an empty screen that he knew he should be grateful for but definitely wasn't.

Fox listened with a growing sense of relief to what Solomon Mullan had to say about the similarities between his sister's case and that of Rebecca Harrington. He had nothing. There were surface similarities, but nothing else. Nothing deeper. She was sure of that. Didn't even need to think about it.

'No record of her ever going to the bar,' she said, scrolling through the casework on her monitor. 'Looks like she overdosed.'

'She was found in the canal,' said Solomon.

'Part of her,' said Fox. 'She'd got tangled in a mooring rope. But she didn't drown, definitely overdosed.'

'Possibly,' said Solomon on the other end of the line.

'Not the first time, either,' said Fox, ignoring Solomon's scepticism. 'And she'd been arrested ...' she scrolled back up, checked, 'seven times for possession.'

'Of?'

'Of heroin, MDMA, Seconal, which I believe is a barbiturate. Diazepam.'

There was silence on the other end of the line, and Fox leant back from her monitor and mentally disengaged. This, all this, was a waste of her time. Eventually Solomon said, 'I didn't know that.'

'Did you know that a note was found on her, addressed to her parents, telling them she was sorry?'

'No.'

'Well now you do,' Fox said. 'So. Was there anything else?'

Solomon didn't answer immediately, then said, 'Any progress on my sister's case?'

'I'm afraid not,' said Fox. 'We've had nothing on this, erm ...'

'Tobes?'

'Tobes. Yes. Yes, him. Nothing's come back yet. If anything does, I'll let you know.'

'Okay.'

'Are we done?'

'Yes.'

'Fine.' Fox looked up at a knock on her door. It opened and her boss's head showed around its edge. She held up two fingers – two minutes – and he nodded his head upwards, my office. 'I've got to go,' she told Solomon. 'And please, next time, give me something more substantial?'

She hung up and looked at her monitor one more time. There was a screen capture of a messaging exchange between Rebecca

Harrington and her potential date included in the case file. She opened it up and read it.

Want to go out sometime?

Maybe. Where u want 2 go?

I love the Gypsy Queen ...

Wheres that?

A barj

Barge?

Sorry. Meant bar, in Hackney.

Lol.

Gluh

?

I mean glamorous. Can't type. Cocktails of infinite variety.

Sounds ☺

It all looked perfectly normal to Fox. Nothing to see here. Move along. She closed the screen capture, then closed down the whole case file. It wasn't her investigation, and as far as she was concerned there was no new information, nothing to warrant further enquiries. Besides, her boss wasn't the kind of person you kept waiting.

Solomon couldn't sleep that night. Around three in the morning he went to the bathroom and rubbed cream into his face without turning on the light. He winced, not at the pain but at the memory of his conversation with Inspector Fox. She must have thought him ridiculous, his theory beneath contempt. And Kay, getting her involved. He shook his head. He wasn't used to being wrong. It was a feeling he didn't like.

He went to his living room and picked up the copied photograph of Rebecca Harrington's date, Caesar. He had dark hair, where Tobes's was blond. Brown eyes, not blue. There was a harder look to his face, something challenging. Tobes's had been softer. But still, wasn't there something there? In the mouth, a ripeness, the bottom lip thrusting forward almost in a pout. Wasn't there? Solomon remembered reading about the difficulty of facial recognition in AI, the complexity of the algorithms, which needed to adjust for different lighting, angles, expressions, all the nuances provided by the myriad of muscles in the face. He looked again at the photograph. Yes, he knew all about faces. And he'd learnt long ago that they were tricky things.

nine

CATO, NAMED AFTER THE CRAZY BUTLER IN THOSE PETER Sellers films, he told her, only she'd never seen them, but anyway, Cato, he was brilliant. Talking to him was like – she tried to think about what it was like, it was like swinging through the jungle on Tarzan's back, the conversation shifting, this way and that, the subjects changing like he was leaping from vine to vine and taking her along with him. Sarah lay back on the grass in the bright sunshine and closed her eyes and congratulated herself on what she thought was not a bad analogy at all. Or was it a metaphor? She didn't know. Didn't care, and anyway, it wasn't a perfect analogy or metaphor or whatever, because Cato was nothing like Tarzan, was funny and sensitive and, what was it? Yeah, brilliant. He was brilliant.

'Are you okay?' he asked her.

She still had her eyes closed so she couldn't see him, but said, 'Yeah. Brilliant.'

'So you haven't?'

'Haven't what?' Sarah was prepared to admit that she'd lost track of this last conversational tangent.

'Seen anything good at the theatre recently.'

'Um,' she said, stupidly she thought, which made her giggle. 'No. I saw *The Book of Mormon*, but that was like two years ago.'

'Enjoy it?'

'Haven't you seen it?'

'Yes.'

'Well then.'

'Well then what?' said Cato, a laugh in his voice.

'Well then, you know it's fucking hilarious,' said Sarah, and chuckled to herself, her head heavy on the warm grass, its smell in her nostrils, all around her.

'Ah. A critic.'

'I wish,' she said.

'I sometimes think,' said Cato, 'that dating, the way we do it now, it's like an audition. You ever think that?'

Sarah opened her eyes and struggled up on to her elbows. The sun was very bright and she blinked against it. 'Say again?'

Cato sighed, and for a moment Sarah thought it was a sigh of impatience, but then he smiled his smile and everything was okay. 'I was thinking, that's all,' he said. 'How we see a picture of somebody, maybe their name, and that's it. That's all you get. And you have to say yes or no. Or swipe right or left, or whatever. And it's a bit like an audition, what an audition must be like.'

'I guess,' said Sarah.

'Unfair, basically,' Cato said. He was sitting cross-legged on the grass and he picked a daisy, pulled the petals off it.

'Well, it worked for us,' Sarah said. 'So it can't be all bad.'

'True,' said Cato thoughtfully, and dropped the daisy and looked at her, smiled. 'That's a good point.' And for some reason, she didn't know why but she was happy to go with it, Cato telling her that she'd made a good point made her almost ineffably happy, which was weird, because, well, basically because she wasn't often happy. Yep, she thought. He's brilliant.

They'd arranged to meet at a pub in town, but when she'd got there, Cato had been outside, called out her name, and when he'd caught up with her he'd asked her if she minded a change of plan.

'Like what?' she said. He looked better than his picture online, somehow more graceful in real life, but with the same crazy tangle of brown curls and amazing blue eyes.

'Like, basically,' he said, a half-smile on his face as if he was both super-confident and very unsure, 'a picnic. Well, even better, a barbecue.' He lifted both arms into the warm blue sky and turned slowly. 'On a day like this.'

Sarah watched him, not sure what to make of him, but it was hot and she didn't fancy sitting inside a pub all day, and if he was boring, or weird, or a nutter, then it made it all the easier for her to run away. 'Sure,' she said. 'Why not?'

'Thank Jesus our Lord for that,' said Cato, nodding for her to follow him, back to where he'd run from when he'd called her name. On the pavement was a cool box, two disposable barbecues on top of it. 'I planned it as a surprise, but then thought you might say no. Which would have been damned inconvenient.' The way he said *damned inconvenient*, like he was an upper-class Second World War fighter pilot, made Sarah laugh out loud.

'And that wouldn't do,' she said, trying for the same accent.

'Hey,' Cato said, as if he hadn't heard, 'you're not a vegetarian, are you?'

'No.'

He wove his fingers together and shook them gratefully at the sky. 'In that case, I'll call a cab and we'll head for a little place I know called Victoria Park.'

*

Sarah thought she might have dozed off, or drifted off, or just followed a train of thought somewhere over the rainbow of ordinary existence, when Cato asked her, 'How are you feeling?'

'Good.'

'You want anything else to eat?'

'I couldn't.' What had they eaten? Couscous and aubergine salad and artichokes in oil and merguez done on the barbecue, halloumi too, and flatbread and hummus and olives, wine ... God. She felt like she was sinking through the earth just from the mass of it all, yet weightless too, floating upwards, which was a contradiction she couldn't quite get her head around, but hey. It was all good.

'Because there's still plenty left.'

'Seriously.' She laughed. 'I'd pop, and I'm already floating above this green planet.' She giggled at this, the image of her, huge and inflated, small people hauling on ropes, trying to keep her from floating away into the ether.

'One more thing,' Cato said. 'For me?'

'Oh Cato,' she sighed, and breathed out, emptied her lungs, wondering whether that might bring her closer to earth, cause her to descend. No dice. Up and up she drifted.

'You said you were floating,' said Cato, some miles below her.

'I am,' Sarah said proudly. From a long way away she could hear the sounds of children playing, laughter, a dog's bark.

'It's the heat,' Cato said. 'That's what makes us float. Look, I've caught up with you, and it's getting ...' He laughed. 'We're getting high up.'

'Mmm,' said Sarah, words beyond her now, even higher above, impossible to reach, to marshal.

'Like hot-air balloons,' Cato said. 'That's what we are. Warm air, up we go. Up, up, up.'

'Up,' said Sarah, repeating Cato's words all she could manage right now.

'It's simple!' said Cato. 'It's physics. That's what we're encountering. But,' he said, 'I have an answer.' He sounded shrewd, to Sarah's ears. What he was about to say was worth hearing, she reckoned.

'Mmm?' she tried to say, though the noise she made sounded strange to her.

'Do you mind?' said Cato, and Sarah felt herself being hoisted up. She opened her eyes to see Cato's face in front of hers, his crazy curls, those blue, blue eyes. He let her go and she came to rest sitting up, her back against something. The cool box? How could that be? Hadn't she just been miles above earth?

She watched Cato hold up a plate with one hand, a metal flask in another. 'Sorbet,' he said. 'With a very special sauce.' He upended the flask and pressed a button and it sprayed smoke over the plate, wisps of it disappearing into the hot still air. He took a spoon and broke off a piece of sorbet. It was yellow, pastel, and it was still smoking. 'Open wide, and we'll get you back down to this green planet.'

Sarah watched the spoon get closer and felt the chill in her mouth, cold, too cold, much too cold. Freezing. She made a sound and Cato leant forward, Sarah could see that he was kneeling on the grass, leaning forward and putting his hand over her mouth.

'This is supposed to happen off stage,' he said. 'People shouldn't be able to hear.'

Her mouth felt cold, so cold it burned yet colder, and then it was just pain, not hot or cold, her teeth feeling like sharp wires were being pulled through them, slicing them, twisting them, pain and cold and then just pain, just pain.

'Does it hurt?' said Cato, but she couldn't answer, could feel her heels beating the soft earth. Had she already landed, come down from the sky? 'There's only one solution. Do you want it to stop?'

It was all Sarah wanted, that this pain, this cheese-wire tearing of her teeth, the cold fire slicing her gums and tongue, that it would stop. She closed her eyes and nodded her head, felt Cato's palm slip against her lips.

'Head back,' he said. 'Head right back. You need to trust me here. I'm going to take my hand away. Now, do you trust me?'

Sarah didn't know, didn't even consider the question or its implications, only wanted the pain to go. Nothing worse could happen, nothing worse than what she was feeling now. Trust was irrelevant. She put her head back.

'You need to open your mouth.'

Sarah opened her mouth.

'You can scream if you like,' Cato said.

Sarah thought she probably already was.

'Open wide,' said Cato.

Sarah opened her mouth, opened her eyes, and saw Cato with a spoon in his hand, and in the spoon, orange that seemed to fight the blue of the day, its brightness unnatural, outglowing the sun's heat, and Cato said, 'I'll be gone in a moment,' and he tilted the spoon, and if anything, though she would never have believed it seconds ago, the pain was even worse.

ten

IT WASN'T OFTEN THAT THE BRAIN POOL HAD A PROPER argument. Its modus operandi was more tetchy debate, particularly between Phil and Fran. But this time it had gone over, crossed the line from discussion to disagreement. Predictably, Solomon thought, Phil was at the middle of it. Less predictably, it was the usually equable Masoud who was bringing it on. And over what? Over whether, in the new show they were preparing questions for, darts should be counted as a sport. Solomon knew that history was littered with examples of wars begun over trivialities, but he couldn't help but think that this was taking it up a level. Or down.

'It is irrelevant,' said Masoud. 'What you think does not matter, it is what the public think. They are going to be watching.'

'And the public watch darts,' said Phil, drinking quickly, agitated, lager disappearing down his neck like he was trying to put out a fire. 'So there you are.'

Masoud shook his head. 'The public watch the Queen's speech,' he said. 'That does not make it a spectator sport.'

'You know what I think?' Phil stopped, eyed Masoud warily.

'No,' said Masoud. 'What is it you think?'

'Phil, maybe you'd like to consider not saying anything for a while,' said Fran. 'Seriously.'

'What I think,' said Phil, ponderously, setting his drink down unsteadily, 'is that this is a cultural thing.'

'Oh marvellous,' said Fran.

'What?' said Masoud. 'Because I'm Iranian?'

'No,' said Phil, 'because you're middle class. And the middle classes,' turning to Fran with a hand held up to head off any objections, 'don't like darts because it's incompatible with their conception of sport as a Graeco-Roman pursuit of the homo-erotic athletic ideal.' He closed his eyes and nodded to himself in approval.

'You just do not like the middle classes,' said Masoud. 'They intimidate you.'

'Ah,' said Phil, picking his glass up with one hand and point-ing at Masoud unsteadily with the other. 'Now. That's not true, not at all.'

'I believe that it is,' said Masoud.

'Nope,' said Phil. It appeared to Solomon that Phil had shot his bolt with his Graeco-Roman hypothesis, eloquence now just a memory. 'Nope nope nope.'

'I had the opportunity,' said Kay, 'to teach, rather than go into research. But I didn't like the idea of dealing with squabbling children. I'm beginning to have the same feeling now.'

'Solomon?' said Fran, looking into their PC's webcam, directly at Solomon in his living room. 'Perhaps you could tell us what you think?'

Me? Solomon thought. 'Um.' He felt a sudden panic, not used to being the centre of attention. 'We could …' Could what? 'Put it to a vote? You know, in the finest Graeco-Roman tradition.'

Kay clapped her hands quickly, quietly, giving Solomon a smile he tried not to read anything into.

'Ah, now then,' said Fran. 'What is it they say about the wisdom of Solomon?' She looked around the table. 'So. Let's see your hands. Who supports the inclusion of darts within the sporting category?'

Phil raised his hand, and so did Kay. Masoud looked at her. 'What?' said Kay. 'I like darts.'

Fran sighed. 'And those against?'

Masoud raised his hand, regarding Phil darkly. Fran raised hers. 'And you, Solomon?'

'Darts conforms to the hand-eye criteria,' said Solomon. 'But it is played in pubs. No darts,' he concluded. 'But Masoud, can I suggest that bridge is out too?'

Masoud smiled. 'I can live with that.'

'Phil?'

He shook his head in disgust. 'The revolution can't come soon enough.' He stood up. 'Excuse me. I'm about to piss myself.'

'Well,' said Fran, brightly. 'Shall we move on to golf?'

When Solomon was with the Brain Pool, he didn't answer his phone, which meant that Luke still hadn't got through to him, which didn't make his mood any better. Just someone else who'd vanished, disappeared off the radar. He was still looking for Robbie White and had got a call that morning from a distant acquaintance he'd met in Chelmsford prison, who'd told him that White had gone to Southend, where his sister lived.

Luke hated Southend, had once got in a fight outside a nightclub there that had violated his parole conditions, even though the fight had had nothing to do with him. Some guy had pushed another guy, everybody starts hitting each other, and the girl he's with catches one right on the jaw, so of course Luke has to get involved, which he does, but it wasn't his fight. He didn't start it, all he was doing was standing up for the girl he was with, and guess what? He ends up doing another ninety days. Exactly, he reckoned, the kind of thing you expect if you're stupid enough to go to Southend.

And anyway, it turned out that *a*, Robbie White's sister was a junkie, and *b*, even if she had seen Robbie, she wouldn't have been able to remember. Luke had had a look around her house, and found a two-year-old in a room at the back tetchily fighting its way out of its cot, but no Robbie White. He'd even considered calling social services, but this wasn't his fight either. See? Southend. No good ever came of going there.

He tried Solomon again, listening to the ringtone in his Audi as he passed the exit for his two-barn-and-an-office lock-up on the A127.

'Hello? Luke?'

'Solomon. Thought you'd died or something.'

'Not yet,' said Solomon. 'I've somehow still been spared.'

'Yeah, well. I've been looking for Robbie. Wanted to know if you'd heard anything.'

'No.' There was silence from Solomon's end, then he said, 'You really think he did it?'

'Course I do,' said Luke. 'So do you, if you're honest.'

'Maybe,' said Solomon.

'He's a scumbag,' said Luke. 'Course it was him. It's been coming. I should have done something about him years ago.'

More silence from Solomon, then, 'I don't know.'

'Well Robbie fucking White does. And soon's I find him, he's going to tell me.'

'I haven't heard from him.'

'No, well if you do, you tell me, yeah? Soon as.'

'I will,' said Solomon. 'But promise me this. If *you* find him, let the police deal with it. Yes?'

This time Luke was silent for a moment, watching the road, the Audi's bonnet swallowing up the white lines of the arterial road. 'You're kidding, right?' he said eventually. 'After all he's done?'

Luke had done time inside and he'd met his share of sociopaths and psychopaths and nutters, but he'd never met anyone quite so ... How could he put it? Irritatingly evil, was how he'd sum Robbie White up. He was as cruel and unpleasant a person as he'd ever met, but he was also, like, really really fucking annoying. Like a bug that wouldn't die, no matter how much you squashed it. No, scratch that. More like a turd you couldn't flush, you thought you'd seen the last of it and there it was again, bobbing back up, refusing to fuck off past the U-bend.

Take, what had it been, two years ago? More? He's at home and Tiff calls him on his mobile, she's crying, saying that Robbie's lost it because she went out and left her mobile at home, so he couldn't call her every half-hour to find out where she was who she was with when she'd be back how much she'd drunk, etc., etc. So now she's sitting in her car, outside the flat, she's locked herself in and she needs Luke to come round, because she thinks he might kill her, really might kill her this time.

When Luke arrives, Tiff's still in the car and he buzzes her flat and Robbie answers, says, 'All right, Luke?'

'I've got Tiff outside, thinks you're going to kill her.'

Robbie laughs through the intercom. 'Think she might've had a bit too much to drink.'

'Oh?'

'You know women, right? Fucking mental.'

'Tiff's my sister,' said Luke.

'Well,' said Robbie. 'Can't choose your family, right?'

Luke got Tiffany out of the car, told her it would be okay, he was there, and together they walked up to the first floor. Luke took Tiffany's keys and opened the door, and before he had slid them out of the lock, Robbie White had come out, taken Tiffany's chin in one hand and spat in her face.

But it wasn't that, it wasn't. Okay, that was bad, but it was afterwards, when Luke had finished with Robbie, Tiffany screaming in the corner of the living room and Robbie on his back, Luke holding his shirt front with one hand, his other bunched into a fist, Robbie White's blood all over the knuckles. Robbie had looked up at him, blood etching his teeth in dark lines, smiled, and said, 'Next time, tell her not to forget her fucking mobile.'

It just didn't make sense, none at all. For Christ's sake, Tiff worked as a stripper. Or burlesque dancer, whatever, Luke didn't care. But that was the thing, nor did Robbie. He never seemed to care at all. Like, Tiff'd spend the week showing her tits to strangers, but soon as she went out on a night on her own, he got all jealous and couldn't take it. It didn't make sense to Luke, really didn't.

Anyway, it shouldn't matter, should all have been in the past. Because three months ago Tiffany had finally thrown Robbie out, and when that hadn't got rid of him, and Luke's threats hadn't worked, she'd had a restraining order taken out on him.

And even though he'd park outside her flat now and then, and make shitty phone calls late at night, she'd moved on.

And now this. It was like Luke had always said. Robbie White. A turd you just couldn't flush.

Solomon turned his mobile off just in case Luke started drinking and decided to call him back up, share with him just what he'd got planned for Robbie White, if he ever found him. It wasn't that Solomon didn't share his brother's antipathy towards Robbie White. He did, but he'd also found him impossible to understand, or relate to. Like with Fox, Solomon had reduced Robbie White to a blunt metaphor, appearing in his mind as a Catherine wheel, spitting angry white-hot spiteful sparks, nothing more. This was what bothered him, the idea that this totem of depthless irritation could have done what he did to Tiffany. He wasn't worthy. Plus, and this was something Solomon did have an instinct for, it didn't seem Robbie White's style. What he would do was beat her up, knock her about and take it too far. It would be obvious, loud, nasty, crass. It felt, though Solomon wasn't much given to exercising his intuition, but it did feel as if something else was at play here, something more sinister, and more intelligent. Though after his first attempt at investigation, he couldn't say that he felt confident in his theory.

Hey. You there?

It was Kay. Careful, Solomon thought. You mustn't let her get too close. Too close and she'll end up seeing you, and then she'll disappear forever.

I am.

Tonight was ... fun.

Did Phil make it home okay?

No idea. Probably. He's a force.

He is.

You didn't tell me. About Rebecca. What did the police say?

Solomon wondered how to answer. It was Kay who had done the work, who had spoken to Rebecca's family, shouldered that emotional burden. He wasn't being fair. He should have told her immediately.

They didn't want to know.

Why?

Rebecca Harrington had a history of drug abuse. She'd overdosed before.

Oh no.

There was a note found on her.

God. Her poor parents.

Solomon waited, feeling culpable, humiliated, with no idea what to add. This had been his idea. Within the Brain Pool, he was infallible. But this was different, more complex and nuanced than the binary question/answer yes/no right/wrong that they usually dealt with. He'd tried something in the outside world, with all of its random events and statistical unruliness. And he'd come up short.

So ... there's nothing in it?

Don't think so.

Hmm.

Hmm?

The photo. You saw something in it.

My imagination.

Maybe. But maybe not. I've never known you to be wrong about anything before.

Thanks.

God, I almost added a smiley face.

Don't.

No.

Well. Thanks for your help.

No problem.

Night.

Night, you.

Night, you. Like the kind of thing somebody would say to somebody else they loved, say it while looking at them, looking at their face.

Solomon folded down the screen of his laptop so that he could see no more. He closed his eyes. The truth was that, like Fox or

Robbie White, Kay was another person Solomon could not fully comprehend. But when he thought of her, what he pictured in his mind was a bird in a gilded cage, an elaborately scrolled and wrought cage, the bird inside splendid and singing happily, but utterly impossible to get to.

eleven

IT WAS INTERESTING, THOUGHT SOLOMON, HOW QUICKLY THE
human brain could adapt to new realities. He was sitting next
to his sister, who was still intubated, still unconscious, and her
sleeping face in the middle of this hospital room had already lost
its power to shock or unsettle. This was now where she lived.
Just as long as she kept living, he thought, that would be okay.
That was something he would be able to cope with.

'You made it out again,' said Dr Mistry, the same doctor
Solomon had spoken with a couple of days ago. 'It's becoming
a habit.'

Solomon nodded. 'And the sooner you get her conscious, the
sooner I can stop.'

Dr Mistry took a torch from his pocket and leant over Tiffany,
lifting one eyelid and shining the light into her eye, then the
other. 'Well, I'd say we're not there yet.'

'No change?'

'Wouldn't expect one. We're keeping her nicely under for
now. She's due an MRI tomorrow, so we'll know more.' He took
a wrist, felt for her pulse. 'I think I mentioned, we don't want to
take any risks with her. She was in the water a while.'

'So what's the prognosis?' said Solomon.

'Well, she's healthy,' the doctor said. 'Excellent muscle tone. What is it she does?'

'She's a stripper,' said Solomon.

'Is that so?' said the doctor, smoothly, barely a hesitation; Solomon had to give him credit for that. He let go of her wrist. 'Well, I'll need to revise my opinion of that profession. Here,' he said, taking a card from his back pocket. 'I meant to give you this.' He handed it to Solomon. On it was a name, *Marija Andersen*, and a title, *Cosmetics*. Below was a mobile number.

'What's this?'

'Someone I know. She does, how would I describe it?' He looked at Solomon, appraising him, said, 'Weaponized make-up.'

Solomon frowned. 'That being?'

'Does a lot of work for film. Turning people into zombies, that kind of thing.'

'Ah,' said Solomon. 'So maybe she can try some reverse engineering.'

Dr Mistry didn't smile at this. 'It's up to you. But she's helped people before. I don't mean to intrude.'

Solomon stood and put the card into his pocket. 'Thanks.'

'There's no shame in it,' said the doctor. 'You're entitled to a normal life. Anyway, I've got my rounds.' He nodded towards Solomon's sister. 'We'll look after her.'

Once Dr Mistry was safely gone, Solomon took the card he'd been given back out of his pocket and sat down again, turning it over in his hands for a long time.

Solomon stayed until Luke got to the hospital and took over from him. That was how it worked, how it always had done. The two of them looked after Tiffany, made sure she had what she needed. Food, clothes, anything, it didn't matter what, they'd do their best to take care of her Maslovian hierarchy of needs. And they also protected her from the outside world, already knowing, from a young age, that it was dangerous and that people in authority frequently meant them harm. They'd learnt that from their days in care, and it was a lesson they never forgot. Was perhaps, though Solomon didn't like to think about it, why he valued precision and elegance, and why the disorderliness of life outside his apartment frightened him so much. Control. Control was everything.

Solomon thought about Dr Mistry. He could have been a doctor himself, he figured. If he'd had the chance. If he hadn't followed his brother in school, hadn't always lived in the shadow of Luke Mullan, the antithesis of the model pupil. School was hard, he'd quickly realized, when teachers were more interested in making you pay for your older brother's misdemeanours than teaching you. So he'd dropped out, done it his own way. Learnt about the subjects that interested him, acquired qualifications when it suited him, enrolling in colleges just to get the exam entrances and collecting A levels like they were stamps. Facts and knowledge flowed into his mind and transformed into elaborate patterns, coalescing into brightly coloured landscapes or entire intricate images, or rendering down into unique sequences, information as a code that he could forever access. He didn't question it, only enjoyed it, this glorious mystery of his own mind. And it hadn't seemed that long before he'd been sitting in a cold room in Cambridge on a sullen April morning, breezing his way through the entrance exam. The thing was, learning wasn't hard, was a lot easier than life, and he'd read the letter offering him a place at Corpus Christi with little more than quiet satisfaction. It hadn't seemed such a big deal at the time.

He jammed the card Dr Mistry had given him back into his pocket and looked over at his sleeping sister. Stop thinking about yourself, he thought. It's done, it's over, so forget about it. What's important is Tiffany, and what was done to her, and that's not over. Far from it.

The hospital's burns unit was in a separate building two streets away from the Royal London, and not part of Dr Mistry's rounds. The woman who had been brought in the day before with severe burns to her mouth and throat was sedated, but nobody in the unit felt positive about her chances of recovery. Her mouth was hidden by an oxygen mask, but beneath that, they knew, was a frightening mess of scorched organs and ruined flesh.

She'd been found walking in Victoria Park, heavily drugged and horribly injured, without any ID on her. They had written *Beatrice* on the whiteboard at the end of her bed because they used a descending alphabetical system for unidentified patients – yes, they'd explain, the same system that's used for hurricanes.

The police had come, taken her fingerprints, taken photographs, asked about dental records but been told that it was way too early, they wouldn't be poking around there for some time, if ever. And so they'd gone away, and Beatrice was lying there, under sedation, and the question that they were all thinking but nobody was saying was not *Will she wake up?* but *Would she even want to?*

twelve

IT WASN'T THAT KAY DIDN'T RESPECT SOLOMON'S DECISION TO keep himself to himself. She didn't know what was different about him, what his exact disfigurement was, and she did, she really did imagine that it was probably quite bad, something that would give your average person pause. But you had to factor her into this situation, and she wasn't your average person, not in an arrogant way, in fact in a totally-not-arrogant way, i.e. she thought she was exceptional in a variety of strange and not especially socially compatible ways, but still. She wasn't your average person. And Solomon probably didn't realize that, and it might perhaps be in both their interests if he did. Maybe.

Plus, and this was true too, she'd been happy when he'd asked her to help with his investigation. Solomon was, after all, the genius of the Brain Pool, the rock star, with his quiet but always assured way of talking, like he just knew. Just knew. And never being seen just added to the legend. She alone knew that it was because he had a physical reason to keep hidden. The speculation within the Brain Pool was that he was *a*, a spy (that'd be Phil, he had some kind of thing about the security forces, probably because he was a commie), *b*, a super-famous crossword setter (which was a contradiction in terms), or *c*, just famous. Okay, there was also *d, e, f, g,* you name it, like he was actually one of the quiz show's presenters, or he did something shady for GCHQ, or he was only five years old and speaking via voice-altering-tech, and doing it all when his parents were asleep, or he was actually dead and beaming it all in from another planet (that one wasn't a real theory). Anyway, the point was, Solomon was a living legend, and helping him investigate his sister's assault was interesting. And she really did want to meet him, whatever he actually looked like. So.

So what?

So she'd call him. He might be a legend, a rock star, a faceless genius. But she was a pioneer in getting organic matter to almost interact with an artificial neurological framework. Almost. Not quite, okay, not nearly, but she was getting closer. So she'd call him. Kay took a deep breath and opened her laptop, sitting at her kitchen counter, a still-half-full glass of wine next to her. Why shouldn't she?

As much as Solomon wanted to talk to Kay, he had an incoming call on his mobile that he couldn't miss. He declined her call on the laptop with one hand, held his mobile in the other and said, 'Yes.'

'Solomon.'

'Robbie.'

'Dude.' Silence for a second, then, 'You got to hear me, man.'

Drunk, Solomon thought. He picked up a pen, clicked it a couple of times. 'What do you want, Robbie?'

'I need your help, Solomon. I've been getting, everyone's telling me, calling me, telling me Luke's out looking for me.'

Solomon took a second to unravel that sentence. 'Luke's looking for you.'

'That's what I'm saying to you, and I'm scared, so you've got to talk to him. You've got to tell him to chill, just like chill the fuck out, you know?'

Solomon didn't, really, and his sympathy for Robbie didn't extend very far past zero. 'Why would I do that?'

'I didn't have nothing to do with it, swear to God, Solomon, I swear to God. It wasn't me.'

'To do with what?'

'Oh come *on*, man, with Tiffany, what the fuck d'you think I mean? I didn't, just, tell Luke, tell him that he's after the wrong person.'

'And why would either Luke or I believe you?' said Solomon.

'Look, listen,' said Robbie, Solomon shaking his head at Robbie's incoherence, his shoddy use of verbs. 'I've got knowledge, man, you understand? I *know* shit.'

'And what is it you know?' said Solomon. On the other end, Robbie took a deep breath as if he was about to jump off something high.

'I know what happened. And I'll tell you.'

This was interesting, thought Solomon, but he didn't allow himself to get too excited. This was Robbie White, and Solomon knew him. Knew that he was about as trustworthy as quicksand. 'Go on.'

'No, man, you've got to tell him. Get him off me, do that, then I'll talk to you.'

'Please,' said Solomon. 'You'll tell Luke what you know when he finds you anyway. Just tell me where you are.'

'*Fuck*,' said Robbie, a desperate expletive, followed by the sound of an impact, and he was gone, nothing on the end of the line. Solomon sat back in his chair and wondered how better he could have handled that call, better handled Robbie. Had he let his own feelings get in the way, enjoying hearing Robbie scared and out of his depth? Possibly he had, although he shouldn't have. It was hardly a rational way to behave. But at the same time, he didn't believe for a second that Robbie knew anything. He was just trying to save his own skin. The most important person in Robbie White's life was himself, always had been. Solomon had often wondered if he suffered from narcissistic personality disorder. He'd suggested it to Luke, but Luke had just laughed and told him that the only thing Robbie White suffered from was being an arsehole.

Solomon's phone rang again. Robbie, again.

'Made me throw my phone,' he said, typical Robbie, finding other people to blame his own failures on. 'Look, oh shit, look, Solomon, I'm sorry, man. Seriously, I'm sorry.' He sounded even drunker now, maybe stoned, definitely out of control.

'What is it you want from me?' said Solomon.

'Want? I just wanted to say, you know. I'm sorry. Just wanted to say that.'

'For what?' said Solomon. 'What did you do?'

'I didn't mean it,' Robbie said. 'Swear. It was an accident. It was, I didn't mean it. I'm sorry.'

'What did you do?' said Solomon again, his voice louder. 'Robbie? Robbie, what did you do?' But Robbie was gone again, and when Solomon tried to call him back, it rang through to voicemail. Leaving Solomon with the question: what exactly was Robbie sorry for?

'I told you,' said Luke. 'Told you he did it.'

'He wasn't making much sense. He was intoxicated.'

'*In vino* whatever,' said Luke. 'We need to find him.'

'*Veritas*,' said Solomon.

'He give you any idea where he was?' said Luke, ignoring Solomon. 'Any clue?'

'No.'

'Okay.' Luke sighed. 'Listen, Solly, are you with me on this?'

'I guess,' Solomon said.

'I'll be around in the morning,' said Luke. 'We'll find him. And when we do, Solly, we'll make him pay for what he did to Tiffany. Yes?'

Solomon stared at the wall opposite him, bare, like all the other walls in his apartment. He wanted nothing to do with this. But Tiffany was their sister. They were meant to protect her. And they hadn't.

'Sure,' said Solomon. 'Whatever you say.'

To speak to three separate individuals in one evening was a social feat Solomon hadn't achieved in over two years, and if he was honest, he didn't feel up to it right now. But Kay had called and he couldn't ignore her, or at least, he didn't want to. So he took the easy way out, and messaged her instead.

Hey. I'm sorry. I missed your call.

No problem. You okay? How's your sister?

No change.

I'm sorry.

Did you need anything? When you called?

No. Yes. Yes, I did.

Kay didn't add anything, and Solomon waited, then wrote:

What was it?

Do you want to go out? Sometime?

Solomon didn't reply, couldn't. He looked at the words, words so genuine, so normal, yet so loaded with threat and humiliation and unhappiness. After a moment, Kay added:

With me, I mean. What do you say?

Say? thought Solomon. What do I say? I say I would love to but the moment you see my face you will smile and pretend that it's fine but underneath you'll be horrified, disgusted, and you'll wish you hadn't suggested it and try to think of ways to extract yourself, to get away without hurting my feelings, to get away and never see me again. I say please, please don't ask me this ever again, because it opens a ray of light, a glimmer of opportunity, and it's better to live without hope, because the reality is that there is none. I say, I like you, Kay, I do, but your life will be infinitely better without me in it, because you are young and pretty and clever and funny, and I am strange and awkward and genuinely monstrous.

Solomon thought for a moment, then typed:

No.

thirteen

LUKE CAME TO SEE SOLOMON TO DISCUSS A PLAN, THE ONLY drawback being, as far as Solomon could tell, that he didn't have one, didn't even have the beginnings. 'Find Robbie White' didn't count, he felt like pointing out, but didn't. 'Find Robbie White' was an outcome, not a strategy. But then he guessed that's what he was there for. What he was always there for. To do the thinking, then point Luke in the right general direction and wait for him to get it done. Which, in fairness, he usually did. Once he had instructions, his older brother proved an unstoppable force.

Solomon was thinking about this while he made coffee in the kitchen and Luke poked around at his hardware in the living room, pretending that he wasn't baffled by it all, the wires, the screens, his brother and the insular life he led. From the living room Solomon heard his mobile, his brother calling out, 'Phone.'

'Who is it?'

A pause, while Luke looked at the screen. 'Fox.'

'Hold on.'

Solomon hurried through, picking it up before it rang through to voicemail. 'Hello?'

'Solomon?'

'Yes.'

'Would you be able to tell me the current whereabouts of your brother?'

'Luke?'

'As far as I know, you only have the one,' said Fox, reminding Solomon of her acid disdain.

'I couldn't tell you,' Solomon said, looking across his living room at Luke and putting a finger to his lips. 'Why?'

'Could you tell me when you last saw him?'

'Yesterday,' said Solomon. 'At the hospital. Is there a problem?'

Luke frowned at him, lifted his hands, *What's going on?* Solomon shook his head, turned slightly.

'And when did you last speak to him?'

Solomon thought before answering, his natural suspicion of authority taking over, his instinct to protect his family. Was there anything to be gained by obfuscating? Probably not. 'Last night.'

'Did he say anything? About what he was doing, where he was?'

'No.'

'No? What did you talk about?'

'Our sister. I imagine that you remember her. You're investigating her case, or at least you're supposed to be.' As Solomon said the words, he closed his eyes, aware that Fox wasn't somebody worth antagonizing.

'I'm aware of my duties, thank you,' said Fox. 'But right now I have another case to deal with. And this one seems rather more clear-cut.'

'Please,' said Solomon. 'Could you just tell me what it is you want?'

'I want to speak to your brother, Luke Mullan,' said Fox. 'Because a little over three hours ago, the body of Robert Lee White was found, murdered. Stabbed to death. And right now, your brother's name is top of a very short list. So, again. Do you have any idea where he might be?'

Solomon turned back to look at his brother. Luke was watching him closely, knew that something was going down.

'I have no idea,' said Solomon.

'I'm not sure that I believe you,' said Fox.

'I imagine that in your line of work you often have to deal with ambiguity,' replied Solomon.

Fox ignored this, said instead, 'You have my number. I urge you to get in contact with your brother and let us speak to him.'

'Of course,' said Solomon.

Fox didn't reply immediately, then said at last, with a heavy dose of sarcasm, 'Thank you.'

She hung up and Solomon looked at the screen of his phone for some time, at arm's length, he didn't know why, then glanced up at his brother. *Luke*, he thought. *What happened last night?*

Robbie White couldn't sleep. He didn't know exactly why. Because he was lying on a thin mattress on a metal floor. Because he only had one blanket, and it wasn't long enough to cover him. And because he was pissed off, pissed off to have to be hiding in the back of a mate's Transit van, parked in a lay-by on a quiet country road like a fucking illegal immigrant. Plus he needed a leak but couldn't be bothered to get out and do it in the hedge. Fucking Luke Mullan. He should have done something about him a long time ago, only he hadn't, because Luke Mullan was a proper legit nutcase and Robbie White installed satellite dishes.

And fucked Luke's sister, which did help, he had to admit. Had helped, before she dumped him, made him look like he couldn't control his women. And now he was lying on a thin mattress in the back of a van, and he was scared. Because Luke Mullan was scary, and what he'd seen the other night, what he'd seen done to Tiff, that was scary too, only he shouldn't have been there in the first place because he wasn't allowed anywhere near Tiff any more, so he couldn't actually say anything. The situation, this whole situation, was completely fucked up.

He heard a car approach, slow down, stop just behind him. The engine sound continued for a few seconds, then cut off. What time was it? He looked at his watch, squinted at the illuminated dials. Two twenty. He almost groaned, but that was another thing, he couldn't make any noise. Because he was hiding, like some kind of rat. Christ.

A car door opened, then closed with a dull thump. He breathed shallowly, the better to listen. Was that footsteps? He strained to hear, turning his head slightly like his ears were aerials, trying to pick up a faint signal, then jumped as a hand banged against the side of the van, a deep metallic boom reverberating inside. Robbie White lay back down, still, mouthing *fuck fuck fuck fuck*, eyes closed tight. How had he found him? Who knew he was even here except Andy, who'd given him his keys? Andy wouldn't have said anything. Except that this was Luke Mullan he was talking about, and if Luke Mullan wanted to find something out, there wasn't a lot anyone could do.

The hand banged again, and immediately afterwards a voice. 'Immigration. We need you to open up.'

It wasn't Luke's voice, that was sure. This voice was clear, sounded ... not posh, but, yeah, clear. Loud and clear.

'In accordance with the Immigration Act 1993 we have the legal right to effect entry into this vehicle,' the voice said. 'We would ask you to open up before that necessity.'

And the voice spoke like exactly the kind of twat who went around at two in the morning looking for people to harass, figured Robbie. Well, look on the bright side. At least it wasn't Luke Mullan. And since he wasn't an illegal immigrant, what did he have to worry about? He hadn't even been asleep.

'Okay,' he said. 'Give us a second.'

He groped around and found his top, put it on, pulled on trainers. He used the light of his mobile's screen to find the keys, stood up as far as he could and blipped the van's doors open.

'It's unlocked,' he said.

The rear doors opened and Robbie looked down at a man in a hi-vis coat, glasses, clipboard in one hand, illuminated from behind by his car's sidelights. *Call that a job?* Robbie thought. *Scurrying about at night, banging on the side of trucks?*

'Listen, I ain't an immigrant,' he said.

'If you could just step out of the van, sir,' the man said.

'You ain't got nothing better to do?' said Robbie, bravado flooding back now he knew he hadn't been found by Luke Mullan, only some immigration jobsworth. 'I told you, I ain't an immigrant.'

'Say you so?' said the man.

'Do what?'

'Come on now.'

'Fuck sake.'

He put both arms up against the frame of the van and jumped down. But as he did so he heard the man shout something, *Choo now* it sounded like, and felt a punch in his side.

He looked down to see that the man in the hi-vis jacket had stabbed him, the knife buried to its hilt halfway up his ribs. His legs gave way beneath him and the next thing he could see was the gravel of the lay-by in front of him, his head lying on tarmac. There was a metal bottle top in front of his eyes and he blinked at it slowly.

'Did you speak?' The voice came from far above him. Robbie didn't answer. He couldn't inhale properly, could hear his breath coming in wheezes, weak, like trying to inflate a punctured football, just couldn't be done.

'Or is the world yet unknowing?' The man squatted and Robbie could see his shoes, trainers. Nike. He tried to breathe again but it hurt, tried smaller breaths, panting like a tired dog.

'I know you saw what happened,' the man said. 'But you didn't tell, did you? Did you?'

But Robbie couldn't speak and the man tutted to himself, stood back up, pushed at Robbie's shoulder with his trainer. 'No medicine in the world can do you good,' he said. 'I wouldn't give you half an hour.'

Robbie closed his eyes and listened to the man get back into his car, the door close, the engine start, and the crunch of the tyres as it slowly pulled away, away into the distance, and he was unconscious by the time the sound of the car's engine was gone.

'I had nothing to do with it,' said Luke. 'Nothing. Swear to God. Christ, Solly, it's not like I wouldn't tell you.' He frowned at Solomon. 'Why wouldn't I tell you?'

Solomon didn't answer, rubbed his good eye instead. This made things very complicated. Made everything complicated, almost exponentially. It was exactly what he didn't need right now, what neither of them needed. Robbie White. Even dead, it appeared, he could prove an irritation.

'Okay, listen. You need to leave, get out of here. Don't go home, don't go to the lock-up, they'll be looking for you there.'

'Obviously,' said Luke.

'So, go to the caravan. It's got everything you need.' He paused, thought. 'You'll need a charger.'

'Got one in the car.'

'Which is where?'

'Two streets away.'

'Okay. You need to go. Don't take the A12, there are too many cameras. Call me when you get there. On the work phone, obviously.'

'Got it.'

Solomon walked to his bedroom, opened his wardrobe and took out a hooded top. The only kind of top he had. He had hundreds of them. No he didn't, he had twenty-three, but still. He had a lot. He walked back to the living room, where Luke was sitting.

'Here. Put this on, don't show your face.'

'Solly?'

'Keep it pointed down.'

'Solly.'

'At the ground. The cameras are above.'

'*Solly*. Fuck's sake shut up and listen. You remember I told you, at the hospital, I had problems.'

Solomon tilted his head, frowned and thought back. Back to the hospital, to Tiff's room, Luke looking tired, hung-over. Telling him about something he had going on. *Nothing good* was how he'd described it.

'Yes.'

'I've fucked up,' Luke said. 'A bit.'

'How so?'

'Been playing in the wrong sandpit.' He laughed, but his eyes looked bleak and worried.

'Meaning?' said Solomon, not interested in Luke's childish metaphors. 'What have you done?'

'I've got some business …' He paused, corrected himself. '*Had* some business. With a guy who, you know, I probably shouldn't be dealing with.'

'So stop.'

'I will. I am.' Luke sighed, sat forward and rubbed his scalp with interlocked hands. 'Jesus. This is a fucking mess. You know?'

'Luke, why are you telling me this?' Solomon had a bad feeling, a sudden sense that he, they, his whole family were a lot closer to the edge of a precipice than he'd realized.

'Just so, you know. I might need your help.'

'I don't—'

'I know. You don't get involved. But this time … Just stay by the phone, Solly. I might need you.'

'Okay,' said Solomon, not feeling okay about it, not at all, something his brother picked up on. Not that it was hard to pick.

'No, not okay. Not Solomon okay-it'll-be-okay-maybe. I need you to stand up right now. I need you. Tiff, she needs you. Yes?'

Solomon didn't like the sound of this, didn't like it at all. But he nodded and looked at Luke, met his eye and said, 'Yes.'

'The phone. Stay by it.'

'Yes.'

Luke stood up and pulled Solomon's hood down over his head, rubbed the top of it. 'It'll be cool.'

'Okay,' Solomon said again, couldn't think of anything else to say. Luke turned to leave and Solomon watched his brother go, close the door behind him. For the first time in a very, very long time, he felt quite alone, and quite scared.

fourteen

WHEN SOLOMON HEARD THE BUZZ OF HIS INTERCOM, HE assumed that it was the police, come to put the pressure on him, face to face. He didn't often get people buzzing his apartment, didn't do visitors. Wasn't keen on the outside world in general.

'Yes?'

'Solomon? It's Marija.'

Marija. Solomon was lost for a moment, then remembered with an almost overwhelming dismay that this was the make-up artist, the one that Dr Mistry had recommended to him. He'd called her, arranged for her to come over. Why? Why had he done it? He'd felt like a teenager ringing a girl for the first time, had hung up once before the call had had a chance to connect. On the second attempt, he'd listened to it ring the other end with his eyes closed in near panic. And now she was here.

'Oh.'

'Is it all right to come in?'

No, thought Solomon, no, it really isn't. No way. I can't do this. He felt sick, genuinely felt like he might vomit. This stranger, this woman, wanted to come up to his apartment and look at him. Examine his face. The thought was too appalling to bear.

'I ...' he said, and stopped. He felt paralysed by fear and dread, entirely unequal to it.

'We can talk,' Marija said. She sounded gentle. 'You don't have to show me, if you don't want to.'

Solomon didn't answer, and after a moment of silence, Marija said, 'I understand. If you'd like me to go, it's not a problem. No big deal.'

No big deal. Perhaps it was this turn of phrase that got through to Solomon, made him step back from himself, look for some perspective. No big deal. So why couldn't he just buzz her up? Well, he could. He could. He really could. And he kept the momentum of this thought just long enough to put out a finger and press the button with the key sign on it. There. It was too late now. She was coming up. Deal with it.

Did it make it worse that she was young and attractive? thought Solomon, as he showed her through to his living room. Or did it make it better? Or didn't it matter? He was having strange thoughts, his mind in mild panic, experiencing tunnel vision. A pretty dark-haired lady was about to look at his face, really look at it, look at it properly.

'Nice place,' said Marija from behind Solomon.

'Thanks,' he said, trying to keep his voice normal, or at least close. To his critical ears, it came out more of a bleat, a frightened goat tethered in a clearing, waiting for some passing apex predator to have done with him. Calm down, he told himself. It'll be okay. It's no big deal.

He made a clumsy gesture at one of his armchairs, and Marija sat down. She had a case with her, a flight case, black and metal. Real-looking. Far too real-looking for Solomon's agitated liking.

Solomon stood, and Marija smiled and said, 'Cup of tea would be nice.'

Making tea calmed Solomon, talking to himself in the imperative, keeping doubt and anxiety at bay. Put the kettle on. Find cups. Introduce water. Steep. Steep some more. Stop thinking. Provide sugar. Sniff milk. Stop thinking. It was safe in the kitchen. The danger lurked outside, in his living room. How long did it take to make tea? Not long enough, was the answer he reluctantly came to, and he breathed deeply, picked up the first tray of tea he'd ever prepared in his apartment and carried it through to where Marija waited for him.

'Thanks,' said Marija. 'So. What do you know about me?'

'Only what you told me on the phone,' said Solomon quietly, sitting down on the armchair next to her, focusing on the tray on the table in front of them. 'You've done this kind of thing before.'

'Many times,' she said. 'You probably think that it must be terrible for me, to have to look at all those injured faces.'

Solomon nodded. 'Yes.'

'But it isn't,' said Marija. 'It's my job, and a job I love. Because I can make a difference, and that's what matters to me.'

Solomon nodded again, didn't answer.

'I won't be shocked,' she said. 'Or horrified, or appalled, or disgusted. I promise you I won't. You said it was an acid attack.'

'Sulphuric.'

'I know what that does,' Marija said. 'I've seen it before. Your eyes?'

'One.'

'Any vision left?'

Solomon shrugged. 'Light, sometimes. If it's very bright.'

'Think you can take your hood down?'

Solomon didn't move for a moment, then reached up and pushed back his running-top's hood. The way he was sitting, Marija could only see the side of his face. His good side.

'I guess it's the other side we're concerned with,' she said.

Solomon nodded.

'Do you want to turn, or shall I get up and walk around?' she asked.

Solomon closed his eyes, took a breath, and turned to look at Marija. The only reaction he saw from her was one of curiosity. Professional interest, he supposed.

'Looks like you got water onto it quickly,' she said. 'Before it got too deep.'

Solomon thought back to Luke's kitchen, the sink, desperately splashing water from the tap. 'Pretty quickly.'

'You go out much?'

'No.'

'Would you like to?'

Solomon considered the question. It wasn't something he'd ever really thought about. He had accepted his fate quickly and without ambiguity. He was monstrous and people mustn't see him. Ergo, he mustn't go out. No debate to be had, none necessary. 'It depends,' he said. 'On what I can look like. On how people will react.'

'And how do they react? At the moment?'

'Poorly,' said Solomon.

Marija laughed. 'They'll do that, people,' she said. 'There's something about faces. Okay,' she said, suddenly all business. 'I'll be honest. I've seen a lot worse. I can help you look more ...' She hesitated. 'Well, normal, let's say it how it is.'

Solomon nodded in silent thanks for her honesty, her lack of sugar-coating.

'The question is, would you like me to?'

Don't think about Kay, Solomon said to himself. This isn't about her, has nothing to do with her. This is about – what was it Dr Mistry had said? His entitlement to a normal life.

'I think so,' he said.

'In that case,' Marija said, 'how about we make a start now?'

Just the week before, Marija told Solomon as she painted on foundation matched to the colour of his good skin, she'd been working with an ex-lance corporal who had been trapped inside a burning patrol vehicle in Afghanistan, the rest of his squad either dead or pinned down by enemy gunfire. She smoothed the foundation with a sponge and told him that the man, the lance corporal, had burns so bad that he needed to wear a transparent mask for eighteen hours a day or the pain would be so great that he would be reduced to tears. And he was the bravest man she had ever met, not somebody who cried easily. She said that there was little she could do for him, but sometimes just talking, just that could help. Sometimes.

'There's not a lot I can do about that eye, either,' she said, her face just inches from Solomon's. It had felt strange to begin with, to have such proximity with another person, but her manner was so unaffected, so reassuringly professional, that very quickly he had forgotten his shame. 'I think we're beyond contact lenses on that one.'

'I figured,' said Solomon.

'I'd recommend an eye patch,' said Marija. 'Like a pirate's. They're cheap, and they also look pretty hench.'

'I'll keep it in mind,' Solomon said.

'Keep growing your hair, too,' she said. 'Cover your ear.'

'What ear?'

'Well,' said Marija, stepping back, 'there is that. The good news is that you're not losing it. Your hair, I mean. Not yet, at any rate.'

With Tiff in hospital, he didn't have anyone to cut his hair anyway. It wasn't like he was going to visit a barber's.

'Okay,' said Marija. 'That's enough for today. You want to take a look?'

Not really, thought Solomon, but said instead, 'Sure.' He stood up and headed for his bathroom. He didn't know why he'd kept the mirror, it had been there when he moved in but it wasn't like he used it. He could have sold it. For sale, mirror, vgc. As new. Unused. He jerked the cord for the light quickly, as if it was electrified, and turned to look at himself.

It wasn't bad. It really wasn't that bad, he thought. The skin looked kind of okay, from a distance anyway. Still creased, wrinkled, but the shininess had gone, that disconcerting artificiality. His ghastly half-boiled eye was still there, peering out, wraithlike, and his mouth just looked ... weird. Like he'd had a stroke, only worse. He held three fingers up, horizontally, to hide his eye. It wasn't too bad. It was ... Not okay. Not normal. But it wasn't horrifying. At least, he didn't think it was horrifying.

He looked at himself for as long as he was able, then walked back to the living room. Marija looked up from where she was kneeling, packing her make-up back into her flight case, and smiled. 'So?'

'Thank you,' he said.

'Better?'

'Better,' he said. 'Definitely.'

'I'll write down what I used,' she said. 'You can order it online. Practise with it, until you feel comfortable. It's a pain in the backside, but nothing thirty per cent of us women don't do every morning.'

Solomon smiled. 'Thank you,' he said again.

'Don't mention it. And keep my card. If you need anything, advice on foundation or just some moral support, give me a call.' She closed the flight case and looked at her watch. 'Oh Lord,' she said. 'I have to run. Don't forget to moisturize once you've taken it off.'

'I won't,' Solomon said, following her to the door.

She opened it, turned to him and said, 'Goodbye,' then kissed him on his cheek, which wasn't something he'd felt for a long, long time.

fifteen

SOLOMON'S APARTMENT WAS IN WAPPING AND WORTH, THE
last time he checked, around a million. All one bedroom of it.
Actually it was probably worth a little more, he thought, remembering the estate agent pointing out just how tall the windows
were, and how luxurious the bathroom was, and just how desir-
able warehouse living remained, particularly when the apartment in question was a proper London-stock-brick Victorian
warehouse with a view of the Thames. He'd bought it four years
ago when it had been worth half what it was today, when he'd
just turned twenty. Even then it had been a lot of money, and
if anybody made the assumption that writing questions for TV
and radio shows paid well, they'd be wrong. It paid lousy.

Most of Solomon's money came from a different source. He
didn't spend a lot of time thinking about exactly where it came
from, although years ago he'd agreed with his brother that it
could not come from trafficking either people or drugs. That
was a rule. Guns, too, they were off limits. And prostitution,
obviously. But what he did know was that Luke brought in a lot
of money, more and more every month. And wherever it came
from, it was Solomon's job to hide it. Get rid of it, magic it away,
and only let it reappear when it was washed clean, cleaner than

clean, ninety degrees of intensive offshore spin-cycle clean. And just as Solomon didn't ask Luke where the money came from, Luke never asked Solomon where the money went to. In any case, he wouldn't have understood. Most people wouldn't. Because what Solomon did with all the money, even he found fairly complicated.

The advantage that Solomon had, and the reason Luke had asked for his help in the first place, was of course his extraordinary brain. He never forgot anything; in fact he seemed to be physiologically incapable of forgetting anything. All the contacts and the cut-outs and the shell companies and the account numbers, all the hundreds and thousands and millions that he sent around the world, they were all stored in his head, appearing when he thought of them as something akin to a giant abstract painting, an elegant, intertwined masterpiece of fabulous colours, intricate lines and exquisite patterns. Nothing was written down, and never had been. Which meant that there was no paper trail, which in turn meant that however good a forensic accountant was, they'd have nothing to follow. Luke often called Solomon his criminal mastermind. It was a title that Solomon had never felt at all comfortable with, principally because it was too near the truth. In fact in its most literal sense, he had to concede, it was entirely accurate.

But. And it was a big but, a crucial but. But, he never had to actually meet anybody. He sat at the centre of the web, and other people did the legwork. Carried the briefcases. Handed over the paper bags filled with notes. Opened accounts, wired money, withdrew it. Got their hands dirty. To Solomon it had always been a theoretical game, an intellectual challenge, nothing more. No more precarious than playing the stock market. Just numbers, when it came down to it. If he could remember the numbers, remember them and keep track of them, and he could, then it would all be fine. Provided he didn't have to interact with the actual people, get involved in the unfathomable chaos of real life, with all its uncertainties and vagaries, it would be fine. It would be just dandy.

Which was why, right now, Solomon was feeling anything but fine and dandy. He was feeling terrified. Because suddenly, it wasn't only about the numbers any more.

'I can't.'

'Solly, listen, you have to. I can't do it. I can't go. It's too risky.'

'I can't.'

'Okay, Solly, okay. Okay, listen. It's fine.'

'Is it?'

'No. No, Solly, no. Of course it isn't, else I wouldn't be asking. But if you close your eyes and listen to me, stop talking, then at least you'll be able to fucking understand. Yes?'

Solomon had the phone pressed to his good ear and had paced a circle around his living room, how many times since Luke had called? Fourteen, fourteen full circles plus around seventy-eight degrees, 5,118 degrees in total. A lot of pacing. 'Yes,' he said.

'Okay. Now listen. This isn't going to be easy, but it needs to be done. Understand? So even if I'm not there. Even if, Solly, yes? Even if I'm not there, it needs to happen.'

Solomon squeezed his phone so hard his fingers ached. 'Okay.'

'Okay?'

'Okay.'

'Well,' his brother said, 'okay then.'

*

Luke thought of it as the Bank of Mullan, mostly because thinking of it as a physical place of granite and marble and polished wood made it feel more real. More real than how Solomon had attempted to describe it, which wasn't a place at all, more a series of companies and entities and faraway accounts, out of reach of Customs and Excise and extradition treaties and tax laws and all the other threats out there who would, if they could, take his hard-earned – or stolen – money away from him. So he thought of it as a real bank, where all his real money was kept, safe and secure. And if Solomon, and only Solomon, knew where it was and how it all actually worked, then that was A-O-fucking-K as far as Luke was concerned. Because Solomon knew *everything*.

What Luke did know was that this bank was full of money that his smurfs brought them, all the little people who acted as cut-outs, depositing many, many small amounts of money, so small that the authorities didn't notice but the Bank of Mullan got richer and richer, its vaults full of money that only Solomon could count.

His brother worked best behind the scenes, invisibly, thinking and planning and making their money magically disappear into the Bank of Mullan. But now Luke was asking him to step into the real world, Luke's world. And this was not good. Because only Solomon knew how to get into the Bank of Mullan, and people might try to make him tell them how to get into it too.

'You said it wasn't going to be easy,' said Solomon, his uncertainty plain to hear, even over the dubious mobile signal.

'No,' said Luke, 'it might not be. But you need to hear why.'

'Do I?'

'Yes. I can't come into town. Can't do it. If they nick me, there won't be bail. I'll be inside for months. Yes?'

'Yes,' said Solomon. 'I get that. So?'

'So. This guy, his name is Arnold. Thomas Arnold. You heard of him?'

'No.'

'No, well I have. Thing is, though, I didn't know I was dealing with him. First I'm talking to a lad from Stepney, next moment this Arnold's on the scene. I wouldn't have gone near him, Solly. No way.'

'What's the problem?'

'The problem is, he's not the kind of person we deal with. Big into women, he traffics them around the country. It's where the money is right now.'

'Luke,' said Solomon. 'No, Luke.'

'I'm sorry,' said Luke. 'It's not what I do, you know that.'

'What did you do for him?'

'Nothing like that,' said Luke. 'I got him some cars. Turns out he's got a lock on the ports, the cars go out, the people come in. The women.'

'So?' said Solomon. 'Just walk away. Write it off.'

'I can't.'

'Yes you can.'

'No, Solly, I can't.' Luke took a deep breath. 'There's a meeting arranged. We need to be at it.'

'We?'

'Let me finish, Solly, Jesus. We can't not go. He owes us money. How's it going to look if we just don't turn up?'

'Who cares? We don't need the money.'

'It's not a question of money, Solly. There's a meeting. We pick up the money, shake hands, it's finished. It needs to be done properly. It's about—'

'Don't say respect,' said Solomon.

'It is,' said Luke. 'That's exactly what it's about. It's how things work. If we don't turn up, we'll lose a whole ton of cash, and he'll take it as disrespect, and do we really need any more grief in our lives right now? Because grief is what we'll get, and serious amounts of it.'

Luke waited for Solomon to process all of that, waited some time. As he waited, he thought about the man he was asking his brother to meet. Thomas Arnold, the kind of criminal who gave criminals a bad name. Or, put it another way, an unpleasant sociopath. Somebody to cross the street to avoid. And never, ever get into business with.

'How much money are we talking about?' said Solomon.

'I got them the cars. We agreed on eighty grand. That's what we need to pick up.'

'Eighty thousand?'

'He'll probably tell you the cars were no good, there was a problem, the bribes went up, the container ship sank, whatever. That's normal. You just hold out, insist on the amount we agreed.'

'And what if I can't get him to pay?'

'You have to,' said Luke. 'Otherwise we look weak, and they'll use us. Try to own us. And we don't want that. Stick to your guns. We agreed eighty thousand. We agreed it. Yes?'

'No.' Luke listened to his brother breathing, agitated. 'I don't think I can do this, Luke. You need to send somebody else.'

'There isn't anybody else,' said Luke. 'It's you and me. You know that.'

'I don't think I can do this,' Solomon said again.

'You can,' said Luke. 'Listen, the meeting's at one of his places. Nothing's going to happen. Trust me.'

'Oh Luke, come on. Please. This isn't what I do. This isn't me.'

'It'll be fine,' said Luke. 'Listen, I'm sorry, okay?' It wasn't okay, Luke knew that, but what choice did he have? 'Just go in, get the money, then walk away. We don't want to be in his debt, and we don't want to be in his pocket. Get what we need, then walk away. Yes?'

Luke listened to Solomon's silence on the other end. Eventually Solomon said, 'I've got to go. Another call.'

'Listen, don't worry about it,' said Luke. 'It'll be fine.'

The last thing Solomon said before hanging up was 'Right,' but Luke couldn't help but think that he sounded far from convinced. Very, very far indeed.

Solomon put down what he had always called, he didn't know why, the Bat Phone, and picked up his ordinary mobile.

'Yes?'

'We've had a look at your brother's mobile records,' Fox said. 'He called you on the same night that Robert White was murdered.'

Solomon closed his eyes tight and tried to get himself balanced, focused. Fox would be talking about Luke's everyday phone. They both had two mobiles, one contract, the other pay-as-you-go. Contract for the normal, the everyday. Pay-as-you-go for business. Fox had pulled the records for Luke's contract phone, the one he'd called Solomon with that night. It was fine.

'So?'

'So, it suggests that you might be an accomplice. You've heard of assisting the commission of a crime?'

'Inspector Fox,' said Solomon, 'don't waste my time. Our sister is in hospital. My brother called me. It's reasonable, in fact it's entirely to be expected, that he'd want to talk. What do you take me for?' He was still rattled by what his brother had asked him to do, and realized that he was coming across as overly aggressive, channelling his brother. Too late now.

'I'm starting to have ideas about you too,' said Fox.

'Would you care to elaborate on that?'

'What do you know about your brother's ... how can I put it? Business concerns?'

'Nothing.'

'Nothing?' Fox did disbelief well.

'Nothing at all.'

'I see. So tell me, what was it your brother wanted to talk about? When he called?'

Solomon took a deep breath, attempted to rein himself in, but knew he was past that point. 'He wanted to talk about why, when our sister is in hospital, clearly the victim of an assault, the police are groping around, giving the impression that they'd struggle to find their own behinds using both hands and a map,' he said. 'And I'm paraphrasing.'

'Mr Mullan, at the moment, I'm only sure that one crime has been committed, and that is the murder of Robert White. I need to speak to your brother, to rule him out of the inquiry.'

'Or implicate him into it,' said Solomon.

'You're not going to cooperate, are you?' said Fox.

Solomon wondered how the investigation into his sister's attack had turned so suddenly into a witch hunt of his family. 'Find out what happened to my sister,' he said.

'Help me find your brother, and I'll have more time to investigate your sister,' said Fox.

'Are you trying to do a deal?' said Solomon. 'That sounds unethical.'

'Just trying to do my job, as efficiently as possible,' said Fox. 'Which strikes me as entirely ethical.' She paused, said, 'Well, you've got my number. Think about it,' and hung up, leaving Solomon standing in the middle of his living room, wondering just how the meticulously planned order and regularity of his life had fallen apart so dramatically, and so frighteningly quickly.

sixteen

WHEN SHE CAME AROUND SHE HAD NO IDEA HOW MANY HOURS, nothing made sense. Nothing. She knew who she was, remembered that, or at least had some vague memory. She knew she was supposed to be booking flights for somewhere, organizing hotels, and she knew, this she absolutely knew, that Ian was going to lose it in the worst way if he found out that she hadn't done it yet, because money mattered to him, mattered a whole heap, and the earlier you made the bookings, the cheaper it was.

But the details, like what day or month it was or why she'd been found where she'd been found, that, that she had no idea how to explain. Her name was Jasmine and she had tattoos, a lot of them, though Ian liked them covered up, so she wore long skirts or trousers at work because, well, because her thighs had ink, and a whole lot of it. So yeah, she knew her name. But what she didn't know, and what she'd kept repeating to the policeman who'd kept asking her, was how she'd come to be discovered by a priest who had at first, apparently, believed she was an angel, a painted angel, fallen all the way down from heaven. And this, this Jasmine knew instinctively, couldn't be true, because she was certainly no angel. She wasn't certain about much, but this, this she was sure on.

'You look like you need a break,' the policeman said. His name was Gary. He seemed nice and he wasn't in uniform, which meant he was a detective, or at least she thought that was what it meant. She had weird pyjamas on and they were scratchy, really scratchy, which wasn't about to do her eczema a ton of good, though apparently she'd been lying on a stone something-or-other for the last two days, so, hey. You know. Whatever.

'It's weird,' Jasmine said. 'If I've been asleep for so long, how come I'm tired?' Her voice sounded like it came from a deep well, somewhere below her. Or above her. Or from somewhere.

'You were drugged,' the policeman, no, Gary, said. 'It takes it out of you, believe it or not.'

Jasmine did believe it, nodding at Gary and yawning. 'I could do with a nap.'

'Yes,' said Gary. Gary seemed nice. 'I'll go. Is it all right if I come back?'

Jasmine looked at him and he seemed to wobble, slip out of focus and then back in, and she smiled and attempted to tell him that that would be awesome, but she fell asleep before she got the chance.

The next time Jasmine woke up, she felt better in that she knew a lot about who she was and how she had got to be here. But she also felt terrified, terrified and cold and confused and amazed, astonished that she was alive and that she hadn't been killed by that man who was worse than anyone she had ever imagined anyone could be. And since she'd woken up she hadn't stopped crying, and the doctors had wanted to give her sedatives, but apparently, from what she'd heard, she wasn't allowed them because the police had urgent questions and they needed answers, like, pronto.

'How are you feeling?' said a doctor, a woman in her forties with a face that was trying its best to look compassionate but really just looked stressed and harassed and unhappy.

'I'm okay.'

'Sure? The police want to speak to you. Do you think that's something you can do?'

Jasmine nodded, raising her head from her pillow. 'I think so.'

'You can stop at any time. My name's Dr Joseph. You just ask for me, and I can stop it. Understand?'

Jasmine nodded again, didn't say anything, and the doctor nodded back and stood up straight and left, left quickly, like she had lives to save or something.

'Jasmine?'

She hadn't seen him but he'd been in the room all along, in the corner, waiting to get at her. Gary. She remembered him clearly. Remembered everything clearly, and wished that she could drift away back to her previous state, where everything had been vague and muffled and a whole lot more manageable.

'Hey,' she said.

'We found your belongings,' he said, pulling a chair up next to her bed. 'Your bag. So we've got your address now.'

'Lewisham. Clare Street.'

'You've remembered?'

'I remember everything.' Jasmine shut her eyes tight to stop tears escaping, so that Gary wouldn't feel sorry for her. Maybe, she thought, if I keep my head back on the pillow, my eyes will reabsorb them and he'll never know how weak I was, and how easily I was beaten by that monster, how easily he got me. That fucken monster. But it didn't work and she began to cry, and cry for a long time, and to give him his due, Jasmine thought, Gary kept quiet until she was done, and that wasn't the kind of thing most men she'd ever met managed.

'So,' he said, gently, when she'd finished. 'You're from Australia.'

'Yes.'

'We've spoken to your parents. They're on their way over. Not sure if that's good news or not.' He said it with a smile in his voice and Jasmine looked at the polystyrene tiles of her hospital room and tried to smile with him, but couldn't.

'It'll be all right.'

'Good. So.' Gary paused, then said, 'Let's take this slowly, okay? You went on a date.'

Jasmine blinked hard before she answered. Fucken tears, she thought. Stop already.

'Liked his profile picture, thought he looked sweet,' she said. 'How wrong did that turn out to be?'

'We've got your phone,' said Gary. 'Got any messages from him?'

'Yeah.'

'Can you share them?'

Jasmine didn't feel like she could handle sitting up, as that would imply a wish to engage with the world, so instead she said, 'Nineteen ninety-four, that's the code. Year I was born. Then go to messages.'

She waited, looked back up at the ceiling while Gary got to grips with her mobile. Tried to remember the exchanges they'd had. She remembered thinking that his messages had been a bit odd, but in an interesting way, a quirky way. A British way. Sweet. *The hour of nine.* Jesus, Jasmine, you waste of bloody oxygen. What were you actually thinking?

'Okay,' Gary said. 'What is he calling himself?'

'Laurence.'

Silence, then, 'Laurence F?'

'That's him.' The name sounded so neutral, so safe, so un-threatening. Laurence. She turned her head, felt her cheek touch the pillow, closed her eyes, listened to Gary read the message exchange.

Drink?

When?

Can u do Saturday?

I can … Where?

The Crypt. Finest distilled liquor.

Liquor??

Website says from Russia argentina pehu I mean peru. Peru!

Interesting … What time?

The hour of nine.

C u then.

She'd arrived at the Crypt, seen the queue and immediately wished that she was somewhere else in the world, anywhere, even back in Perth, anywhere rather than having to queue up in some losers' bar in Shoreditch along with the other losers. She did hip. She didn't do out-of-towners' hang-outs, even if she was an out-of-towner herself. She had standards. She had long legs and a whole heap of very cool and expensive tattoos, and she was young, and she was pretty, and no. No no no. She wasn't doing the Crypt, wasn't queuing, however quirky and sweet Laurence was. Even if the place served liquor from Peru.

'Hey. Hey! Jasmine!'

She'd turned and there he was, with all his crazy curls, which were the only reason she'd swiped on him in the first place.

So, what made you go for him?

His crazy curls, and his quirky way of writing.

That sounded almost like a romantic story, right? Right? Maybe, but what she'd then turned and said was:

'Is this for real?'

'No,' Laurence said, pushing his crazy curls away from his eyes. 'It's a big, big mistake.' He laughed and looked away from her, like he was shy, only he was older than she was so, like, maybe he wanted to grow up a bit? Anyway, he said, 'Look, I know somewhere else. A lot quieter, and a lot cooler. If you're still up for it.'

Jasmine had looked at him, his curls, his cuteness, even though he was older than her. There'd been something about him, something vulnerable, that had made her relent.

'Okay. But it had better be close, yeah?'

She remembered getting into a taxi, and remembered Laurence offering her something to drink and her drinking it, because she was a fucken idiot, and then she didn't remember anything else until she was sitting on something uncomfortable in a place where every breath she took felt like age and stone and cold. And she remembered Laurence, only he wasn't Laurence any more. He was now a cold person full of anger and muscle and concentration who had shed a skin and assumed another persona, who had become somebody else. Somebody Jasmine would have crossed a street to avoid, so much hate did he emanate, like if she put out a finger his force field might shock her.

'Presently,' he said, 'through your veins, a cold and drowsy humour will run.'

'What?' It was dark, where they were, and quiet, Laurence's voice echoing slightly, even though he wasn't talking loudly, was in fact talking quietly and precisely.

'No warmth or breath will suggest you're even alive,' he said. 'Like death.'

'You're going to kill me?'

Laurence paused, then said, 'Like death, stiff and stark and cold.'

'Why?' she said. 'Why am I here?'

'To free you.'

'Free me?'

'From your current shame.'

Jasmine said nothing, felt her heart beat, so hard that in the silence she believed that she could hear it. She didn't understand, none of it, couldn't make it out, could barely make Laurence out, sitting next to her. Laurence reached for her arm and held it, and she felt a sharp prick but he was so strong that she couldn't jerk her arm away.

'Please don't,' she said. 'Please.'

'Hold,' said Laurence. 'In forty-eight hours, you will awake, as from a pleasant sleep.'

And that was everything that Jasmine could remember.

'How long?' she asked Gary.

'How long what?'

'How long was I there? In that church?'

Gary lifted his shoulders slightly. 'It's hard to say. You were found on a Friday. From what we can work out, you could have been there for two days.'

Forty-eight hours, thought Jasmine. A pleasant sleep. 'Two days? In church, without anyone finding me?'

'The congregation's small,' said Gary. 'Somebody comes in on a Wednesday, and the priest comes over on a Friday, for the service. So yes, it could have been that long. You'd been given a lot of ...' Jasmine heard Gary go through his notebook. 'Propofol. It's used for keeping people under.'

'But ... why?' said Jasmine. That's what she couldn't understand. 'Why?'

'That,' said Gary, 'is why we need to speak to him. So, Jasmine, if you feel up to it, could you tell me exactly what he looked like?'

seventeen

TIFFANY'S ROOM AT THE HOSPITAL WAS ON THE SEVENTH FLOOR, but Solomon always took the stairs, because biomechanics dictated that when people walked upwards on staircases they naturally looked at the steps, rather than up at the other people passing on the way down. A lift, now, that was a different prospect. That was bounded by simple problems of physical dimension. In a lift there was nowhere to hide, unless you faced the wall, and a man in a hooded top and sunglasses facing the wall in a lift one metre by one metre by one and a half metres, 1.5 cubic metres, wasn't something that was likely to go unnoticed. So Solomon hiked it up to the seventh floor each time he visited his sister, reasoning that at least he was getting some exercise, something he didn't get a lot of, seeing as he'd barely left his apartment in two years.

It had been five days now since Tiffany had been put into an induced coma, and Solomon had done his research. Five days in a coma was a long time, too long, unless there was a good reason for it. He sat next to her bed and watched her chest rise and fall, holding her limp hand and squeezing it, hoping for a squeeze back despite knowing that it wasn't going to happen, because, you idiot, Solomon thought, she's been placed in a *coma*. He'd spoken to the nurse but she'd told him that he needed to speak to Dr Mistry, and after waiting for two hours he'd asked a different nurse who had told him that Dr Mistry had already left for the day. So instead he just sat and watched his sister in her hospital bed, and wondered who, if anyone, was out there looking for whoever had put her here.

The afternoon passed, Solomon reading and thinking and listening to his sister's vital signs, until visiting hours ended and he headed home. He walked the three miles to Wapping, not in any kind of mood to deal with the stares of strangers. Or, if he was honest, in any hurry to get to the coming evening, with all the uncertainty and unmanageable outcomes that it promised. Because at nine o'clock he was expected at Thomas Arnold's office, to act as his brother's proxy and get down to some hard bargaining with a notoriously unpredictable criminal he had never met and could not properly imagine. He didn't want to do it, wasn't even sure that he could do it.

The rush-hour traffic crawled past him as he walked, surrounding him with the heat of bus exhaust and the smell of petrol and hot tarmac, the sun still strong even though it was gone six. The reality of it all, the cars and people and sounds and smells of London, seemed at odds with what he was expected to do later. It didn't feel real and he supposed that he was still in denial of some kind, unable to fully believe that he was going to turn up at Arnold's office, walk in, sit down and open negotiations. He might as well be asked to walk into a cage of lions and tame them, so outside of his capabilities it all was. So rather than think about it, he counted paving stones, estimating how many he would cross before he reached his apartment, and feeling some infinitesimal measure of satisfaction at being within a hundred of his original estimate when he turned the key in his building's front door.

Inside, he opened his laptop and saw with a feeling of mild dismay that he'd missed several calls from the Brain Pool, which he only now remembered was meeting that evening. He thought of Kay and considered giving it a miss, something he had never done before. He wondered how it would be, with her. He hadn't spoken to her since she'd asked him out on a ... what was it? A date, that's what it was, that's what she'd asked him out on. God. But instead he checked that his webcam was disabled, and made the connection.

'Solomon, you're with us,' said Fran. They were all there, Phil, Fran, Kay and Masoud, Phil taking a healthy gulp of lager and swallowing it before adding, 'Welcome.'

'Hello,' said Solomon. Masoud raised a hand, but Kay did nothing except glance at the camera of whoever's laptop was being used, then look quickly away.

'So, now that we are all here,' said Fran, 'shall we begin? Solomon, since you were last, you can be in the chair.'

Which meant, you can try to answer the questions we've prepared. 'Okay.'

'Are you sure?' said Phil.

'This show is intended to be challenging,' said Fran.

'Even so.' What Phil meant, Solomon knew, was that just because he might be able to answer the questions wasn't necessarily a reliable indicator that anybody else would. He didn't get put in the chair often. It was Kay or Masoud, usually.

'How is your Chinese history?' said Masoud.

'Reasonable,' said Solomon. He liked Chinese history, its order and regularity, imagining it as a rather ornate bar chart, every bar of a different colour, each corresponding to one of the various dynasties. He much preferred Chinese history to European, which he could not help but picture in his mind as an overrun marketplace, goods and belongings spilt everywhere, plenty of slashing and screaming, with somebody in the middle being burnt alive. 'Not too bad.'

'Can you tell us when—'

'Which calendar are we using?'

'Jesus,' said Phil, to nobody in particular. 'Is he for real?'

'The Gregorian one will do,' said Fran.

'Okay,' said Solomon. It suited him. He had no idea how the traditional Chinese calendar worked, only that it had fewer days each month. And the years were 355 days long, or at least he thought so. No, that was right. They were. Good.

'So,' said Phil. 'Can you tell us when the Zhou Dynasty ended?'

'No,' said Solomon.

'To the nearest century,' said Masoud.

Solomon thought. 'Eighth,' he said. 'BC.'

'The Han Dynasty?'

'Ended?' said Solomon.

'Yes.'

'Third,' he said. 'AD. Two hundred and twenty.'

Phil took a slug of lager, then shook his head. 'Unbelievable.'

'Tang?'

'Tenth. Nine hundred and seven, AD.' He watched the group, Masoud and Fran smiling at him via the webcam, Phil sitting back in his chair, apparently disgusted by Solomon's freakish knowledge, and Kay playing with her glass in front of her, not looking.

'Hmm,' said Fran. 'Already I'm thinking this is too easy.'

Solomon shrugged, even though nobody was with him to see. 'I don't think so. About right.'

'Solomon's easy is another man's bloody impossible,' said Phil.

'Phil.' Fran spoke to him like she was warning a misbehaving dog.

'Just saying.'

'Kay?'

Kay didn't answer immediately, then said, not looking up, 'I don't know. Solomon is ...' She stopped, then said again, 'I don't know.'

Fran looked at her but didn't say anything. 'Masoud?'

'What I think,' Masoud said, 'is that you, Solomon, are a quite extraordinary person.'

'Hear hear,' said Fran, and Solomon didn't know what to say in response, so instead he just watched Kay, who sat silently for a few moments and then picked up her rucksack, stood, and left without saying a word.

Thomas Arnold's office was in Bethnal Green, which meant that Solomon had to take the Tube to get there, something he hated doing, even though London Underground etiquette was to sit down and not talk to anyone and, if possible, not look at anyone either. Solomon sat with his elbows on his knees, his hood up, head down, Ray-Bans on even though it was gloomy this far underneath the city, hoping that he wouldn't have to stand up and surrender his seat to anyone old or pregnant, which of course he would do, that also being Tube etiquette, along with being the right thing to do.

He got out and walked up Cambridge Heath Road, through the warm evening, the sun almost set but the streets still full of people. The address he'd been given was underneath a railway arch that advertised car washing on an A-board on the street outside, a drive-through operation where you turned in to the arch, men jet-washed your car, and you came out the other side cleaner and £20 lighter. It was still open even though most businesses on the street had closed, and he waited at the entrance until a short man in a plastic apron turned and said, 'Yes, boss?'

'I'm here for Mr Arnold.'

'He know you?'

'He is expecting me, yes.'

The man looked Solomon up and down and didn't give the impression that he liked what he saw. 'What you called?'

'I'm called ... I'm Mullan. Please, just tell him Mr Mullan's here.'

The man nodded, something sceptical in it, like he'd be personally surprised if Solomon got any nearer to Thomas Arnold than he was now, and disappeared into the gloom, the brightness of the setting sun casting the arch into near blackness. People walked past Solomon on the pavement as he waited, young couples out for the evening, a pair of drunks urgently discussing where they'd get their next drink from, a woman on a phone telling the person on the other end that there was no way he was seeing his daughter, no way, he couldn't just call the night before and expect to see her, who the fuck did he think he was?

'Mr Mullan?' The man was back, scepticism replaced by an apologetic servility. 'Mr Arnold says to come with me.'

Solomon followed the man, the gloom and his Ray-Bans plunging him into near darkness. The man stopped and opened a door and light from behind it spilt out into the dark railway arch. He didn't go in, just gestured with his hand, a brushing motion as if to hurry Solomon up, don't keep Mr Arnold waiting.

Inside was a carpet-tiled office with a desk, a couple of chairs and a TV on the wall that was showing a football match. It was being commentated on in a foreign language, and it took Solomon a couple of seconds to realize that it was Greek. Panathinaikos, he recognized their away strip. Behind the desk was a large man wearing a tracksuit and eating pistachio nuts. He had dark curly hair and a large, wide scar running from his forehead down to his jawline, interrupted by his eye socket, which had no eye in it. The scar looked old and was thick, as if a line of electrical cord had been inserted into his skin. He watched Solomon as he came in, then glanced up at the TV, reached for a handful of nuts, looked back at Solomon and nodded at him, looked back at the TV, shelling a nut at the same time and eating it. He watched a couple of passes, then looked back once again at Solomon.

'You want to sit down?' Arnold shelled another nut and put it in his mouth. He had big wet lips and his earlobes were fat, which Solomon had read was a sign of early heart disease, but given that Arnold must have weighed twenty stone, that wasn't the only indicator.

'No,' said Solomon.

This got Arnold's attention, and he turned his body away from the TV so that he was properly facing Solomon for the first time. His eyelid was almost closed over the socket of his missing eye, and sunken, nothing beneath to fill it out. 'Oh?'

'My hope is that this won't take us long,' said Solomon. In and out, that was what Luke had said. We don't want anything to do with this man.

'You always talk like that?' said Arnold.

'I just—'

'You want to take your glasses off, your hood off, at least.'

'I'd prefer not to.'

Arnold shrugged. 'How'd you do business with a man whose face you can't see?' He put another nut in his mouth, chewed and nodded to himself. 'Huh?' He turned back to the football, then changed his mind and said, an edge to his voice now, 'So sit down. Sit. *Sit.*'

Solomon stayed standing for a moment, looking at Arnold, who was chewing busily and watching him without amusement. He cursed Luke silently, then pulled out a chair and sat down, head lowered, looking at the carpet tiles, which appeared older than he was, and in an even more desperate condition.

'So,' said Arnold. 'You're Luke Mullan's brother.'

'Yes.'

'Good guy, from what I hear.'

'I'm here for the money. Eighty thousand. I can't stay.' Solomon had a sudden strange feeling, a reawakening of some atavistic childhood fear, of being lured into a monster's lair that he would never get out of. He listened to Arnold chewing on his nuts, and heard the Greek commentator's voice rising in excitement as Panathinaikos launched a counterattack.

'I heard he's got trouble,' said Arnold. 'That right?'

'It's nothing serious,' said Solomon.

'Mmm,' said Arnold. Solomon tried to place his accent but couldn't. London, certainly, but something else, and he didn't think it was Greek. Or Turkish. 'What's up with your face?'

'I'm sorry?' said Solomon.

'Your face,' Arnold said. 'Come on. Look at me.'

'I'd rather not.'

'Need to see your face,' Arnold said. 'If we're going to do business.'

Solomon hesitated, then took off his Ray-Bans and put them in his pocket, took his hood off, and did his best to meet Arnold's eye. He tried to fight a rising panic. He shouldn't be here. He didn't know what he was doing. Why was he doing what this man asked him to?

Arnold looked at him and nodded, still chewing on his pistachios. 'Huh.' He reached down and picked up a blue plastic bag, put it on the desk. 'Here. Hundred thousand.'

'Eighty,' said Solomon, alarms triggering in his head. Luke had said eighty. 'We said eighty.'

'Eighty, that's yours,' said Arnold. 'Twenty, I want you to do something for me.'

'No,' said Solomon. 'We don't have any other business.'

'What I heard,' said Arnold, as if Solomon hadn't spoken, 'is you're the clever one. You know how much I'm putting through that place outside?' He gestured at the arches outside his office door.

'No.' And I don't want to, thought Solomon. I want to go home, to my apartment. To order and normality.

'Put it this way,' said Arnold, placing both elbows on his desk and giving Solomon his full attention for the first time. 'Even if I get one car washed every minute, twenty-four seven, charge each customer a hundred pounds, even then I can't get enough money through. And I've got ten of these places. You get me?'

Solomon got him. Arnold was washing his dirty money through his businesses, but he had too much of it. He'd cook the books so it looked like the business was making more money than it was, and hide his illicit profits in with his legitimate income. But he was putting too much money through, and it was going to show. Probably already was.

'I do things the old way,' said Arnold. 'What I hear about you, you're smarter than that.' He sat back in his chair, grabbing another handful of pistachios as he did so, started shelling them. 'Fucking pistachios, you start on eating them and it's impossible to stop, you know?'

'No,' said Solomon.

'No?'

'No. No, I won't launder your money. No way.' Solomon's hands were shaking and he clasped them together so that Arnold wouldn't notice. This was exactly what his brother had told him not to let happen. Don't get involved. Get the money and leave. We want nothing to do with this man. God, life. How did people manage it?

Arnold considered what Solomon had said, then replied, 'You get a lot of girls, looking like that?'

'What?'

'I can get you anything you want. She won't care. Young, young as you like.'

'No.'

Arnold nodded to himself, then turned and watched the TV, where Panathinaikos were playing out a goalless draw. Solomon recognized the other team as Iraklis 1908. He looked at the blue plastic bag on Arnold's desk and wondered what would happen if he stood up, took out twenty thousand, then left with the rest. Just turned and left. He knew that would never happen. Luke, maybe Luke could have done it. He pictured Luke standing up, standing over Arnold and throwing the twenty grand onto his lap, saying, 'No dice.' God, he wished his brother was here.

'Your sister's in hospital, that right?'

Solomon didn't answer.

'Your brother, who knows where he is? Your sister is all on her own. So you can do this for me, make my money disappear, then come back. All clean. I heard you can do that.'

Arnold paused but Solomon didn't say anything to fill the silence. He just wanted to get out of there. Just wanted to hear the click, that click of his apartment door. The click that said, you're safe. You're home, safe.

'Okay, so. Come here and pick up your money. Now, or the offer ends and I find another way to make you play ball. Understand?'

'I don't think my brother will be happy.'

'Fuck your brother,' said Arnold. 'You know anything about me?' Arnold stopped chewing and became very still, and Solomon realized that he was angry, that this man was on the edge of losing control of himself.

Solomon closed his eyes, then took hold of the arms of his chair, stood up and walked to the desk. He picked up the blue bag. Thomas Arnold let out a long breath, then turned to him and smiled.

'Okay, so, okay. Good. I want it back in seven days. Understand?'

'Seven days?' said Solomon. 'No. That's too soon.'

'It's when I want it,' Arnold said. 'Here.' He wrote a number down on a sheet of paper, handed it to Solomon. 'You call me. Yes?'

Solomon took the paper without answering, then turned and headed towards the office door. As he reached it, Arnold said, 'Hey? If you want a girl, I can get you one. They don't mind me, they won't mind you. We're not so different, me and you.'

Solomon stopped, feeling Arnold's gaze on his back like an

electric current. He put his hand on the handle of the door and said, slowly and as calmly as he could, 'How I look doesn't define me. Believe me, we are entirely different.'

He didn't wait to hear Arnold's answer, just opened the door and walked as quickly as he could out of the gloom of the archway and into the noisy evening of voices and sirens and marginal safety.

eighteen

KAY WAS PREPARED TO ADMIT THAT SHE WAS BEING STUPID. More than stupid. Petulant, selfish and unreasonable. Yes, all of those things. She didn't have any right to resent Solomon for not wanting to see her, had no idea what he looked like, what his reservations might be, his fears or anxieties or, well. She didn't know. Didn't know anything about him, that was the thing, but she wanted to. She wanted to know him because so far everything she'd heard from him was brilliant, smart and certain, and that was good enough for her.

So, okay. There was always more than one way to skin any particular cat, that she knew, given that so far the approaches she'd taken to making organic material interface with code numbered she didn't know how many. A lot. And not a lot of success on the horizon either, or at least none that she could see.

She couldn't keep Solomon's aborted investigation out of her head. She was honest enough to question why that was, whether it was because she thought there was still something in it, or whether it was just a way to get to him. But whatever, it kept playing on her mind. She went over the facts. Rebecca Harrington, found dead of an overdose in a canal. Just after an online date with a man called Caesar, going for cocktails at the Gypsy Queen. And the police had it down as suicide. So what? What was so remarkable about that? Nothing, except that Solomon's sister had been found in the same canal, after an online date, the same drugs in her body. That was a coincidence too far. Or did she only think that because it meant she and Solomon had some kind of connection, some shared experience? Around and around it went in her head. God, it was pathetic. Like some kind of lovelorn teenager, obsessed by a pop icon she'd never even met.

Yes, but still. She didn't have anything better to do, and she was passing the Gypsy Queen on her way home anyway, so she might as well go in, mightn't she? Have a look? No reason not to. She could try a cocktail. It was a nice evening. So. So that's what she was going to do. Dammit.

The Gypsy Queen was a traditional glaze-tiled pub off Hackney Road, which had once been grand and had then gone into a steady decline, its original fittings ripped out in preference to pool tables and fruit machines and Sky TV, until some enterprising owner had ripped out those pool tables and fruit machines and Sky TV screens and restored the whole place to its glory years, with the additional veneer of craft ales and a menu that offered gourmet burgers made with rare-breed steak. Kay looked at the list of beers, and searched the back of the menu, but the one thing she couldn't find was cocktails, not even one. Not even a mojito.

'Help you?' said the barman, a young man with horn-rimmed glasses and an arm full of tattoos.

'Do you do cocktails?' said Kay, taking a seat at the bar.

The man looked uncertain. 'What kind of cocktail?'

'Mojito?'

'Don't think so,' said the man. 'What's in it?'

'Rum. Mint.'

'Well we haven't got any mint, far as I know,' he said. 'I can do you a rum and Coke.'

'No thanks.'

'It's not Coke Coke,' the barman said. 'It's locally made. Organic.'

Please, thought Kay. Organic Coke? Wasn't the whole point of Coke that it was full of refined sugar and about as antithetical to artisan sensibilities as it was possible to get? 'It's okay,' she said. 'Did you ever do cocktails?'

'Not, you know, as a thing,' the barman said. 'No.'

'Okay,' she said, her mind turning.

'So …' said the barman, after a few moments.

'Hmm? Oh, nothing then. I'm fine.' She sat still at the bar for a few more moments until she came to a decision, then got down off the stool and left, the barman watching her curiously as she walked out of the door.

Solomon had found it difficult to sleep, imagining, in his standby-red-light state of consciousness, that the blue plastic bag full of cash on his living-room coffee table was alive, possessed of a malignant power that was seeping into him through the walls as he lay in bed. And Arnold. Solomon couldn't think of him as a person, instead he could picture him only as a castle, a huge dark castle filled with the savage cries of a furious ogre. It was as much as his mind was able to comprehend. He'd eventually found sleep at four in the morning and had woken at midday, which wasn't that remarkable for Solomon, who didn't have much to wake up for at the best of times. And that particular day he had more reason than normal for staying in bed and keeping the world at bay. His sister was in a coma, his brother was on the run, and he was on the hook for twenty grand of a criminal's dirty money.

A week ago things had been, if not fine, then at least manageable. He had once read a study of homelessness that had concluded that for most people, losing everything was just a string of three instances of bad luck away. The loss of a job and a spouse, and one long-lasting illness was all it took. One day, everything was fine; a month later, it had all gone to hell. Well, this irredeemable mess had only taken Solomon one week to arrive at. He closed his eyes against the light of the day spilling through his curtains and tried to think of a way out of it all, but in his mind there was no light to be found.

What was it that Thomas Arnold had said? *We're not so different, me and you.* That had got to Solomon, hit a nerve, had been more than he was willing to take. *How I look doesn't define me,* he'd replied. *Believe me, we are entirely different.* How true was that? Solomon thought of Kay, of her generosity, of the time she'd called him with her hair pinned up. *Night, you.* That was what she'd said. And later she'd asked him for a drink, asked him out. And he'd said no. Solomon groaned in his bed, out loud, a sound equally despair and frustration. Because he did want to see her, he just didn't dare. Which meant, did it not, that he allowed how he looked to define him, control him, dictate his choices. At least Arnold, with his horrific scar and missing eye, made no effort to hide. Jesus. He picked up a pillow and pressed it over his head, dismayed by his groggy logic. Did that make Arnold *better* than him? Did it?

*

143

Kay hadn't slept well, turning the Gypsy Queen's mysterious and inexplicable lack of cocktails over in her mind, trying to reach a conclusion that didn't point in a sinister direction. She'd wondered whether she should tell Solomon but had worried that it might look needy, after the last exchange they'd had. *I know you don't want to go out with me, but I've been scurrying around town looking for excuses to call you up anyway.* No, she'd need something more than a missing cocktail menu. There was nothing worse than looking needy. Nothing less sexy. That was practically scientific fact, and she was a scientist, so.

She'd lain in bed and thought of Rebecca Harrington's parents. Her bereft father, her quietly angry mother. They'd told her that there was a suicide note. No, no they hadn't. Solomon had told her, because the police had told him. Whatever, there'd been a note. And if she hadn't killed herself, then, well, it didn't make sense. Why write a note if you're not going to kill yourself, unless … Unless somebody made you?

Which was why Kay was now back outside Rebecca Harrington's parents' council building. She didn't feel at all certain about what she was about to do, on the far reaches of what constituted a reasonable theory. A long shot, that's what it was. But still. She'd thought it through and believed that, on balance, Something Wasn't Right. Which was good enough for her, what with the whole Solomon situation.

'Hello?'

'Jean? It's Kay. I came to see you a few days ago. About Rebecca.'

There was a pause on the intercom, then Jean said, 'Yes?'

'Can I ask you one more question?'

There was a longer pause this time, Kay standing in silence only broken by the shouts of some nearby kids playing basketball.

Then the buzzer sounded and she pushed open the building's door and made her way up to the third floor. She walked along the open balcony to Jean's door, realizing as she did that she had no plan, no strategy for approaching this. Her imagination had gone only as far as buzzing Jean's number, telling her who she was. What now?

Jean was waiting beside her open front door, looking, if anything, even tinier than before. She hadn't put make-up on and she seemed both older and more desolate. God, Kay thought. What am I actually doing here?

'Hi,' she said. 'Thank you for seeing me.'

'What do you want?' said Jean. 'I gave you all I had.'

Kay paused, then said, too quickly she knew, 'She left a note. Rebecca, I mean. Did she leave a note?'

Jean tilted her head, then said, carefully, 'Yes.'

'And was it ...' Kay had no clue how best to ask the next question. 'Did it seem like her? Like something she'd write?' Idiot, she thought. It was a suicide note. They're not something people write often. But Jean didn't seem to think the question was untoward.

'It didn't seem like her,' she said. 'No. But the police said, well, they told me that it was normal. When people aren't in their right mind. They said they write strange things. They said I shouldn't worry about it.'

'Do you think I could see it?' said Kay.

'Why?'

'I don't know,' said Kay. 'I mean, well.' God, what did she mean? 'I just think there might be something going on. Something not right.'

Jean looked at her for some moments, then nodded quickly

and walked back into her flat. Kay waited on the doorstep. She could still hear the sound of the kids playing basketball, and the distant drone of a helicopter somewhere over the other side of the building.

Jean came back out of the gloom holding a clear bag with a piece of paper inside. 'Here,' she said, handing it to Kay with two fingers, as if it was contagious. Kay took it and held it up. The bag was a freezer bag, and inside was a piece of notepaper torn from a spiral-bound pad, one edge ragged, written in blue pen.

I am done.
Farewell, kind mother. Father, long farewell.
Rebecca

Kay read it twice, three times, then looked at Jean. 'This is her handwriting?'

'Yes. But it doesn't sound like her.'

Kay hadn't known Rebecca, but she had no difficulty believing that it wasn't her style. The words would sound strange coming from anyone. 'And the police didn't think it was strange?'

'They didn't want to know. Weren't interested. I said to them, you really think she wrote this? They said, she weren't in her right mind, so who knows?' She put out a hand and Kay gave the note back, the piece of paper small and pitiful inside the bag.

'I'm sorry,' Kay said.

'You still think something ain't right?'

'I don't know. Maybe. I'll let you know.'

'You do that.'

'I'm sorry,' Kay said again. 'To keep bothering you.'

Jean shrugged. 'Ain't no bother.'

'Where's Jim?'

Jean shrugged again, and sighed. 'Ain't seen him for a couple of days,' she said. 'On a bender, I expect. Like he used to do when Becky was a kid.' She sighed again and Kay saw the suspicion of tears, but Jean turned around before they fell. 'Looks like I've lost them both,' she said, and walked back into her flat again, this time closing the door behind her.

nineteen

FOX WAS BORED, VERY BORED. THE CONFERENCE SHE WAS AT was entitled 'Policing Diversity: Considerations for a Post-Western Community'. She didn't walk the beat any more, so she didn't really give a damn about 'South Asian Terms of Engagement' or 'Women, Islam and Street Diplomacy'. As far as she was concerned, this was just a box-ticking exercise, one more course to put on her record, one step closer to her next promotion. That was the only reason she was sitting in a hot lecture room in Hendon, sun streaming through the windows and no air-con, surrounded by over-eager fellow officers who actually, properly seemed to be taking this nonsense seriously. They were taking notes, for God's sake.

Her mobile rang again, and this time she decided to take it, three missed calls being, to her mind, too many for comfort. Besides, it'd give her a rest from this latest speaker, a pudgy man in glasses who seemed to think that being from a minority conferred some special status, some kind of extra-legal protection from arrest, regardless of whatever crime you'd actually committed. She took her mobile out of her bag and stood up, and before she'd reached the door said, 'Fox speaking.'

'Inspector Fox?'

'Yes.'

'Hi there. My name's Gary, Sergeant Gary Bright. I'm calling from Islington nick.'

A sergeant? She'd got up to speak to a sergeant? She sighed and looked back through the windows into the room she'd just escaped. Oh well. Speaking to a sergeant still beat listening to an overweight man talking about diversity. 'Yes?'

'I understand you're in charge of the Tiffany Mullan case.'

Fox frowned and didn't answer immediately, calculating her answer. In the end, she just went for, 'That's right. And?'

'Well, I've picked up a case that has, or at least might have, similarities.' He paused, then added, 'Maybe.'

Fox sighed, then attempted interest. 'Really?'

'She was found drugged, after a date. Somebody she'd met online. Only we can't find him, seems he doesn't exist. Does that sound familiar?'

First Solomon Mullan with that, what was her name? Rebecca Harrington. Now this. Fox closed her eyes and lifted her face to the ceiling, taking a moment to compose herself. 'Possibly,' she said.

'So I was wondering if you could share the file with me,' Sergeant Bright said. Not Gary. Fox liked to keep things formal. 'Let me take a look?'

'Let me just understand,' said Fox. 'The victim's female?'

'Yes. Early twenties.'

'Found drugged?'

'That's right. Like Tiffany Mullan.'

'Okay, hold on,' said Fox. 'Slow down. Where was she found?'

'In a church.'

'A church?'

'In Finsbury Park.'

'Any injuries on her?'

'No,' said Sergeant Bright. 'Though she was drugged.'

'You said. Any idea what kind of drugs?'

'Propofol. It's a sedative.'

'You know that Tiffany Mullan was drugged with pentobarbital? It's a barbiturate.'

'Well ...'

'They're very different drugs.'

'Still,' said Bright. 'There are similarities. Between the cases.'

'Possibly,' said Fox again. Keep it vague, don't commit to anything, she thought. Don't encourage him. Sergeant Bright had the same eager sound that a lot of the officers in the room she'd just left had. She didn't like it, not one bit.

'Actually, I was surprised,' said Sergeant Bright.

'Oh?'

'That you were taking the case. Isn't organized crime more your area?'

Oh spare me, thought Fox. She pinched her eyes with a thumb and forefinger, then forced herself to put on a smile before she answered, the better to sound pleasant. 'Normally, yes. But you know how it is. Not enough officers. It's about whoever's got capacity, or at least it is over my end.'

'I know that feeling,' said Sergeant Bright.

Behind Fox, the door to the lecture room opened and a man's voice said, 'Sorry, could you keep your voice down? We're trying to listen.' Fox turned and gave him one of her looks, one of the looks that had, she suspected, helped get her to the rank of inspector so quickly. It was the kind of look people found hard to deal with. Hard to even fathom, the depth of hostility it contained. The man, short and balding, with glasses, quickly scuttled back into the lecture room.

Fox walked further down the corridor, then said, 'So. What was it you wanted?'

'Your file. On Tiffany Mullan. I wondered if you could share it with me.'

'Tell you what,' said Fox. 'I picked the case up first. How about you share what you've got with me, and I'll be in touch.'

'I—' began Bright, but Fox interrupted.

'After all, I've got more experience, and I'm further into the investigation. If I find anything, I'll let you in on it.'

'Well, I mean—'

'Good. Listen, I'm in a meeting, so I'm going to have to go. Get whatever you have over to me. And Bright?'

'Yes?'

'Good work.'

She hung up before he had a chance to protest. Jesus. Things were starting to get a little complicated, and Fox was aware that she was playing with fire with this one. Pretty soon she might have to do some proper investigating, which hadn't been the original idea. She'd have to be careful. She'd have a think about it back in the lecture room. At least it would give her something to do.

'He gave you what?'

'Twenty grand. On top of the eighty.'

'Why?' Solomon held the Bat Phone away from his ear. It wasn't often Luke raised his voice, at least not to Solomon, but that was what he was doing now.

'Because he's making too much money to wash it through his

businesses, and evidently you've told him that it's a particular speciality of mine. So thank you for that,' said Solomon, not raising his voice but sounding equally irritated.

'And you took it? Jesus, Solly. This, exactly this, is what I didn't want to happen.'

'It's not as if he's an easy man to say no to,' said Solomon. 'And I was there on my own.'

Luke was silent for a moment, then said, 'No. I hear you. He's a horrible bastard, he really is. But Solly, he's got us now.' Solomon listened to his brother groan on the other end of the line, a note of despair in it. 'You know? Thomas Arnold has got us. Shit.'

'What was I supposed to do?' said Solomon. 'It's you who got involved with him, not me.'

'I know, I know,' said Luke. 'Listen, I'm not angry with you. It's me, this is on me. Shit,' he said again. 'Okay. Let me think.' He was silent, and Solomon listened to the whistle of the bad connection, then Luke said, 'Any news on Tiff?'

'Still the same,' said Solomon.

Luke sighed. 'Is that bad or good?'

'I don't know,' said Solomon, even though he thought it was probably bad. There was no need to share his fears with Luke. What could he do, hiding out in a caravan on the edge of Essex?

'Okay,' said Luke. 'Let's contain this. Do whatever it is you do with his money. I'll sort it out when I get back. Yes?'

'Which will be when?' said Solomon.

'Yeah, well,' said Luke. 'Just stay safe. Do what you need to do. Yes?'

'Okay.'

'I'm sorry,' said Luke.

'Okay.'

'Stop saying okay.'

Solomon did, but only with difficulty. 'I'll call you,' he said, instead, and hung up. He was in his living room, sitting at his desk, and behind him he could feel Arnold's money from where it sat on the coffee table, like some uninvited malevolent spirit that had taken up residence in his apartment and couldn't be exorcized. Which was ridiculous, Solomon knew, irrational and ridiculous, but still. *Do what you need to do,* Luke had said. The problem is, Solomon thought, I don't know what to do. I have no idea.

He was interrupted by the sound of a notification, and he looked up at his screen and saw a message from Kay.

Hey. Are you there?

No, thought Solomon. No, I'm not. I don't exist. Nothing to see. Nothing worth seeing. But instead he leant forward and typed:

Yes.

Need to speak to you.

Okay.

Now?

Okay.

Solomon watched his screen as if it was a dangerous animal until the call icon appeared. Incoming call from Kay. He checked his webcam was disabled and hit the green receiver icon. Onto his screen came a video image of Kay. She had her hair up again, just a few stray curls hanging down, and Solomon felt a lurch in his chest, a freefall sense of despairing desire.

'Hi, Kay.'

'Hi, Solomon. How are you?' She sounded formal, Solomon thought. Distant.

'I'm well.'

'So, okay, so I need to speak to you.'

'I'm listening.'

'It's about your sister. Well, might be. I'm not sure. But I think it is.'

'Is ...?'

'Is about your sister. Well, actually it's about Rebecca Harrington, but it might have something to do with ... I mean, I don't know. I'm not sure.'

'Okay ...'

'You remember that Rebecca was going on a date, to drink cocktails? At the Gypsy Queen?'

'Yes.'

'So I was in the Gypsy Queen, well, I was passing it and I just thought, you know. Since it had been mentioned. Remember?'

'The bar. Yes.'

'Right. So, I was passing it, and I remembered it, so I went in. Just to, I don't know. For a look.'

'For a cocktail?'

'Well, see that's the thing,' said Kay. 'Exactly that. Because they don't do them. Cocktails. They don't even have a cocktail menu. Zero cocktails. I asked for a mojito and the man said, what's in it?'

'Rum, mint ...'

'He didn't have any mint.'

'So you think ...'

'Wait, that's, that's not even the beginning. It got me thinking,

154

and I remembered the suicide note, and I'm thinking, well, something's not right here, with the whole zero-cocktail situation, and if there's something up, then that suicide note, that can't be right either. With me?'

'Yes,' said Solomon. 'Causality.'

'That's exactly it,' said Kay. She nodded, sounded excited. She had a pen in her hand and she shook it at the screen. 'Causality, that's exactly what I was thinking. So I went back to Rebecca Harrington's parents' place.'

'You did?'

'Uh-huh. And I asked Rebecca's mum, Jean, I asked her about the note. And she said that there was something up with it, but the police had told her that often suicide notes can sound funny because, you know, the people who write them aren't, by definition, in their right minds.'

'Kay,' said Solomon, 'you didn't need to do this. Not on your own.'

'No, well.' Kay laughed, a self-conscious sound, and looked down, away from the screen. 'Anyway, doesn't matter. You want to know what it said?'

'The note?'

'Yes. It was in this, like, this freezer bag, Solomon, it was the saddest thing. Just the saddest thing. And it said, *I am done. Farewell, kind mother. Father, long farewell. Rebecca.*'

'That doesn't sound right.'

'Exactly what I said. And what her mum said. It's not right. Solomon, nothing about this is right, the more I think about it, the more I believe it.'

'The police said it was suicide.'

'The impression I get,' said Kay, 'is that this was a troubled young lady who the police couldn't be bloody arsed to waste precious resources on.' She paused, then added, less forcefully, 'Is what I think, anyway.'

Solomon couldn't help but smile at Kay's sudden righteous anger. But she was right, or at least, what she said sounded plausible. After speaking to Fox, he'd given up this angle, any connection between his sister and Rebecca Harrington. Maybe he'd given it up too easily.

'So,' said Kay, looking straight at the screen so that Solomon had the impression that they were making eye contact, even though they weren't. 'I thought I'd tell you. See what you think.'

What Solomon thought was that Kay was unlike most people he'd ever met. What he said was, 'I don't know. I need to think.'

Kay blinked, then said, 'Sure,' as if Solomon had dismissed her, which wasn't what he'd meant, was far from it.

'I mean, sorry, Kay, I mean, this is unexpected and I don't know what to make of it. That's what I meant.'

'Okay,' said Kay, but she still sounded hurt.

Solomon blinked his eyes closed, then said, 'I'm sorry. About last time. Turning you down. You know, when you asked me—'

'It's fine.'

'No, Kay, please, it's not. It's just—'

'I was out of line. It's fine.' Kay shook her head, not looking at Solomon. 'Look, I just thought you'd want to know.' She looked away from the screen, and said, 'I need to be somewhere. Let me know how you get on.'

'Kay,' said Solomon, but she put up a hand and waved her fingers, and the picture cut out as she hung up the call. Solomon sat looking at the blank screen for a long time, wondering how he'd managed to get it so wrong. It wasn't often that he felt stupid, but right now, he wouldn't trust himself to tie his own shoelaces. He stood up, and as he turned, he saw the blue plastic bag full of money, money he had accepted from a criminal he'd been pre-warned about. He picked the bag up and threw it against the wall, banknotes fluttering down to the floor like a lottery winner's celebration. Solomon watched them sourly. Luck, he couldn't help but think, was something he'd been short on recently.

twenty

RENAISSANCE DRAMA WASN'T ONE OF SOLOMON'S STRONGEST areas. He had, he was willing to admit, a kind of inverted snobbery when it came to Shakespeare. Shakespeare was the establishment, the canon, the knowledge that you got by going to the right school, by doing education the right way or, put it another way, by having it bought for you. He'd done nothing the right way, had learnt what he'd learnt the hard way, and he'd given Shakespeare a miss. Pretty much all of early-modern and Jacobean drama with it: Marlowe, Middleton, Jonson, Webster, the lot. Which still didn't, and this he knew, *really* didn't excuse the fact that Rebecca Harrington's date was as good as forcing references from *Antony and Cleopatra* down everybody's throats, and not being particularly subtle about it, either.

Gypsy Queen. Caesar. And now this suicide note, which basically stole Cleopatra's dying words and retasked them for he didn't know what reason. Couldn't guess. But he had the link. What was even more irritating was the fact that as Solomon read the play, he had to admit that it was pretty good. More than good. It was extraordinary, an intoxicating journey of unexpected metaphors and extended conceits, of exquisite poetry and explorations of human frailty and hubris that endured to this day. In fact, although he knew this on one level, when he thought of what he'd read, he perceived it in his mind as a rolling green landscape interwoven with mile-wide ribbons of silk of every conceivable hue, the entire terrain trembling and humming slightly with the power of the language it was built upon. Which only made him feel more of a fool for having wilfully avoided it for the last twenty-something years.

So, have you done?
Come then, and take the last warmth of my lips.
Farewell, kind Charmian; Iras, long farewell.

And Rebecca's suicide note:

I am done.
Farewell, kind mother. Father, long farewell.

Cleopatra. Egypt's Queen. The Gypsy Queen. Solomon stared at the text of the play on the screen in front of him and thought of Kay, of how, if she hadn't made the effort on his behalf, he would never have made this connection. He felt, how had Shakespeare put it? Robbed of his sword. Belittled, outwitted, humiliated. The question was, by who? What intelligence lay behind this, and was it the same one that had put his sister in a coma?

His intercom sounded and Solomon walked to the hallway and picked up the entry phone. 'Yes?'

'Delivery.'

'For?'

'Solomon Mullan?'

'Third floor,' he said. He couldn't remember ordering anything but, given that everything he ever received was ordered online, it was easy to lose track. Still, he left the chain on his door. He'd rather let the delivery person think he was a strange recluse than let them look at his face. Anyway, he *was* a strange recluse.

'Mr Mullan?'

'Just leave it outside the door.'

'Need you to sign.'

The delivery man passed an electronic device through the gap in the door and Solomon took the pen and signed, passed it back, then waited until the man was gone before opening the door. On the floor was a package about the size of a shoebox. He picked it up. It was light, felt almost empty. He took it inside and cut it open along the joins with a knife. Inside was inflatable plastic packaging, and in the middle an opaque white plastic bag. He took it out and cut it open, and took out a single black eye patch. *A box that size, just for this?* He'd forgotten he'd ordered it, or perhaps more accurately, had tried not to remember.

He walked to his bathroom and put it over his eye and looked at himself in the mirror. What was it Marija had said it made people look? *Hench.* A new word he hadn't been familiar with, denoting machismo and substance. He examined his crumpled, shiny, ruined skin, his mouth, half lipless and pulled down in sour disapproval, curls thankfully spilling over his missing ear. Hench wasn't the word he'd have chosen. Plus, and this was something he hadn't considered, wearing an eye patch didn't exactly render him inconspicuous. Still, though. He'd ordered it, and he needed to visit his sister. He looked at the pots of make-up that Marija had left him and decided that he might as well get to work.

Before he left his apartment, Solomon sent an invitation to the whole of the Brain Pool for a special, unscheduled meeting. Wasn't that the point of the Brain Pool? If there were gaps in anyone's knowledge, then there was always someone to fill it. And for Solomon, Shakespeare was less a gap, more a chasm. He got an immediate reply from Phil, confirming what Solomon had long suspected, which was that Phil had about as active a social life as he himself did.

The worst thing about putting on Marija's make-up was that it involved him looking at himself in the mirror, something that ranked very near the bottom of things that Solomon relished doing. He applied the foundation as thickly as she had done, building up layers and smoothing it so that it looked almost normal. Nothing to be done about his mouth, but with the eye patch on he could just about pass, he figured, for a pock-marked pirate who had recently suffered a medium-size stroke. And that, he was prepared to accept, counted as a significant improvement.

No hood, no sunglasses. That was the deal. Go out and face the world. Why not? If Thomas Arnold could do it, so could he.

Solomon did it in stages, like a novice runner approaching a marathon. Milestones, knocking them off, one at a time. First, get to the bus stop. Don't count the paving stones. Look up. Watch people, traffic, the sky, shopfronts, life. He felt his pulse race, the almost illicit thrill of parading himself, an exhibitionist rush. Exposing himself, baring himself to the world. Next, wait for the bus. Number 276. Step out, off the pavement, put up a hand, make it stop. Get on, card to the reader. Eye contact with the driver. Done. Stand, hold the strap, sway with the bus and check out who's on board. Jostling kids at the back, pensioner up front with shopping trolley, across from grim-faced older lady, large, dressed for church even though it was a Thursday, looking around in disapproval for something to disapprove of. Passengers looking back at him, showing curiosity but no fear, no disgust. A victory, a triumph, and no small one.

Solomon stepped from the bus and walked up the sunlit street towards the hospital with a surge of hope in his chest, a memory to hold onto. Of a journey in which he was a participant, a fellow traveller, not a timid onlooker, hidden, ashamed. As he walked, he thanked Marija, and not even the combined spectres of his comatose sister, his wanted brother, Kay's distance and Thomas Arnold's menace were enough to smother this new discovery. This new and unexpected invitation to participate in Life.

Dr Mistry was in Tiffany's room when Solomon arrived. He turned at the sound of the door opening and put his fingers to his lips and gestured Solomon back out of the room, back into the hospital corridor.

'Is there anything wrong?' said Solomon.

'No, no, I just don't want your sister disturbed,' said Dr Mistry. 'She's awake.'

'Awake?'

Dr Mistry wagged his head. 'Kind of. Out of her coma. And I know you'll want to speak to her. Which is fine. But she's showing some memory loss, and I don't want her upset, so, please. Don't talk about what happened, don't ask her about it.'

'Okay.'

'The official line, for the moment, is she had a fall. Yes?'

'Yes.'

'A couple of minutes. No longer. All you need to do is reassure her, everything's okay, that kind of thing. Manage that?'

'Yes.'

'All right. Good.' Dr Mistry tilted his head. 'Marija?'

'I gave her a call.'

'It looks better. A lot better. The eye patch is a nice touch.'

'Thanks. And, well.' Solomon wasn't used to expressing gratitude, or any kind of emotion. 'Thank you. For giving me her number.'

'No problem,' said Dr Mistry. 'All part of the service.' He smiled, then said, 'Two minutes. Yes?'

'Yes,' said Solomon. 'Two minutes.'

Dr Mistry nodded, then turned and walked away down the corridor. Solomon pushed open the door to his sister's room, walked to her bed and sat down. Tiffany was still lying on her back and her arm was still in a cast, but the tube that had been forced down her throat was out and she looked close to normal. Peaceful.

'Solly?' Her lips barely moved, her eyes stayed shut, but it seemed to Solomon a minor miracle to hear her voice, as gloriously unlikely as a weeping statue of the Virgin Mary.

'Hey, Tiff,' he said. 'Welcome back.'

'I'm in hospital.'

'You are.'

'Why?'

'You had a fall,' Solomon said. 'A bang on the head.'

Tiff sighed and moved her lips but didn't say anything.

'Don't talk,' said Solomon. 'You need to rest.'

Tiff sighed again and Solomon watched as tears formed at the corners of her eyes and fell down her face into her hair.

'No,' said Solomon. 'There's no need to cry. Tiff, it's okay. You're back with us now. You're going to be okay.'

'I can't remember what happened.'

'That doesn't matter,' said Solomon. 'What matters is that you're back with us.'

'Where's Luke?'

'He's around. You know Luke. He's been in every day.'

'Solly?'

'Yes?'

'Can you hold my hand? I keep thinking that you're a dream.'

Solomon reached out and put his hand over his sister's. 'I'm not a dream,' he said. 'I'm real.' He squeezed Tiffany's hand and said, 'More real than ever.'

Solomon got the Circle Line home, taking the escalator down into the depths of the Underground, stewing in its Victorian pre-air-conditioning heat. There were signal problems somewhere on the line and he had to wait for a train, feeling a part of the tutting, head-shaking crowd massing on the platform, no longer watching from the wings. Eventually a train arrived and Solomon got on and stood near the doors. It was even warmer inside the carriage, the base temperature of the Tube raised by too many warm bodies in an enclosed space. The train left the platform but didn't make it far into the tunnel before it stopped in a series of belligerent shudders. Solomon felt sweat in the small of his back, just above his waistband, more sweat prickling his hair. He wondered, too late, whether the make-up Marija had given him was waterproof.

He didn't know. He closed his eyes and willed the train to start moving. He only had two stops to go. Not far. Shouldn't be long.

It wasn't yet rush hour, and even though the train had been delayed, it wasn't crowded. There was a group of teenagers who should have been at school talking loudly and laughing, keeping up a steady level of bad language, *fuck bitch shit* punctuating every sentence. The tallest of them, wearing a cap with a large gold sticker on it, was looking at Solomon, a half-smile on his face. He elbowed a kid next to him, whispered something, and they both cracked up, exaggerated laughs, shaking their heads and fist-bumping each other. Solomon turned away from them and looked up the carriage. The train began moving, then stopped again, the air brakes hissing. Behind him the kids were still laughing and Solomon heard one of them, he didn't know which, say, 'Think it is, fancy dress? Shit,' followed by more laughter. The carriage didn't move and Solomon touched his face and looked at his fingers, a smear of peach-coloured foundation on them. He could feel his heart beating faster and he willed the train to start, to just go. He'd get off at the next stop, hike it home. Just *move*.

'Yo, bruv.' A voice behind him, closer than before. 'Yo.'

Solomon turned and immediately faced the tall kid, who had come towards him. 'Are you talking to me?'

'What's with the patch, man?' The kid was sixteen, seventeen, but bigger than Solomon.

Solomon shook his head, said, 'Leave it,' and turned away again.

'Yo, just axing, bruv,' the kid said. 'Hey.'

Solomon didn't turn, knew kids well enough, kids in groups. Never give them the oxygen. Never react. But he also knew that it wasn't a foolproof technique.

From behind he heard somebody laugh, another voice say, 'Do it,' and he felt fingers pull at the elastic of his eye patch and flick it over his head, the patch flying off. He looked around and said, as firmly as he could, 'You need to leave me alone,' but was stopped from finishing his sentence by the look on the tall kid's face, something between shock and delight.

'Shit, bruv, the fuck happened to your face?' he said, then turned and said to his group, 'You believe this?' He turned back to Solomon and now he really was laughing, shaking his head in fascinated revulsion. 'Man, that is fucked up,' he said, and Solomon returned his stare but inside was thinking, *No, no, this is not happening, this cannot be happening.*

'Hey,' said a voice behind him, and he turned to see a man, a clocked-off builder in a high-vis jacket, holding his eye patch. 'Leave the man alone, hear me? Go on, piss off.' The man held Solomon's eye patch out and Solomon took it, and he tried to say thank you but was stopped from getting the words out by the look on the man's face, which he could only describe as pity, pure pity.

The train started to move and Solomon got out at the next station and walked home with his eyes focused on the paving stones beneath his feet, automatically counting them in his head. When he got to his apartment he threw the eye patch away and lay on his bed without taking his clothes off and put a pillow over his head, and as the day grew dark around him all he could think in his head was *stupid, stupid, stupid stupid stupid.*

twenty-one

'FOR SOMEBODY WHO DOESN'T KNOW SHAKESPEARE,' SAID FRAN, 'that's a mightily impressive connection to make. You didn't have a lot to go on.'

'Cleopatra as the Gypsy Queen, and Octavius Caesar as a key player,' said Solomon. 'That should have been enough, on its own.'

'I would never have made that connection,' said Masoud. 'Not in an aeon, and I love Shakespeare.'

'*Farewell, kind Charmian; Iras, long farewell. Have I the aspic in my lips? Dost fall?*' said Fran, quoting from memory. '*If thou and nature can so gently part, the stroke of death is as a lover's pinch.*'

'So who wrote it?' said Phil, interrupting her. He seemed in an especially abrasive mood tonight, Solomon couldn't help noticing.

'Shakespeare,' said Kay. 'Even I know that much.'

'Ah,' said Phil enigmatically, before going back to his drink.

'Ah?' said Fran. 'What does *Ah* mean, Phil?'

'Please,' said Masoud. 'Do not tell me that you are one of them.'

'One of who?' said Kay. Phil picked up his glass and scrutinized the underside without answering.

'One of those people who believes that it wasn't Shakespeare. Who wrote the plays,' said Masoud.

'No evidence to suggest he did write them,' said Phil.

'But of course, there is a lot,' said Masoud. 'There is plenty.'

'And plenty to suggest he didn't,' said Phil.

'Perhaps we could get back to—' said Fran, but Phil cut her off.

'Jointly written, if you ask me,' he said. 'A collaborative effort. Shakespeare being a cipher. A totem.'

'This would be your Marxist reading of the plays,' said Fran.

Phil tipped his drink towards her. 'An anarchist reading,' he corrected her. 'But yes. If you like. The collected works of the Southwark Players.'

'The who?' said Masoud.

'A writing collective,' said Phil. 'Subversive.'

'Bullshit,' said Fran, a rare epithet.

'The evidence,' said Phil, now waving his glass around in an elliptical pattern at nobody specific, 'is mounting.'

'No it most certainly is not,' said Fran tartly. 'And please, nobody offer to buy Phil anything else to drink.'

Phil put down his drink, glowered, then sat back and belched. Definitely had a few before the meeting, Solomon thought, though Phil, having got his theory off his chest, seemed somewhat happier.

'So, Solomon,' said Fran, looking into the camera, straight at him. 'It is a strange message, but it seems quite obvious what the theme is.'

'Yes,' said Solomon. 'But the question is why? Why write a coded message into a ...' He almost said *suicide note*, and stopped himself. The Brain Pool didn't need to know everything. 'A note to your parents?'

The Brain Pool had no answer for that. Solomon hadn't expected them to. But he figured that it was worth putting it out there. These were, after all, the smartest people he'd ever met, Phil included.

'Shakespeare obsessive?' said Kay.

'Perhaps it was Phil,' said Fran, making Masoud bark with laughter, an outburst Solomon had never seen from him before. Masoud laughing, Fran swearing. This was turning out to be quite the night for the Brain Pool.

'So anyway,' said Fran. 'You said you had another.'

'I'll put it on screen,' said Solomon. He brought up the message exchange between Tiffany and the man who called himself Tobes.

Drink?

When?

Can u do Saturday?

Day off! Where shall we go?

To a convent.

???

Convent. A bar. Dwkd. I mean awkward. Have you been?

To Convent? No.

You should!

OK ...

What hour now?

??? Hour?

Time. What time.

Oh. 9?

C u then.

'So what are we looking at?' said Fran.

'A message exchange that might be connected,' said Solomon. 'Maybe.'

'And you cannot tell us what this is about?' said Masoud.

'I'm sorry,' said Solomon. 'I can't.'

'That first message,' said Fran, 'sounds like a suicide note. Which it isn't, is it? Because if it was, the police would need to be involved.'

'The police are probably aware,' said Kay. 'But they're not as bright as we are.'

'That is certainly true,' said Phil.

Solomon should have expected the Brain Pool to be shrewd enough to see through his obfuscation. He took a deep breath. 'Look,' he said, 'I'm sorry. I'm asking you to help me, but I have no right to, and I apologize. And I can't tell you anything about this. So, I, well.' He stopped, ran out of things to say, not used to public speaking. Even if it was from behind a computer screen.

'No, Solomon, no, we weren't asking ...' said Fran.

'It is fine,' said Masoud. 'It is intriguing. Please.'

'Solomon,' said Phil, sitting back upright with difficulty. 'If it helps you, then we consider it a privilege.' He nodded to himself and added, 'Yes we do.'

Fran turned to Phil in what looked like astonishment, then turned back and said, 'Yes. Yes, of course. So. Solomon. What should we be looking for?'

'I'm not sure,' said Solomon. 'A link. Some kind of connection.'

'A convent,' said Fran. 'Sounds possible.'

'Possible?' said Solomon.

'Shakespearean,' said Fran. 'There was Isabella.'

Measure for Measure,' said Masoud.

'She wanted to join a convent, yes,' said Fran. 'Who else?'

'*Romeo and Juliet*,' said Phil. He waved his head slowly at the table, then intoned in a voice deeper than his normal delivery, '*Come, I'll dispose of thee amongst a sisterhood of holy nuns.*'

Fran watched him in bafflement, then said, 'And *Hamlet*. *Get thee to a nunnery.*' She looked at the laptop screen on the bar table, at the message Solomon had shared on it. '*Where shall we go? To a convent.*' She frowned. 'It's not quite there. But it's like ...'

She stopped, and Kay watched her, then said, 'Fran?'

'I don't know. It's like, maybe, I'm not sure. Is it like the conversation is being manipulated? As if it's being shaped, directed?'

'How do you mean?' said Solomon.

Fran sat up straighter and looked at the screen closely. 'Twice the phrasing has been off, and the man, or whoever this is, has pretended it was a mistake. He writes *a convent*, but he means Convent, a bar. Phil,' she said, 'can you find *Hamlet*? The full play? It doesn't matter who wrote it, for now.'

'I can,' Phil said, tapping at a tablet.

'Search within it. *Hour*, that should do.'

'A second,' said Phil, then, to himself as he searched, '*Upon your hour ... At this dead hour ... Thy fair hour ... What hour now?* Gotcha.'

'*What hour now?*' said Fran. '*Hamlet*. And the famous exchange, Hamlet and Ophelia, where he tells her, *Get thee to a nunnery*. And in the message, *To a convent.*'

'It is hidden,' said Masoud. 'But it is there.'

'It's certainly there,' said Phil. 'And you're not going to tell us what this is about?'

'Phil,' said Fran, warning.

'I'm sorry,' said Solomon. 'I really am. I can't. But this is, it's …'
It wasn't often he was impressed by others, but this seemed of
another magnitude. 'Astonishing.'

Fran and Phil said nothing for a moment, then Fran cleared
her throat and said, 'Well. Solomon. Coming from you, that is
very kind.'

'So …' said Kay, breaking the awkward silence that followed.
'Do we have a connection? Or at least, put it another way, if you
like, I mean, do we have enough of a connection?' She frowned,
thinking back over what had been said. 'There's some kind of
mind at work here. Shakespeare, yep, we've got it. But is that the
connection? Or is there more?'

'Cleopatra, Ophelia,' said Masoud. 'They are both tragic heroines.'

'Yes,' said Fran. 'And look at the power dynamic. A man,
presumably, arranging a date with a woman. The roles. Mark
Antony, Hamlet.'

'The names,' said Phil. 'Who was writing to Cleopatra?'

'Caesar. Octavius Caesar, Mark Antony's rival.'

'And the other?' said Fran.

'Tobes,' said Solomon, again putting it together as he said it.
'To be. To be or not to be. To be, but twice. Plural.'

'This is smart stuff,' said Fran. 'This isn't obvious.'

'It's taken, what? Fifteen minutes?' said Solomon. 'I've been
looking at this for days.'

'You've got us all here,' said Phil. 'We're a team.'

'A collective, surely,' said Fran.

Phil bowed his head, slowly. 'Such a thing has been proven to
work,' he said.

'So what have we got?' said Kay. 'Somebody who, what? Plays

the role of a Shakespearean character and, I don't get it. Tries to make his date into a, what was it you called them, Masoud? Tragic heroines?'

'Maybe,' said Masoud. 'Very probably, from what I have seen.' He turned to look straight at Solomon and said, 'And this is something that the police know about?'

'They know,' said Solomon. 'But unfortunately, they don't think it's sufficient to justify a formal investigation.'

'But you do?' said Fran.

'I don't know,' said Solomon. 'I just … It was curious.' He watched Kay to see her reaction to this lie. She didn't blink.

'Well,' said Masoud. 'It is certainly that.'

'So,' said Phil. 'Another case solved by the Brain Pool. Are we finished here?'

'I think so,' said Solomon. 'Thank you. Thank you, everyone.'

He watched a general nodding and chair movement, Fran hauling up her handbag, ready to go. Kay stayed seated, looking around the table, then said, 'Am I missing something?'

'Sorry?' said Fran.

'Nothing,' she said. 'Ignore me.' She waited for the rest of the group to stand, then looked straight at Solomon and mouthed, 'I'll call you,' before the screen went blank as Masoud cancelled the connection.

Solomon didn't count the minutes, but still noticed that thirty-seven of them had passed before Kay called him. He checked his webcam was disabled and accepted the call.

'Hello,' he said. 'Is there anything wrong?'

'I didn't want to say anything,' said Kay. 'You know, with everyone there. But don't you think we're missing something?'

'From the messages, you mean?'

'Not exactly, no,' said Kay. 'More ...' She paused. 'We've all been, okay, I haven't been, but the rest of you, you've all been very clever, working it out. But isn't there, you know, I mean there must be, right, a chance, a big chance, that these poor women who've been found, that they're not the only ones. Right?'

Solomon had been playing with a pen, but he stopped, his whole body frozen. A sense of dread washed through him.

'Solomon? Are you there?'

Solomon swallowed and took a breath, then said, 'I'm here.'

'Well? What do you think?'

What Solomon thought was that the past couple of days had proved to him that he was stupid; more than stupid, way beyond stupid. An imbecile, a simpleton. 'I think you're right,' he said.

'That there are more?'

'That there could be, yes.'

'So what do we do?'

Solomon thought of Fox, her indifference to his sister's case. Her preoccupation with his brother. He wondered who, if anyone, might actually care.

'I don't know,' he said. 'But something. We need to do something.'

twenty-two

IF IT HAD ONLY BEEN FEAR, OLIVIA THOUGHT, THEN THAT would be … not okay, but better. It was the combination, that was what made it so … so beyond. Beyond anything she'd ever felt before. Dread, and horror. But with it the not knowing. Not knowing why she was here. *Why?*

She could imagine her mother. *I told you so.* That's probably what she'd think, even though her daughter was trapped in a black pit that smelt of oil, a car parked over the grille that covered it. *I told you so.* That would be about right. *Why did you have to move there in the first place?* The same question she always asked her. As if Cheltenham was the epicentre of the cultural universe, and Hackney was the end of the world. Her mother, withering away in a seven-bedroom town house, surrounded by meaningless trinkets, memorabilia from a life not worth remembering. *You did what? One of those dating application things?* Actually, she would never say that, because she would never have heard of such a thing. Not unless it featured in the *Times* crossword. *Oh, Olivia.* She'd say that. She'd certainly say that. Because she'd assume that this, her daughter being held captive in a black concrete hole, was Olivia's own fault. And the worst thing about it? She'd be one hundred per cent right. It *was* all her own fault.

Olivia listened carefully, stilled her breath to be sure. She hadn't heard any noise, any sound at all, for a while. A long while. No distant traffic, no footsteps, no unexplained creaks or rustles. Nothing. She had found the metal lid of a paint can and had been using it to chip away at the rusty iron of the grille near one corner of the pit. The pit was the size of a dining table and not high enough to stand up in. Olivia thought it was probably a mechanic's pit for working on the underside of cars, but she had never actually seen one, not for real. Her kind didn't really do garages. The grille was made of criss-crossing metal bars as thick as a biro and it was old, the metal orange and flaking at the joints. But the paint lid was made of soft metal and kept folding and cutting into her hands, which had been bleeding for a long time now. She didn't know how long she'd been there, had woken up in the pit. All she knew was that she'd been put there by Demmy, because he was the evil bastard who'd tricked her into meeting him for a date, drugged her, and imprisoned her in a concrete crypt with only the dark dirty underside of a car to look up at.

And the way he'd trapped her. Her mother wouldn't believe it. Olivia didn't believe it. She'd known something was off from the beginning, that message exchange she'd had with him. With Demmy. Ridiculous name to begin with, and then the things he'd written. Just weird. Just weird, and she'd met him anyway. And why? Because she'd liked his photo. *Because you liked his photo?* Yes, Mother, yes. Because you were always right, I *am* an idiot, and yes, I liked his photo.

Olivia kept scraping, trying to keep a good grip on the paint-tin lid despite the blood, which made it slippery, and thought back to the message exchange, the memory of it, and her stupidity, giving her an angry motivation.

Want to go out?

Sure. Know anywhere good?

Forest? (bar)

Where's that?

A barren detested vale.

???

Okay, Hackney.

Hilarious. When?

Tuesodlq

?

I mean Tuesday. Can't type.

Good for me but I work late ... When's good for you?

At dead time of the night.

?

Any time. I meant any time. God. Hello?

Okay ... 9?

9 is good.

See you then.

C u.

At dead time of the night. And no alarm bells had started ringing. She pushed at the bar she was working on in disgust and felt it give, the joint where it met another giving way, rusted and weakened. She stopped and sat down with her back against the concrete side of the pit and looked up at the grille, barely visible in the gloom. The squares of the grille were maybe ten centimetres apart. She'd need a gap of at least forty by forty centimetres to get through, which meant ... She counted. Sixteen, she'd have to cut through sixteen bars, four on each side of the square she'd need. She'd counted them before, many times, and every time they'd come to twenty. And she'd got through three. Which left thirteen. Thirteen bars to cut through, using a paint-tin lid that was getting worn away a lot faster than the bars were.

She closed her eyes and tried not to think about the pain in her hands, and whatever lay in front of her, the reason she'd been put in this pit in the first place. She tried to empty her mind, still it, silence it like the silence outside the pit. But she couldn't, couldn't, because the second she stopped moving, her mind filled with taped footage of men being decapitated in front of cameras, of women mutilated and left in ditches, of broken people kneeling in cages, meekly awaiting the inevitable. Why was she here? What was planned for her?

Olivia had never been to the Forest bar before, a dark basement down a flight of stairs off a street behind Hackney Road. And it had been a forest, or at least kind of, twisted trunks of trees snaking between the floor and the ceiling, the space thick with them so that even now she didn't have a good idea of how large the bar actually was, where it began and ended. She couldn't even work out how the owners had got the trees in in the first place. Demmy had been waiting for her, had stood up from a table near the entrance when she came in. He looked like his photo, maybe a bit older than she'd imagined, but no disappointment. What had she thought? *He'll do.* Yes, that's what she'd thought.

'Olivia?'

'Demmy. Hi.'

'Let me get you a drink.'

'I'll go,' Olivia said. 'What are you having?'

'No,' said Demmy, very solemnly. He had dark hair, and although she hadn't thought before, she wondered where he came from, what his background was. Greek? Iranian? Some place where male chivalry was still taken seriously, maybe.

'Okay,' she said. 'A vodka and tonic.'

'Take a seat,' Demmy said. 'I'll be back.'

The bar was lit by green wall lights and a large neon sign that said *Forest* in glowing cursive green. It was nearly empty, Tuesday night not being weirdly-themed-cocktail-bar night, Olivia supposed. Music was playing, but softly, and the bar was kind of … what? she wondered. Peaceful. Weird but peaceful. Okay, so it was some stupid hipster doomed-to-failure folly of a bar, but it was kind of cool, at the same time. She still couldn't work out how they'd got the tree trunks in.

Demmy came back holding two drinks, made a show of working out which one belonged to who, then handed one of the glasses to Olivia before sitting down.

'Cheers,' he said.

'Cheers,' said Olivia.

'Not been here before?' said Demmy.

'No. It's kind of cool, though.'

'In a weird way,' said Demmy.

'Exactly,' said Olivia. They were silent for a while, for too long, and Olivia tried to think of something to say, then eventually said, 'So, what do you do? For, you know. A job.'

'Oh,' said Demmy. 'This and that. You know?'

Olivia didn't, not really, but Demmy didn't offer anything else. Olivia drank, to fill the silence, then said, 'What kind of this and that?'

'Whatever comes along,' said Demmy.

Olivia watched his face but couldn't read anything in it. He seemed comfortable, unconcerned, but Olivia wasn't about to spend an evening with somebody who wouldn't answer questions. She didn't do evasive. She drank some more, then said, 'For example?'

'Well,' said Demmy. 'For example, I ...' He paused, then said, 'How's your drink?'

'Fine,' said Olivia. Actually, it was strong, was what she thought, already feeling its effects. She'd need to be careful. She suspected it was a double. 'So? For example?'

'Well,' he said again, 'I wanted to be an actor.'

'Tough profession,' said Olivia.

'Tell me about it,' said Demmy. He said it forcefully, ending with a laugh to soften the delivery, take the edge off. 'So now I do other stuff. How about you?'

'PR,' said Olivia. 'For a start-up.'

Demmy nodded but didn't ask for any details. Instead he looked at his watch, then said, 'What do you think about the trees?'

Olivia looked around the bar. Was it her imagination, or were there more now than there had been before? Probably something to do with the lighting. 'I can't work out how they got them in.' This date wasn't going well, was what she was actually thinking. There was already an undercurrent of tetchiness in their exchanges, some incompatibility in the chemistry. She drank some more. She'd finish her drink and go, she thought. One drink to be polite, then off.

'The trees, though summer, yet forlorn and lean,' said Demmy. 'Here never shines the sun.'

'What's that?' said Olivia. The inside of her mouth felt strange, as if it was swelling, her tongue fat and stupid.

'Overcome with moss and baleful mistletoe,' Demmy said, ignoring her. He was silent for a moment, glancing around the bar, then looked directly at her. 'Wouldn't you say?'

'I don't understand what you mean,' said Olivia, talking carefully, making sure that the words came out right. *Enunciating.* That was the word.

'Here never shines the sun,' Demmy said. 'Here nothing breeds.'

Olivia had had enough. She tried to stand up, but her legs wouldn't move, wouldn't do what she wanted them to. She pushed her drink away from her and it tipped, but Demmy caught it before it overturned.

'Do you hear it?' Demmy said.

Olivia tried to speak but couldn't. Instead she shook her head and realized that she was crying, from fear of this man opposite her who she didn't know and didn't want to know.

'A thousand fiends, a thousand hissing snakes,' he said. 'Ten thousand swelling toads. You don't hear them?'

Olivia pushed at the table with her hands, as hard as she could, but Demmy shoved back and then stood up and said loudly, as if performing for an audience, 'Olivia? Olivia? Are you feeling okay?'

He came around the table and picked up Olivia's arm, wrapping it over his shoulder, then lifted her to her feet. Her legs felt as if they were made from cloth, as solid and substantial as flannel. She had no more strength or coordination than a stuffed toy, a patchwork doll. Demmy walked her towards the door and pulled it open, the night air a distant tingle on her skin. And as he dragged her up the stairs, he whispered to her, a hiss as inhuman as a reptile, *'First thrash the corn, then after burn the straw.'*

Olivia didn't know what Demmy had put in her drink, but she felt nauseous, like a hangover but worse, thirsty and tired and weak, as if she hadn't eaten for a long time. And a headache, like sharp explosions going off in the back of her skull. The smell of oil in the pit made her feel sick, excess saliva collecting in her mouth and her stomach heaving.

She heard the sound of a door opening, closing, then dull footsteps on concrete. She put the paint-tin lid behind her, between her back and the wall. The footsteps came closer, and then stopped. A dark shape appeared between the lip of the concrete pit and the underside of the car.

'Why am I here?' Olivia said. 'Hello?'

She saw the shape move, but it didn't answer, just made a clucking sound, a sound of disapproval.

'What are you going to do to me?'

The shape took a deep breath, then said, *'First thrash the corn, then after burn the straw.'*

Olivia remembered hearing him say that before, a memory associated with trees and toads and darkness and the hissing of snakes. 'What do you mean?' she said, her voice more a desperate shriek. 'What? What do you mean?'

But the shape just made the same clucking sound. It stayed there for some moments, looking down at her, and then disappeared. Olivia heard the sound of footsteps, this time getting quieter and quieter, and then the closing of a door, leaving her once more alone, alone in her pit.

twenty-three

'WE'RE CLEAR ON WHAT OUR ROADMAP IS, YES?'

'Yes,' said Fox. She watched her immediate superior, Chief Inspector Goven, as levelly as she could. He was a good gaze-holder, she had to admit. Hated to admit, but there you were. He just did not give one shit who he stared down, or how he came across as he did it. And how he came across was as one colossal ball-breaker, an overweight, grey-haired, red-faced, almost-certainly-divorced ball-breaker. 'Yes,' she said again. 'We're clear.'

'Good.' He was standing up behind his desk, looking down at Fox, who had foolishly sat down without waiting to see what he did. She'd knocked on his office door, he'd opened it, then gestured her to sit. She'd sat. And he hadn't. So Fox had been looking up at him for the last five minutes, and would be for she didn't know how much longer. However long it took him to make his point. 'Because I need you to be a team player on this one. I like team players. What I don't like is coppers who sign up for one thing and then go off on their own little expedition. Understand?'

'I understand,' Fox said, 'but sir—'

'So if you understand,' he said, putting his hands on his desk and looming over her, 'maybe you could explain to me just what you think your mission is.'

'Bring in a medium-to-large player in organized crime,' she said.

'Because?'

'Because?' Fox said, confused by the question and sounding, she knew, stupid. Christ, she hated coming across as stupid.

'Because you're a key member of Task Force Jehovah,' said Goven. 'And you've got hard targets to hit. This is your KPI, and if you don't hit it, you're going nowhere. Understand?'

'Yes,' said Fox. 'We're on the same page.'

'So okay, tell me again. This girl, this ...'

'Tiffany Mullan. Luke Mullan's sister.'

'Right. I thought, you told me there was nothing to it. You told me, and I have it in writing, that she was just a way in to Luke Mullan.'

'She was.'

'Was.'

'Well,' said Fox. She paused, chose her words carefully. 'It depends on what we want to do with this new information.'

'This new information being that some junkie was found in the same canal that she was.'

'Just after a date. Or a supposed date.'

'This Tiffany Mullan,' said Goven. 'Is she a junkie too?'

'No. Not as far as I'm aware.'

'Coroner's report?'

'For Rebecca Harrington? Suicide. There was a note.'

Goven stood up straight and turned his back to Fox. Fox watched the semicircle of sweat on his shirt, just above his waist. Watched him breathe in, out, in, out, deeply.

'So,' said Goven, slowly, 'there's basically no link at all between the two of them, except that they both fell into the same fucking canal?'

'There's more,' said Fox.

'There'd fucking well better be more,' said Goven. 'Because your time might be worth eff all, but mine isn't. Understood?'

Fox took a deep breath. 'I had a call from Islington nick. Another girl had been found, drugged, after a date.'

'Drugged? What, dead?'

'No, just drugged. She'd been out for two days.'

'And?'

'And the sergeant there—'

'The sergeant.' Goven turned back to Fox. 'Really? The *sergeant*?' He shook his head, then said, 'Go on.'

'This ... sergeant, he'd heard about the Tiffany Mullan case and thought there might be similarities.'

'Why?'

'Because the girl, the one who'd been drugged, she'd been on a date. With some guy she met online and who couldn't be traced.'

'Where was she found?'

'In a church.'

'A what?' Goven tapped the side of his temple with three fingers, hard. 'God help me. A church?'

'And drugged.'

'Barbiturates? Same as Tiffany Mullan?'

'No.'

'No. So you've got the mystery date. That's your link.'

'Not my link. Sergeant Bright's.'

'Right. The sergeant. And this didn't come down from his superiors?'

'I don't think so,' said Fox. 'He wanted my case notes, but obviously there aren't many, given that we're going after her brother. So I told him to send me his, since I picked the case up first.'

'Okay.' Goven nodded, seemed almost satisfied by this action. Getting a compliment from Goven was rare, Fox thought, trying to remember a time he'd praised her and coming up short. 'Heard from him since? This sergeant?'

'No.'

Goven nodded again. 'So, let's recap.' He put an index finger to a thumb and said, with a heavy dose of unfriendly sarcasm, 'If I may?'

Fox nodded.

'Number one. We have Tiffany Mullan, a stripper, found in a canal, head wound, barbiturates in her blood.'

'Yes. After an online date.'

Goven nodded. 'Two, we have this Harrington disaster, found in the same canal, suicide note. Supposed to have had a date, but the coroner ruled suicide.'

'Yes.'

'So we can forget her. Finally, we've got a girl found drugged in a church. After a date. Maybe.'

'A date who can't be traced.'

'They all use fake names nowadays, you know that,' said Goven. 'Fake profiles. Proves nothing.'

'Maybe not,' said Fox.

Goven nodded once more, this time to himself, and then to Fox's surprise sat down. He leant back and swivelled his chair slightly, left then right, holding Fox's gaze as he did it, which made Fox respect him a little less. That kind of thing was fine for Bond villains, but come on. Please. At last he said, 'I need to know we're aligned here.'

'Of course,' said Fox.

Goven leant back in his chair. 'I run organized crime. We can agree on that.'

'Yes.'

'I don't run Helen Fox's home for druggie slags.'

Fox didn't answer at first. This was harsh, even coming from Goven. This was beyond harsh. Fox suddenly realized that she had entirely underestimated how angry, how furious, Goven was. She didn't answer, instead did her best to hold his bleak stare.

'Can we agree on that?'

'Yes,' said Fox, 'although I must object—'

Goven sat forward in his seat and brought both hands down flat on his desk. 'Shut up. Shut up. Do not say another word. Yes? Do not answer that.'

Fox didn't answer.

'My job,' said Goven, 'is to bring in criminals. Criminals who contribute to the underground economy, who launder substantial amounts of cash. This is my job. It's what I have been tasked to do. And if I don't do this, I don't just get shit from the Chief Constable. I get shit from the Home Office, I get ministerial-grade shit, the kind of shit I do not want. The kind of shit I will not have.' He paused, took a breath. 'Inspector Fox, understand this. I will sell you, your colleagues, your family, anyone I think might help, I will sell them all, crucify the lot of them, to avoid one second of one uncomfortable meeting with one government minister.' He rubbed his eyes, then pulled his hand downwards over his face. He fixed Fox with his gaze and spoke slowly and deliberately. 'Let me be even plainer. You are facing a fucking existential decision here. Bring one more speculative dead-woman hypothesis to me, instead of the warm body of Luke fucking Mullan, and you will be out of a job. Do you understand me?'

Fox blinked. 'Yes,' she said.

'Are we aligned?'

'Yes.'

'Task Force Jehovah is all I care about. And it is all you care about. It is the only thing that matters, because I have got targets to hit and I will hit them, with or without you. Because my pension matters more than you. Yes?'

'Yes.'

'Luke Mullan. You told me you'd bring him in. Didn't you?'

'Yes.'

'Then, Inspector for-the-moment Fox, I suggest you fucking bring him in. And soon. Because it's been too long already, and as you can probably tell, my patience is very nearly run out.'

'Sir.'

'I picked you because I thought you were a career copper. Some posh sort with a chip on her shoulder, trying to prove her parents wrong, make it through the ranks instead of becoming an investment banker, which I will bet my bollocks they'd have preferred you did. This is your reputation as much as mine, if I'm right. So get out there and start knocking on some more doors, start rattling some more cages, and get me a fucking result before you end up knocking on your mummy's door, telling her that you fucked up and can you come home for a while, to regroup because the nasty police force was way beyond you.' Goven breathed in deeply and closed his eyes, leaning back again in his chair. 'Once more. Are we aligned?'

'Yes,' said Fox. She barely managed to get the words out, thinking of her parents, of her mother, her baffled and betrayed expression when Fox had told her she was joining the force. Goven might be a stone-cold bastard, but he'd had her right, skewered her right where her heart ought to be, if she hadn't sold it long ago. She had to make this job work. If she didn't, her parents would have won. And she could not allow that.

'Then good,' said Goven. 'Good. And do yourself a favour. The next time you knock on that door, you make sure you've got Mullan handcuffed to your wrist. Because you're on my list now, and it is a list, let me assure you, that it is very fucking difficult to get off.' He paused, reached for a pen, picked it up and then said, looking at it rather than at Fox, 'Now piss off.'

Outside in the corridor, Fox felt her ankle give on one of her high heels, and put a hand out to the wall to steady herself. She needed to make a decision, she knew that. Make a decision about her career, about how serious she was about it. But even as she thought this, she realized that that decision had been made long ago, had been made the moment her parents had told her that she was making a mistake, that she would regret it, that she would never make it. Not in an environment like *that*. But she would make it. She would play the game. Be a team player, get aligned, get on board, get a result. This she would do. Whatever it took, and however it played out. She had targets to hit, the team had targets to hit, and she was going to make sure they hit them. Whatever the hell it took.

twenty-four

'YOU KNOW HOW MANY OF THEM THERE ARE?'

'I know,' said Solomon. He'd never regretted not studying Shakespeare in detail, but he did now. This was a hole in his knowledge that he was trying to fill. 'Let's start with the key texts, the canonical ones. Who have we got?'

'Cordelia, Desdemona, Juliet, Lavinia, Ophelia,' said Kay.

'And Cleopatra.'

'Obviously. I mean, not obviously like *duh, obviously*, but, you know. We've been through it.'

'Yes,' said Solomon gently. 'I know what you mean.'

Kay sighed. 'It feels too big.'

'How do you mean?'

'Just ... I don't know.' It was the evening after the Brain Pool meeting, and Solomon was talking to Kay over his laptop. He didn't know if it was his imagination, but he thought Kay might be wearing make-up. Eyeliner. He supposed he could find out for sure by comparing the images from tonight with cached images from previous conversations, but he figured that might be creepy, or a key indicator of some especially deviant tendency. Besides, he didn't want to think about make-up, not after what had happened on the Tube. Stop thinking, he thought. You think too much. Enough.

'Solomon?'

'Sorry. I think we need to break this down. Approach it systematically. Okay. We know about Ophelia and Cleopatra. So we just need to choose somebody else.'

'Desdemona.'

'Okay. So, Desdemona. Victim of?'

'Othello.'

'Yes, I mean, what happened to her?'

'Well, Othello smothered her. Because he thought she was unfaithful, even though she wasn't, but he wouldn't listen to her, and basically he acted like, well.' She stopped, then said, 'He was a moron.'

Solomon smiled. 'We're together on that one. So the thing to do is look for news stories where a woman was suffocated.'

'Exactly how I like to spend my Thursday nights.'

Solomon was silent, then said, 'You're right. I'm sorry, Kay, this isn't your problem. You shouldn't be doing this.'

'No, I didn't mean it like that,' said Kay. 'It was meant as a joke.'

'Yes, but—'

'Oh God. I'm such an idiot.' She put her hand to her forehead and shook her head, her eyes covered.

'No, Kay, come on ...'

'Why do I always get it wrong?'

'You don't,' said Solomon. 'I just mean—'

'I can't even ask you on a date without basically scaring you off. What's the matter with me?'

'It wasn't you,' said Solomon. 'Really. It's just ...' He couldn't think of what to say, then realized he knew exactly what to say, just didn't want to say it. So he did. 'It's just that I look like a monster, and you will be horrified. You will be. I guarantee it.'

Kay looked up at the camera on her laptop, as if by staring hard enough into it, she'd see behind the avatar, get some idea of what Solomon meant. Then she said, softly, 'Don't you think I should be the judge of that?'

'Kay ...'

'I'm an intelligent person. I know I don't always sound it, but I am. I'm brilliant and I often make good decisions. Like, more often than not.'

'I'm not ready,' said Solomon. 'For people to see me.' He paused, then said, 'For you to see me.'

'Me?'

'You. You especially.' Solomon willed himself to stop, to go no further, to reveal nothing more. Kay didn't need to know how he felt. What good would it do? None. It could only do harm.

'You mean that?' said Kay.

'I ...' Solomon swallowed and blinked back a tear. 'Please, can we just get back to work? Kay? Please?'

Solomon had been to see his sister earlier, who had been pleased to see him but distracted, frustrated at her loss of memory. She'd told him that she felt like when she'd forgotten some actor's name in a film; she knew it but just couldn't think of it, like it was *there*, somewhere, but she couldn't access it. She'd sighed and swallowed and said that she didn't even know if she wanted to remember it, didn't know what had happened to her, what had been done to her. And Solomon had sat and held her hand, and wished that Luke had been there, that they were all together, like they'd always been before.

And so afterwards Solomon had called Luke on the Bat Phone, and listened to Luke tell him about exactly how shitty everything was right now, how he couldn't even wash his clothes so he'd given up on underwear, how he was living on tinned food, eating it out of a can and basically living like some kind of outlaw, which he guessed he was, like fucking Robin Hood or something. Solomon had never imagined his brother in the same terms as Robin Hood, had never placed him in the same moral bracket. He'd rob from the rich, sure, but he'd also rob from the merely wealthy too, and from the well-to-do, and the comfortably off, in fact anyone who had possessions worth enough to make the risk/reward equation make sense. Which included anybody who owned a high-end BMW, and Solomon had met people who could barely afford their rent yet who still somehow owned high-end BMWs. All of which had passed through Solomon's mind as he listened to his brother complain about his enforced exile in an old caravan in the deepest, darkest Essex countryside.

'This is depressing,' said Kay.

'Sorry?'

'All this. Searching for news stories about women. Makes me actually never want to leave my flat again.'

'Too much?' said Solomon. He watched Kay. She was twisting a loose strand of hair around and around one finger, a mannerism he now recognized. She made an effort not to, would occasionally catch herself doing it and stop, almost guiltily. He imagined that she'd been warned about it as a child, perhaps by an over-strict mother.

'No, just ... It's like trying to find a needle in a haystack. The number of women, the number of victims. You already know how bad it is, kind of, but then you actually start looking ...'

Solomon glanced down at his notes. A litany of outrages, of stabbings and rapes and beatings and humiliation heaped on humiliation. Kay was right. You started to look more closely and the statistics became human, flesh and bone and blood and suffering.

'Oh.'

'What?' said Solomon.

'I've found something.'

'What have you—'

'Oh God. Solomon.'

'Kay?' Solomon watched her, reading something on her screen intently. She looked horrified, her mouth slightly open, her head still.

'I don't know ...' she said, then stopped and continued reading. 'Oh, no.'

'What is it?'

'I'll send you a link,' said Kay. She didn't look up, kept staring at her screen. Solomon heard the sound of a notification, a link to a news story. He clicked it and a web page opened on his screen.

BURN HORROR IN VICTORIA PARK

A young woman suffered horrific burns to her face and mouth after reportedly ingesting the hot coals from a disposable barbecue. Onlookers were shocked to see the as-yet-unnamed woman collapse in front of them on a busy day in east London's Victoria Park. Police are trying to trace a man she was allegedly on a date with immediately prior to the incident. She remains in hospital in a critical condition.

'Portia,' said Solomon.

'I've got the reference here,' said Kay. 'From *Julius Caesar*. *With this she fell distract, and, her attendants absent, swallowed fire.*'

'And this was ...' Solomon checked the date of the story. 'Five days ago.'

'I don't understand,' said Kay. 'I mean, how? How could he even have done it? In a park, in broad daylight?'

'It might not be him,' said Solomon.

'Eating hot coals,' said Kay. 'It has to be. Solomon?'

'Yes,' said Solomon. 'You're right.'

'We need to go to the police with this. You know the officer working on your sister's case, right?'

Solomon thought of Fox, of her cold disdain. 'Yes.'

'So you need to go to him and tell him what's going on.'

'Her,' said Solomon. 'And I already have done. You know that.'

'I know,' said Kay. 'But Sol, this is something else. This is ... There's somebody doing this, it's obvious. Isn't it?'

Solomon didn't register her question, hadn't got past her use of his name. Sol. She now called him Sol. It felt like, no matter how much he resisted, something unseen and intangible was pulling them closer. It made him frightened.

'Solomon?'

'Yes,' he said. 'Yes, I know. I'll speak to her. I promise.'

After they had finished, Solomon went to the bathroom and stood looking at his reflection for a long time. Then he took out the make-up that Marija had left him and once again applied it to his face, building up the layers, taking care. He went to the kitchen and found the eye patch that he had thrown away and put it back on, then brushed his hair so that it covered his ear. He looked at his reflection, turning his head, trying different angles. The light in the bathroom was on a dimmer and he dialled it down, trying to match the kind of light you might find in a restaurant at night. A dark restaurant. A romantic restaurant. He took a step back and regarded himself, tried to be impartial. Did he look like a monster? Not really, he didn't think so. A little odd, with the eye patch. Eccentric, maybe. No, odd. But if he could meet Kay in a restaurant, then ... Then maybe. Perhaps. Some day.

He looked at himself one last time and then began to wipe the make-up off again. He'd think about it. He didn't need to make a decision now. No rush. *Sol.* She'd called him Sol. He dried his face with a towel, and sighed into its giving softness. Hell, he didn't know.

twenty-five

OLIVIA HAD TAKEN OFF HER TOP AND TORN IT INTO STRIPS and wrapped her hands in it, anything to get a better grip on the paint-tin lid that was her only hope of salvation. She'd had a long internal debate about the wisdom of removing her top, leaving her in only a bra, wondering whether it would act as a provocation, put her at further risk. Rape, that was what she worried about, whether being essentially half naked might put ideas in the mind of whoever had imprisoned her. But then she took an impartial look at her position, imprisoned in a pit with a grille on top and a car parked over that, and figured that whether she was wearing a top was neither here nor there. Whatever that monster had planned for her was going to happen, was already decided. All that mattered was getting out of there before he came back. And to do that, she needed to tear her top to pieces and get to work.

It was lighter than it had been before, Olivia guessing that the early morning was turning to day. She could see the underside of the car parked above her, its pipes and welds and angles, could see the top foot or so of the pit she was in. The rest was in deep shadow, completely black. She held her hands up and inspected them. They were caked in dried blood, her nails ragged. It wasn't like they were used to hard work. She didn't do manual labour, never had done.

She thought of work, of her work. She should be there, she had appointments to keep, people to speak to. Nothing on site, though, only phone calls, one with a media agency in New York. Would anyone miss her? Probably not; the company she worked at, the start-up, was chaotic at the best of times. It was mostly young people, the default assumption if somebody was late in being that they'd probably had a heavy night and were still sleeping it off. No, nobody would miss her, not for hours and hours, maybe not all day. And what if they did? It wasn't like they were going to go to the police. That wasn't going to happen. That, Olivia told herself as she worked away at a rusting steel joint, was definitely not going to happen. So stop thinking about it, and work harder. The only way you're getting out of here is if you get yourself out. So work harder.

To motivate herself she thought again of her mother. She imagined what she'd be doing right now. She'd be awake and up. Dressed immaculately. She always dressed immaculately, even if she had nothing to do and nowhere to go. She would rather die than open the door to the postman in a dressing gown. No. No, that wasn't possible. So. Right now, she might be:

Having her hair washed and set.

Taking the car out for a drive.

Playing bridge with her friends, who she didn't like.

Talking on the phone with one of those friends, discussing how much they both mutually disliked the others.

Visiting the shops. Never 'going shopping'. No, her mother visited shops.

Watching her cleaner clean, no doubt inadequately.

Doing the *Times* crossword.

Counting the ways in which Olivia had *a*, let her down, *b*, defied her, *c*, ignored her, *d*, embarrassed her, *e*, failed to meet her standards in any of thousands of small yet inexcusable and unforgivable ways.

With these thoughts Olivia worked away harder and harder at the joint of steel, continuously, for minutes, pushing, scraping, bending, bleeding. Eventually she stopped because there was another thought in her head that she was trying to smother, to bury with anger at her mother. But the thought would not stay away and she looked at the joint, and at the paint-tin lid, which was worn into an almost unusable crescent, and accepted the thought, which was that she was making zero progress. None at all, not even the ghost of an impression on the remaining joints. She was getting nowhere.

She had worked her way through four joints. Four in how many hours? Two? Three? How long did she have? Demmy would be back sometime. Where was he anyway? She'd need to work her way through twelve more bars to make the forty-by-forty-centimetre hole she figured she needed, the absolute minimum she needed to squeeze through. There was no way, absolutely no way. It was the work of a week, or a month. And her paint-tin lid was almost worn away. There was no way.

She sat down on the floor of the pit and looked up at the sharp concrete edge of it, delineated clearly now in the light flooding in from whatever windows there might be in the space beyond. Okay, she thought. Okay, Olivia, think. Breathe. You need to get yourself under control. Take control.

Where was Demmy, and when would he be back?

He'd left an hour ago.

Early morning.

So, logical conclusion: he had a job.

Even monsters needed to work. Didn't they?

So, logical extension: he'd be back eight or nine hours after he left.

So, she had time.

Hell, it was only a theory. But she needed something, and this would have to do. She had eight hours left to save herself. Which wasn't much, but it was something.

What she didn't have was a tool to work with.

She got on all fours and felt around on the floor of the pit. No, she thought. Be methodical. You've got eight hours. Do this properly. She made her way to one of the short walls of the rectangular pit. Do a sweep, she thought. Make sure you don't miss a single centimetre. The floor was grainy with old detritus, tiny pieces of metal and scraps of cloth and paper. She brushed the palm of her hand over the surface, feeling the sharp gravel and metal against her skin. She worked from side to side, crawling backwards, slowly, careful not to miss anything in the utter blackness of the pit's bottom.

Nothing.

Ow. Sharp.

Nothing.

Nothing.

What was that? A screw, or a bolt. Not big enough.

Nothing.

A rag. Keep that.

Nothing.

Shit. That hurt. She was bleeding. Again.

Nothing.

Nothing.

Another screw.

And another.

Nothing.

What was that? Round. Metal. Another paint-tin lid?

She lifted it up and looked at it in the dim light just beneath the grille. It wasn't a paint-tin lid. It was round and metal and had a hole in the centre. The edge of the circle was gritty, like sandpaper, and sharp. It hurt her finger as she ran it across. She didn't know what it was. She'd never done manual labour. One thing was for sure, it was a whole hell of a lot better than that crappy paint-tin lid. It looked substantial, strong.

Olivia felt a brief burst of adrenaline, a flush of faint hope. She crouched down, then took a firm grip of the circle of metal and ran it along the joint where two bars met. The circle's edge cut into the webbing between her index finger and thumb. Shit, it really was sharp. She took the rag that she'd found and wrapped it around half of the circle, then tried again. The circle caught on the metal and made a loud rasping sound. It left bright steel where she dragged it across the bar. She did it again, and again, and again, and could see a shiny groove where her metal circle's edge had removed old steel. Again, again, again, her heart beating faster as she worked. This was happening. This was really happening. She had eight hours. She had eight hours, and she had a real chance. She closed her eyes briefly, in thanks to she didn't know who. Now, Olivia, she thought, get to work.

twenty-six

FOX DID NOT WANT TO SPEAK TO SOLOMON MULLAN, NOT OVER the phone, definitely not face to face. Particularly not *his* face, she thought, without a twinge of guilt. She had enough to worry about. But he had been insistent on the phone, telling her that the information he had was important, critical, that lives were at stake. She thought he was probably delusional, already slightly demented from his hermit lifestyle, pushed over into fantasist la-la land by what had happened to his sister. Which was, she still maintained, most likely an accident. Almost certainly an accident. Yes, she was still happy with her initial assessment. Drug-addled stripper slips on a canal towpath. Case closed, as far as she was concerned. It was the brother, Luke Mullan, that she cared about. That she had only ever cared about. Take on the sister's case to get to the brother. And now she had Luke Mullan in her sights, she didn't want to hear any more conspiracy theories from Solomon Mullan. Didn't need any more distractions. But somehow, and she still didn't understand how, somehow he'd managed to get her to say yes. To agree to a meeting. She must be losing her grip.

'Send him up,' she said into her desk phone, slamming it back into its cradle. Idiot, she thought. Haven't you got enough on your plate? She closed her eyes and tried to will herself calm, assume a professional demeanour. Hear him out and move on, she thought. Just hear him out.

There was a knock on her door and she paused, took a deep breath, and said, 'Come in,' as evenly as she could. The door opened and a woman in uniform, Fox couldn't remember her name, stood aside to let Solomon Mullan past. He looked just as he normally did, sunglasses on, hood up, shuffling along and staring at the floor, a walking apology for the way he appeared. *Spare me*, thought Fox. *Just, spare me.*

But she said instead, 'Mr Mullan. Please sit down.' She indicated the chair in front of her desk, but he didn't look up, just walked to it and sort of folded himself down into it, focusing on the edge of her desk nearest him.

'Thank you for seeing me,' he said in his precise, considered way.

Fox ignored his thanks, said instead, 'Mr Mullan, I am very busy. I do hope that what you have to say to me is worthwhile.'

'I have new information,' said Solomon.

'Pertaining to?' said Fox.

'Pertaining to the likely scenario that multiple women are being targeted by the same person.'

'Please tell me,' said Fox, staring coldly at the top of Solomon's bowed and hooded head, 'that this isn't a continuation of the theory you brought to me last week.'

'I would prefer to call it a validation of that theory,' said Solomon.

Fox closed her eyes and willed herself to stay silent. Count to five, she thought. No, scratch that, count to ten. 'Go on,' she said eventually, her voice barely more than a whisper, a reluctant croak.

'It's the messages,' said Solomon. 'I always thought they were strange.'

'The messages?'

'Between my sister and her prospective date, and between Rebecca Harrington and the person she'd arranged to meet. There was something about the messages, an inconsistency in the grammar. An unconventional syntax.'

'Haven't we been here before?' said Fox. 'Rebecca Harrington's death was ruled a suicide.'

'And I believe that verdict was incorrect.'

'Mr Mullan, please ...'

'Both messages make clear reference to Shakespearean plays,' said Solomon. He spoke clearly but quietly, and Fox had to listen carefully, his words aimed towards her office floor.

'To what?'

'Shakespearean plays,' said Solomon. 'That, and the similarity of their circumstances, stretches coincidence too far.'

'I'm sorry, Mr Mullan, I'm struggling here,' said Fox. 'You're going to need to start making some kind of sense.'

'In Rebecca Harrington's suicide note, she explicitly references *Antony and Cleopatra*, by paraphrasing her last words. *Farewell, kind mother. Father, long farewell.* These aren't the words of an uneducated drug user.'

'Uh-huh,' said Fox. She knew *Antony and Cleopatra*, had read the play at school. 'So ...'

'And then,' Solomon continued as if she hadn't spoken, 'she's found dead, an apparent suicide. Like Cleopatra. In the play.'

Fox reached out and picked up a pen. She drew an exclamation mark on a piece of paper in front of her, then a question mark. She almost added *WTF*, but stopped and said instead, 'Sorry, Mr Mullan. This is a waste of my time. Of our time.'

'And then there's my sister,' he said, still in that same precise and quietly determined voice. He took off his sunglasses, rubbed his eyes, still looking at the floor. 'In her message exchange *Hamlet* is referenced, the implication being that she was being cast in the role of Ophelia.'

Fox thought back to the exchange. 'Really?'

'Her prospective date used the phrase *What hour now?* I always thought it sounded unnatural. It turns out that Hamlet asked the very same thing of Horatio, in the play.'

'In *Hamlet.*'

'Yes. And then the reference to the Convent bar. There's a clear parallel with Hamlet telling Ophelia, *Get thee to a nunnery.*'

As Solomon had been speaking, Fox had been drawing an untidy black circle, going over it again and again until the paper gave way underneath. She didn't have time for this. Solomon Mullan, she decided, was insane.

'Mr Mullan, I'm afraid I'm going to have to end this meeting.'

'But you can't,' said Solomon, sounding surprised. He glanced up quickly, giving Fox a brief glimpse of his hideous white eye. 'I haven't finished.'

'But I've heard enough,' said Fox.

'My sister was found drowned,' said Solomon. 'Like Ophelia. The comparison is almost exact.'

'No, Mr Mullan, it's—'

'And then there's Portia. From *Julius Caesar.*' Solomon was talking rapidly now, louder. 'She swallowed hot coals, just like a woman found in Victoria Park only days ago. She'd been on an online date, too. Ophelia, Cleopatra, Portia. The evidence is ... You can't ignore it. It's impossible to ignore.'

Not impossible, thought Fox. Nowhere near. She frowned at him, at the top of his head, his face once again turned towards the floor. Either he was mad, or this was some crazy way of compromising her investigation, forcing it in a different direction. She had to admit that although what Solomon Mullan was saying sounded mad, the way he was saying it seemed rational enough. So maybe this was a plan, a diversionary strategy. It didn't matter which, really. What mattered was getting him out of her office before he could muddy her real investigation any further.

'I'm going to have to ask you to leave,' she said. 'I agreed to this meeting in good faith, but had I known you were going to bring me something like this, I would not have made the time.'

'This,' said Solomon, 'is your job. Police work. Running an investigation, and conducting it thoroughly.'

'My job,' said Fox, trying to keep the fury out of her voice, 'is to target criminals. Not run down bizarre conspiracy theories brought to me by solitary fantasists.' That was probably going too far, she thought, without much remorse. She was beyond pissed off.

Solomon nodded at the floor. 'I see,' he said. 'You're unwilling to listen. Tell me, Inspector Fox. Just what is your agenda here?'

'My *agenda*?'

'What exactly are you investigating?'

'When did you last see your brother?' said Fox.

'I haven't seen him since I last spoke to you,' said Solomon.

'Where is he?'

'I don't know.'

'We're done here,' said Fox.

Solomon shook his head. 'You can't ignore this.'

Fox picked up the phone and hit zero for the front desk. 'Fox here. Could I have a couple of uniforms ...'

'I'm leaving,' said Solomon, standing up quickly. He dropped his sunglasses and he bent down and picked them up, fumbling at them in panic. Despite her anger, Fox couldn't help but feel some pity for him. His existence must be genuinely miserable, unremittingly so. She watched him open her office door and pause in its frame, considering something before walking through, leaving the door ajar behind him.

'Hello?' said a voice coming from the phone receiver she was still holding in her hand.

'Don't worry,' said Fox. 'He's gone.' And please, she thought, let that be the last I see of him. As she gazed at her open door, she thought of Sergeant Bright and his theory about the woman he was investigating, who'd been found asleep, drugged. How he too had thought there might be similarities with Tiffany Mullan's case. She felt a brief shiver of uncertainty, a quick but deep lurch of anxiety that she was ignoring something, rejecting something significant. She thought back to the message exchange that Rebecca Harrington had had. *Infinite variety*, wasn't that it? But no. No, she didn't have the time. This wasn't her investigation, and nobody had brought her compelling evidence. She didn't have the time, and she didn't have the evidence. She put the receiver of her phone back on its cradle, firmly. Luke Mullan. That was what mattered, and she'd find him no matter what.

Solomon wasn't new to feelings of frustration, but this, this feeling he had after his meeting with Fox, this was something else. He could feel it in his nerve ends, in his fingers, a furious buzz. Due to Fox, but also himself, his weakness, his … what? His *impracticality*. He just couldn't hack it out there, always on the back foot, behind on points because of his face, his hideousness. And Fox, that tall ice-covered mountain, too steep and too slippery to get any purchase on, entirely unassailable.

He needed to call Kay but he didn't want to, didn't feel equal to it. To admitting his failure to persuade Fox about what was happening. Because it *was* happening, he was sure of that, sure that he wasn't deluded or … What was it she'd called him? Fox? A solitary fantasist. But he wasn't solitary, because he had Kay, too. And the Brain Pool. So he wasn't a solitary fantasist, he was just a hideous misfit who couldn't win round an indifferent and probably corrupt police officer.

His negative cycle of thoughts was interrupted by a call coming through. Kay. He checked his webcam and accepted the call, experiencing his customary lurch of impossible desire at the image of Kay on the screen, her hair unpinned, unruly ringlets spilling artlessly around her shoulders.

'Hey,' she said.

'Hello, Kay,' said Solomon.

'I have news,' she said. 'Are you ready?'

'Um,' said Solomon, not sure that he was, but Kay continued regardless. 'I've been looking for a pattern, some kind of, I don't know, method I suppose you'd call it. To what's been going on. Because otherwise it's just … Well, I mean there's got to be a pattern, it's not like this is random, you know?'

Solomon nodded. It was true. There had to be a design behind it all. Something predictable. 'And you found something?'

'Maybe,' Kay said. 'We haven't got all the data, so it's hard to know. But looking at the dates, first we had Rebecca Harrington. That's Cleopatra. Then your sister, for Ophelia. And last week it was Portia. And if you look at the plays, they're in reverse

209

order. Chronologically. I mean, there are a couple missing, there's no Desdemona, and *Othello* comes between *Hamlet* and *Antony and Cleopatra*. But assuming we've just missed her, then what's happening is this person, whoever it is, what he's doing, or she ...' Kay paused for breath, then said, 'They're working through tragic heroines, going backwards in time.' She stopped and looked up at the screen and shrugged. 'Maybe.'

'It feels like a reach,' said Solomon.

'The data supports it,' said Kay.

'It's an incomplete data set.'

'True,' said Kay. 'But the pattern's there.'

'Okay,' said Solomon, nodding. 'It's a reasonable hypothesis.' One of thousands, he thought, but instead said, 'So that means ... Who's next? Potentially?'

'Juliet.'

'Another suicide.'

'Right. First she was drugged, so it looked like she was dead, and then she woke up and Romeo was dead, so she ... Well, it's complicated. Shakespeare, you know?'

'I know.'

'So the way I see it, she's next.'

'And after her?' Solomon thought, then said before Kay could answer, 'Lavinia. *Titus Andronicus*.'

'That's the last one.'

'God,' said Solomon.

'I know,' said Kay.

'Raped, hands cut off, tongue cut out,' said Solomon. 'It's not possible.'

'I don't think we're there yet. It's got to be Juliet.'

'Okay.' Solomon didn't say anything else, and there was a brief silence. Kay twisted a strand of hair with a finger, then looked up at the screen.

'So how did it go? With the policewoman? What did she say?'

'She said …' Solomon rubbed his face, suddenly itchy where his scarred skin was. 'She didn't want to know.'

'What?'

'She wasn't interested. She thought I was crazy.'

'But … What about the evidence?'

'She said I was a fantasist. She wouldn't listen.'

'I don't understand.'

'She's got her own agenda,' said Solomon.

'These are real women,' said Kay. 'She must care.'

'I'm sorry,' said Solomon. 'I tried, I really did.'

Kay was silent, shaking her head. 'What are we going to do?'

'I don't know,' said Solomon. 'But Kay? I promise you, I'll think of something. I promise.' Kay looked up at him again, and Solomon was doubly glad that she couldn't see him, couldn't meet his gaze. Because he was making a promise he had no idea if he could keep.

twenty-seven

THIS IS HAPPENING, THOUGHT OLIVIA. THIS IS DEFINITELY happening. She didn't know how long it had taken, didn't know how long she had left, but she was getting there. She'd cut through eleven bars, almost three sides of the square she'd set herself. Five left. She adjusted the rag, the one she was using to hold the sharp-edged circle of metal she'd found, refolded it so that it was an effective barrier between her hands and the blade. Because it was sharp, really sharp, and was going through the rusty bars of the grille above her about, she didn't know, about a hundred times faster than that paint-tin lid she'd started out with.

She felt the rasp and snag of the blade as she worked it against the latest bar. Her plan was to cut through three sides and then use brute force, pull the grille down as if it was a trapdoor and the last side was hinged, really work at it until it snapped. So this bar, bar number twelve, could be the last one she needed to cut through. This thought made her scrape and rub harder, ignoring the pain in her hands, which were cut and bloody and kept cramping up as she struggled to get a good enough grip on the circle of metal.

As she worked away, she felt the blade of the circle bite deeper and deeper into the bar until it suddenly gave way. She dropped the blade and hooked her fingers into the grille and pulled it, the area she'd cut out hinging down towards her. Up, down, up, down, she felt the resistance lessen and lessen, the hinge growing weaker and weaker. Screw it, she didn't even need it to fall off, that would do. There was a space, a square hole, forty centimetres by forty.

Looking up at it, it didn't look so big. Not big enough. Olivia wasn't huge, but she wasn't tiny either, and that hole didn't look big enough. And the underside of the car was so close to it, only a few centimetres above the grille. How was she going to squeeze through that hole, then bend enough to get between the grille and the car? She didn't know. Didn't think she could do it. She'd miscalculated, spent the last however many hours on wishful thinking, nothing else. There was no way she could fit through that hole, fold herself out from under the car. No way.

She sat down on the floor of the pit and looked up at the sharp ends of the cut bars, their tips shiny where they'd been cut through. She had no top, had torn it up hours ago. She thought of the news reports, the speculation. *She managed to cut through the grille holding her, but appeared to give up.* Her mother, nodding along to that, in sad recognition of her daughter's innate failings. *Well, she always did. Give up, that is.*

Olivia got up, put her head through the hole she'd made. It was in the corner of the pit, at least she'd thought of that. Not made it right in the middle. She was almost standing. She felt her shoulders against the underside of the grille, both sides, which meant that the hole was too narrow. She turned so that her shoulders were diagonally across the square hole. How was she going to lift herself up? She thought, then ducked back down into the pit. She put her hands above her head, got them through the hole first. She rose up, feeling the jagged ends of the bars nagging and tearing at the skin of her arms. She leant forward and reached out, getting a hand on the underside of the car, its front bumper. She pulled and immediately felt the cut bars dig and rip into her chest. She closed her eyes and pulled and heaved, but the bars just dug in further, snagging on her skin. If she pulled any harder she'd just impale herself on them. This wasn't going to work. It would kill her, no way she could pull herself up and over them.

She let herself sink back into the pit. Okay. This wasn't the end. This was a setback. She needed to cover the ends of those bars. The bars on the edge she had to drag herself over. She could do that. She had ... What did she have? She had shoes. She had ballerinas, and she could put them over the bars, and haul herself over the soles. That would work. She took them off and placed them over the bars, pushing them on as securely as she could. She worked herself back through the hole, again feeling the bars' edges cut into the skin of her arms. But her front was protected by the shoes, and she leant forward again and grabbed the car's bumper and pulled. And pulled, and heaved, all of her strength, and felt her feet leave the floor of the pit and her body begin to slide up and out, out of the pit.

She pulled and wriggled, her legs shimmying, her bare feet dancing as she worked her way out. Her head banged against the underside of the car, her shoulders scraping metal. Then one of the shoes she'd placed over the bar ends fell off and she immediately felt a stabbing sensation as the bar cut into her stomach, and she let go of the car's bumper and slid backwards, the exposed bar ends raking into the flesh of her chest as she fell back into the pit. She pulled herself into a foetal position, the pain so great that she could barely breathe. She wept quietly, her head on her knees, trying to ignore the agony where the bar ends had cut into her.

After some time, she didn't know how long, the pain began to subside, and instead of pain she felt anger, a cold anger, that she had been put in this pit, that she had been so easily duped, that somebody had had the arrogance to think they could do this to her. No. No, she wouldn't allow it. No way.

She scrabbled around for her shoes. Okay, this can work. She found the remains of her T-shirt and used them to tie her shoes to the bar ends, working the scraps through the bars and around the soles of the shoes, pulling the knots tight. Reef knots, that was what she needed. Left over right, right over left. She worked as quickly as she could, aware that she'd spent too long on the floor of the pit, feeling sorry for herself. She needed to move, and fast. Once again she pushed her way through the hole, arms first, leaning forward to grip the car's bumper. She pulled and heaved and again felt her feet leave the floor of the pit. Pull, she thought. Just bloody *pull*.

Behind her, somewhere beyond the car, she heard a sound, the same sound she'd heard earlier, of a door opening, then closing. She stopped, listened. He was back. She closed her eyes, concentrated on her fingers. Get a grip. Now pull. She heaved and squirmed and felt her legs flailing behind her, felt the pain of her damaged chest and stomach dragging over the soles of her ballerinas. Felt her waistband snag, bucked desperately and got over it, the bar ends at her back cutting into her skin, her head and shoulders banging against the underside of the car, her target a narrow band of light between the floor and the car. Her arms burned with the effort and she bucked harder, squirmed and writhed until she felt a shift in balance and understood that more of her was out of the pit than in. She pulled and pulled, her head now level with the car's bumper, her thighs sliding over the edge of the hole she'd made. She was out.

She crawled commando-style out from under the car and stopped, listened. No sound. *Where was he?* She looked behind her, through the gap between the bottom of the car and the floor. She couldn't see anything, no legs, nobody approaching, just the space she was in, some kind of large shed. *Where was he? There must be another room. He must be out there somewhere, in another room.*

Olivia looked about and saw a pile of tyres in a corner, stacked seven or eight high. She ran across and ducked behind them. It was quiet. She crouched down and tried to control her breathing, then peered around the side of the stack of tyres. The shed was still empty, just a big space with a corrugated roof and pieces of machinery and car parts in the corners and against the walls. The car she'd been under was an old Ford, a rusting orange Escort with no engine and a missing driver's door. And in the opposite corner to her, a doorway. A dark doorway. Which now had a man standing in it.

twenty-eight

OLIVIA DUCKED BEHIND THE TYRES AGAIN AND CLOSED HER eyes. She could just stay where she was. Maybe he wouldn't find her. Maybe he'd just figure she was gone, and he wouldn't bother looking. Maybe she was already as good as free. She listened to Demmy's footsteps as he walked towards the car, and the pit that she'd escaped from. Maybe it would be okay.

Except it wouldn't, would it? she thought to herself angrily. It just wouldn't, no way. You need to get out of here, get away. So okay, okay. Here's what she'd do. She'd wait until he got to the car and looked underneath. And while his back was turned and he was trying to make sense of just exactly what was going on, working out how she'd escaped, she'd go. Not run. Walk, walk silently and quickly. She didn't have shoes on, so she'd make no sound. She'd walk silently and quickly and once she was through the doorway she'd run like hell. That's what she'd do. But to do that, the first thing that needed to happen was she needed to open her eyes and see what was going on. That's what she needed to do first. So, Olivia? Olivia, bloody open your eyes and take a look.

She put her head around the side of the stack of tyres and watched Demmy walk towards the car, the car between her and him. He looked different from the night before, all character in his face gone, no expression on it at all. He stopped a metre away from the car and said softly, 'Come, Olivia, now is the time to enjoy that nice-preserved honesty of yours.'

He waited, his head cocked to one side. It was very quiet in the huge shed. He frowned, then said, 'Olivia?' He walked to the car and rapped on its roof with his fist, making a booming sound in the silent shed. 'Olivia?'

He dropped down out of view, and immediately Olivia moved, coming out from behind the stack of tyres and walking sideways, her back to the wall of the shed, keeping as close to it as she could. The car was still between her and Demmy, but she was moving around it and she'd need to get past it and into potential view before she made it to the doorway. Exposed, in the open, she realized that she had lost her bra and that she was bare-chested and bare-footed, smeared in blood and muck. She kept moving.

'Olivia!' Demmy's voice was suddenly loud, panicked, and Olivia walked faster and faster. As she skirted the walls, the car gave up its protection and she could see Demmy, only metres away, kneeling down and looking into the pit.

'Olivia!'

She got to the doorway just as he shuffled backwards and began to stand. She turned and went through it into another shed, this one narrow and dingier, a grimy window in one wall, both edges lined with workbenches, tools, vices, car parts. She ran through it and reached the door, a cracked round black plastic handle on it that she turned and pushed. Was it locked? She pulled instead and it rasped open, its bottom dragging along the ground, the noise loud, too loud, far too loud.

'Olivia!'

The voice was close, so close, and Olivia ran outside, into some kind of yard, old car parts scattered everywhere, the ground earthy and strewn with sharp stones, which skewered the soles of her feet as she ran. Through the yard, onto a track that led between trees, grass growing down the middle, rutted each side. She ran and ran, not knowing where the track led, further into the woods or out, out into salvation. Her lungs hurt and her breath rasped roughly in her throat.

'Olivia!'

The voice was still close but not as close as before, she didn't dare look behind to see, had to keep going, the track she was running down juddering in her exhausted vision, every strike of her feet against the hard rutted ground sending a jolt of pain through her body. Up ahead she could see a pole with a sign on it, green with white lettering that she couldn't read, and beyond that an opening-out, something grey, tarmac, a road. She kept running, aware that she was making a noise, an involuntary keening sound. She reached the end of the track and ran into the road just as a pickup truck came around a bend and she collided with its bull bar, aware of the squeal of brakes as she was thrown high into the air before everything turned black.

twenty-nine

'SO SHE'S OKAY?'

'She's okay. She still can't remember what happened, but she's out of danger.'

'Thank fuck for that,' said Luke. 'Not being there for her … You know?'

'I know,' said Solomon. He was standing in an outside seating area, benches provided for those patients who still needed to smoke, even though they were literally surrounded by disapproving healthcare professionals who probably watched them exhaling toxic fumes thinking, why do we even bother? The reception on his mobile wasn't great, but that was probably due to Luke calling in from the Essex interior. 'You'll be back soon. You won't have to hide forever.'

'You think?'

'Yes,' said Solomon, with as much certainty as he could manage.

'Because I learnt something interesting the other day,' Luke said.

'Oh?'

'A mate of mine gives me a call. Tells me he's heard there's a copper after me. Says he knows her. Name of Fox.'

'Go on.'

'This mate of mine, he tells me I want to look after myself, 'cos she's heading up some kind of heavy-duty organized-crime task force. Tells me that's what she does; she's some rising star in the war on illegal money.'

Solomon frowned. 'Then why did she take Tiffany's case? That's got nothing to do with ...' He stopped talking. 'Oh.'

'Explains why she doesn't give two shits about finding who did that to Tiff.'

'She never cared.'

'Course she didn't. She saw it as a nice juicy chance to get her hands on me.'

Solomon crossed to a bench and sat down. 'That explains a lot.'

'Doesn't help us much though, does it?'

Solomon looked up at a man in a dressing gown fumbling with a pack of cigarettes, eventually working one out of the full packet, then lighting it with a trembling hand. He was hooked up to a drip and was old and looked ill, and Solomon couldn't help but think he might not get to the end of his packet of twenty. He closed his eyes and tried to concentrate.

'Solomon? You there?'

'I'm here.'

'What about Arnold? When does he want his money?'

'Soon,' said Solomon, calculating. 'Day after tomorrow.'

'You've got it?'

'I'll have it.'

'Okay.' Luke was silent for a moment, then said, 'What are we going to do?'

'I'll think of something.'

'Yeah?'

'Yes,' said Solomon, quietly.

'You promise?'

'I promise,' said Solomon. He gazed into the middle distance, at nothing, and felt something forming in his head, an idea, or the beginnings of one. 'I absolutely promise you.'

'Well okay,' said Luke. 'You're the man.'

'I am,' said Solomon. 'I certainly am. I'll call you back.' He cut the call and closed his eyes again. He stayed perfectly still, but was perturbed by what he was feeling, a strength of emotion he was unused to. Fox had played him, played him from the start, and he was angry. Actually angry. He understood that he felt emotions, shame being top of the list; in fact if he was to draw a pie chart of his emotional range, the shame portion would be the entire pie except for the narrowest of slivers that would contain, possibly, fear and loneliness and frustration. But anger? Solomon thought of his sister, of what had been done to her. Of the other women, whom nobody cared about. Fox didn't, never had done, never would do. She had lied to him, outmanoeuvred him, made a fool of him. And all the while, other lives were in danger – no, had been irrevocably damaged. Yes, he was angry. And he was right to be angry, it was perfectly normal. It was acceptable. It was to be expected.

His job was suddenly clear, and he had no doubt about whether he was equal to it. He knew that he was. If the people whose job it was wouldn't do something about this, then he would. And he would redeem his brother and avenge his sister in the process. Because that was his job, his role in the family. He might be disfigured and he might be despised, but he was still a borderline genius. And that was what would count, ultimately.

Solomon got up from the bench and left the hospital, walking in the direction of his home. It was a warm day, but overcast, and a light rain fell, hitting the pavement's thermal mass and releasing rich smells of stone and fuel. As he walked, he broke the situation down, examining it, mining it for hidden strengths, unseen advantages.

One thing he did have was information. Knowledge that others didn't know he had. And that gave him power.

Specifically, he knew that Fox was working for organized crime.

Specifically, he knew that Tobes, or Caesar, or whatever he was called, was choosing women to play roles of his choosing.

Specifically, he knew that Thomas Arnold didn't have a clue about how international offshore money laundering worked.

Solomon crossed Tower Bridge, stopping halfway across to watch a motor launch scud through the wash from the other river traffic, throwing up dirty brown spray as its prow slammed into waves before careening over them. Purpose, that was what he needed, purpose and momentum. He started walking again, thinking about the problem at hand.

He also knew what they wanted, what these people wanted. He knew their motivations, which meant he knew how to get to them. And that gave him leverage.

Specifically, he knew that Fox wanted to haul in a criminal, somebody big.

Specifically, he knew that Tobes, or Caesar, or whatever he was called, wanted to find a new victim.

Specifically, he knew that Thomas Arnold wanted somebody to wash his money clean, the more of it the better, because his clumsy car-washing scheme was about as sophisticated as a prawn cocktail and would land him in prison eventually. And sooner rather than later, in Solomon's opinion.

So, okay. Solomon had the beginnings of a plan. What he didn't have, and what he definitely needed, was an ally. An accomplice. Somebody who was brave, whom he trusted and who trusted him, and who, crucially, was a female. With an accomplice like that, he thought, he had a chance. All he needed was an accomplice. Plus, of course, and at this Solomon sighed unhappily, a fair amount of luck.

Back at his apartment, Solomon scribbled down a rough critical-path analysis while he had it in his head. It soon became a flow diagram of bewildering complexity, the vast variables at play, the unreliability of the human factors and the preponderance of unknowns keeping him drawing and redrawing until even he couldn't completely understand the scope of what he was planning. He stopped and looked down at his Byzantine scribblings. It looked less like a simple plan, more like a wiring diagram for a monumentally ambitious nuclear reactor, and he screwed it up and threw it into a corner of his living room. It was always the same. As soon as real life intruded, actual people with their individual needs and motives and general unpredictability, things got difficult. No, not difficult, impossible, the introduction of human variables putting his calculations beyond the capacity of any theoretical model.

Logic and process wasn't going to help, not with this. The fundamental plan was fairly simple, he told himself, more in hope than conviction. Fairly dangerous too, at least in parts, but only for him, not for anybody else. Not for Kay. Because she was part of the plan, or at least she might be. Needed to be, if Solomon was honest.

Purpose and momentum, he thought. Purpose and momentum. He opened his laptop and sent her a message:

Can you talk?

He waited, staring at the screen. A moment later, a reply:

Yes.

He dialled her number. Purpose and momentum. He needed to get her on board but he needed to be honest, tell her what was happening. What the dangers might be, the potential costs. Get her on board with eyes wide open.

She accepted his call and her face came on screen. She was at her lab desk, holding a pen, her hair pinned up. Maybe she always had it up at work. Maybe it kept it out of Bunsen-burner flames. Idiot, Solomon thought. God, he was nervous.

'Hello, Kay. I hope I'm not disturbing you.'

Kay didn't reply or move, and Solomon waited, assuming that his screen was frozen, some glitch in their connection, a band-width issue. But then he saw Kay blink, which didn't happen with frozen images.

'Kay? Can you hear me?'

Kay blinked again, then said, 'Oh.'

Solomon felt a surge of terror and looked at his screen. His webcam, he hadn't disabled his webcam. His webcam that was, right now, beaming an image of his wrecked and hideous face to Kay's screen, an image so horrifying that it had robbed Kay of words and movement.

He grabbed his mouse and turned the camera off, too late, way too late. She'd seen him. Seen his face. She of all people, she had accepted a call and been confronted with that. He wheeled his chair away from his desk, back, back, and put his head in his hands in dismay and horror. How had this happened? How had he done this, made such an unspeakable mistake?

'Solomon? Are you there?'

Solomon didn't answer, couldn't answer. He kept his head in his hands, frozen with shame and dread.

'Solomon? Please, Sol. If you're there, tell me.'

She would now be looking at his avatar, the question mark, spinning around. Only there was no question any more, was there? She knew. She'd seen him and she knew, and so that was that.

'I don't know if you can hear me, Solomon, but I want you to know that I'm sorry if I appeared surprised, or shocked.' Kay spoke slowly and clearly, every word considered. 'I just ... I just wasn't prepared. That's all. That's all it was. Solomon?'

But Solomon couldn't answer, didn't have the words, and instead he wheeled his chair back to his desk, one hand partially covering his eyes so that he didn't have to look at Kay, didn't have to see her expression of guilt and pity and, underneath, disgust. He reached out with his other hand and took hold of his mouse again, and just as Kay said, 'Solomon, please,' he cut the connection and her face disappeared.

thirty

SOLOMON WOKE TO THE SOUND OF KNOCKING. HE CHECKED the time. Eleven o'clock. He'd fallen asleep early. The knocking wasn't loud, but it was insistent, a quick rapping that didn't sound like it was going anywhere. He lived in an apartment building. Who could be knocking? Nobody could get in from the street, so maybe someone from a neighbouring apartment. Maybe they needed help. Maybe the building was on fire.

He got out of bed and walked to his door. The rapping continued, not loud, but somehow ... How would he describe it? Determined.

'Hello?'

'Solomon? It's Kay.'

'Kay?' What was she doing here? How had she got here? How did she know where he lived?

'Can you let me in?' Her voice was muffled through the door, but it was her, it was definitely her.

'I ...' Solomon was frozen with panic. She couldn't come in, of course she couldn't. No way. 'I don't think ...'

'Let me in,' Kay said.

'Why are you here?'

Kay rapped on the door again. 'I'm not going anywhere. You'll have to let me in sometime.'

Solomon thought. 'Hold on,' he said. 'Two minutes.' He walked to his bathroom and warily eyed the make-up that Marija had left him. He'd used it before, he knew the ropes. He took a deep breath and picked up the foundation, opened it and started painting it on his skin, working up the layers, smoothing it out. He worked as fast as he could, but wasn't anywhere near finished when Kay started knocking on the door again. He thought he heard her call something, it sounded like 'You can't hide,' and he called back, 'One minute,' before going back to work. Hurry, but don't rush, he thought. God. He was applying make-up in the bathroom mirror. What was he thinking?

'We have you surrounded.' That was definitely what Kay had just called through the door. He tried to ignore her, kept applying the foundation as quickly as he could.

'Come out with your hands up.'

He was almost done. Eye patch, where was it? No, clothes. He wasn't dressed, was only wearing a T-shirt and boxers. He went to his bedroom and pulled on a pair of jogging bottoms, then found the patch. Another look in the mirror. Not great. Far from great. Better, but not great at all.

'This is your final warning.'

One more look. Enough. It was what it was. He turned off the light, then switched it back on and put away the make-up containers. Then he went to his door, stopped, turned back to dim the lights in the entrance and in the living room. Get the lighting right. Okay. He went back to the door, stood at it. Okay. He was doing this. He was.

He turned the latch, and pulled the door open.

'At last,' said Kay. She still had her hair up and was wearing a white shirt and jeans, trainers. She smiled. 'Can I come in?'

Solomon stood back out of the light of the corridor outside and nodded. 'Yes. Come in.'

She brushed past him cheerfully. Solomon paused, then closed the door and followed her into the apartment. She was standing in his living room, looking at his desk, the screens, the wires.

'Um,' said Solomon, not a thought in his head.

'Got anything to drink?' said Kay.

Solomon didn't drink, not really. He thought. 'Scotch.'

'That's it?'

'Yes.'

'Oh. Well I'll have that then. Have you got any ice?'

'No.'

'That's okay. I'll just have it neat.'

Solomon went to the kitchen and reached down a barely touched bottle of Teacher's. He poured two glasses and took them into the living room, put them on the coffee table. Kay was sitting in one of the armchairs. Solomon stood.

'How did you find me?' he said.

Kay frowned, as if the question was redundant. 'It wasn't hard.'

'You hacked me?'

'Like I said.' Kay reached forward and picked up a glass, took a drink. 'It wasn't hard.'

'How did you get in?'

'A man with a dog. A Pekinese. The dog, not the man.'

'Oh.' Solomon didn't know what else to say. He'd imagined that he lived in a remote bubble, secure, unreachable. It turned out that Kay had found him within a couple of hours. He bent down and picked up the other glass, but didn't drink.

'Listen, Solomon, I needed to see you. I couldn't just leave things like they were. I just, well, I just imagined you thinking about how I'd reacted, my face, it must have been ... Well, I just needed to see you, talk to you properly. Because however I seemed, it wasn't ... I mean, it wasn't that bad.' She winced and closed her eyes briefly. 'Sorry. That sounded a lot worse than I thought it would.' She paused, then said, 'And could you sit down? You're making me nervous.'

Solomon sat down.

'I like the eye patch,' said Kay.

'Anything's an improvement, right?' said Solomon, wishing that he could make himself sound less bitter.

'Don't say that,' said Kay.

Solomon didn't say anything. He could smell the Scotch as it evaporated up from his glass. Kay was silent too, and they sat like that for some moments. Then Kay said:

'Well?'

'Well what?' said Solomon.

'I came to say what I just said.' Kay downed her Scotch. 'I don't know. I guess I hoped you'd say something. React.'

'I don't have anything to say,' said Solomon.

'Solomon, please.'

'I don't know why you came,' he said. 'You shouldn't have come.'

Kay didn't reply immediately, and Solomon sat, his head bowed, his customary apologetic pose. Then she muttered something he didn't pick up.

'Sorry?'

'I said, *Don't you get it?*'

'Get what?' said Solomon, confused. What was he missing here?

'Jesus, Solomon.' Kay put her glass down firmly, annoyed. 'I came because I'm like you. That's why. I'm the geek. The one no one understands. Or wants to talk to, or be stuck with at the school disco. The one nobody wants a second date with. Forget how you look for a moment, think about who you are. You're weird. You're odd. You probably always were. Just like me. Only now, you've got a face to match. And do you know what? I think you like it. I think it makes things easier. I do. I really do. You get to hide away and assume that nobody will like you, because of how you look. But me? Me, I have to live out there in the world, where people talk to me and chat me up and ask me out on dates, and I know they don't like me. I know, because it's proven, because they don't invite me out on a second date. Ever. Why? Because I'm the geek. And no one understands me. And you know what?' She took a breath, exasperated. 'I think you might. I think you might understand me and like me and maybe want to spend time with me. But since you spend your life hiding behind that absurd question-mark avatar like you're some kind of enigma beyond imagining, it's hard to tell. You know?'

Solomon nodded down at his glass, and then looked up at Kay. 'But I look hideous.'

'I don't care how you look,' said Kay. 'I care about how you talk, and how you think. I care about who you are, because I think that we, you and me, I think we could have something.'

Solomon shook his head. 'I can't believe that.'

'You should,' said Kay. 'Because I believe in you.'

'You don't know me.'

'I already know enough.'

Solomon shook his head again. 'Kay ...'

'It's fine,' Kay said. She picked up her glass and looked at it in disappointment. 'I've said what I had to say. I know it's hard for you. But I've said it, and you can do whatever you want with it. Have you got any more Scotch?'

Solomon nodded and went to the kitchen and came back with the bottle. He poured a decent measure for Kay.

'Thanks,' she said. 'Now. Since I'm here. There was something else. What the hell are we going to do about this madman?'

Solomon explained his plan to Kay, or at least as much as he could explain without giving away key details of his other life, chiefly his extensive criminal activities. Kay listened and drank Scotch, watching his face. It made Solomon uncomfortable but he didn't say anything, didn't want another dressing-down.

After he finished, Kay nodded to herself, then said, 'And if, let's just say if this works, then I'm supposed to meet this person on my own?'

'The police will be there.'

'They will? I thought they didn't want to know.'

'I'll make sure they do.'

'How?'

'I can't tell you that,' said Solomon. 'You need to trust me.'

'Right.'

'You can say no. You probably should.'

'I trust you.'

Kay said it with such simplicity that Solomon was momentarily overwhelmed. 'Kay, I ...'

Kay yawned. 'I'm tired,' she said. 'Do you have a spare bed?'

'No. Only mine.'

'Then I'm going to sleep in it.' She stood up, a little unsteadily. Solomon stood too. 'Which way am I going?'

'I'll show you.' He led Kay to his bedroom and she put her

arms loosely around his neck and said, 'Goodnight,' before kissing him softly on his good cheek. She let go and sat on the bed and then flopped backwards and lay quite still. 'Wake me up at eight,' she added, and Solomon watched her for a moment before heading for the sofa.

thirty-one

A HYPOTHESIS, SOLOMON KNEW, WAS WORTH NOTHING WITHOUT testing. And Kay's hypothesis that his sister's attacker was enacting the roles of Shakespearean tragic heroines in reverse chronological order was plausible, but untested. And so he had devised a test, a brute-force, unsophisticated test that he had no idea would work or not. But at least, he told himself, he had optimized the test so that it stood a chance of success.

The plan was to dangle Juliet out there as bait, and see if anybody bit. To give the plan a bit of help, Solomon had just finished hacking the API of the dating app that all the victims had used. Now, Kay's new, entirely false, profile was being served up as a matter of priority to every registered male in a five-mile radius. Not only that, she was now called Julia, loved doing 'cultural stuff', and was interested in meeting somebody who enjoyed the theatre. It struck, Kay and Solomon reckoned, the right note. A wannabe sophisticate who gave her unworldliness away with the word 'stuff'. Wide-eyed, try-hard and vulnerable. Somebody who might provoke contempt in their target, get him to bite. That was the idea. And Julia, the name, close to Juliet but not quite there. As far as bait went, it was as targeted as they could get it. Now, it was time to test the hypothesis. Was Juliet the next on the list?

It might work. It should work. And of course, though Solomon was too shy to say this to Kay, she was very pretty. Which, too, would help. Though even the thought of this, of Kay's attractiveness, simultaneously caused Solomon to doubt whether they could ever be together in the future, whether there was any possibility for them, this unlikely matching of Beauty and the Beast, or at least some approximation of that. Stop thinking, he told himself. You think too much.

Solomon had left Kay at his apartment and was now, once again, waiting for a meeting with Inspector Helen Fox, head of an organized-crime task force and utterly indifferent to the matter at hand. But he had a plan for this too, and it was a good one. Or at least he thought it was, though a lot depended on the outcome, especially as one of the outcomes could very well be the injury or even violent death of one Solomon Mullan.

'Would you like to follow me?'

It was a different uniformed officer this time, but the same route behind the front desk of the police station and down a corridor, up a flight of stairs to Fox's frosted-glass door. She hadn't even answered Solomon's call, Solomon being put through to her voicemail. But what he'd got to offer her was juicy enough that she'd called back within five minutes and made time the next morning, no problem, yes, certainly she could fit him in. What time was he thinking?

The uniformed officer knocked and Fox called, 'Come in,' and there they were, once again, Fox and Solomon, sitting across a desk from one another. Fox smiled, both a rare and not very attractive sight, Solomon couldn't help but think.

'So,' she said. 'You said you could tell me where your brother was.'

'That's not what I said,' Solomon replied. 'No.'

Fox stopped smiling. 'You told me you could bring him to me.'

'I said I could give you something you want.'

'And I want your brother.'

Solomon nodded. He was wearing his eye patch and make-up, and he met Fox's gaze with no problem, his head erect, assertive. 'Well, I'm afraid that's never going to happen.'

Fox narrowed her eyes. 'Are you wasting my time again?'

Solomon ignored the question, said instead, 'I'm here to do a deal. That's what I said. Specifically, I told you that I could give you what you wanted.'

Fox sat back in her chair and eyed him doubtfully. 'Go on.'

'Have you ever heard the name Thomas Arnold?'

Fox gave away the smallest tic, a slight twitch at the corner of her mouth, nothing more. Not a bad poker face, Solomon thought. But I saw it.

'Possibly,' she said.

'He traffics women, amongst other things, and launders a lot of money. Of course, my brother is entirely innocent of anything you might believe he has done, or is involved in. But I'm willing to bet that the illegitimate earnings you have erroneously ascribed to him are significantly less than those of Thomas Arnold.'

Fox frowned briefly. 'Meaning?'

'Meaning,' said Solomon, 'that Thomas Arnold is a far bigger fish than you believe my brother to be.'

Fox rubbed an eye with her forefinger. 'I'm still listening.'

'I can lead you to Arnold with half a million sterling of dirty money in his hands,' said Solomon.

Fox stood up and turned to the window, looking out over the car park outside. 'Really?' she said, her voice an attempt at disbelief mixed with sarcasm, but excitement a clear undertone.

'Really,' said Solomon.

'And how will you manage that?' she said.

'That isn't a concern of yours.'

'What time frame are we talking?'

'Two days. Three tops.'

'That's too soon,' she said, her back still to Solomon.

He smiled. 'Fine,' he said. 'Then we're done here.'

'Wait.' Fox turned and tried out another smile, this one more ghastly than the one she'd worn to greet him. 'Let's say the timing works. Let's go with that, see where it takes us.'

'Let's do that.'

'So the next obvious question is, what do you want? In return for this ... what did you say his name was?'

'Please,' said Solomon. 'You know who he is.'

Fox's smile flickered, rallied, then gave up the ghost. 'What do you want?'

'I want you and two officers of your choosing to be present when I bring you the man responsible for my sister's near-drowning, the murder of Rebecca Harrington and several other violent attacks on women.'

Fox closed her eyes as if Solomon had just delivered bad news she wasn't willing or able to process. Eventually she said, 'This again.'

'This again.'

She sat down, closed her eyes briefly, then opened them and said, 'You don't know any Thomas Arnold. You read his name in the press and made this money story up to get me to cooperate with your insane investigation. You are a fantasist, and you need to leave my office, now.'

Solomon took out his phone and placed it carefully on the desk in front of him. 'Would you like me to call him?' he said.

'Thomas Arnold? Yes. Yes, I would love you to,' Fox said.

Solomon picked his phone back up and found Arnold's number. He called it and put it over the phone's loudspeaker. The two of them listened to the ringing tone, then a man's voice as he picked up.

'Arnold.'

Solomon put a warning finger to his mouth, then said, 'Mr Arnold? It's Solomon Mullan.'

'Yeah?'

'Just a courtesy call to tell you that everything is in place.'

'Better be,' said Arnold. There was noise his end, the sound of machinery and cars. 'Listen, not a good time. You've only got till tomorrow, remember?'

'I remember.'

'Got to go. I'll be seeing you.'

'Oh, and Thomas?'

'What you call me?'

'Sorry, Mr Arnold. Same place?'

'Make it the afternoon. Got to go.'

Arnold hung up and Solomon looked over at Fox. 'Recognize that voice?'

Fox nodded, distracted. She thought for some time, then said, 'And what do you want me to do? When you ... How did you put it? Bring me this person.'

'Question him.'

'About what?'

'The women.'

'But Mr Mullan,' Fox said, leaning forward across the desk towards Solomon, 'I don't buy your theory. Remember?'

'Just ask him for his name. Ask him for his name, and then ask my companion what name he gave her. They won't match.'

'So?'

'So watch him. Watch his reaction. You're a police officer. I was under the impression you had some kind of second sense for when things aren't right.'

'So all you want me to do is question him.'

'Well,' said Solomon, 'it would constitute a start, wouldn't it?'

Fox narrowed her eyes at this, then sat back and watched Solomon, thinking. Eventually she said, 'Arnold first. Then I help you.'

'Hold on,' said Solomon. He dialled his own number, waited for the call to go through to voicemail, then said, 'I'll need you to guarantee your help.'

Fox took a breath, then said, clearly, 'I promise that I will supply myself and two officers.'

'At a place and time of my choosing,' said Solomon.

'At a place and time of your choosing.'

'In return for my help apprehending Thomas Arnold.'

'Really?' said Fox, then sighed. 'In return for your help getting hold of Thomas Arnold. Good enough?'

'Thank you,' said Solomon, ending the call. 'That's good enough.' He stood up and put his phone away in his pocket. 'I'll be in touch. You'll need to be ready to move.'

'I'll be ready.' Solomon turned to leave, but Fox said, 'Mr Mullan?'

Be careful, he thought. This is where she gets an attack of guilt and conscience and tells me to be careful because I am going after a violent criminal on her behalf.

'Yes?'

'Don't balls this up. Understand?'

He left Fox's office and took the stairs to the ground floor with a smile on his face. Clever he might be, but he'd seriously over-estimated her on that one.

Kay was gone when Solomon got back to his apartment, a note on his coffee table thanking him for the Scotch and the use of his bed, and signed off with *Solomon & Kay, Private Investigators*. Solomon sat in his living room and read it over and over, stopping each time at the sign-off. Private investigators, yes, but with no experience and a plan that had so many unknowns in it that it barely counted as a plan at all, more an optimistic series of desirable-though-unlikely outcomes. And he was putting Kay right in the centre of it.

But then, he had Fox signed up and ready. The risk was minimal, or at least it was contained. Kay would never be alone. The real risk, he couldn't help but think, was with Arnold.

Solomon got up and walked to his bathroom and removed the panel along the bath. Inside was a plastic bag. He pulled it out and counted out £35,000. He'd need that. That was part of the plan. No criminal, he figured, was likely to turn down the offer of extra money. Free, easy, clean-as-a-whistle money, and one hell of a lot of it, too. He went back to the living room and lay back and closed his eyes. He hadn't got a lot of sleep the night before, with Kay in his bed, her presence in his apartment like a tantalizing promise that could never be realized. He should sleep. He needed to be on his game tomorrow, even though he still wasn't precisely sure what the game was, what the rules were, or how it should be played.

thirty-two

'I MEAN, SERIOUSLY. OKAY, SO IT'S NOT ACTUALLY *ME*, IT'S somebody called Julia who we made up, I get that, but still. Pizza Hut? I said I like cultural stuff, not … not *stuffed crusts*, for God's sake.'

'No,' said Solomon, his webcam on so that Kay could see his face, read his expression.

'Stop smiling,' she said.

'Sorry. Any more?'

'Any more? Well done, Solomon I'm-a-genius Mullan, for hacking the API so well that I'm being courted by, currently, seven hundred and sixty-three not particularly eligible bachelors.'

'It worked, then.'

'It did. Yes, it certainly worked. I started off actually answering them, you know, getting into a conversation with them, to see if they were our nutter rather than just, you know, A. N. Other nutter. But there's no way, I can't reply to them all.'

This was a problem. Kay was inundated with date offers from men and couldn't keep up with the demand. And if she wasn't replying to them all, drawing them out in conversation, there was a chance they'd miss their target. They would discover him in a turn of phrase, wording that seemed off, clumsy, anachronistic.

'Here's another. *I'll buy you dinner if you buy us breakfast.* This is the world we live in. It's actually not funny.'

'I'm out of the loop on all this,' said Solomon. 'I've not been dating.'

'I was kind of aware of that. Sorry, too blunt. Meant to be funny. Hey, here's another one. *Do you look as good in real life as your profile picture, or is it one of those over-flattering ones?*'

'Wow,' said Solomon. 'That is pretty precise. And direct.'

'Direct it is.'

'Did you reply?'

'Yep. I said yes, it was taken before the head-on collision.' Kay stopped and put her hand over her mouth and closed her eyes. 'Oh God, Solomon.'

Solomon laughed. 'At least you didn't say acid attack.'

'I'm such an idiot. Oh *God. Idiot.*'

'It's okay. Got any more?'

'Hmmm? Only about seven hundred. Someone told me that they love me. Just that. *I love you.* On the basis of what? This world.'

'I'm sorry,' said Solomon. 'Listen, I've got to go. I'll call you later.'

'Yeah, later. If I'm still here. I might have run off with any one of countless available men.'

'Good luck with that,' said Solomon.

'Bye.'

He disconnected and sat smiling for some moments, before remembering what it was he needed to be doing. He found a backpack and stuffed the £35,000 into it, then put on his Ray-Bans and pulled his hood up. Time to go and swindle Thomas Arnold.

On the way, he stopped off at the hospital, where Tiffany lay asleep, peaceful, a half-smile on her lips. Solomon watched the fragile rise and fall of her chest underneath the thin hospital blanket, examined the delicate bones and veins of her face. He sat there for a long time, enjoying a calm that he did not want to leave. But he had to, and eventually he stood up and kissed his sister softly on the forehead and walked slowly and reluctantly away.

Outside the arch of Thomas Arnold's car wash a man was parked, half on the kerb, half on the road. The car was a white Mercedes and the driver got out as Solomon approached. He was dark-skinned and wearing Ray-Bans like Solomon's but also a tight black T-shirt that showed off large biceps. One of the workers at the car wash came out, a short man in his fifties in overalls and rubber boots. He said something to the man that Solomon couldn't make out, and gestured with his arms.

'I ain't going anywhere,' the man said. He seemed angry.

'But you can't park here,' the worker said.

'You seen this?' the man said. 'Fucking scratched my paint-work when you washed it.'

The worker looked at the man's car. 'No,' he said. 'That isn't a new scratch.'

'Calling me a liar?'

'No, but—'

The Mercedes driver cuffed the car-wash worker with an open hand to the side of the head. 'So what are you gonna do about it?'

'I'm telling you,' the worker said. 'We did not make that scratch. How could we? We don't use sharp items to wash the cars.'

The Mercedes driver raised his hand again and the other man cowered away into the railway arch. As he backed into it, Thomas Arnold came out and hit the Mercedes driver on the head with a long piece of metal, it might have been a wheel-nut wrench. The driver staggered briefly and Arnold dropped the metal bar and hit him with his fist, knocking him to the pavement, then kicked him repeatedly. Passers-by stopped and watched, a woman putting her hands over her young child's eyes.

'Fucking get into your car and fucking fuck off,' said Arnold, his words synchronized to his kicks. He stopped and looked down at the still form of the man, then spat on him, before turning and walking back into the arch.

The onlookers stood in shocked stillness, the Mercedes driver lifting himself up onto all fours, shaking his head like a stunned slaughterhouse beast. Solomon watched the scene with dismay. This was the man he was about to deal with, a man who used violence in a way that seemed casual, trivial. He could feel his resolve ebbing, dwindling like sand through a cupped hand. He had his plan, or what passed for one. But did he have the courage to see it through?

Arnold didn't seem to be perturbed by what had just happened, didn't even seem to be breathing heavily, which, given his bulk, was remarkable. He was wearing a purple tracksuit and standing behind his desk, and he looked at Solomon waiting in his doorway and said, 'Huh.'

Solomon didn't know if that was an invitation to come in or

not, but he walked in anyway, given confidence by what he was holding in his bag.

'Unbelievable,' Arnold said. 'These people, they try and get away with anything, I'm telling you.'

Solomon half expected him to add, 'It's criminal,' but Arnold didn't; instead he sat down and said, 'You going to keep those sunglasses on?'

'Yes,' said Solomon, taking the chair across the desk from him.

'Huh,' Arnold said again, an inexpressive sound that might have conveyed surprise or, equally, indifference. 'So. You got my money?'

'Yes.'

'Okay, so.' He pointed a hand at his desk and smiled, the skin crinkling around his empty eye socket. 'Put it there.'

Solomon lifted his bag and unzipped it and pulled out the money, piled it on the desk. Arnold watched him without speaking and when he'd finished said, 'That's not twenty thousand.'

'It's thirty-five.'

Arnold nodded as if he understood, which he didn't. 'So I've got thirty-five grand,' he said. 'Okay, where did it come from?'

'You invested it wisely,' said Solomon. 'I can forward you the paperwork.'

Arnold nodded again, this time Solomon was sure in complete bafflement. 'You what?'

'It's how it works,' said Solomon. 'I take the money, send it overseas, it comes back into the system and I invest it.' He paused, wondering how much detail to give, how much nonsense he could get away with. 'It's called structuring,' he said. 'It's what I do.'

'So, what, in seven days I make fifteen grand?'

'You did this time,' said Solomon. 'Your investments can go up or down, depending on the market.'

'How often do your investments go down?'

'Never,' said Solomon. 'Not yet, anyway. But like I say—'

'Yeah, yeah, I get it,' said Arnold. He nodded to himself and leant back in his chair, watching the pile of money as if it was a dead animal that might suddenly come back to life and scuttle away. He closed his good eye and remained still for a long time, so long that Solomon wondered whether he'd gone to sleep. Then he abruptly sat forward and said, 'How much can you take?'

'Sorry?' said Solomon.

'Can you deal with? Money? How much can you deal with?'

'Mr Arnold, I've returned your money. As far as I'm concerned, our business is concluded.'

'Concluded? You mean finished, innit?'

'That's what I mean, yes.' Play hard to get, Solomon thought, wishing he felt more in control than he did.

'See, the thing is, I didn't say it was fucking concluded, did I? So it isn't. Understand?' Arnold licked his lips, his tongue fat and wet.

Solomon didn't reply, just watched him through his Ray-Bans and tried to hold his nerve. This was one of those unfathomable human-interaction-type variable situations he found it impossible to predict.

'I need you to do something else for me.'

'I'm sorry, but—'

'Wasn't a question,' said Arnold. 'It wasn't a request. It wasn't a please-Solomon-Mullan-help-me deal. I need you to do something for me. Now, nod.'

Solomon didn't nod.

'Nod, or this, what we're doing here, this is finished and I move on to your sister.'

Solomon took a deep, audible breath and said, 'Okay.'

'So okay, now we're communicating,' said Arnold. 'I have a lot of money that I can't fucking get rid of. I'm talking bags, man, bags. You're going to help me.'

'How much?'

'How much can you deal with?' said Arnold. 'Shit, how many times have I got to ask the same fucking question?'

'A hundred thousand, tops.'

'No way,' said Arnold. 'You can do better than that.'

'It's too risky.'

'Can't have this money lying around,' said Arnold. 'I need you to take more.'

Solomon blinked behind his Ray-Bans, squeezed his eyes tight, then said, 'Five hundred.'

'Thousand?'

'And that is it. Seriously. We'll have forensics all over us if we go any higher. That's the limit.'

'Half a million?'

'Yes.'

'And how much do I get back?'

'That depends on the markets,' said Solomon. 'And the risk. High-risk investments yield more.'

'How much?'

Solomon shrugged. 'Nine per cent.'

'So how much do I get back?'

'The five hundred, plus forty-five.'

'Thousand?'

'Yes.'

Arnold laughed. 'In seven days?'

'It will take longer,' said Solomon, then wondered why he even cared, why it even mattered. If his plan worked, he'd never have anything to do with the money. 'Ten days, maybe.'

Arnold laughed again. 'So now we're doing business.'

'I guess.'

'Okay.' Arnold stood up and came round the desk. Solomon stood too, his head lowered, away from Arnold, as if the man carried a bad smell about him. Arnold walked past him and out of his office, and Solomon grabbed his empty bag and followed him. Arnold was waiting for him in the arch where the car-wash workers were hosing down the floor with power washers, the space filled with the hiss of the machinery, the air damp with a fine mist.

'You better not be fucking with me,' said Arnold. 'You won't be the first person I've hosed off this floor. You get me?'

Solomon nodded, his view of Arnold thankfully obscured by the film of moisture on his Ray-Bans. 'I get you.'

'So I'll see you tomorrow. I'll call you, tell you where to meet. Yes?'

'Okay.'

Arnold turned and walked away and Solomon headed towards the light at the entrance of the arch, which looked, through the mist of his sunglasses, like some heavenly promise of redemption and safety.

It was gone eleven when his door buzzer sounded. He lifted the intercom's handset and heard Kay's voice on the other end.

'Sorry, no man with a dog. You'll need to let me in.'

He buzzed her in and left his apartment door ajar, before

fleeing to the bathroom and locking himself in, going through the make-up procedure that was getting easier, becoming a familiar ritual.

'Hello?'

'I'll be out in a minute,' said Solomon, his heart beating faster, his hand becoming more unsteady at the sound of her voice. He finished, looked at himself, put on his eye patch and unlocked the bathroom door, hesitated, then opened it and walked through.

Kay had found the Scotch and was in the living room, pouring it into two glasses. She smiled when she saw Solomon and held up a glass for him.

'Here.'

'Don't you sleep?' he said.

'Lab hours,' she said. 'It's open all night, and there was something I had to check on. A result,' she said, saying *result* as if it might have earth-changing potential.

'How was it?'

'A disaster,' said Kay, frowning exaggeratedly. 'Oh well, what the hey,' she added, smiling suddenly and taking a healthy drink of Scotch. 'There's still an outside chance that what I'm trying to do isn't impossible, biologically speaking. And the good news is, if it *is* possible, which I very much doubt, but if it is, not only do I get more funding, I probably win the Nobel Prize.'

'Well,' said Solomon. 'That would make it worthwhile.'

'Wouldn't it?' Kay sat down, and looked up at Solomon. 'But that's not why I'm here. I think, in fact I'm about ninety-seven per cent sure, that I've found our man.'

thirty-three

'THAT DOES SOUND STRANGE.'

'Strange? It's him. It's got to be.'

'What does he look like?'

'Weird glasses, curly hair, nice smile. Here.' Kay passed her phone to Solomon. The shot was of a man, maybe thirty, smiling at the camera, mousy curly hair and glasses that he recognized. He would. They were Ray-Bans, Clubmasters, black-framed at the top, metal below, sixties throwbacks.

'What's he calling himself?'

'Demmy.'

Solomon thought. 'I can't think of who that might relate to.'

'Okay, but look at the language.'

Kay handed Solomon her phone and he read the message exchange again.

Want to go out?

Sure. When?

Friday?

Cool. Got somewhere in mind?

Some secret hole.

Hole?

Watering hole.

Obvs. Anywhere specific?

Do you know Mr Todlq's?

No. Sounds … weird.

*I mean Mr Toad's. Which also sounds … weird. But it's
pretty cool. All drinks freshly distilled.*

What time?

At dead time of the night.

Sorry?

Any time. I meant any time.

Verily! How about 9? Hello?

See you at 9.

Solomon had read *Romeo and Juliet* and so he knew every
word. He tried to pick the references for this exchange, the key
words, where they were found in the text, but nothing stood out.
He looked at Kay, who raised an enigmatic eyebrow at him.

'What have you got?'

'Juliet's speech, when she dies,' said Kay. 'It fits. Listen.' She
read off Solomon's laptop. '*Or, if I live, is it not very like the horrible conceit of death and night, together with the terror of the
place – as in a vault.*'

'And?'

'And it fits. *Death and night, together. Dead time of the night.*
Night, death. The connection's there.'

'It's not perfect. It doesn't fit perfectly.'

'Your sister's exchange wasn't a perfect match either.' Kay sloshed more Scotch into her glass and waggled the bottle enquiringly at Solomon, who shook his head. 'He wrote *convent*, but the play used the word *nunnery*, remember? And here, he writes *secret hole*, and the text says *vault*. But it's the same thing.'

'Maybe.' Solomon didn't like ambiguity. He preferred the scientific method, trusted it. The method that painstakingly erased ambiguity, until only certainty remained.

'There's more,' said Kay. '*All drinks freshly distilled*. That's got to be a reference to Friar Laurence.'

'*And this distilled liquor drink thou off*,' said Solomon, quoting from memory, the scene where Friar Laurence gives Juliet her sleeping draught. 'Yes, I buy that.'

'And this place? Mr Toad's? It's some kind of stupid hipster artisan gin distillery or something.'

'*Some say the lark and loathed toad change eyes*,' said Solomon.

'Sorry?'

'It's in *Romeo and Juliet*,' said Solomon. 'Juliet in denial that morning is coming. *The loathed toad*.'

'All the references are here,' said Kay. 'It's him, Sol. It's him.'

Solomon should have felt excitement, but instead he felt the opposite, a dull and culpable dread that he had ever conceived this hideous plan that would put Kay within touching distance of Rebecca Harrington's killer, his sister's attacker, a man who could force women to eat hot coals. What was he thinking?

'It's too dangerous.'

Kay tilted her head slightly, frowned. 'What?'

'This. I don't like it. I was wrong, and now I would like to stop it.'

'You want to *stop* it?' said Kay.

'Yes.'

'Just like that.'

'Yes. Kay, it's—'

'It's not your decision? You're damn right it isn't, Mr I've-got-a-God-complex. What, you think that because it was your sister who was attacked, you're running the show? You're the moral arbiter of this little escapade?' Kay paused for breath, then said, 'These are real women who are being attacked, killed, mutilated, and no one in authority gives a shit. But guess what? I do. I do, I really do. So no, Solomon, no, the decision is not yours and yours alone to make. Understand?'

'I didn't mean—'

'I'm sure you didn't. You just suddenly thought, when confronted with actual real life instead of the theoretical kind that you prefer, you suddenly realized that this might actually be a teeny bit dangerous.'

Solomon had no response to that statement, could find nothing inaccurate in it to object to. Instead he said, his head bowed, 'I don't want you to get hurt.' Kay didn't reply, and so he added, 'You mean a lot to me.'

'I do?'

Solomon nodded at his carpet.

'Sol?'

'Yes?'

'Look at me?'

Solomon looked up slowly, feeling his face flush in embarrassment, further embarrassment on top of the customary shame he felt for looking the way he did.

'I'm sorry,' said Kay. 'But this is something I choose to do. You do understand that?'

'Yes.'

'And anyway, you're bringing your very own rent-a-cop, aren't you?'

Solomon thought of the elaborate choreography he still needed to pull off, delivering Thomas Arnold to Fox before she'd commit to providing protection for Kay, and of course getting Thomas Arnold into Fox's hands without Arnold murdering Solomon for basically trying to sell him down the river. 'Yes,' he said, with as much certainty as he could.

'Okay then,' said Kay, raising her glass. 'This is exciting. Sol? This is really, really exciting. Plus, it's got a hell of a better chance of coming off than any experiments I've got going on in the lab.'

Kay called a cab and Solomon didn't ask her not to, didn't suggest that she stayed. After she left, he washed her glass and stood for a time at the sink in the kitchen, trying to justify to himself what he was doing. He thought of Tiffany, still lying in hospital, and of the other women who were at risk or who had already been victims of his sister's attacker. Kay was right. This was bigger than him, bigger than any qualms he might have. But still. It was too messy, too incoherent, there were too many variables involved for him to feel confident. He just could not be sure, about anything.

His phone rang and he went to the living room and answered. 'Yes?'

'Arnold here. Tomorrow.'

'Tomorrow.' Tomorrow was Wednesday. Kay's date was on Friday. The timings worked, just.

'I'll have the money. You got a car?'

'No.'

'Then get a taxi. I'll be at Thurrock services. M25.'

'I can do that.'

'I know you can. I'll be there at three, north corner of the car park. Silver Golf, licence ends YHW.'

'Yankee Hotel Whisky,' said Solomon.

'Whatever,' said Arnold. 'Tell the taxi to park somewhere nowhere fucking near me, and walk. Understand?'

'Yes.'

'And you'll be alone.'

'Yes.'

'So we're golden,' said Arnold. 'Three tomorrow. Silver Golf. North side. Yes?'

'Yes,' said Solomon, again.

'Yeah, and Solomon?'

'Yes?'

'Don't be fucking late.'

Solomon held his dead phone to his ear for a moment, then dropped it on the sofa. As a child, he'd been taken to a theme park, and he and Luke had gone on a roller coaster. He remembered being hauled up a steep metal track, remembered the clanking, complaining sound of the chain as it winched them up and up and up, his whole body pressed back into his hard plastic seat as they were lifted almost vertical. But most of all he remembered a feeling of things being out of control, of events taking on a momentum he no longer had a say over. He had closed his eyes and spoken quietly to himself as he had been flung around the track, his brother hooting and swearing with delight next to him, and he had promised himself that he would never, ever put himself in such a situation again. Yet here he was.

Still, though, he did have a quasi-ally in this. He looked at his watch. Almost one in the morning. It was too late to call Fox, but he couldn't wait until morning, wouldn't be able to sleep. If things were in motion, if there was a momentum he couldn't change, then she needed to be caught up in it too. He picked his mobile back up and called her number.

'Christ's sake, know what time it is?'

'Yes,' said Solomon. Fox didn't sound as if she'd just been woken up. She sounded awake and alert and as displeased as usual to be hearing from him.

'So? What is it that can't wait?'

'I've got a meeting with Thomas Arnold tomorrow at three p.m.'

There was the briefest of pauses. Solomon imagined her reaching over to her bedside table for her notepad, then she said, 'Where?'

'Thurrock services.'

'Three p.m.'

'Yes.'

'How much money is he bringing?'

Solomon hadn't asked, but he figured that the higher the amount, the more committed Fox would be. 'Between four and five hundred. Thousand.'

'Okay. What's the plan?'

'He's parking in the north corner. Silver Golf, licence ends in YHW.'

'Yankee Hotel Whisky,' said Fox.

Solomon closed his eyes and made a mental note to stop quoting the NATO alphabet. He was clearly in bad company. 'That's right,' he said.

'You're supposed to be alone?'

'That's what he said.'

'Okay. I'm going to need you to wear a mike. We can sort that out tomorrow. Do you own a jacket? Actually, scratch that, a hooded top'll do, so wear that. I'm going to prepare you a script. Only when you've delivered what we need are we going to step in. Understand? You don't get him to say what we want, we won't be getting involved.'

'That wasn't something we discussed.'

'Sorry?' said Fox. 'We're discussing it now, aren't we? This is a fluid situation.'

'I'm taking all the risks here.'

'Mr Mullan, you're accepting half a million pounds from a notoriously violent criminal. Do you need me to remind you that this was your idea?'

'No.'

'We'll be there. But we're not going to expose ourselves to a man like him unless we know, know beyond doubt, that we've got him nailed to a cross. I hope a man of your intelligence can understand that.'

Solomon could, although he didn't like it. 'Okay.'

'Okay. So. It's gone one, tomorrow's a big day. I want you to go to bed, and be in my office at nine. Think you can do that?'

'I'll be there.'

'Okay. Good. Then I'll see you tomorrow. And Solomon?'

He was surprised to hear Fox use his Christian name. This was a first. 'Yes?'

'Try to get some sleep.'

thirty-four

'WE WON'T BE GIVING YOU A TWO-WAY,' SAID THE MALE OFFICER who was threading a cable through the front of the hooded top Solomon had just taken off, sharing space with the drawstring. 'The boss says we only need to hear. A two-way's bulkier, needs to be close to your mouth. Too obvious. This, we can just keep it all in here.'

'What's the range?'

'Two hundred metres you get perfect sound,' the officer said. He was about fifty and his glasses were so thick Solomon wondered how he'd been allowed onto the force in the first place. 'Three hundred's your maximum.'

'Lithium?'

'That's right. Know your stuff, do you?'

'I read something somewhere,' said Solomon. 'It can't have a long life.'

'Half an hour if you're lucky.' The officer was sitting at a desk and he looked up at Solomon and said, 'You won't need that long.'

'I hope not,' Solomon said.

'Easy,' the officer said. 'In and out.'

Solomon was in a room somewhere on the ground floor in the back of the police station. It was lined with metal shelves and on the shelves were large translucent plastic boxes full of equipment, shabby paper labels glued to them, marked with words like *Receivers, Close #1, Range*. One was marked *Spares/repairs*, and filled with a tangle of various-coloured wires, which didn't reassure Solomon. Nothing in the room suggested that he was amongst cutting-edge surveillance practitioners. More enthusiastic amateurs with limited funds, and probably limited experience to go with it.

'Right, you're done,' the officer said. 'It's activated remotely, so you just forget it's there.' He picked Solomon's top up and handed it to him. 'I'll take you back upstairs.'

Solomon had arrived at nine, and Fox had been waiting for him at the station's reception, which was another first. She hadn't seemed exactly pleased to see him, but she had managed a smile. Which was more than his brother had earlier, when he'd called him. Luke hadn't had much to smile about when Solomon had told him his plan. He had, conversely, done a whole lot of swearing.

'No fucking way.'

'I have to,' Solomon said.

'You want to do over Thomas Arnold? Are you insane?'

'It'll get him off our backs.'

'If it works. If you don't get killed. If he doesn't put a price on your head, which, Solly, he probably will, even if your plan comes off. You're out of your mind.'

'Well,' said Solomon, as calmly as he could in the face of his brother's fury, 'it's too late anyway. It's done.' The roller coaster's already gone, he thought. And there's nothing that can stop it.

'Solly, do not do this. Do. Not. Do this.'

'It's too late,' Solomon said again.

Luke was silent for a moment, then said, 'This is on me. I got you into this.' Another pause, then, anger mixed with frustration, 'But you couldn't keep things fucking simple, could you?'

'Listen, Luke, I have to go.'

'Please, Solly. Don't do this. I'll come back, I'll get it sorted. Call this off.'

'I'll call you later,' said Solomon. 'When it's done.'

Solomon had hung up on Luke's anguished '*Solly.*' He shouldn't have told him, should have waited. What purpose had calling him served? Maybe just that Solomon felt scared and alone and wanted to hear his big brother's voice, borrow some psychological strength. Well, that hadn't worked.

'Get any sleep?' asked Fox, an attempt at concern, at human warmth.

'A little,' said Solomon. 'Enough.'

'Good. Shall we?'

She set off for her office, walking fast, so fast that Solomon had to hustle to keep up with her. He had to admit that she had a presence, an aura of capability that he was grateful for. He'd never felt more out of his depth in his life, more uncertain. She hurried up the stairs to the first floor and was holding open her door by the time Solomon caught up. He sat down opposite her, Fox's desk in between them.

'So,' she said. 'Are you ready for this?'

'I think so,' said Solomon.

'Well, you're not,' said Fox. 'No way. In fact, I'm very much in two minds about whether we're going to go ahead with this.'

Solomon took his Ray-Bans off and set them carefully on the desk, then looked up and met Fox's gaze. 'Why is that?'

'Why? Because I suspect that you are a fantasist, and so I have to question your state of mind and your ability to carry out a task such as the one you're faced with today.'

Solomon nodded. 'And conversely, I suspect that you are a police officer driven by ambition rather than integrity, and I have to question your judgement and priorities.' He paused. 'But I'm here now, and I've got Thomas Arnold on a hook, and I seriously doubt that you're about to give that up, given your ambition. So please, Inspector Fox, let's just get on with this, shall we?'

Solomon delivered all of this without once looking away from Fox. Her eyes widened as he accused her of putting ambition before integrity, and narrowed as he told her that he didn't believe she would give up the chance of nailing Arnold. But after a brief pause she nodded, took a deep breath and said, 'All right. In that case, let's get you wired up.'

Back in Fox's office, she handed Solomon a piece of paper. 'Think you can remember this?'

Solomon took it, glanced at it and handed it back. 'Yes.'

'Mind reading it properly?'

'I have done.'

'Solomon ...'

'It won't work.'

'How do you mean?'

'He's not an idiot,' said Solomon. 'So what do you hope to gain by treating him like one?'

'I don't follow,' said Fox.

'*You want me to launder this, the same way as last time?*' Solomon said, quoting from the script Fox had shown him. 'You don't think that's a little ... blunt? Obvious?'

'We need him to admit to it. We need him to admit to money laundering. The money on its own, he could explain it away. Maybe, with the right lawyer. We need something on record.'

'He won't go for it,' said Solomon, thinking of Arnold, his volatility, and underneath that, his shrewdness.

'You don't get the choice,' said Fox. 'You do this my way, or you don't do it at all. I call it off.'

'You won't do that,' said Solomon. 'No. You want him too much now.'

'I'll call it off,' said Fox, snapping her fingers, 'like that.'

Solomon shook his head. 'You won't. Anyway, I know how to play him. Remember, I've met him. I know how he works.' He imagined Thomas Arnold, his clumsy metaphor of a castle barely containing a furious ogre. Did he really know him?

'So what's your plan?' said Fox.

'Annoy him,' said Solomon. 'Get him to lose his temper.'

'And what will that achieve?'

'He'll lose his discretion,' said Solomon. He thought back to Arnold's attack on the man outside the railway arch, his loss of control. 'Trust me, I've seen it.'

Fox shook her head. 'No. No, I can't agree to that. I'm already taking enough of a risk without you going off piste like this. No way.'

You're taking a risk? Solomon thought. 'Inspector ...'

Fox stood up. 'Okay, we're done. You think I won't call time on this? Think again, Mr Mullan.' Back to Mr Mullan, thought Solomon. 'I'll have that wire removed and I'll have forgotten you by the end of the day. I've got other targets. Your brother, that's one. He's still on my list. Murder. Remember?'

Solomon tried to summon up some leverage, think of

some way to outmanoeuvre Fox, but came up short. She held the cards here. And anyway, once he was face to face with Arnold, there wasn't a lot she could do. He nodded up at her and said, 'Fine.'

Fox sat back down. 'In that case,' she said, handing the script back to Solomon, 'do you think you could read this properly?'

Solomon's taxi was an unmarked blue Saab with a sticker in the back window that said it was licensed for private hire. His driver wasn't the man with the thick glasses who had fitted his wire, which he was glad of. His driver was a fit man wearing a bulletproof vest beneath his shirt and a gun on his belt. The car was in a secured car park behind the police station and another officer, also fit, was bending over a map spread out over its bonnet. The day was hot and both officers were wearing sunglasses, Oakleys, though Solomon suspected that they were the sort of men who liked to wear sunglasses whatever the weather. Anything to help up the badass factor. The second officer also had a gun. Fox was standing next to the second officer, looking at something he was pointing to.

'Solomon?' she said. 'I need you here.'

Solomon joined her. The map on the Saab's bonnet showed the layout of the services, the buildings, the petrol station, the arrangement of the parking. The second officer had his finger on the north side and didn't acknowledge Solomon's presence.

'The target'll be here,' he said. 'Steve'll park here.' He pointed to another area, more parking but far away from Arnold's position. 'And we'll be here.' He pointed to an area outside the service-station's border but close to Arnold's position. 'Backup's here.' He pointed this time at an area below Arnold, but close by.

He took his finger away and stood up straight, acknowledging Solomon for the first time. 'You're Mullan?'

'Yes.'

'Sergeant Hayes.' He didn't offer to shake hands, instead turned to Fox. 'Do we know how many will be with the target?'

'No.'

Hayes nodded. 'Understood.' He turned to Solomon. 'We'll go when Fox gives the word. You won't know when that is, but we'll come fast and aggressive. There will be noise. There will be shouting. All I need you to do is step backwards. Understand?'

'Yes.'

'Step backwards and create distance between yourself and the target. What we don't need is a hostage situation. He won't go for you immediately. There will be confusion. In that time, create some distance.'

Solomon nodded. 'I understand.' He did, although he hadn't considered a hostage situation before and it did nothing to reassure him.

'Excellent. If there is shooting, I want you to lie on the ground, facing the gunfire. That will make you the smallest target possible.'

'Makes sense.'

'And face *our* gunfire,' Hayes said. 'We know how to shoot, so we won't hit you. The target, if he fires and misses, we don't want him hitting your head.'

Solomon nodded, unexpectedly impressed. 'Got it.'

'Fine,' said Fox. 'So we're all set.' She took a sheet of paper from underneath the map and placed it on top. 'I just need you to sign this.'

'What is it?'

'Basically,' said Fox, 'this covers us if you get killed or injured, or suffer irreparable psychological damage, or, I don't know, twist an ankle. Whatever happens, you freely and without duress accept that doing this is your choice, that we do not accept any blame or responsibility, and no lawsuits are going to come our way.'

She handed Solomon a pen and he signed, and Fox folded the paper and tucked it into her inside jacket pocket. She looked at her watch. 'Time to go. Remember, go by the script and get what we need.' She didn't add 'or else', didn't need to. If Solomon didn't get Arnold to say what they needed, he'd end up with Arnold's money. Money the police would take from him. Leaving him half a million pounds in debt to a gangster famed for his brutality. If he didn't get Arnold to implicate himself, he was as good as dead. No, Fox didn't need to add 'or else'.

As he got into the back seat of the blue Saab, Solomon knew also the enormity of what he was getting into. And he was way, way more scared than he had been all those years ago, getting winched up to the top of that roller coaster. This ride up the M25 was worse, exponentially worse.

thirty-five

SOLOMON WAS ALONE IN THE BACK ON THE DRIVE TO THURROCK services, Fox taking a separate car so that she could get into position. The driver, Steve, didn't say much. He asked Solomon if he was sure that he'd memorized the script, was sure that he knew what Thomas Arnold needed to say. Solomon nodded and pulled his hood as far over his head as he could and closed his eyes behind his Ray-Bans. In any case, it was too late for talking. Everything was in motion and the only thing that mattered was what happened when he was face to face with Arnold. Get him to state, unambiguously, that he wanted the money to be laundered. Get that word. *Laundered*. Make him say it. Get him to say it without raising suspicion. Without Thomas Arnold beating him to a pulp, or worse.

The unmarked Saab made it past the A13 exit before they hit traffic, illuminated signs overhead warning of a vehicle fire ahead. Steve looked at his watch and sighed. Half past two, just past. Plenty of time yet. The traffic slowed to walking speed and Solomon wondered what would happen if he just opened the door and stepped out and forgot it, forgot the whole plan. Just walked away. But that wasn't a solution. Arnold would find him. He didn't strike Solomon as the kind of man who readily accepted being stood up. Stop thinking, he told himself. It is what it is. It's too late. Way too late, and if you don't like the plan, then you shouldn't have thought of it.

His mobile rang and he took it out and looked at the number. Luke's. He rejected the call and Steve turned around in his seat and said, 'You'll need to turn that off. Might interfere with the wire.' Solomon nodded and powered it off just as they left the M25 and headed into the Thurrock services.

'You ready?'

'Yes,' said Solomon. No, he thought.

'We've got a few minutes. Anything you want to clarify?'

'No.'

'Remember, don't let him get hold of you. We don't need that kind of complication.'

'Understood.'

'Take a step back—'

'I understand,' said Solomon. 'At this point, anything you say is unlikely to help me, unless of course you've forgotten to tell me something significant.'

'I haven't.'

'Good,' said Solomon.

Steve took a short breath as if preparing to reply, but thought better of it, and they sat and gazed through the car's windscreen for several minutes in silence. Then Steve said, 'It's time.'

The walk from the south-east end of the car park to the north took less than two minutes, and would have been quicker except that Solomon was in no hurry. Was in the opposite of a hurry, whatever the term for that might be. A state of extreme reluctance, he supposed. Disinclined. Uneager. Was that even a word?

God, he was scared, his thoughts nonsensical. His knees felt strange, as if they'd had all their strength removed, as weak as a tiny child's.

The corner of the north side of Thurrock services was almost empty and the silver VW Golf wasn't hard to spot. Licence ending YHW. Yankee Hotel Whisky. Hadn't he decided to stop doing that? It was parked nose forward, its rear against the bushes that formed the perimeter of the car park, rubbish – bottles and plastic bags and old cans – scattered underneath. Beneath the vast overcast Essex sky it was about as unromantic a spot as Solomon could imagine, as ugly and unloved as his own face.

The passenger door opened and Thomas Arnold stepped out, wearing a dark green tracksuit, white stripes down the arms and legs. The driver's door opened almost immediately afterwards and another man, almost as big as Arnold but younger, immaculately groomed black hair, black T-shirt, got out and watched Solomon over the car's roof. Solomon stopped. Arnold turned and opened the back door of the car and pulled out a duffel bag. Eastpak. Solomon recognized the brand from where he was standing, ten metres away.

'Well?' said Arnold, holding the bag in one hand. 'You going to come and get it?'

Solomon forced himself forward, closer and closer to Arnold. This was it. This was the moment that mattered.

'Here.' Arnold held the bag out towards Solomon, but he ignored it. Arnold frowned. 'Take it.'

'Before I do,' said Solomon, 'I need to understand some things.'

'What kind of things?' said Arnold.

Solomon took off his Ray-Bans and forced himself to look

Arnold in the eye. One eye against another. 'Like, where did this money come from?'

'Oh shit,' said Fox, a rare epithet. She had activated Solomon's wire, or rather Sergeant Hayes had, and she was listening to the exchange through headphones from the other side of the hedge, in the back of a small van that told the world that it delivered car parts nationwide.

'What's he doing?' said Hayes.

'Stick to the script,' said Fox, to herself, ignoring Hayes. 'Just stick to the bloody script.'

'Baker?' muttered Hayes into his radio, picking up on Fox's anxiety. 'Are you ready to go?'

'Ready,' said a man's voice.

'Stand by,' said Hayes. 'Something's happening.'

'Roger,' said the man, Baker.

'The script, the script,' said Fox, repeating the words as if it was a mantra, as if they held a mystical power, could steer the situation back in the right direction. 'Stick to the bloody script.'

'Fuck did you say?' said Arnold, more surprised than angry, as if he'd just seen a frog talk.

'Only, I was speaking to Luke,' said Solomon, 'and he told me that you make your money by trafficking women around the country, from overseas. And I have to be honest with you, I have an issue with that specific type of ... industry.'

'Industry.'

'A moral issue,' said Solomon. He was off, the roller coaster now at full speed, and all fear was gone, replaced by the unfamiliar thrill of control entirely relinquished.

Arnold turned his head and gazed into the middle distance for a moment, before turning back to Solomon. Now he was angry. Very still and very controlled and very, very angry.

'You see,' said Solomon, 'I just don't think that kind of thing is right. So I don't think I can take the money.'

Arnold attempted to drag a smile through his fury and was about to say something, to reply, but Solomon interrupted him.

'It all just feels a little sordid.' That ought to do it, he thought, feeling an emotion verging on the delighted. I'm being brave, he thought. That's what's happening. I'm being brave, like Luke.

'You'll take my fucking money,' said Arnold, 'and you'll bring it back to me when it's clean, when you've done whatever it is you fucking do to it so it can't be traced. Because if you don't, you silly little cunt, I will murder your sister, and I will murder your fucking brother, and I'll make sure you're there to watch it.'

'I'm just not convinced I can do it,' said Solomon. 'Sorry.'

'Sorry?' Arnold took a step towards him. 'No. No no no. You launder money, and you'll fucking launder mine. Under-fucking-stood?'

At the word *launder*, Solomon heard shouting from behind him, loud and aggressive and coming nearer. But Arnold was already approaching him, and although he remembered to step back, it was too late and Arnold took hold of Solomon's hooded top and pulled Solomon towards him, turning him and putting a massive arm around his neck. Solomon could hardly believe how strong Arnold was. The man in the black T-shirt Arnold had come with reached into the car and came out with a black gun, which he fired, once, twice, three times in the direction of the police who were approaching, dressed in black, black baseball caps on their heads.

Arnold now had a knife in his other hand and he held it against Solomon's neck.

'Back,' he shouted. 'Back back back.'

One of the approaching policemen was on one knee holding an automatic rifle, and he fired it once and the man in the black T-shirt slipped down the side of the Golf, out of view. Solomon was struggling to breathe, Arnold was gripping his throat so tightly, and the sides of his vision were beginning to darken and cloud. He heard shouting but it seemed to be coming from much further away than it had before. And then he felt an impact in his back and Arnold let go of him, and Solomon fell to his knees, the day brightening around him as he sucked in oxygen. He turned, and Arnold was lying on the ground and Luke was standing over him holding a hammer in one hand, a spectacle that Solomon initially suspected was some kind of vision or hallucination, right up until Luke said, dropping the hammer onto the ground and joining Solomon on his knees, 'Jesus, Solly, *that* was your plan?'

'Where the hell did he come from?' said Fox, watching as Luke Mullan was handcuffed by a sergeant from the tactical squad. 'Okay, take him and Arnold. I want both of them. Is anybody hurt?'

'Only the shooter,' said Hayes. 'Haven't got any update on him.'

'Well,' said Fox. 'Go and check that bag. Make sure it's got money in it.' She watched Hayes cross to the scene of the shooting, black-clothed policemen all over it, Luke being pulled up by his upper arms, his hands cuffed behind him. Arnold was still unconscious, that's if he wasn't dead, Fox thought, remembering the impact of the hammer that Luke had swung.

Where had he come from? He must have been hidden before they got there. They hadn't had time to do a sweep, it had all happened so quickly.

She walked over to Solomon, who was still breathing heavily. She had no idea what to make of what had just happened. It hadn't gone down anywhere near how she'd planned it. Someone had been shot. That meant paperwork, and a lot of it, and this operation hadn't been properly sanctioned or organised and it had turned into a complete shitstorm. But then, she had Thomas Arnold. And as an unexpected bonus, she had Luke Mullan too. Plus she'd taken half a million of dirty money out of circulation. In fact, she thought as she walked, this was a result, an unexpected and excellent result. And her boss, Goven, he'd make sure that any potential recriminations concerning the way the operation had been conducted would go away. Because she had just ticked a lot of boxes, hit a lot of targets. Smashed her KPIs. Which was, in the final analysis, all that mattered.

'Are you okay?' she said to Solomon, looking down at him, still on his knees.

'You can't take Luke,' he said.

'Of course I can. In fact, I must. He's wanted for murder.'

'I gave you what you wanted.'

And more, thought Fox. 'Yes, you did,' she said. 'But I'm afraid that's hardly relevant. I can't give wanted criminals immunity, just because they're related to you.'

'Please. Let him go.'

'Even if I wanted to, I couldn't,' said Fox. 'And I really don't want to. But you're free to go.'

Solomon picked his Ray-Bans up from where he'd dropped them, put them on and stood up. 'Please.'

'No can do.'

He sighed and looked upwards at the sky. 'But we still have an agreement?' he said.

'Sorry?' said Fox.

'An agreement. You'll provide officers.'

'Oh.' She'd forgotten, lost in her personal triumph. 'Yes. Whatever. Now, if you'll excuse me.' She looked at Solomon and shook her head. 'Why didn't you just follow that bloody script?'

thirty-six

THE GREAT CHARACTERS ALL HAD FATAL FLAWS. THE ONES
that were remembered. Hamlet had his indecision, Othello was
brought down by his jealousy. And this one, the woman calling
herself Julia, her flaw was hubris. Like Cassiopeia. She thought
she was clever, smarter than he was. *Verily*. In her message she
had written *Verily*. Why? To reel him in? To whet his appetite?
Women nowadays didn't say *verily*. She had given herself away,
and now the trap was set. Who did she think she was?

He didn't need a stage, not for this. Or rather, no stage was big
enough for what he had planned. It would be played out in the
real world. And that world would sit up and take notice.

'Jonny?'

He looked up from where he was sitting, in the still-warm sun
outside the hospital's main sliding doors. 'Yes?'

'We need you.'

'Right.'

'A and E, bed eleven. There's a lot of blood.'

Jonny looked at the cigarette he had been smoking. There was
still half left to be smoked. Half a cigarette. He stood up and
mashed it out in the steel ashtray, feeling the dying heat of the
embers in the tips of his fingers.

'Now?'

'Yes,' Jonny said. He followed the ward sister back inside the hospital and went to the room where the cleaning products were kept. He would need a bucket and a mop and disinfectant, and water, plenty of water. Blood diluted and spread when it was cleaned, mingling with the water and taking on a different kind of life, diffuse and unmanageable. He turned the tap on and waited until the bucket was half full, then took his mop and bucket and disinfectant spray to Bed 11.

'Took your time,' said a male nurse, peeling off bloody gloves with an air of great irritation. The bed was empty, but there was blood on the bedclothes, the floor, the curtain. Jonny thought of *Macbeth*, the desperate cry, *Out, damned spot.*

'The curtains will need changing.'

'So change them,' the nurse said.

Jonny idly imagined drowning the nurse in his half-filled bucket, the surprise he would feel at having his head pushed under, his first inhalation of warm water, here, in a small cubicle in a busy hospital. Jonny did not doubt that he could do it.

The nurse left and Jonny got to work. He didn't think of it as a job. More as a role he had taken on. One that gave him the keys to the hospital's pharmacy, which had come in useful of late. And still would, or so he hoped. Once the trap was successful and events played out as he envisaged. A success, a huge success. Immaculately staged, brilliantly executed.

The blood mingled with the water, tendrils of red unfurling and dissipating, a gentle submission. The water turned a rosy colour, becoming paler and paler as the blood was diluted further and further. *Verily*. The hubris. The arrogance. To imagine that he would not pick up on it. *Lavinia*. The last performance hadn't been successful; in fact it had been a disaster. A fiasco, the stage abandoned, the player escaped. This time it would be different.

He reached up and unclipped the curtain of the cubicle, suddenly thrust into the public eye, patients and doctors and nurses and relatives watching him at work, pushing a mop, eliminating the essence of someone unknown from where it had lain, spilt. Let them watch. It was just a role, just another role. Let them all watch.

thirty-seven

SOLOMON WOKE THE NEXT MORNING WITH A GROAN AND immediately wished that he could go back to sleep, sleep for the entire day, anything to avoid having to acknowledge that the day before, his brother had been arrested for the murder of Robbie White. Not only that, but he'd been arrested trying to help him, Solomon, out, because Solomon's idea of a plan was about as sophisticated as an aubergine. As nuanced as a headbutt. He lay in bed with his hand over his face and worked his way through what had happened. Luke had been arrested. But so had Thomas Arnold. Fox had got her man, and the money. So she was still on the hook. She'd agreed to help Solomon in exchange for Arnold, and that was still on, despite the collateral damage he had suffered along the way. If this was chess, Solomon thought, he had just sacrificed his queen. Luke, his brother, the only person he knew he could rely on. What had he done?

It was Thursday. Which meant that tomorrow was Friday. Yes, Solomon, that's an established truth, he thought, still only half awake, his thoughts trapped in a pre-conscious vestibule of doubt and dread. And on Friday, Kay was supposed to be meeting a killer. If his plan from yesterday lacked finesse, then where did it leave tomorrow's? It was unthinkable, impossible; it couldn't happen, he couldn't allow it. But then he remembered Kay's reaction when he'd suggested to her that they call it off. She was determined, and Solomon suspected there was little he'd be able to do to talk her out of it.

He got out of bed and put on coffee and while it was brewing walked into the bathroom and rubbed cream into his face, taking care not to look at the mirror. Why did he even have it? A question he must have asked himself a thousand times. But today he had even more reason not to look at it, his feelings of shame and inadequacy amplified by the disaster of yesterday. Of what had happened to Luke, because of him. Because of him, and him alone.

He poured coffee and drank it standing up in the kitchen. He'd need coffee before he called Fox. He didn't imagine it would be an easy conversation.

'Yes?' she said, impatient, irritated, clearly in no mood to speak to Solomon. But then when had she ever been?

'Have you charged my brother?'

'He's helping us with our enquiries.'

'You only have twenty-four hours to hold him without charge,' said Solomon. 'Are you going to charge him?'

'No, I have longer,' said Fox. 'You're aware that he's suspected of murder? That's a serious crime. I can hold him for ninety-six hours, should I need to.'

'Can I see him?'

'No.'

'I think you owe me that.'

'I'm not aware that I owe you anything,' said Fox.

'But you do,' said Solomon. 'We need to talk about tomorrow.'

'Tomorrow?'

'Your side of the deal. You and two officers of your choosing at a place and time of my choosing.'

'Sorry,' said Fox. 'Tomorrow? No way. Haven't got time.'

As he spoke to Fox, Solomon scrolled down the front page of a news site. Shots fired, he read. Man injured, Thomas Arnold arrested. Another man helping with enquiries. That would be Luke, Solomon supposed. 'I imagine that you're dealing with the fallout from yesterday.'

'A man was shot,' said Fox. 'These things tend to get noticed. Attract attention.'

'I'm guessing you wouldn't welcome more attention,' said Solomon.

'Meaning?'

'Meaning, I have a recording of you promising to provide me with assistance, in return for my help in apprehending Thomas Arnold. I imagine that if the press got hold of that recording, it would give yesterday's operation further scrutiny.'

Fox sighed and didn't answer for some time, Solomon picturing her rubbing her eyes in irritation. An ice mountain she might be, but Solomon had a toehold, and he wasn't letting go.

'Christ. Okay. What do you need?'

'Just you and two other officers. Plain clothes. I need you to be in a bar called Mr Toad's at nine o'clock.'

'Mr Toad's.'

'Yes.'

'And then what?'

'And then I will point out a man, and you will question that man.'

'Right, I remember. Ask him his name. Check him out. Remind me, on what grounds?'

'On the grounds that he is misrepresenting himself. Using a fake name.'

'That's pretty thin.'

'Still, you have agreed to help, and I have that agreement on record.'

'What did you say the name of the place was?'

'Mr Toad's.'

'Really?'

'Nine o'clock.'

'I need to go.'

'You'll be there?'

'Yes, for Christ's sake, yes, I'll be there. Are we done?'

'Yes.'

'Goodbye, Mr Mullan.'

Fox hung up and Solomon closed his eyes and took a deep, long breath. It was done. The plan was still on track, or at least kind of. He would find the man responsible for what had been done to his sister. Luke he'd worry about later.

Kay was at the lab and couldn't be disturbed, so Solomon applied Marija's make-up and put on his eye patch and walked to the hospital, taking his time, trying to enjoy the bright sunshine and the sense of freedom that his new, acceptable appearance gave him. He took the lift up to Tiffany's room and looked through the window. She was awake and sitting up. He tapped on the glass and she smiled when she saw him, waved him in.

'Hey, Tiff.'

'Solly! You turned into a pirate or something?'

'What do you think?'

'Hmmm.' She tilted her head to one side. 'Not sure. Where's your parrot?'

'It's supposed to look hench.'

'That what they told you?' She giggled. 'Only joking. You look all right, you do. What is it, make-up?'

'Something like that,' said Solomon, sitting down on the chair next to her bed. Just hearing his sister's voice, its cheerfulness and artlessness, made him feel immediately better.

'Well, it looks good. You look good.'

'Thanks.'

'Bring me grapes?'

'I forgot.'

'Some brother.' Tiffany frowned, then said, 'Talking of brothers, where's that Luke? Hasn't come to see me once.'

'He's around,' said Solomon. 'He sends his love. You know what he's like.'

'Thought he must be in prison or something. Again.'

'Not yet,' said Solomon, glad not to have to lie to his sister. 'Anyway, how are you? Got any memory back?'

'No. Worst blackout of my life. The doctor says it'll take time.' She shrugged. 'Could be worse. Least I'm still here.'

'Yes. I'm glad about that.'

'Should hope you are.' She frowned again. 'Are you all right? You look like you've got things on your mind.'

'I'm fine.'

'No you ain't. Don't have to tell me if you don't want to.'

'Really, Tiffany, I'm fine.'

'Suit yourself. Here, you want to make yourself useful?'

'Yes.'

'Go out and get me as many magazines as you can carry.'

'What kind of magazines?'

'The glossy kind. Duh.'

On his way out of the hospital, Solomon realized that he was glad he had come to see his sister, more than glad, grateful. Because there she was, a good, kind, honest person who had had violence visited on her by somebody who was not worthy, who had no right to touch such goodness, to violate such innocence. And if that counted for Tiffany, then it did so for every other woman who had suffered at his hands. And although it was dangerous, and although it might end in tragedy, Solomon now knew that what he and Kay were doing was both right and necessary. Sometimes logic and reasoning only took you so far. This was something that even Solomon recognized. Sometimes you just had to do what you thought was right, regardless of the consequences.

thirty-eight

MR TOAD'S HAD ONCE BEEN A CINEMA, BUT THAT CINEMA HAD long closed, probably, Solomon imagined, because it'd only had one small screen, and today's consumer wanted choice, and wanted that choice to be big, loud and in Dolby 5.1 surround. Where film titles had once been displayed over its entrance it now read *MR TOAD'S*, and next to the words was a stylized cut-out toad in a top hat triumphantly holding up a glass of something transparent and presumably alcoholic.

This Friday night it was busy and warm, and people were standing outside on the pavement holding plastic cups filled with more translucent liquid. Judging by the noise level, that liquid was alcoholic too. It had been years since Solomon had been to a bar, and he unconsciously slowed down as he got closer, like a showjumper approaching a challenging fence. He couldn't see Fox outside and so he took a moment to centre himself and pushed his way through the crowd on the pavement, into the bar.

Inside, the crowd was thinner. There was a large, dim open space, with a long bar taking up the entire back wall. To Solomon's left were three tall copper stills that looked like they were working, a tangle of piping leading up into the ceiling. There was no music, only the buzz of conversation and laughter.

He looked around and saw Fox standing with two men, all of them drinking and giving the impression that they were tourists who had stumbled upon the place by mistake and weren't at all sure that the accident was a happy one. He couldn't see Demmy, though he knew that faces were tricky things. Clubmaster glasses, curly hair. That was all he had to go on. He scanned the crowd. No. He wasn't here. Not yet.

He took out his phone and texted Kay to let her know that it was safe to come, that they had it covered. He hadn't been sure that Fox would show, even given the leverage he had over her, but she was here and it was safe. There wasn't a lot that Demmy, or whatever the guy's real name was, could do. He would recognize Kay, approach her, Solomon would give Fox the nod, and that would be that. Whatever happened from then on was out of his hands, out of their hands. Either Fox did her job or she didn't.

Solomon waited at the bar and a man with a moustache with waxed ends asked him what he wanted.

'Gin and tonic.'

'House gin?' the man asked. Even though it had been a long time for Solomon, he couldn't remember ever having been offered the house gin.

'Fine.'

The man made his drink, pouring gin from a height, out of a bottle with a thin, curved metal spout in the end. Solomon paid and turned, leaning back against the bar and watching the room. He tried to think of the last bar he had been to. The truth was, even before the accident, he hadn't been particularly sociable. He never seemed to have much in common with the people he met. He did like football, which had always helped, although the level of detail he was able to go into did sometimes lose people.

'Nice eye patch, pal,' said a man who had just arrived at the bar. 'That's a new one. Tattoos, beards, now eye patches. Fucking hipsters. What's next?'

Solomon didn't reply, noting the level of drunken challenge in the man's voice. Better not to say anything. He thought of Luke, what Luke would have done in this situation. The man wouldn't have got past 'Nice eye patch'. Wouldn't have made it to 'pal'.

'Two lagers,' the man said to the barman. 'Pints of.' He turned back to Solomon. 'Got a wooden leg to go with it?'

'No,' said Solomon quietly.

'Say what?'

'No,' said Solomon. 'I don't.'

'Yo ho ho,' the man said, more contempt than humour in the delivery. Solomon looked across at Fox, who caught his eye and raised an eyebrow. Solomon shook his head at her. No. This wasn't their man. Just some drunken idiot looking for an easy target.

The man paid and picked up his drinks, said to Solomon as he left, 'You know you look fucking ridiculous, don't you?' Solomon watched him walk away, an unsteady swagger. This, this was exactly why he didn't ever want to go to bars.

The bar was filling up and Solomon people-watched while he waited for Kay to show. He checked his watch. Ten to nine. There was a group of men in suits, talking loudly and laughing, probably came for a drink after work and didn't fancy leaving, wanted to put off heading home for the weekend to where children and wives and responsibilities lurked. Smaller groups were dotted about, the people young and fashionable, beards and black-framed glasses and too-short trousers, which after his years in self-imposed exile Solomon now recognized as a thing, too-short trousers worn with shoes but no socks. It was strange how styles changed, particularly if you weren't around to witness the slow evolution. Rip Van Winkle, or something like that, as if he had woken up to a world subtly yet irrevocably altered.

He was nervous, his thoughts running in strange directions, disconnected, agitated. This was the bar where Demmy had chosen to meet Kay. Solomon tried to imagine how he did it, what went down. He had read about date rape, Rohypnol slipped into drinks. He guessed that was what Demmy did. Hadn't both Rebecca and Tiffany been found with drugs in their bloodstream? He watched a young woman laugh loudly and lose her balance, a man next to her having to hold her up, the man laughing too. Did he slip them drugs and then, when the effects took hold and they could no longer stand, put an avuncular arm around them and walk them outside? That would be one way to do it. That would be the obvious way to do it.

Kay came into the bar, pushing her way through the crowd. Her hair was down, ringlets spilling over her shoulders, and she was wearing make-up and a dress, a short yellow dress. Solomon felt a surge of adrenaline that he could not entirely put down to apprehension or fear. She looked beautiful; of the crowd yet apart from it, somehow unattainable, no, unclassifiable, in a way that he could not properly articulate. A mystery, he guessed. He wondered just how strong this house gin was.

Kay saw him and went cross-eyed briefly to acknowledge him, which made Solomon smile but also made him ineffably sad for a reason that he could not precisely identify. Then she walked towards the bar and stood a couple of metres from him. He had sent Fox a shot of Kay, and now he caught the inspector's eye and she nodded, a perfunctory and weary concession. Solomon didn't care. She was here and she would do what she'd promised. That was all he cared about.

He checked his watch again. Two minutes past nine. He should be here. Demmy. He'd said nine, so he should be here. Glasses, curly hair. Solomon watched the crowd, its fluidity and movement, the laughing, the shuffling, the different groups like disparate tribes, all in opposition to each other. As if some kind of underground invitational contest had been organized and here they were, waiting, waiting for the bell to ring, for something to happen. *Solomon*, he told himself. *Stop drinking that gin.*

Kay was waiting to order her drink, her elbow on the bar, a note in her hand to attract the barman. A man next to her put his hand over hers, covering the note, and said something to her, close to her ear, no way that Solomon could hear. Kay smiled and shook her head and took her hand away from beneath his. The man didn't have glasses on and his skin was dark, south Asian, but Solomon turned to Fox anyway, in case, even though he had shared the photo of Demmy with her. She knew what she was looking for. Fox caught his gaze and shook her head. He couldn't see from this distance, but he imagined that she rolled her eyes as well.

Solomon had been nursing his drink for half an hour now, and he began to feel an absurd guilt that he wasn't spending enough money to rent his place at the bar. He drank the last of his glass and turned and ordered another gin and tonic.

'House?'

'What's its strength?' Solomon said.

'Its strength?' said the barman. 'Let me think. It's organic. It's locally brewed. It creates jobs. That what you mean?'

'No,' said Solomon. 'Just ... Forget it. I'll have a beer.'

'Meant to be a joke,' said the barman. 'No offence.'

'None taken,' said Solomon. 'How about a Corona?'

The barman sighed, and said, 'Coming up.'

Solomon took his Corona. He'd forgotten that bar people always pushed a segment of lime into the top, which Solomon now pushed through into the bottle, which in turn messed with its pouring. Which Solomon enjoyed, because it gave him a chance to ponder the vagaries of nano-wave dynamics while he waited for Demmy to show. He waited, and he drank, and he tried not to look at Kay, whose presence he imagined he could actually feel, next to him though two metres away. Impossible to *actually* feel, but he could feel her anyway.

A man in glasses, Solomon didn't get a good look at the frames, walked to the bar and stood next to Kay. Curly hair. Glasses, and curly hair. Solomon looked at his bottle of Corona, suddenly imagining it as a weapon. It could serve a purpose. Was this Demmy? Solomon checked his watch. Nearly quarter past nine. Late. It had to be him. Didn't it? He looked over once again at Fox, who was watching, for the first time intently.

'And you think that's funny? In what, and I want you to be precise, exactly in what way do you think that meets the criteria of funny?' Kay had taken a step away from the man in glasses and was looking up at him with contempt. No, Solomon corrected himself, not contempt. Anger. Solomon glanced over at Fox. She was standing where she always had been, but her two companions were making their way over.

'Kay?' he said loudly, not looking at her, talking into the room. 'Is it him?'

'No,' said Kay. 'No, it's just a dickhead. Who's going to piss off, and take his woeful chat-up lines with him. Yes?'

'Lesbian,' the man said, which made Kay laugh.

'Off you go.'

'Going.'

Solomon held a hand up and Fox's officers stopped and did, in Solomon's opinion, a not-especially-subtle about-turn.

Twenty past nine. Solomon looked at Kay, who shrugged.

'What do you think?' said Solomon. 'Keep waiting?'

'Maybe,' said Kay. 'If I have to. I'm not used to this.' She gestured out at the bar. 'Meat market.'

'He'd be here,' said Solomon. 'If he was going to show.'

'I haven't seen him.'

'Me neither.'

'Or me,' said Fox quietly, appearing like some kind of cold wraith in the midst of the bar's warm noise. 'Eff why eye, we're going. Off. Obligation fulfilled, evening wasted, as anticipated.'

'Are you Inspector Fox?' said Kay.

'Yes.'

'She's exactly like you described her,' Kay said to Solomon.

Fox didn't react to this, although Solomon imagined that it would give her pause for several days, something he could not help but love Kay for. One of many things.

'It's a no-show,' said Kay, after Fox had left, taking her colleagues with her.

'Yes.'

'Shit,' said Kay. 'Something we did? Scared him off?'

'Don't think so,' said Solomon. 'Don't know.'

'What are we going to do?'

'Regroup,' said Solomon. 'Rethink.' He had no idea.

'You have no idea,' said Kay. 'But that's okay. We'll think of something.'

They walked outside and Solomon ordered a cab for Kay. 'I'm sorry,' he said.

'Why? Not your fault.'

'No,' said Solomon. He sighed. 'Why wasn't he here?'

They stood outside the bar in silence, and Kay's taxi pulled up. 'You want to share?'

'No,' said Solomon. 'You're not going my way. I think I'll walk.'

'Don't feel bad,' said Kay. 'You did all you could.'

'Maybe,' said Solomon. He watched Kay get into the cab, watched until it was out of view, then turned and walked back through the dark streets to his apartment.

thirty-nine

THE TAXI STOPPED AT A RED LIGHT AND HE WATCHED THE dark silhouette of her head and shoulders. He was in the car behind, but it didn't matter. She wasn't looking for him. She didn't know she was being followed. Again, her hubris amazed him. This woman who had said that her name was Julia. Who had said that she loved doing 'cultural stuff'. Who enjoyed the theatre, and wrote *verily* in text exchanges. He could laugh, it was all so obvious. So clumsy and amateurish.

There were two of them, he knew that now. He had seen them talking together in the bar. Her and an accomplice. A man and a woman, hubris combined. Salmoneus and Cassiopeia. It didn't matter. They had walked into the trap and now he was following her, and soon she would be part of his next performance. Julia-not-Julia whose name was now Lavinia.

The lights changed and the taxi headed down Victoria Embankment, the street lamps painting the car's roof orange. It took a left over Southwark Bridge. He followed, and as they crossed the Thames marvelled at the city's beauty, the buildings either side of the river lit up and those lights reflected by the always twisted and churning water, black and restless. This city, he thought as they drove across the bridge. What a stage, its scale and history a perfect backdrop. He wound down his window and let the night air in, breathing it in deeply, feeling an affinity with his surroundings, a shared ambition and greatness.

They drove for some time down a main route he could not name. At last the Prius took a left and he followed, keeping his distance now that the streets were narrower, even though it was dark and there was no way that the driver ahead or the woman in the back knew they were being tailed. No way at all. They took a left, another, then a right, the streets becoming narrower at every turn, more oppressive, tower blocks hemming them in, squeezing them tighter. The Prius indicated once more and pulled over on the left in front of a row of terraced three-storey Victorian houses. He passed and stopped twenty yards further up the street and wound down his window. He waited, watching the taxi in his rear-view mirror. The woman would get out, and the taxi would go, and then it would all be in the performance.

The taxi pulled away and he reversed back down the street to take its place. The woman was walking up the steps to the front door of the town house.

He opened the door and threw a mobile phone at the bottom of the steps, a soft clatter. 'You dropped your phone,' he called out.

The woman who wasn't called Julia turned. 'God,' she said, and walked back down. He got out of the car and crossed the pavement, bending to pick the phone up.

'It's fine,' the woman said. 'I can—'

He stood up and pressed the cloth into her face with one hand, holding the back of her head with the other. She struggled, but he was too strong, so strong that he had time to check up and down the street before dragging her back to his car, opening the back door and easing her in. She slumped backwards across the seat and he pushed at her and folded her legs in clumsily as if she was an awkward piece of luggage. Then he stood up and looked around. There was nobody there, nobody to see what had happened. It had all been over in seconds, perfectly performed. And if he could do it out here, in the world, there was no doubt that he would have been able to do it on the stage. If they'd let him. If they'd appreciated his talent. It didn't matter, not now. When they read about it, they would be amazed. His, they would finally realize, was a particular kind of genius.

He got back into the driver's seat and pulled away. He had a long way to travel, and he needed everything to be in place before the night ended. He looked into the rear-view mirror, where the woman was unconscious on the back seat. *Lavinia.*

forty

IT WASN'T UNTIL FOUR O'CLOCK IN THE AFTERNOON THAT
Solomon acknowledged to himself that he was panicking. Until
then he had been worried, but he had kept his worst fears sup-
pressed, endlessly spinning less catastrophic scenarios in his
head, telling himself that these were the more reasonable expla-
nations for Kay's absence, the more plausible. She was at the
lab. She was out running, shopping, she'd gone to a gallery, the
cinema. Any one of a hundred, a thousand possibilities.

He had tried messaging her at eleven but there had been no
reply. Fine, he'd thought, she's not online. Nothing remarkable
about that. He'd tried again at midday, then called her mobile.
No answer, so he'd sent her a text, asking her to call him. At one
o'clock he'd called her lab.

'Hello?'

'Hello. Could I speak to Kay Spinazzi, please?'

'Can I say who's calling?'

'Solomon Mullan.'

'I'll have a look.' He had waited, hoping, willing her to be there,
to come to the phone. He had listened to background noises, the
faint sound of two people talking and laughing, then footsteps
approaching.

'Sorry, she's not here.'

'Has she been in today?'

'Don't think so. Who did you say you were?'

Solomon had hung up and sat in his living room, telling himself to stay calm, to think rationally. He had Kay's address from the night before when he had ordered her taxi, and now he ordered another, pacing his apartment while he waited for the cab to turn up, then heading down to the street anyway, anything to keep moving, to avoid thinking. The taxi had arrived and he'd sat in the back, his hand wrapped around his mobile, hoping to feel it vibrate, to hear Kay tell him breathlessly that she was sorry she'd missed his calls, no, she hadn't realized that he'd be worried, she'd just fancied a walk and had lost track of time. But no call came, and he arrived at her address and walked up the steps to her house and rang the bell. He waited for a couple of minutes, was about to ring again when the door was opened by a man with a beard, wearing a dressing gown.

'Yeah?'

'Could I speak to Kay, please?'

The man looked Solomon up and down. Solomon was wearing make-up and his eye patch, but the man's gaze made him feel suddenly ashamed and inadequate. 'She's not here.'

'Well ... Do you know when she'll be back?'

'Search me. Don't think she came home last night. Must have got lucky.'

'She didn't come home?' Solomon couldn't keep the panic out of his voice.

The man frowned. 'Is there a problem?'

'Are you sure she didn't come home?'

He shrugged. 'Pretty sure. Is there a problem?' he asked again.

'No,' said Solomon. 'Just, if she comes back, could you tell her to call Solomon? It's very important.'

'Solomon.'

'Yes.'

'Okay.' The man stepped back into the house, then stopped. 'You want to come in?'

'No,' said Solomon. 'Thanks.' He turned and headed back down the steps and walked up Kay's street, hurriedly although he had nowhere to go and no plan. Kay was missing. She hadn't come home. She hadn't come home because, obviously, yesterday at the bar they'd thought they were oh so clever, when actually they were idiots. No, scratch that, *he* was an idiot. Solomon Mullan. There was a word for it. Hubris. Imagining that they were two steps ahead when they were one behind, always had been. Solomon hadn't even stopped to maybe consider it. And now Kay was missing and it was on him, completely on him.

He passed a park and he walked in and sat down on a bench. The day was warm and overcast and he closed his eyes and tried to think. He tried to tune out the traffic noises and the sounds of kids playing and think, really think. Had he actually done any proper thinking yet? Probably not. He'd got by on arrogance and hubris, mostly. Believing that he must be better than his foe, that if he was morally better then it must follow that he was superior in every other regard.

But who *was* this foe? Who was this person who had attacked his sister, who was causing violence to women? He took a deep breath and realized – no, he didn't realize, he acknowledged for the first time that he had no idea. None. In his mind there was nothing, a blank, an empty space. He could not understand this person, could not fathom him, could not guess his motives or comprehend his actions. He, Solomon, had been busy constructing plans to catch somebody whom he had no knowledge of beyond the superficial. The complacency of his behaviour suddenly appalled him. What had he been thinking?

So. He leant forward and put his head in his hands and tried to put these reflections aside, exchange them for a more profitable train of thought. He had acknowledged that he did not understand this person. Part of the larger picture, of how he understood facts and knowledge systems and binary problems, but did not have an instinct for people, could not get a handle on the messy business of real life. So, he needed help. He needed help, and fast.

He took out his mobile and called Inspector Fox.

'No,' she said. 'No, we're done. It's a Saturday and you've already wasted my Friday night. Enough.'

'She's missing,' said Solomon. 'Kay's missing.'

'I saw her last night.'

'She didn't get home.'

'Maybe she met somebody.'

'No. I put her in a taxi.'

'At what time?'

'Just after you left. Nine thirty.'

'So, maybe she went out somewhere else afterwards.'

'No,' said Solomon. 'No, she's missing.'

'Mr Mullan, it's only been a few hours since she was last seen. She's a grown woman. You don't think you're being … alarmist?'

'I just know that—'

'I've had enough of listening to your theories, the things you somehow know to be true. If she doesn't show up, report her missing. This has nothing to do with me.'

'You're a police officer.'

'Correct,' said Fox. 'I'm not your therapist. So please, stop treating me like it.'

'I—'

'Goodbye. Please don't call again.'

Fox hung up and Solomon sat staring at the screen of his mobile, sitting on the park bench. He had no idea what to do next, and he needed help. And if Fox wasn't going to step up, then he had only one more place left to turn. He got off the bench and headed out of the park, looking for a cab.

Solomon had only just crossed Southwark Bridge, the Thames sparkling in the evening sun, when his mobile vibrated. He entered his code and looked at his messages. A new one, from Kay. He opened it, his fingers clumsy, his hands shaking.

233038422852186516762398811179543892

He read through the numbers, then hit reply.

Kay? What does this mean?

He waited, watching the screen, feeling the taxi's motion as it turned corners on the way back to his apartment. Then, a new message:

That is all you get.

Solomon replied with a single question mark, but got nothing back. All he had was a string of numbers, which at first glance meant nothing. He sat in the back of the cab and closed his eyes. They must mean something. They had to. But he could not say what.

forty-one

'RUN THAT PAST US AGAIN, SOLOMON, IF YOU COULD,' SAID Fran. 'And please, try to calm down.'

'Kay is missing, and I believe that she has been abducted by the same person who attacked my sister and engineered the note that you have already seen, Rebecca Harrington's suicide note that used references from *Antony and Cleopatra*,' Solomon said.

'But how?' said Fran. 'How was she abducted?'

'I don't know,' said Solomon.

'And why do you think that this is the case?' said Masoud. 'Do you have evidence?'

'We found out who he was,' said Solomon. 'And by we, I mean Kay and I. And we, well, she, she arranged to meet him.'

'Oh Solomon,' said Fran. He watched her face on his laptop screen. She looked dismayed. Worse, disappointed.

'The police were there,' said Solomon. 'I thought it would be safe.'

'Then what happened?' said Fran. 'What went wrong?'

'I don't know,' said Solomon. 'I think ... I think he knew. That he was watching us, when we thought we were looking for him. And maybe, I don't know ... He didn't turn up, but then perhaps he did, and I think maybe he followed Kay.'

'How did he know who Kay was?' said Fran.

'Well, he had her photo,' said Solomon. 'It was a date. We wanted him to think he was meeting her for a date, so he needed to see her.' He stopped, then added, pointlessly, 'It's how it works, nowadays.'

'Solomon, no. How could you have?' said Fran. 'How could you have put Kay in danger?'

'I think that's enough, Fran,' said Phil. He was turning his pint with his fingers on the table in front of him and he spoke quietly but firmly. 'I imagine that young Solomon's feeling enough guilt right now.'

'And I should think—'

'I said enough,' said Phil. 'We're here to help, not castigate. We're not going to nail him to the cross for this.'

Fran thought about saying something else, stopped herself, then nodded. 'You're right, Phil. Solomon, I apologize. It's just that I'm fond of Kay.'

'I think we all are,' said Phil. 'All the more reason to listen to Solomon and try to help. So.' He looked directly at the screen, at Solomon. 'Do you have anything?'

'He sent me a list of numbers,' said Solomon. 'Let me share my screen.' The numbers replaced his avatar, so that the Brain Pool could see them:

233038422852186516762398811179543892

'He sent you that?'

'From Kay's phone, yes. I replied, and all I got was a message. *That is all you get.*'

'That was the message?' said Masoud.

301

'Yes.'

'And these numbers.'

'Yes.'

'Do they mean anything to you?'

'No.'

'From what I remember,' said Fran, 'the hypothesis was that this person was casting women in the role of tragic heroines. By women, I mean his victims.'

'Yes,' said Solomon. 'Kay had a theory, that these heroines were being chosen in the opposite order Shakespeare wrote them.'

'Cleopatra,' said Masoud. 'Who else was there?'

'Ophelia. And Portia.'

'She wasn't a tragic heroine,' said Fran. 'She was just a heroine, and a good one.'

'I mean the Portia from *Julius Caesar*,' said Solomon, 'not *The Merchant of Venice*. There was a story in the paper, about a woman who had been forced to eat hot coals.'

'My God,' said Fran. 'And you think that was him?'

'She'd been on a date,' said Solomon. 'It all fits.'

'And the police,' said Masoud. 'They know all this?'

'All of it,' said Solomon. 'They're not interested.'

'Sounds right,' said Phil. 'Doesn't serve their purposes. Too intellectual. Beyond them. Shouldn't be the thin blue line, should be the thick one, you ask me.'

'Yes, thank you, Phil,' said Fran. 'So who did Kay think was next?'

'Juliet,' said Masoud. 'No, Solomon?'

'Right. And we put the hypothesis to the test, and this person, whoever he is, he used references from *Romeo and Juliet* in his messages to Kay.' Solomon thought back to them, the mentions of death and night, toads and distilled liquors. They couldn't have got that wrong.

'GPS coordinates?' said Phil.

'I thought of that,' said Solomon. 'They don't correspond, no matter what I try. Cyclical, repetition, polynomial, I've tried algorithms, can't find a pattern they match. Phone numbers, post office protocols, IP addresses. These numbers mean nothing, whatever I do with them. Either he's a mathematical genius, or it's something else.'

'Alphabetical?'

'No. I ran it through everything I could think of, and it only returns random strings of letters.'

'The text,' said Masoud. 'Have you gone to the text? *Romeo and Juliet*?'

'First thing I tried,' said Solomon. 'Look at the first five numbers. Act Two, Scene Three, line thirty, word three.'

'And?'

'And I get the word *the*. From the line, *Full soon the canker death eats up the plant.*'

'It sounds reasonable,' said Fran. '*The*. Often the beginning of a sentence.'

'Yes, but look at what comes next. Which number.'

'Eight.'

'That should designate the start of the next sequence. It should denote the act number, but *Romeo and Juliet* doesn't have eight acts,' said Solomon. 'So the pattern doesn't work.'

'How about if you use the first six numbers of the sequence,' said Fran. 'Act Two, Scene Three, line three hundred and three, word eight.'

'There are only ninety-four lines in Scene Three,' said Solomon. 'It doesn't work.'

The Brain Pool were silent for a moment, Phil busying himself with his drink.

'Oh God,' said Fran, breaking the silence. 'Poor Kay.'

'The question I have,' said Solomon, 'is why? I don't understand this person. Why is he doing this? It's so ... theatrical.'

'Because he wants people to appreciate him,' said Phil. 'That's obvious, right? To him, this, all of this, it's a performance. I'll bet my house that your man's a failed actor who's now got some shitty job, and he's eaten up by resentment, watching his contemporaries make it. Classic narcissistic personality. Can't get my own way? Then I'll show you.'

'It explains the theatricality,' said Fran.

'He's transferred his animosity,' said Phil. 'From the theatre to the world in general. All the world's a stage, right?'

'That's crazy,' said Solomon.

'Won't argue with you there,' said Phil. 'I expect he's psychotic.'

'Then what do we do?' said Solomon.

'Keep running those numbers,' said Phil. 'He wants you to find him. He won't have made it too hard, that's not what he wants. He wants the attention, I expect he wants to be caught.' He nodded. 'Definitely. Otherwise, how does he get the reviews he wants?'

'All the world's a stage,' said Fran. 'And we're his audience.'

'We all are,' said Phil. 'We just don't know it yet.'

'The answer is in those numbers, I have to agree with Philip,' said Masoud. 'But Solomon, the police need to be dealing with a situation like this.'

'I know,' said Solomon. 'I know. And I've tried. I just can't see how—'

'So here's what we do,' said Phil, setting his drink down and sitting up straight in his seat. 'We all report Kay missing. Each one of us. Fran, call me and leave a message on my voicemail. Say that you're Kay, and that you're worried because somebody's been following you. Call Masoud and tell him the same thing. Got it?'

'That's illegal,' said Fran.

Phil waggled a hand. 'It's a grey area. But if Masoud and I play it to them, it'll mean they have to act immediately. Yes?'

'All right,' said Fran slowly.

'Good. Solomon, keep running those numbers. There's something there, there's got to be.'

'How do you come to know so much about how the police work?' said Fran.

'I'm an anarchist,' said Phil. 'It's my duty.'

Solomon broke the connection and called Fox. Again. He had called and called, left messages, but had no reply. Outside it was dark, the day almost over. He looked again at the string of numbers he had been sent. The answer was there. And if he could find it, then the police would have to listen. He went to the kitchen and made coffee, then sat back down in front of his screen, wondering what else was left to try.

forty-two

GOD, SHE WAS SO ANGRY, SO ANGRY AND FULL OF RAGE WITH nowhere to direct it. Solomon, I trusted you. I trusted you to steer a way through this, to elegantly weave through the variables and arrive at a safe harbour, trophy in your hands. And you fucked it up. How could I have trusted you, how could I have believed that you were infallible, like some supernatural being, sent from the stars to challenge and liberate and, ultimately, love me? How could I have been such an idiot?

And how could I have fallen for it? How? Some random in a car pulls up and tells me I've dropped my phone and, what? I giggle like a sixteen-year-old out on the town for the first time, five too many sambucas in me, and I patter, I remember it and I actually did, I actually *pattered* down those steps in my little dress into the jaws of some crazy who I *already knew was out there*. The idiocy of it all was almost worthy of an independent inquiry, a jury of peers who could look at it cold-bloodedly and work out a five-point action plan to ensure that This Never Happened Again.

But she was grateful for the anger, was trying to guard it, shield its heat from the cold threat of terror that was close, and getting closer. She was in a pit, her hands tied behind her back, bound tightly together with something hard and sharp. Cable ties, she thought. The pit smelt of earth, damp and claylike, and the edges of the pit were ragged and moist, but in the absolute darkness she could see nothing at all. So she sat in the darkness and tried to retain her anger, keep it hot, and think of the things that this monster wanted to take away from her, but that she would not allow. The things that even in this hideous black pit she would not, *would not*, let him take from her.

Like her work. Her experiment. The One. She had been engaged in it for three years already and it looked like lasting for a whole lot longer, and she needed to be around to see it. Because she'd put so much of herself into it, it had been her idea, her yet-to-be-proven stroke of genius, her revolutionary use of enzymes to bridge the organic/composite divide and create artificial life, genuinely artificial, quasi-sentient life. And that was worth living and breathing and fighting for.

She had done the science bit already. She'd tried to move the board covering the pit she was in, but there was no way it was going anywhere. She'd got to her knees, then her feet, and used her back, pushing up with her legs. She'd read somewhere that your legs were stronger than your arms by some ridiculous factor. But the board hadn't moved, hadn't even buckled. She'd tried digging with her hands but she could barely move them, they were bound together so tightly. And so she'd made the reluctant but pragmatic decision to conserve her strength for the unlikely event that she was in a position to get away, to make a break for it.

What else did she not want to lose, would not accept losing? Solomon. Because even though she was trapped in a pitch-black pit beneath an immovable board, she knew that Solomon was out there, and she still believed in him, at least kind of, despite her fury. He was quiet and shy and awkward but he had something, there was something other-worldly about him, assured in a way she had never encountered in anyone before. He was out there and he would be looking for her, and just the thought of that made her feel better. Not much better, but better, better-ish. She didn't know why, could never have explained it. Yet there it was. She had an unshakeable faith in a young, unassuming, diffident man with a face most people couldn't bear to look at. Why, she could not say.

It was dank and not warm in the pit and Kay only had on the dress she'd worn to the bar, and as hard as she tried, she couldn't get it to cover more than about sixty per cent of her body, the rest of it cold and getting colder, unable to generate warmth against the cool soil. She wondered whether it was day or night, and how long she had been trapped here. A few hours? A day? Longer? Her anger was dwindling, was almost gone, no match for the chill fear that this pit was pushing out from its sides. No match at all.

Okay, she was scared. She nodded, acknowledging her state of mind in the blackness. She was scared, and that was fine, but at least she wasn't panicking. No, she wasn't panicking yet. And why? Because, along with her kind-of belief in Solomon, she also knew, or at least was pretty sure, what was coming. What was planned for her. She was Juliet, and Juliet killed herself after, as far as Kay could recall, a fraught chain of events involving a sleeping potion and a gullible boyfriend. So this wasn't finished. She wasn't going to die down here; she was going to have her apparent suicide carefully stage-managed. Which meant that there would be a confrontation with her tormentor, she would have to see him again, at least once. And although she was scared, she knew that she wouldn't be left down here forever, to starve to death. She would have her confrontation, and they would see. Or Solomon would come to the rescue. Whatever. It wasn't over yet.

There was a noise above her, footsteps on the board, and she called out, 'Help!'

No response.

'Help. Please, I'm trapped.'

Nothing.

'I'm trapped. Please. Help. You have to.'

Still nothing.

'Call the police. Just call them. Get them here, now.'

She stopped yelling and listened. The footsteps had stopped. She held her breath and felt the perfect silence, the damp indifference of the soil walls. She narrowed her eyes to concentrate better, even though she was in absolute darkness. And then she heard a voice, a man's voice, muffled through the board over the top of her pit, so muffled that she struggled to make the words out.

'First thrash the corn, then after burn the straw.'

'What? What did you say? Hey! I'm trapped. Down here.' Kay banged on the board above her with her knee, as hard as she could, shouting, 'Help! Help me!'

'First thrash the corn, then after burn the straw.' The voice was louder this time, and Kay was sure that she'd heard right. She heard the sound of footsteps again, this time moving away, and she slumped down into the corner of the pit and pulled her knees up under her chin. That had been him. But it obviously wasn't time yet, time for whatever he had planned. And what

was that he had said? *First thrash the corn, then after burn the straw.* She didn't recognize that from *Romeo and Juliet*, had never heard it before. She didn't know what it meant, but it had the ring of violence to it. And for the first time since she'd found herself in the pit, Kay began to feel a terror she was not sure she could control.

forty-three

CHRIST, FOX WAS TIRED. WHAT A WEEK SHE'D HAD. SHE'D RUN A successful operation but had still had to put up with all kinds of crap from senior officers who wanted to know who had sanctioned what, who'd okayed the wire and the use of firearms and the presence of an informant, and the money, so many questions about the money. Where had it come from? If it had been made under exploitative conditions, if there was a human cost to it, then where should it go? How should it be redistributed? Who gave a toss? thought Fox. Give it to the donkey sanctuary. She didn't care. They didn't need to know where it came from; they had Thomas Arnold and Luke Mullan in custody, and Thomas Arnold on tape talking about laundering the money they were so conflicted about. They should be promoting her, not wringing their hands. In fairness, her superior, Goven, had eventually told them all to piss off and leave her alone, but still. And this Solomon Mullan, like a fly she couldn't swat, always buzzing around her, one crazy theory after another. She'd had enough of this week and yet here she was, working another Sunday. Enough. Enough already.

But the truth was that, although she'd had a hell of a week, she hadn't slept well, either. She had a feeling, a nagging feeling, like when you leave home and remember you might have left the stove on, but by that time you're so far away that going back is too much of an ask, so you leave it. You leave it, but you can't forget it. That was the feeling she had. And it was all down to that one phrase. *Cocktails of infinite variety.* The phrase that had been in Rebecca Harrington's message exchange with her date. Because Fox had recognized it back then, immediately, recognized it from *Antony and Cleopatra.* But she'd had other things on her mind, other priorities, so she had ignored it. She was ninety, well, okay, seventy per cent certain that it meant nothing. But it was there, the feeling, and it wasn't going away.

She opened the door to her office and sat down behind her desk. She had a day of paperwork ahead of her, the aftermath of her, let's not forget, *successful* operation to put a major money launderer behind bars. She looked without enthusiasm at the papers stacked on her desk. This was no way to spend a Sunday. She should be hanging out with friends, meeting for lunch, spending the day drinking and laughing. Yeah, right. As if that ever happened. She'd long accepted that she wasn't the drinking-and-laughing type. Or the having-lots-of-friends type either, come to think of it.

There was a note on her desk. A sergeant had called from Islington nick, wanted Fox to call back. Whoever it was had left a mobile number, but not a name. Fox didn't recognize the number, and anyway, it was Sunday. How important could it be? And even if it was, frankly, she didn't care, not right now. She had forms to complete, actions to justify. She took a pen out of her desk tidy and got to work.

*

By lunchtime, Fox had had enough. She put down her pen and leant back in her chair, rubbing her eyes. She didn't want to be doing this. Admin. Couldn't somebody else do it? She was management, she shouldn't be filling in forms. She should be making decisions, and delegating the small stuff to some fresh-faced sergeant. Speaking of sergeants, she remembered the note that had been on her desk. She dug it out from beneath her papers. Still didn't recognize the number, but what the hell, she'd call it anyway.

She picked up her mobile and dialled the number, listening to it ring the other end. It went through to voicemail, where a Sergeant Bright asked her to leave a message, which she didn't. Sergeant Bright. She recognized the name but couldn't place it. She put her phone down on her desk and left her office, wondering if there was anything edible being served downstairs. The canteen was closed, a cleaner mopping the floor, and Fox swore and walked through to the front of the station, wondering where would be open on a Sunday. A uniformed officer was putting a poster up, and Fox gave it a glance, then stopped.

'Who told you to put that up?' she said.

'This? Just came through.'

The poster's headline read, *Missing*, and underneath was a shot of Kay Spinazzi.

'Came through from where?' she said.

'I don't know,' said the officer. 'Just an email. Asking us to circulate the poster.'

Fox's feeling of unease increased, suddenly ratcheted up. She'd ignored Solomon Mullan, but he'd got somebody to listen. Now it was official, and she ... Shit. She was implicated, she was part of this, and if it all went south, then she'd be in the firing line. She'd ignored Mullan and now, somewhere, there were other officers looking into it. She felt a surge of fear, of dread. *Cocktails of infinite variety.* She shouldn't have ignored it. Maybe she shouldn't have ignored it.

Fox turned and went back upstairs to her office, her hands tingling in near panic. As she walked along the corridor, she remembered the name, it came back to her. Sergeant Bright. The officer who'd suggested there was a connection between Tiffany Mullan and ... she couldn't remember who. The woman who'd been found in that church. Shit. What did he want? She got to her office and saw that she'd missed a call. From Bright. God. She sat down and put her hands on her face, fingers over her eyes. Okay, she thought. Okay. Breathe. You need to jump on this, jump on this now. Before it's too late. If it's not already too late.

She returned Bright's call, listened to it ring through again.

'Sergeant Bright.'

'Sergeant, it's Inspector Fox.'

'Yes, Inspector. Thanks for calling me back.'

'No problem.' Calm, she thought. Speak calmly. 'How can I help you?'

'Right, yes. Well, I came across another case, not one of ours, but I heard talk of it.'

'Yes?'

'A young woman who had been abducted but escaped. This was several days ago. She was hit by a car and taken to hospital.'

'And this relates to me how?'

'She'd been on a date, somebody she met online. One of those swipe-if-you-like-me things. She'd been drugged and woke up in a pit.'

'But she escaped.'

'Right. So anyway, I thought I'd share it with you.'

'Thank you.' Fox breathed slightly easier. It didn't sound like there was a strong link. 'Anything else?'

'Nothing specific. I'll forward you the case details. Well, apart from one thing, the reason it got me thinking.'

'Oh?'

'Just something odd. A phrase, the one thing she can remember her abductor saying.'

'Which was?'

'Hold on.' She waited. 'Here we are. *First thrash the corn, then after burn the straw.* Apparently that's what he said.'

'Which means?' said Fox, scribbling it down, feeling her sense of dread washing back, stronger than last time, a tide coming in, some kind of reckoning arriving.

'No idea,' said Sergeant Bright. 'It's a line from Shakespeare. From *Titus Andronicus*, that's all I know.'

Fox felt an urge to vomit. She closed her eyes and concentrated on breathing, slowly, gently.

'Inspector Fox?'

'Thank you,' she managed. 'I'll be in touch.'

She hung up and dropped her phone as if it was suddenly too hot to hold. She scratched her head with both hands. Her heart was beating too fast and she could feel sweat prickling on her scalp. Shit shit shit. Oh God. Oh shit. She sat motionless for minutes, running scenarios through her head. They all ended with her getting fired, or at the very best demoted, with no chance of career progression. She needed to act. At least if she acted, it would be recognized; her superiors would be able to see that she'd tried. Made an attempt at redeeming the situation.

She picked her phone up again and called Solomon Mullan. He answered on the second ring.

'Inspector.'

'Solomon, I need to—'

'You need to help me. Kay has been abducted and—'

'I know,' said Fox. 'Listen to me.' Solomon sounded manic, on the edge. They both were. 'Are you listening?'

'Yes.'

'I have some new information,' she said.

'Yes?'

'Other cases,' Fox said. 'That have just come to my attention.' Which was true, or at least half true.

'What other cases?'

'A woman was found drugged, last week. It might be related.'

'Drugged? Where?'

'In a church,' said Fox.

'What happened?'

'She was discovered. Alive. She'd been there for a couple of days.'

'Asleep?'

'Yes.'

'Oh, Jesus,' said Solomon. He sounded more panicked now than he had when he picked up. 'Juliet. That was Juliet.'

'Sorry?'

'We were wrong. Kay and I, we—'

'There's something else,' said Fox. 'Another case. This time the woman escaped.'

'When?'

'Recently.'

'How recently?'

'Several days ago,' said Fox. 'That's all I know. But Solomon, she remembered her abductor quoting a line from Shakespeare.'

'*Titus Andronicus*,' said Solomon.

'Yes,' said Fox, momentarily astonished. 'How did—'

'It doesn't matter. Inspector, I need your help.'

'Of course,' said Fox, as if her assistance had never been in question.

'Stay by your phone,' Solomon said. 'I'll get back to you. Just be there. Can you do that?'

'I'll be here,' said Fox. 'But what exactly—'

'I'll get back to you,' said Solomon, and cut the connection, leaving Fox with a silent phone to her ear and an almost overwhelming sense of dread and culpability. This could be her career, right here.

forty-four

KAY WAS TRAPPED SOMEWHERE BETWEEN SLEEP AND WAKE-
fulness, the cold against her flesh piercing her sleep, her bound
hands painful, but her mind too exhausted to break the delicate
surface of consciousness. In this fitful state she dreamed, and in
this dream the cover of the pit she was in had been removed and
she was looking up at the silhouette of a man, black against the
dark night sky above him, and he was whispering down at her,
repeating the same words, again and again.

First thrash the corn, then after burn the straw.

She turned and twisted, half asleep, senselessly trying to find
a comfortable and warm position in the pit. In her dream the
man left, and the sky above her was now bright, a bright blue,
full daylight. And Solomon appeared at the top of the pit, no
eye patch or sunglasses, and his face wasn't scarred, and he was
handsome and perfect, his curly hair framing his face as he
looked down at her. Only now the pit she was in was deep, so
deep, and Solomon was reaching down and she was reaching
up, but their hands couldn't meet, would never meet, and she
was crying, and it was no good, no good at all, because she was
trapped in her pit forever.

Kay writhed and shivered in her pit, and dreamed, dreamed

of being saved by Solomon, but in her dreams he was too late, always too late. She didn't blame him, though. No, she didn't blame him, because she loved him and at least he was trying. At least he was doing that.

Titus Andronicus. Solomon looked back at Kay's message exchanges with her abductor, the man who had called himself Demmy.

> *Do you know Mr Todlq's?*
>
> *No. Sounds … weird.*
>
> *I mean Mr Toad's. Which also sounds … weird. But it's pretty cool. All drinks freshly distilled.*
>
> *What time?*
>
> *At dead time of the night.*

He got the play up on his computer, *Titus Andronicus*, the full text. Searched for 'toad'. An immediate hit:

> *The thousand swelling toads, as many urchins,*
> *Would make such fearful and confused cries.*

He searched for 'distilled'. Another result:

> *Upon whose leaves are drops of new-shed blood*
> *As fresh as morning dew distill'd on flowers*

Finally, 'dead time of the night'. Another hit. Solomon leant back in his chair and read:

And when they show'd me this abhorred pit,
They told me, here, at dead time of the night,
A thousand fiends, a thousand hissing snakes,
Ten thousand swelling toads, as many urchins,
Would make such fearful and confused cries
As any mortal body hearing it
Should straight fall mad, or else die suddenly.

Titus Andronicus. He had latched onto *Romeo and Juliet*, rationalized the references, the imperfect references, reached an erroneous conclusion based on imprecise data. Latched onto *Romeo and Juliet* without exploring any other possibilities. He had been wrong, wrong the whole time. It was Lavinia. Kay had been cast as Lavinia, who was attacked and raped and mutilated by Tamora's sons, Chiron and Demetrius. Demmy. Raped, her hands cut off and her tongue cut out. No. No, it couldn't happen. It couldn't. He had to stop it, had to be allowed to stop it.

The numbers. Run the numbers, according to your original hypothesis. That they match the text, that they correspond to acts, scenes and lines in the play.

23303842285218651676239881179543892

Okay. First, 233038. Act 2, Scene 3, line 303, word 8. Solomon found the scene and counted lines. Such a long scene, he forced himself to count slowly. Get it right. Here was the line:

For, by my soul, were there worse end than death.

The eighth word. *End.* He wrote it down, moved to the next sequence. 42285. Act 4, Scene 2, line 28, word 5. He counted again, quicker this time, and found the line:

But were our witty empress well afoot.

The fifth word was *empress.* Solomon moved on, through the next five sequences.

Act 2, Scene 1, line 8, word 6.

Hill.

Act 5, Scene 1, line 67, word 6.

Buried.

Act 2, Scene 3, line 98, word 8.

Pit.

Act 1, Scene 1, line 79, word 5.

Twenty.

Act 4, Scene 3, line 89, word 2.

Hours.

End empress hill buried pit twenty hours.

Twenty hours. How long had it been since he'd received the message? He checked his phone. 18.47. Twenty hours from then was 14.47. What time was it now? Gone two. 14.28. Nineteen minutes. There were nineteen minutes left to find her. Solomon opened another window and pulled up Google Maps, typed in *Empress Hill.* One result, in Epping. He called Fox, who answered immediately.

'Yes?'

'I think I know where she is. Where Kay is.'

'How?'

'Doesn't matter right now. Empress Hill. It's in Epping.'

x

'What is it, a street?'

'Yes. The information I have is that she is buried in a pit at the end of Empress Hill.'

'She's *what*?'

'We have nineteen minutes to find her.'

'Slow down. How do you know this?'

Solomon forced himself to stay calm, to speak clearly. 'I've been sent a message. A cryptic one. Specifically, it reads *end empress hill buried pit twenty hours.*'

'Twenty hours. What's that, a deadline?'

'It leaves us nineteen minutes.'

'I'll send a car,' said Fox, 'and meet you there. Give me your address.'

Solomon gave Fox his address and she hung up. He went back to his screen and stared at the map, at Empress Hill. Kay was there, and he was here, and he was too late. He couldn't be too late, but he was. Because there were nineteen minutes left to find her, which wasn't long enough. Wasn't nearly long enough. He bunched his fists and rubbed his head, as hard as he could. Too late. Much too late.

forty-five

HIS GOAL WAS AUTHENTICITY, STRIPPED OF ARTIFICE AND theatricality. His ambition was the purest form of performance possible. His drama was real, played out on the world stage, his players entirely genuine, experiencing the emotions rather than acting them out. Feeling the fear and the pain on the most visceral level. It was that realism, that authenticity, that made his art so pure. That made his art of the highest form possible, an emphatic riposte to all those who had doubted him and his ability.

Lavinia was still there. They hadn't found her. She had been in her pit for nearly twenty hours now and they hadn't found her. He thought of his pursuers. If they were coming, they would have been here by now. Perhaps the challenge had been too cryptic for them. They could not understand. But the thought of them out there, looking for him, gave his role an extra dimension, heightened the tension. For wasn't Demetrius caught in the end? Caught and murdered? He welcomed the tension to the role. It added to the authenticity.

It was nearly time. Nearly time to thrash the corn. In the forest behind him there was a recently felled tree; that was where it would happen. The axe was new and unused and had a blade that was sharp enough to cut skin when you rubbed your thumb along its edge. Lavinia's wrists were not thick and should not be enough to trouble the blade when it came down. For the tongue there was a knife and pliers, although how that would play out was still uncertain. The cutting-out of a tongue was a difficult act to imagine. It was a difficult act to imagine and would be a difficult act to carry out. But for the sake of purity and authenticity, it was necessary.

He walked across the forest clearing to the board. Two oil barrels filled with concrete were on top, lying on their sides, held in place by wooden chocks. They would take some shifting, he knew, because he had rolled them on there in the first place. He should get to work. There was little time left, just over thirty minutes. He was nervous. This was a key performance, the apotheosis of all that he had been working towards. The key performance, but the most challenging. He took a deep breath, then stepped forward onto the board.

From Wapping to Empress Hill in Epping was 18.2 miles. Imagining a constant speed of sixty miles per hour, it would take 18.2 minutes. Reduce that speed to fifty miles per hour and it would take 21.84 minutes. Up it to seventy and it would only take 15.6. The police car Solomon was in was using its lights and sirens, but it was still doing nowhere near sixty. Or fifty. Another red light ahead, another queue of traffic to navigate, the cars pulling to the left and right to create a passage for the police car to crawl through. At forty miles per hour, it would take 27.3 minutes to travel 18.2 miles. At thirty miles per hour it would take 36.4. But they didn't have that amount of time. Solomon looked again at his watch. 14.44. He'd waited seven minutes for the police car and had been in it for three, and they hadn't yet done four miles. There were three minutes left. To travel 18.2 miles in three minutes would involve driving at 364 miles per hour. There was no chance.

His phone rang. Fox. He picked up. 'Yes?'

'I've got officers on the scene, at Empress Hill. There's nobody there.'

'There has to be.'

'Nobody. An empty pit, but nobody there.'

Solomon thought of the play, of *Titus Andronicus*. The exact wording. *Exeunt DEMETRIUS and CHIRON, dragging off LAVINIA.* She might not be there, but she had to be close.

'Where is the pit? In a forest?'

'I don't know. I'm not there yet. *Get out of the fucking way,*' she shouted at someone or something on the other end. 'Traffic's murder.'

'She must be close,' said Solomon. 'Tell them to find her.'

'They're waiting for extra officers,' said Fox. 'They want reinforcements.'

'There's no time.'

'They haven't been briefed on the situation. They won't move until they get reinforcements, or I get there.'

'How far out are you?'

'Hold on.' He heard her ask somebody, presumably the driver. 'Seven miles away.'

Solomon checked his watch. Twenty-eight seconds left to go. To cover the distance, she'd need to travel at … He thought for a moment. Nine hundred miles per hour. Too late, much too late. 'Please,' he said. 'Just send help.'

'Doing my best,' said Fox. 'I'll call you if I hear anything.'

Solomon sat back as they hit the A406 and stayed left to take the M11, the lanes clear in front of them, their speed approaching a hundred. They'd be there soon, they had to be right behind Fox. They'd be there soon, but not soon enough.

First she'd heard the sound of something heavy being moved above her. Then he'd pulled away the board covering the pit she was in, daylight flooding in. She'd had to close her eyes, she was so unused to the light, to any light at all. He'd thrown down a crate and she'd stepped onto it and he'd pulled her out, over the edge of the pit. She was in a forest clearing, the sunlight warm against her cold skin. He stood there looking down at her.

He didn't look like his photo, the photo he'd used for his online profile. He wasn't wearing glasses and his hair was short, very short. Without the curls and the glasses his face was difficult to describe. White, blank, characterless. Just a face.

'Let me go,' she said.

'No, I won't do that,' he said.

'Please.'

'I cannot.'

Kay was kneeling on the ground, bare dirt covered with patchy ivy. She tried to stand up, her bound hands making her as unsteady as a toddler.

'Please. People will be looking for me.'

'Yet they haven't found you.'

'They will.'

He smiled. 'All too late. Come.'

He held her by the arm and pulled her.

'Where are we going?'

'To a barren detested vale.'

326

'No.' Kay struggled free from his grip. 'No. I don't want to.'

'*Where never shines the sun.*' He intoned the words as if possessed, as if another voice was speaking them, using him as a mouthpiece. '*Where nothing breeds.*'

'What? Please, I don't know what you're talking about.'

'I think you do.'

'No,' said Kay. It was true. She didn't. She didn't recognize anything of what he was saying. Whatever it was, it wasn't in *Romeo and Juliet*.

'Come.' He reached for her again, and Kay stepped to the side, leaving him off balance, then launched herself at him, colliding with him shoulder to shoulder. He staggered and put a foot out to steady himself, but his foot slipped on the edge of the pit and Kay slammed into him again and he fell backwards into the pit.

Kay turned and looked at the forest surrounding the clearing. Which way was safety? She didn't know, and she didn't have time to think. She ran, her sandals not easy to run in, through the trees. She couldn't put her arms out to push aside the branches of the trees, and they caught at her as she ran, snagging on her skin. The floor of the forest was uneven, covered with tree roots and pieces of wood, dead branches and whole rotting trunks, and with her hands bound behind her she couldn't run fast, couldn't properly balance. She felt as if she had only just learnt, had yet to master the complex act of running. Behind her she could hear him shouting, not far away, not far away at all, and she raced ahead, through branches that tore and clawed and cut her skin until her foot slipped on a rotting log and her ankle turned beneath her with a popping sound, then pain, huge pain, and she lay on her side looking up at the blue sky through the trees as his voice got louder and louder and closer and closer.

By the time Solomon arrived, Fox was already out of her car and talking to two uniformed officers. They were at the end of a residential street that had a wooden fence at the end with a gate set into it. Fox looked up as Solomon got out of the police car.

'Let's go,' she said.

'This is it?'

'Backup's two minutes away,' she said. 'You want to wait for them?'

'No.'

'So let's go.' She nodded to the officers and they went through the gate and up a trail, which narrowed to almost nothing before coming to a clearing. In it were two oil barrels on their sides, and a pit half covered by a large wooden board.

'*Tumble me into some loathsome pit, where never man's eye may behold my body,*' said Solomon.

'Sorry?'

'Nothing,' said Solomon. 'She should be here.'

'She may be near,' said Fox. 'But where? We've got the whole forest to search.'

Solomon looked at the trees surrounding them. He couldn't even see the trail they'd come by. Somewhere in there was Kay. But like Fox said, where? They could search for weeks without finding her. He felt a sick wash of dread and despair. They were too late, and now she was gone, and it was all down to him and the false assumptions he had made.

'We've got more officers arriving,' Fox said. 'We can search properly. By grid. We'll find her.'

'Maybe,' said Solomon. He didn't say anything else, but

thought of Kay and what her abductor had planned for her. Rape, her hands cut off, her tongue cut out. They might find her, it was true. But finding her wasn't what Solomon was worried about.

'I've asked for a helicopter,' said Fox. 'I'm waiting. They'll have thermal imaging.'

Solomon nodded, gazing around him at the quiet forest, the silence broken by the crackle of one of the officer's radios. The officer responded, then left the clearing, the way he had come. To meet the backup, Solomon supposed. Fox walked to the pit and looked down into it, then turned to Solomon and was about to say something when they heard a sound. Fox stood quite still, listening.

'That was—' said the officer, but she silenced him with a finger and a look. The three of them stood silently, and heard the sound again. This time it was clearer. A woman's voice, screaming in fear or rage, coming from within the forest.

'You, stay there,' Fox said to the officer. 'Let's go,' she said to Solomon, and took off running, Solomon right behind her.

She had run away but he had pursued and caught her, and the fear and pain that she was experiencing was true and real and right, an authenticity he could hardly have dreamt of. Here, in this forest, in its dark interior, the performance was coming together in a way that no ordinary stage could have replicated or rivalled. His hand was clamped around Lavinia's neck, and she was whimpering and sobbing, her eyes closed tightly from the terror and the pain, her ankle clearly broken, bent at a hideous angle.

'First thrash the corn, then after burn the straw.'

He took his hand away from her throat and stood up. Here would do. Here would be perfect. The log that she had fallen over would serve as the block. He unbuckled his belt and opened his trousers, then paused. He wasn't ready. He had not considered this, the act, the act and the moment, and he wasn't ready. With Lavinia sobbing and her ankle broken and her face covered in dirt and tears and snot, he had not considered this. That the act would be difficult, that the pressure and the setting would affect him like this. Affect his performance. He felt a slow build of anger and shame. Authenticity. He needed authenticity, but he was not ready.

'What are you going to do?' said Lavinia, looking up at him.

'First thrash the corn, then after burn the straw.'

'You keep saying that,' she said, anger beneath the fear. 'I don't know what it means.'

'Why, Lavinia,' he said, 'of course you do.'

'Lavinia?' she said. 'I'm not ...' She closed her eyes. 'Oh no.'

'Of course you know.'

'I'm not Lavinia,' she said. 'Please.'

He bent down and rolled her over and put the sharp edge of the axe against the black cable ties that held her wrists.

'They told me, here, at dead time of the night,' he said, summoning up his darkest tone, his most ominous expression, as befitted the scene. *'A thousand fiends, a thousand hissing snakes, Ten thousand swelling toads, as many urchins ...'* He cut through the ties and pushed her shoulder to get her on her back again. *'Would make such fearful and confused cries, As—'*

'Please.' This time the word was not an entreaty but something else, something mocking, disdainful.

'As any mortal body hearing it,' he said, ignoring her, *'Should straight fall mad, or else die suddenly.'* He stopped and stood up straight, then repeated, *'Or else die suddenly.'*

'You're not on stage,' she said. 'You're not an actor. You're ...' She paused, searching for the word, closing her eyes tightly in pain before opening them again and looking right at him. 'You're ridiculous.'

'No, Lavinia, no ...'

'I'm not Lavinia. My name is Kay Spinazzi and I'm a research scientist. And you ...' She stopped, caught her breath as pain racked her. 'You are, I don't know what you are. A joke.'

'No,' he said, heat flushing his face. 'I am ... You don't understand. This is ... purity.'

'You don't have a cl—' She stopped again, pausing a moment to master her pain. 'A girlfriend, do you?' She laughed, a brief snort of breath before she winced in pain once more.

'*Nay, then I'll stop your mouth,*' he said.

'Have you actually listened to yourself?'

Enough, he thought. The purity and authenticity was now in the balance, his performance compromised and hers not right, not right at all. Where was the fear? He needed to bring back the fear or it was lost, the performance ruined. He bent down and took hold of her arm and dragged it over the log. She struggled and he dropped her arm and stepped on her broken ankle, which made her scream.

'No,' she said. 'No, don't.' She tried to sit up, and this time he stamped on her ankle, making her scream again, and then her body went limp as she passed out. Even better, he thought. The performance was back on track, purity and authenticity restored. He arranged her arm over the log, taking his time, then picked up the axe and took aim at her pale wrist.

*

'Kay,' Fox shouted as she ran, Solomon close behind. 'Kay Spinazzi.' The trees were thick and they had to fight their way through, warding off branches with their arms. 'Kay Spinazzi, if you can hear me, shout. Kay Spinazzi.'

They leapt over logs and dead branches, slippery with rot, heading towards where they had heard the scream. Solomon saw a glimpse of yellow, bright against the dark greens of the forest.

'Here.'

Fox stopped and they pushed through a tangle of ivy and branches. Kay was lying on her back, unconscious, as if asleep, her legs carelessly arranged and one arm thrown above her head across a log, the end of it a mess of flesh, the bright flash of bone, and blood that pulsed from it rhythmically, turning the ivy leaves around it dark red and glistening.

forty-six

'SHE'S GOING INTO SURGERY,' SAID FOX. 'THERE'S A CHANCE she'll keep the hand.'

Solomon nodded, looking at his own hands, Kay's blood still visible beneath his nails, caked into the sides. He'd tied a tourniquet around her arm as tightly as he could, and carried her out of the forest, Fox walking beside him, holding Kay's arm up above her, keeping her partly severed hand from moving as Solomon hurried back over the uneven forest floor. They'd put her into the back of a police car and it had taken off, getting her to hospital within minutes, blood being pumped back into her, dragging her away from the edge of death, morphine easing that journey. Her blood was on Solomon's shirt, his trousers, so much blood. He closed his eyes and saw again the mess of her wrist, the ghastly white of her carpal bones. He knew what microsurgery could do nowadays, knew that however bad it had looked, there was always a chance. But something about the visceral gore that he had seen outweighed his rationality. How? How could anything be salvaged from such wreckage?

'So,' said Fox. She rubbed her eyes with a thumb and index finger, a very human gesture.

Solomon looked at her as if for the first time, seeing a person, somebody with feelings and failings, flesh and blood below that icy exterior he had not been able to fathom, to get a toehold on. Just a person, and one who was exhausted, he thought. Exhausted, and probably ashamed.

'So,' he repeated.

'Let's say that I accept your theory, as crazy as it sounds.'

'You should,' said Solomon. 'I believe that it's been amply borne out by events.'

Fox nodded. 'Fair enough. So the question is, who is he?'

Solomon shook his head. 'I don't know.'

'Well, let's start with some hypotheses,' said Fox. 'Like ...' She stopped and yawned. 'Jesus, I can't think. Do you want a coffee?' She stood up.

'Yes.'

'Be right back.'

Fox left and Solomon sat alone in her office. Fox had asked the same question that Solomon had been asking himself for hours. Who was he? Who was this man who killed and tormented women, who used them as unwilling actresses in his own performance? Solomon didn't know, but he felt like he was getting closer. There was something nagging away at him, an anomaly, something that didn't fit, though he couldn't say just what.

He closed his eyes and imagined all that had happened and all that he had learnt since the morning the hospital had called him to tell him that his sister was in a coma. He imagined a landscape, panoramic, the events appearing as features of that landscape, abstract shapes and patterns of different sizes and prominence. He stilled his breathing and concentrated, exploring that landscape, travelling through it, over it. He lost himself in it, no longer in Fox's office but somewhere else, in his own theoretical wonderland, a place where he understood the rules completely because they were his rules, and his alone. Who was he? Phil's words: *He wants you to find him.* If that was true, then there had to be something. Solomon had to have missed something, something that had been there all along. He receded into the landscape of his mind, immersed in it, looking, seeking, deeper and deeper. There was something there. There had to be. He could feel it.

'Didn't know if you took sugar, so I didn't give you any,' said Fox, coming back into the office carrying two Styrofoam cups.

Solomon held up a hand, eyes still closed. He tried to stay where he was, lost in his thoughts, in his landscape, because he was beginning to see something, see it clearly, the thing that he had been looking for. Above the landscape, against the pristine blue sky, were three silver clouds. Three silver clouds that stood apart. Three anomalous silver clouds.

Caesar.

Dwkd.

Mr Todlq's.

'What?' said Fox. 'What's wrong?'

'Caesar,' said Solomon.

'Caesar.'

'*Julius Caesar.* Portia in *Julius Caesar.* She's tragic, but she's not iconic. Not like Ophelia, or Juliet.'

'I don't follow,' said Fox.

'He chose her for a purpose, a particular purpose. There's always a purpose.'

'Again, I don't—'

'Jonathan,' said Solomon.

'Jonathan?'

'I think his name is Jonathan.'

Fox frowned. 'Why?'

'I need more data,' said Solomon. 'That case you told me about. The woman who was found asleep in the church.'

'Drugged.'

'Right. Do you have her message exchange? When she set up her date?'

'Hold on.' Fox picked up her phone and dialled a number, listened to it ring then said, 'Sergeant Bright? ... Uh-huh. I need something from you ... The message exchange the woman from the church had ... Yes, could you send it to me immediately? Thank you.' She hung up and looked across her desk at Solomon. 'What have you got?'

'Nothing yet,' he said. 'A theory.'

'The name Jonathan is more than a theory.'

'I need to be sure,' said Solomon. 'Has anything come through?'

'Not yet,' said Fox, looking at her computer. 'Like I said, Jonathan isn't a theory. It's a name.'

'It could be,' said Solomon. 'The data's incomplete.'

'I ...' began Fox, then stopped and looked at her screen. 'Hold on ... Yes. Here it is.'

'Open it,' said Solomon, closing his eyes.

Fox clicked open the email attachment from Sergeant Bright. 'Okay.'

'There should be a misspelling in it, probably followed by the words *I mean*.'

Fox read the JPEG of the phone screen that Bright had sent her. '*Website says from Russia argentina pehu I mean peru.*'

'How did he misspell it?'

'P-E-H-U.'

'Chamberlain,' said Solomon. 'Possibly.'

'What ...?'

Solomon shook his head. 'I need you to do the same for Rebecca Harrington. You've got that exchange?'

'Yes.'

'So, same process. Any misspelling followed by the words *I mean*.'

Fox found the file and opened it up, and read, '*Gluh ... I mean glamorous*.'

'Spelling?'

'G-L-U-H.'

Solomon nodded to himself. 'Huh.'

'Okay,' said Fox. 'You're going to need to tell me what's going on.'

'Have you ever heard of Caesar's cipher?'

'No.'

'It was used by Julius Caesar,' said Solomon. 'It's one of the simplest. You replace each letter with the one that comes three places later in the alphabet. So A becomes D.'

'So ...'

'So in the exchange with my sister, he wrote D-W-K-D. He tried to pretend he meant *awkward* but mistyped it, only it doesn't add up. The letters aren't close enough together on the keypad to be easily confused. Meaning that it was mistyped on purpose.'

Fox nodded, and frowned at the same time. 'Okay,' she said slowly.

'In Caesar's cipher, that sequence, D-W-K-D, translates to A-T-H-A. There are almost no words that contain that sequence of letters. Jonathan is one of the few. Jonathan or Nathan, but Nathan is less common.'

Now Fox shook her head. 'You've lost me.'

'Do you have a piece of paper?'

Fox took a sheet from the printer beneath her desk and pushed it across, then handed him a pen.

'Okay,' said Solomon. 'Start at the beginning. The first victim. Rebecca Harrington.'

'Cleopatra,' said Fox, unable to keep the guilt from her voice. *Cocktails of infinite variety.* The phrase she'd tried to forget, but that had kept gnawing at her.

'Right. So in her message exchange, we've got G-L-U-H. Which becomes D-I-R-E.'

Fox frowned, thought. 'Right. Counting back three letters.'

'Next should come Cordelia and Desdemona,' said Solomon. 'The hypothesis must be that they were victims, but haven't yet been identified as part of the pattern.'

'Yes,' said Fox, trying not to imagine her role in that investigation, the glory it might offer.

'Let's assume that one of these victims' message exchanges contributes C-T-E-D-B, and the other Y-J-O-N.'

'Why?' said Fox.

'Stay with me,' said Solomon. 'Next is Ophelia. D-W-K-D becomes A-T-H-A. Yes?'

Fox watched him in silence. He looked up at her briefly, then continued.

'Portia comes next, but we don't have her message exchange, though we should be able to get hold of it, as her case is being investigated. But I would expect that it would provide N-C-H-A.'

'Why?' said Fox, again.

'Wait,' said Solomon. 'Then comes Juliet, P-E-H-U becoming M-B-E-R. And finally Lavinia, O-D-L-Q becoming L-A-I-N.'

Fox shook her head. 'Which means?'

'Which means that we know his name,' said Solomon. He wrote out the deciphered words, the ones he knew for sure and the ones he had postulated. That he had postulated but that he was eighty, no, ninety per cent sure of. They had to be right. He turned the sheet around, and Fox read the words:

D-I-R-E-C-T-E-D-B-Y-J-O-N-A-T-H-A-N-C-H-A-M-B-E-R-L-A-I-N.

'Directed by Jonathan Chamberlain.' She looked up from the sheet of paper. 'That's not possible.'

'Possible, certainly,' said Solomon. 'I would say probable.'

'Jonathan Chamberlain,' Fox said again. 'And this from, what? Two sample sequences?'

'The hypothesis came from two samples,' said Solomon. 'The data just keeps confirming it.'

Fox looked at him across the desk. 'You are extraordinary.'

'No,' said Solomon. 'It was there all along. I was just too slow to see it.' Stupid, he thought. Stupid, stupid, stupid. How could he have let this person fool him for so long? He felt ashamed, disgusted. There was no excuse. This was basic stuff.

'But why?' said Fox. 'Why leave this trail?'

'Because he wants to be caught,' said Solomon. 'He wants the attention, the admiration, the limelight. Deep down, that's what he wants. *Directed by*. He wants the celebrity. No.' He paused, realizing that at last he had a proper understanding of him. 'He doesn't want it. He needs it.'

Fox leant back in her chair and turned her head to look out of the window. She stayed in that position for some time, Solomon happy for the interlude. Then she reached out and took the pen that she'd offered Solomon and went back to gazing out of her window, holding it in both hands, turning it slowly.

'He parcelled out his name,' she said, eventually. 'Right up until the end.'

'He had a plan,' said Solomon.

'A schedule,' said Fox. 'The plays he would perform.'

'Or direct.'

'So he has a background in it, in theatre. You'd say?'

'A failed actor,' said Solomon. 'He couldn't make it on stage, so he decided to take it out on the world.'

'All the world's a stage,' said Fox.

'Exactly.'

'But he wanted the acclamation, so he seeded his name throughout.'

Solomon shrugged, suddenly sick of this person, this man with his grandiose resentments and tiresome parlour games. *Directed by Jonathan Chamberlain.* It was monstrous, beyond his imagination. 'I guess,' he said.

'So let's find him,' said Fox. 'I'm in. Let's go.'

forty-seven

VENGEANCE IS IN MY HEART, HE THOUGHT. HE UNLOCKED THE door to the room and turned on the overhead strip lighting, which flickered and buzzed before throwing a rancid yellow light over the shelves of linen: sheets and towels and pillow covers. He reached up, then stopped at a voice behind him.

'Jonny?'

He took down his hand and without turning around said, 'Yes?'

'Where were you yesterday?'

'Ill.'

'You didn't let anybody know.'

'I did.'

'Oh? Who?'

'Jean.'

'Jean's on holiday.'

He turned around slowly and gave the ward sister a smile, goofy and guilty. 'Oh. I forgot. Sorry.'

'I'm going to have to give you a warning.'

'Okay.'

'*Okay?*' The ward sister looked at him with disgust, shaking her head. 'Is that the best you can do?'

Jonny considered telling her to go to hell, thought about taking a step towards her, laying his hands on her. He could leave her in here, hide her body underneath the piles of laundry. She wouldn't be discovered for hours, more than enough time. He could, he really could. He *wanted* to. The ward sister watched him, and she must have seen something in his expression because she took a step back, out of the small room, out into the corridor.

'Not good enough,' she said, all power and confidence gone from her reproach, and she turned and walked away, Jonny listening to her footsteps hurrying down the corridor. It didn't matter. He wouldn't be here much longer anyway.

Vengeance is in my heart, he thought, reaching up for what he had come for. *Vengeance is in my heart, death in my hand.*

'What is it?' said Fox. Solomon was looking at his phone, which had just vibrated. He glanced up at her.

'A message. From Kay's phone.'

'Can't be ...' started Fox, then, 'Oh. From him.'

'It must be.'

'What does it say?'

'It says, *Vengeance is in my heart, death in my hand.*'

'Which means?'

'It's a line from *Titus Andronicus*,' said Solomon. '*Vengeance is in my heart, death in my hand, Blood and revenge are hammering in my head.*'

'So you've pissed him off,' said Fox. 'That's no surprise.'

'No,' agreed Solomon. 'So. What have we got?'

'No Nathan Chamberlains, but I've got a Jonathan Chamberlain. He's an actor, or was, hasn't done anything for the last three years.'

'What kind of acting did he do?'

'Adverts, mostly,' said Fox, reading her computer screen. 'A couple of bit parts in soaps. Nothing much. Nothing you could make a living from.'

Failed actor, thought Solomon. 'Is there a photo?'

'Here.' She turned her screen so that he could see. A man, curly hair, white. It could have been him. There was no reason why not. If it was him, then he had not so much a face, more a blank canvas upon which could be laid any number of variations.

'Anything else?'

'Date of birth, agent details. Though if he hasn't worked for three years, his agent's probably dropped him.'

'So how do we find him?' said Solomon.

'Well,' said Fox, typing as she spoke. 'Let's see if he's got a criminal record.' She typed some more, hit return, and waited, looking at her screen. 'Nope. Okay, we can at least find out where he lives.'

'He'll be local,' said Solomon. 'He must be. All the victims have been in east London.'

Fox typed some more, then shook her head. 'Nothing local. I've got a Jonathan Chamberlain in Wimbledon ... No. Too old, nearly seventy.'

'Nobody closer?'

'No.'

Solomon frowned, then shook his head. 'Can't be him.' He thought some more. 'Are we sure that it's his real name? Jonathan Chamberlain?'

'How do you mean?'

'Stage names,' said Solomon. 'A lot of actors have them. We could be looking for the wrong name.'

'Maybe.'

'We could call his agent,' said Solomon.

'It's Saturday.'

'It's worth a try. They might know something.'

Fox nodded, picked up her phone and called a number. Solomon watched and waited. Fox shook her head at him, said, 'Answering service,' then stopped and picked up a pen and wrote down a number, before hanging up. 'She left a mobile number. For emergencies.' She paused. 'What kind of emergencies do actors have? Bad reviews?' She called the number she'd noted down, and Solomon watched again, and listened.

Vengeance is in my heart, he thought. He waited for the lift door to open, then walked out into the freshly polished corridor, gripping the pillow tightly. *Vengeance is in my heart, death in my hand.* The corridor was empty and quiet and smelt of cleaning products. It had been easy, finding out who he was, too easy. Solomon, the name stored in Lavinia's phone, wasn't a common one. Solomon, who had a disfigured face. He'd noticed that at Mr Toad's, even though he'd been wearing make-up to cover it. A quick search on the internet had thrown up a news story about an acid attack on a Solomon Mullan. Mullan. So that was the connection. Yes. It made sense.

Vengeance is in my heart, death in my hand, Blood and revenge are hammering in my head. He'd ruined everything. Solomon Mullan had ruined it all, had sullied its purity, had destroyed its authenticity. The scene had been perfect. The forest setting, Lavinia's terror, it had all been perfect. And then, just when he'd been ready to strike, he'd heard the voices and his stroke had missed and he'd had to run. Solomon Mullan had ruined it, and he would have to pay for that, would have to be made to suffer. Suffer in a way that would stay with him for the rest of his life.

'So, Jonathan Chamberlain,' said Fox, putting her phone down. 'Not Oscar material, is what his ex-agent reckons.'

Solomon had listened to one side of Fox's conversation with the agent, but it was the agent who had done most of the talking. 'Oh?'

'A bit try-hard, is what she told me. Try-hard, and very needy. She said that everything was always somebody else's fault, and that she regretted ever having taken him on. A persecution complex, was what she told me.'

Solomon nodded. 'That sounds right.'

'He hated directors, would develop obsessions about them. When they turned him down for roles. Then *she* dropped him, and he fixated on her, wouldn't stop calling her and telling her how deluded she was, how misguided. She said she thought about going to the police, but he gave up in the end.'

'And? His name?'

'Right. Jonathan Chapell, two Ls. She said he thought it sounded too Protestant, so he changed it. Didn't do him much good, though.'

'Chapell. That's not a common name.'

'No, it isn't.' Fox typed into her computer again, Solomon watching her. 'No criminal record,' she said, 'but I've got an address for a Jonathan Chapell in E8. Athestone Road. Hold on.' She typed some more. 'That's a match. The date of birth is the same as Chamberlain's.'

'You've got him?'

'Looks like it,' Fox said.

'So let's—'

Fox held up a hand. 'This is where things get complicated,' she said. 'I need to bring a team in to handle this.'

'It's just one man.'

'Who is extremely dangerous,' said Fox. 'And we don't want to miss him. We'll have to watch his home, and his place of work.'

'If he's got one.'

'Easy to find out,' said Fox. She typed some more. 'National Insurance number's all you need, and to get that, all I need is a name and date of birth, which I already have. Give me ten minutes and I'll have his whole life in front of us.' She read her screen. 'Current employment, Royal London Hospital. We'll have to—'

'Royal London?'

'Yes.'

Solomon stood up. 'We've got to go. Now.'

'What?'

'*Vengeance is in my heart*,' said Solomon. 'And my sister is in that hospital.'

He pushed open the door without knocking. She was awake, and looked up when he came in.

'Hello,' she said. He had a brief, fond feeling of something approaching nostalgia. Ophelia. She had been so sweet, so biddable. But then she had been full of barbiturates.

'Hi,' he said. 'How are you feeling?'

'Better,' she said. 'Are you a nurse?'

'Not exactly,' he said. 'No. No, I'm not a nurse.' He smiled, and whispered, 'I don't like nurses.'

She smiled briefly back, then frowned and said, 'Then who are you?'

'I am your sweet prince, here to sing you to your rest.'

Tiffany's eyes widened, then she closed them and said softly, 'I know who you are.'

'You do?'

She nodded, her eyes still closed but tears leaking through, running down her cheeks. She didn't say anything.

'You remember?'

She nodded again, her lips squeezed tightly together.

He took a step towards her bed and stood above her. He dropped the pillow he was holding onto her legs and took out a long black cable tie. She didn't open her eyes. He put the cable tie through the metal tubing of her bed frame, running the free end through the tie's eyelet, forming a large loop. He took a scalpel from his back pocket.

'Put your hand through this,' he said.

Tiffany opened her eyes and looked at the cable tie, then up at him. 'I don't want to,' she said.

'If you don't, I will cut your throat.'

She shook her head. 'Please,' she said.

'You have to. You have to do it.'

She blinked slowly, then nodded and put the hand of her good arm through the loop of the cable tie, and he pulled it tight with a zipping sound.

'Why are you here?' she said.

He put his finger to his lips. '*Shh.*' He crossed to the other side of the bed and took out another cable tie, pulling it tight around her other arm, the one in a plaster cast. 'Just to be sure,' he said.

She watched him do it and didn't say anything. She blinked away her tears, but more came to take their place.

'You see,' he said gently, 'your brother, Solomon, ruined something very precious of mine. Something that meant a great deal to me. So I have decided to take revenge on him by taking away something precious of his.' He picked the pillow up from where he had placed it on the bed.

'No,' said Tiffany. 'Please don't.'

'It won't hurt,' he said. 'You just need to remember not to panic.'

'No.'

'It will be like a long sleep,' he said. 'Just that.'

'Please,' Tiffany said again.

He shook his head and placed the pillow over her face. 'It's too late. It's all your brother's fault, and it's far, far too late.'

Fox had taken a car herself and called it in as she drove. The hospital was close by, less than a mile in a straight line, and they had pushed and battered their way through the traffic, Fox laying on the horn and screaming out of the window at any cars that didn't move quickly enough. They had made it in three minutes and Fox had left the car at an angle across the street in front of the hospital, doors open, lights still whirling, throwing panicked blue across the hospital's stone facade.

Solomon ran through reception, Fox just behind him, up the stairs and down the corridors he had walked so often to see his sister. Past open wards, past a nurses' station, an X-ray department – Christ, it had never seemed so far on previous visits – left at phlebotomy, his legs not moving fast enough, Tiffany's room not arriving quickly enough. Another corner, this was the corridor, past door after door after door, a waiting area, another door, and this was his sister's room.

He opened the door and saw the bed and a man standing over it, a pillow in his hand, clamped over his sister's face, her legs thrashing, the covers kicked off. The man looked up and said, calmly:

'I can't get her to die.'

'Away from the bed,' said Fox, moving past Solomon and spraying liquid into the man's face from a black canister. He let go of the pillow and stepped backwards, and Fox rounded the bed and reached for his arm, but as she did, he cut her across the face with a scalpel. Fox took hold of his hand and bent it backwards and he dropped the scalpel, and she stepped back and sprayed him again, a sustained burst. He made a mewling sound and staggered into the corner of the room, his fists covering his face.

'A hand?' she shouted to Solomon.

Solomon joined her, but he only watched as she took out handcuffs and efficiently cuffed one of the man's wrists, then turned him and brought his other arm behind his back, securing both wrists together. Solomon turned to his sister, who was gasping for breath, arching her back, lifting her whole body from the bed as she tried to take in air.

'She'll be okay,' said Fox.

Solomon turned back to Fox. Blood was pouring down one side of her face, the lips of her wound ghastly, so deep that Solomon had a glimpse of her teeth through her cheek.

She sucked in breath and staggered, nearly fell. 'How bad is it?' she asked him.

forty-eight

'THEY TRACED DESDEMONA AND CORDELIA,' SOLOMON SAID. 'OR at least, the women he cast them as. In Greece. He took a holiday there three weeks ago. They were both British tourists. One, Desdemona, she survived. But not Cordelia.'

'God,' said Kay. 'I can't imagine.'

'And you?' said Solomon. 'How are you feeling?'

'Alive,' said Kay.

'Your hand?'

'I can move my little finger.'

'The doctor says you should get all sensation back.' Solomon paused. 'You know, when I saw it, in the forest, with the blood … I don't know. It was like my rational mind was telling me that there was hope, but there was something …'

'Hey, Solomon?'

'Yes?'

'Keep it light, could you?'

'Sorry.'

'Anyway, I'm tired. Will you come back soon?'

'Yes.'

'Promise?'

'I promise.' Solomon stood up. 'I'll see you.'

'See you.'

Solomon left Kay's room and headed for the exit, yet another hospital visit over. How many had there been in the last few weeks? Nineteen. He knew the number, of course he did. He never forgot. As he walked out of the hospital, he thought about Kay, about how much she meant to him. He pictured her in his mind, the image of her that he had. A bird in a gilded cage, the cage elaborately wrought, the bird inside splendid, singing happily. He realized now, or at least he thought he did, why she was in that cage. It was not to keep her trapped. No, it was to protect her from any monsters outside, monsters that would bring harm to her, and compromise that blissful happiness she possessed. That cage was there, he realized, to protect her from him.

He felt the sunlight on his face outside the hospital, and stopped at the top of the steps. He closed his eyes against the strong light, and stood still for some time. Behind him was Kay, somebody he cared about more deeply than he would have imagined possible. But he would break the promise he had just made to her; he had no choice. He would not be back to see her. Wherever her life took her, whichever direction, she would be better off without him. He had known that from the beginning. He hoped she would find success, that he would next see her face in a scientific journal, or on the front of a newspaper, hailing her great breakthrough. She was beautiful and intelligent and she deserved it, she deserved success and happiness. He was hideous and would bring her only horror.

He took a deep breath and rubbed a tear away from his wretched skin. There. It was decided. He opened his eyes and slowly walked down the steps of the hospital, and out of her life.

*

Luke was waiting for him outside, parked on double yellows with his hazards flashing, standing next to the car, daring the world to tell him to move. Which, of course, it didn't.

'You good?'

'Yes,' said Solomon.

'So,' Luke said. 'We going out?'

'No,' said Solomon.

'What? I'm out of jail, Tiff's out of hospital, that fucking psycho's locked up and you're not coming out for a drink?'

'I just want to go home,' said Solomon. 'If that's okay.'

Luke looked at Solomon, and shook his head. Tiffany peered out of the window and said, hopefully, 'Just one?'

'Sorry,' said Solomon.

'Sorry,' said Luke, unable to keep the disdain from his voice. 'All right. I'll drop you off, then me and Tiff'll get on it. And I mean, on it.'

Solomon got into the back seat of Luke's Mercedes and they headed off.

'Hey, Solly,' said Luke.

'Yes?'

'You're our hero, you know that?'

'Don't.'

'It's true,' said Tiffany. 'We love you.'

Solomon didn't reply. He looked out of the passenger window and tried to estimate, given the market penetration of Mercedes in the UK, the current overall traffic density, and the distance (which was 2,578 metres), how many Mercedes, of any model, they would intersect with on the way back to his apartment.